The Con

Mark Knowles

Table of Contents

3

FOREWORD

The night watch

In AD 6, after a disastrous fire, the Emperor Augustus created Rome's first dedicated fire-fighting corps. The 'vigiles' (literally, 'watchmen') replaced the haphazard system of dragooning poorly-trained, sometimes reluctant, public slaves into duty to supplement the private bands of the better off citizens. They were disparagingly known as 'Spartoli' ('bucket carriers') in reference to the buckets of coiled rope sealed with pitch that they carried with them. Under the overall command of a Prefect, the vigiles were organised along quasi-military lines into 7 battalions ('cohortes') responsible for patrolling the 14 regions of the ancient city. Each cohort was made up of 7 'centuries', each of which comprised roughly 70-80 men. A Tribune was in charge of each cohort, and a Centurion commanded a century.

'Sebaciaria'

Derived from the Latin for tallow, a hard animal fat used in the manufacture of candles, Sebaciaria refers to an especially dangerous duty – one month long – that every watchman would have to perform at some point. The available evidence does not allow us to say with certainty what this duty was, but a frequent phrase amongst the graffiti discovered on the walls of watchmen's barracks ('sebaciaria feci' and 'tuta', 'I completed Sebaciaria' and 'safely') suggests a sense of relief the men felt upon completion of this tour that was more significant and remarkable than after regular duties. It clearly involved torches and lamps, and probably required the Sebaciarius to light up patrol routes for his colleagues and for others using the streets at night. A badly placed torch in a tightly packed city like ancient Rome could have catastrophic consequences. In addition to dealing with fires, watchmen would frequently encounter criminality. The concept of a professional police force would not crystalise for at least another 1500 years and the watchmen would be expected to deal with what they saw with very little training and infrastructure: in the ancient world, 'restorative justice' as we know it would have been summary and brutal.

This story, which is based on true events and documented characters, begins midway through one such month of Sebaciaria.

Structure of The Watch in February AD 205

PREFECT (Junius Rufinus)

Deputy Prefect (G. Balbus)

7 tribunes

49 centurions

Total force: (including detachment of 4 cohorts at Ostia & Portus) = c.3500 men

'Duties of the Prefect of The Watch'

"Severus and Caracalla Emperors, to Junius Rufinus, Prefect of The Vigiles, greetings. You are hereby authorized to punish with the rod or with the cat-o'-nine-tails the janitor or any of the inhabitants of a house in which fire has broken out through negligence. In case the fire should be occasioned not by negligence but by crime, you must hand over the arsonists to our friend Fabius (Septimianus) Clio, Prefect of The City. Remember also that one of your duties is to discover runaway slaves and to return them to their masters."

"... The Prefect of The Vigiles also deals with cases of ... housebreakers, thieves, harbourers of thieves, robbers ... unless in any particular case the offender is of such ruffianly and infamous character ... that the case is handed on to the Prefect of The City ..."

– Justinian, DIGEST, 1, XV

PART I

Rome, XXIV Februarius
Rome was suffocating under thick fog.

It crept through the refuse-strewn alleyways. It drifted up the seven hills and infiltrated the deserted temples of the Capitoline. It curled round the creaking timbers and boardwalks of the wharves that abutted the River Tiber, coating the hulls of the skiffs and cutters huddled against them in a clammy sheen. Rome was so shrouded in fog that there was no separation between earth and clouds.

The watchmen now approaching the docks were tired, hungry and fractious. Compounding their misery, they had all, at various points throughout the night, bumped into objects that had materialised in front of them too late to be avoided.

"You're disgusting, d'you know that? And you make this smacking noise when you chew."

The squat vigil merely shrugged and continued munching the sticky honeycomb.

"It'll have been out all night on that post. A dog's probably pissed all over it or something."

"Adds to the flavour."

His burly friend shook his head and looked away. They had all had to patrol for a double watch of six hours in anticipation of the trouble usually associated with the Terminalia festival, lighting up extra routes for the security of those citizens joining the all-night procession to the temples atop the Capitoline Hill. On this day, neighbours of the various districts put aside whatever grievances they might have had with each other and spilled out onto the streets to honour the god of boundaries with gifts of garlands, wine and sweetmeats. Excessive drinking and fragile bravado typically resulted in blows being exchanged with strangers from other areas of the

9

city. This night, however, the mood had been subdued: the watchmen put it down to the effects of the dispiriting fog and bitterly cold air.

Shivering against the roof of a disused warehouse, the informer looked on as the four spectral shapes emerged from the early morning mist. The pale aura cast by their torches highlighted strong physiques topped by lobster-tailed helmets, and fragments of their gruff conversation – broken by their footsteps - drifted up to him. As they materialised, their words produced wispy tendrils in the cold morning air.

"Wait." The tallest of them – a tribune - raised his hand and the conversation halted abruptly. "Over there, by the wharf."

The watchmen approached the crumpled form that the informer himself had discovered only minutes before. He would have missed it on his walk home along the dockside had the fog not broken when he glanced towards the water and noticed the dark shape on the stone step, just above the waterline.

The tribune bent down, with his back to the spy. He saw him wince, as he knew he would.

"Shit," he muttered. "It's a little girl."

"Damn it; look at the state of her!"

The tribune took off his helmet, revealing curly grey and black hair and thick stubble, and tossed it across the quayside. It clattered to a stop by the rotting building in front of the informer. He stood and tugged his fingers through his hair, bellowing a curse to the gods. The informer noticed how the other watchmen exchanged nervous looks.

They fell silent. Their faces, smudged with the smoke from their torches, bowed towards the body as if in prayer. She was fourteen or fifteen years old and once strikingly pretty, the informer knew. But he had grimaced when he lifted a clump of matted hair with his little finger and seen the ugly crater in her skull, caked with congealed blood, marking the site of the blow that had, he hoped, killed her instantly.

"So, now we just shove her in the river, let old Father Tiber look after her?" asked the short one with the bulbous nose, bulging eyes and the Syrian accent, whom the others had called 'Bulla'. The informer knew this was a nickname meaning 'lucky charm', which he assumed was ironic given that he resembled a frog. He saw him toss something into the river and lick his fingers. "She drifts to the other side, she becomes the Fourteenth's problem, no?"

"Right, I'm moving her." The one with the physique of a boxer or wrestler crouched by her.

"Damn you both, no!" The sharp tone of the tribune stopped him. "I found her and she'll not just end up in a pit like any other beggar we come across. There'll be people out looking for her."

He knelt down again and and his belt tools clanked against the cold stone of the quayside. He pulled up his hood and whispered a prayer to Mars the Avenger. Then he kissed the tips of his fingers and closed the girl's eyes for the last time before taking a long, deep breath and retrieving his torch.

"Get back to the Watch House and drag everyone out, no excuses." He nodded to the smallest man of the group who jumped up onto the quay and sprinted off into the fog.

The one named Bulla hesitated. "Er, tribune? If she doesn't go into the river, shouldn't we just report this to the City Prefect? Someone murdered her, no?"

"Correct, we should. But we're not. Do it, man! Cover her in that blanket. Titus, rope the area off. That post there twenty … no, forty paces to the merchant ship over there," he said, pointing to a galley that dwarfed the craft bobbing next to it. "I don't want anyone tramping through here without my permission."

A rule breaker. The informer smiled to himself. Interesting.

He watched Titus dash off into the mist, rope looped around the crux of his elbow, with an agility that was surprising for such a big man. His bones now throbbed and he tried adjusting his position to keep his blood circulating. Immediately after his gruesome discovery he had heard the footsteps of the watchmen and blind panic had seized him, for there would have been only one conclusion for the vigiles to have drawn, as he stood frozen over the corpse. His eyes had darted about for somewhere to hide before seeing the roof of the disused building on which he now lay. He was freezing and he struggled to prevent his chattering teeth from betraying his presence.

But he couldn't slip away, not just yet. Experience – and necessity - told him to wait a little longer. He was a quadruplator and a successful job could earn him one quarter of the estate of a convicted man: he had endured worse conditions than these to gain that bit of information, or that one slight against the Emperor, that he needed. And times were tough: there were far too many informers in the city, most of them rank amateurs, who would do a bad job for a pittance. The situation developing below could be lucrative: the tall tribune had been right when he suggested that this victim was no mere beggar: she was of noble stock. He pulled the hood of his cloak further over his face and gritted his teeth.

Just a bit longer …

Ten minutes later, hobnailed footsteps clicked down the dockside behind him and a short, clipped conversation ensued that he couldn't quite pick up. Then the footsteps approached, slower now, and several more figures moved into view. They were all clad in similar dirty yellow cloaks and equipped with mattocks, rope and cudgels.

"Tribune Ambrosius," announced the newcomer, a handsome man with dark features. He was out of breath. "What's going on? My lot are supposed to be helping out after a fire on the Pincian Hill but your man insisted …" his voice trailed off as he noticed the body.

"Take a look."

The watchman stepped down onto the platform and flinched as he drew the blanket beneath her chin. "Right," he said, wiping his hand on his cloak, "er … so give us a quick report and we'll hand over to the Urban Cohorts. You can all get back to barracks for some rest."

"No."

Ludo gave him a look. "No? What d'you mean no?" He glanced at Bulla and Titus, who folded their arms. "Why put your own neck on the line for that lot?"

"It stays with us. I found her." Ambrosius held his stare and Ludo shrugged.

"Fine. Tell us where you want my men."

"Have a couple on the ropes and a couple more searching the gaps between the buildings. The girl was struck with a heavy weapon, something rounded, not long like a cudgel. Might tell us something about who did it. And maybe one of them can knock on some doors in case there's anyone sleeping in those buildings."

The informer frowned, both confused and impressed. What on earth was he doing?

Ludo issued a few instructions to his detachment of watchmen. The informer could read the body language of people that would rather be somewhere else. Somewhere warmer, probably. As one of them walked to his post, almost underneath the informer, he whispered in his colleague's ear but his words were loud enough to be heard from twenty feet above.

"Shame. She'd have been a tidy little piece!"

"What was that?" Ambrosius stalked over. The other watchmen stopped and turned.

"Me, tribune? I …!" A stinging cuff round the head silenced him. The informer winced.

"Have some respect, you ignorant little bastard!"

Ludo hurried over and positioned himself between them.

"Easy! Easy, tribune! I've got it! I'll handle it!"

"Get a grip of them, Ludo!"

Ambrosius wheeled away and gripped a splintered mooring post, letting his anger subside. Though it was anybody's guess where his thoughts were at times like this, when his explosive temper consumed him, Bulla and Titus had learned the hard way to give him space, and the rest of Cohort IV had followed their lead.

Distracted by the fracas, the informer had not noticed that a pallid sun had crept over the horizon and that the fog was dissipating. He began to creep away from the edge but then, from the corner of his eye, saw Ambrosius become rigid, as if struck in the back by an arrow. His head snapped around towards the girl's body and he dashed back across the dockside, beckoning Titus and Bulla over. Ludo also sauntered over to them.

"There's something this girl wants to tell us."

Titus nodded. "Ambrosius, I was just thinking now that something's not right with her."

"Wow, very observant musclehead! Her head is all caved in and she's cold as stone," snorted Bulla. "But apart from that, she's fine!"

"Go on," said Ambrosius, ignoring him.

"Well, I figured with an injury like that, there should be blood all over the ground. But there isn't much: the rest is all over her clothes." They both jumped down and Titus cradled her head, revealing a dark patch of dried blood. He gently lowered it again. "The water level hasn't risen and it's not rained, has it? So where's it gone?"

"It's not gone anywhere, Titus. She wasn't killed here. Look at this," said Ambrosius removing her stiffened arm from under the blanket. "I didn't think anything of it before but she's clenched her fist. Help me prise it open. Ludo, get me a torch."

Together, they managed to move her rigid fingers away from her palm. The slack skin of her wrist felt like freshly plucked poultry, and Bulla could only wonder how Ambrosius was so unfazed by it. Ludo's torch hovered over them a few moments later.

The fog was disappearing fast: just rags of it drifted past now. The informer could hear his own heart pounding. He knew he should leave immediately

"See how her thumbnail is long and manicured. But the index finger – look – it's bent back; her middle finger – the same. And the ring finger. The little fingernail is intact. And look; dried blood on her palm, though she's not dug her nails into it because the skin's not broken. Bulla, give me your knife."

"It could be from anywhere. I don't see what you're getting at." Ludo wrinkled his nose.

Ambrosius took the knife and tried to scrape underneath the middle fingernail, but her fingers were so stiff and unyielding that he was unable to manoeuvre the blade.

"Forgive me, missy." He wrapped two of his fingers around her middle finger and wrenched it back. It cracked and yielded a little. The informer flinched in revulsion.

"Oh fuck!" Ludo wheeled away to retch. "How in Hades can you do that?"

"Just keep the damn light on us! There it is. So she put up quite a fight after all." Bulla and Titus peered at the tip of the blade on which there was a very small peel of skin. "Good girl."

"So that's not her blood on her palm?"

Ambrosius was distant again, as if confronting unpleasant images only he could see. He took a deep breath. "Bulla, pull her stole above her waist."

The watchman hesitated for a second then nodded.

"Bastard violated her." Ambrosius could only glance at the livid bruising and dried blood around the girl's wispy pubic hair. When he turned away on his haunches and tried to stand, he became light-headed. Titus gripped his arm and helped him up, but Ambrosius brushed him off and moved away.

The other vigiles were watching intently. Titus glared at them and they looked elsewhere. The informer had the distinct impression that the big man was very protective of his tribune. Bulla lowered the skirt and covered the body with the blanket.

There were a few moments of heavy silence along the dock and the informer sank lower against the roof, planning his escape down the rickety staircase at the back of the warehouse. Ambrosius was staring at the first floor window of the decaying building behind the body and scratched his chin.

"She was thrown out," he declared, breaking the silence, "but she missed the water."

The other watchmen turned to see what he was looking up at and the informer froze in abject panic. He closed his eyes and waited for the shouting as they saw his cloak etched against the skyline.

But Ambrosius was concentrating upon a pair of faded green shutters which, unlike the others, were slightly ajar. He approached the door and withdrew a mattock from his belt. When he tried pushing against it, it didn't yield, but the informer could hear old timbers creaking in protest. There was a pause and then a crashing blow of metal on wood, making the informer flinch. A final kick with the flat of Ambrosius' boot and the entire door was sent toppling to the floor.

The informer was already rolling away from the edge of the roof, taking advantage of the racket below. He felt like a child again, giddy at having picked someone's pockets in the forum, scarcely believing his luck to have escaped. As he scrambled down the stairs, he was already planning how he would present the information to his patron.

He wouldn't want to be in the tribune's shoes, that was for sure. The Praetorian Prefect was not a forgiving man.

II

Bulla, Titus and Ludo followed Ambrosius inside with a pair of torches that crackled in the dusty, heavy air. As their eyes adjusted to the gloom, they made out stacks of crates, an old desk covered in a dustsheet, upturned amphorae and grain sacks strewn about the floor. At the far side of the room there was another door. Ambrosius pointed to it and the others nodded. He replaced the mattock in his belt and withdrew his baton. They approached the door, more cautiously now.

Ambrosius kicked hard at the door and it burst open. In front of him was a small entrance room at the back of which was another door. A weak stripe of light at the bottom suggested that it lead onto a street heading away from the docks, back towards the city. Ambrosius waited for the torch before moving into the chamber. Apart from a narrow passageway to his left that led to a flight of stairs, the room was empty.

Or at least it appeared so.

As they made for the stairs, Titus noticed something on the floor as the light from his torch brushed over it.

"Ambrosius! Over here!"

It was only a partial boot print but it was clearly outlined in dried blood, and it pointed towards the door. Ludo found the next one, tracking back towards the gloomy staircase.

"There's more," he muttered. "Watch where you step …"

"Wait! You're right: just wait a minute. Bulla, I need your knife again."

He disappeared for a few moments and from the first room came the noise of fabric being torn apart and wood splintering. He returned bearing a section of dustsheet and a crate lid.

"Hold this," he said, presenting the lid to Bulla. He threw the cloth over it and twisted the drapes around underneath so that the material became taught across the surface, like the skin of a drum.

"Go on, and avoid stepping on the blood."

With Ludo at the head, the four watchmen ascended the rickety staircase, noting how the prints became clearer. Ludo rounded the corner and stopped in his tracks. He thrust his torch into the gloom.

"Ye gods!" The dancing flames etched a look of horror on his face. Ambrosius pushed past him and stopped dead. There was blood everywhere: in pools on the floorboards, in spatters on the wall and, most sinister of all, on the dirty sailcloth laid out in the centre. More than this, however, and what would linger in the memory of all of the watchmen, was the evil stench of fear itself. It screamed at them in the silence. Even as the men entered the room and skirted the sailcloth, the cloying, pungent whiff of stale urine, clotted blood, bodily fluid and death assaulted their senses. Bulla and Ludo gagged, barely managing to retain the contents of their stomachs. Titus' fist gripped the torch handle so tightly that his knuckles turned white and his eyes were wide with fury and incomprehension.

Ambrosius made for the shutters and prodded them open, noting the dried blood on the peeling paintwork of the slats. He ignored the stares of the vigiles posted outside and the people that were now gathering at the rope cordons. The view to the crumpled body was blocked by the step and screened by the fog but it was in line with the window and perhaps six feet from the building; a considerable distance, which could only mean that she was flung out of it with brutal force. He shook his head: of all the unanswered questions, this was the most puzzling. Was she hurled out in a fit of rage after scratching her attacker hard enough to bend her nails? Had he looked out and assumed she had been swallowed up by the Tiber or was it a crude effort to simulate an unprovoked street assault and divert attention from the building? But there was nothing of any interest in here; nothing to link either the girl or her killer to it since it had long since fallen out of regular use.

He rubbed his tired eyes and steeled himself to finish the task. He retrieved the dustsheet and crate lid and returned to the centre of the room. Bulla was frowning at him.

"What are you going to do with that?"

"Just an idea … Bulla, Titus, Ludo: have you avoided this area?"

The three looked at the patch of viscous, drying liquid in the centre of the room, in the midst of which was a boot print. The distinctive pattern of hobnails embedded in the sole was defined in the blood: three columns of five with an extra one by the big toe. They all nodded. "Then you'll be witnesses to this."

Gripping the cloth twisted behind the lid, he pressed the crate over the boot print and held it there for a few moments. With equal care, he raised the lid and turned it over. There, on the tautened side of the cloth, was a clear impression of the boot.

"I think that's the best likeness we'll get."

Bulla's hands were on his hips. "You are going to compare this with everyone's boots in Rome?"

"No," Ambrosius replied without a trace of irony. "That's your job."

Bulla gave him an incredulous look.

"Of course not you fool. Have a final sweep round the place, then we'll get out of here."

"Good," said Ludo. "And then we should light it up and destroy it. It feels like Charon's bedroom."

"I remember swearing an oath to put out fires, not start them."

"Bulla, fold up that sailcloth. The blanket out there's too small to wrap her in."

The Syrian saluted with mock insolence and set about the task without enthusiasm, whilst the others gave the room a final sweep. The oppressive pall of death hung heavy in the air and they were all keen to go. Bulla had folded the cloth and was on his haunches examining something small.

"What is it?" asked Ambrosius.

He dropped it into the palm of his hand and poked it. It was shaped like a flattened sphere with a small hole in the back, and the torchlight picked out streaks of milky red minerals.

"I'll tell you exactly what that is," said Ludo. "That's an ear stud, but the pin's missing. It's Sardonyx, a semi-precious stone. My wife's got a Sardonyx brooch. Fucking expensive it was too."

"Where was it?"

"There, under the blanket in a gap between the floorboards."

Ambrosius scratched the stubble of his chin. Fatigue was beginning to play tricks with his memory. With the summer would come his fortieth year; what had happened to his once agile mind? "She was wearing no jewellery. Are her ears pierced?"

"I think so," said Ludo, "but I've also seen some young, aristocratic dandies about town wearing ear studs like that."

"Fine, good work Bulla. Pouch it and we'll take it with us. Is there anything else?" They shook their heads. "Then let's get out of here."

They heard the scratching when they were back on the stairs, like a large animal clawing at wood. Ambrosius held up his hand, stopping Ludo's complaints about his wife in mid-sentence. The noise stopped, then resumed louder before stopping again.

A powerful blow made the door in the entrance chamber rattle. The watchmen clattered down the stairs, weapons drawn. In response, footsteps scuffled on the other side of the door and then skittered away. Ambrosius dropped his shoulder and barged it open, stumbling onto the slippery cobbles outside. The retreating figure half turned towards him, already ten strides away. A hood concealed his face and in the poor light he couldn't get a good look at the features. The four men set off after him but, for all save Ludo, the long shift they had already endured had stripped speed from their tired legs.

"Get back here!" yelled Ambrosius.

The man was approaching a stone archway at the end of a narrow alley and reached into his cloak, discarding a long, thin object that clattered to the floor.

Murderer! An image of the girl's innocent young face flashed before Ambrosius' eyes. Rapist! He couldn't let him get away!

But the strength in his legs was fading fast and he knew they would tie up in seconds. The hooded figure turned left, skidding but regaining his balance, and disappeared from view. Ambrosius felt a shove in his back and he stumbled as Titus' sturdy frame barged past.

"Sorry trib," he mumbled, sprinting clear. He turned left several strides ahead of them and also disappeared.

They emerged onto a street that threaded towards the Cattle Market. During these twilight hours, the narrow streets belonged to the poor. All along the way, unwashed scavengers eked out their existence in search of scraps or bones, shuffling between the shopkeepers who had already begun to open the pavement awnings and raise the shutters ahead of a long day's trade. The fugitive, pursued by Titus, startled several of them as they stepped onto the pavement and barged them aside. The road surface itself was invisible under its coating of dung and refuse, and Titus knew that, if he were forced over the steep kerb, his pursuit would be over in a heartbeat.

And yet, though his burst of energy was flagging, Titus did not stop. He had not boxed in six years, and in that time had added spare weight to his frame in no time at all. He tried to ignore the sensation that he was running through ever-thickening mud and focused on the figure who kept flicking desperate glances over his shoulder.

In a last ditch effort to shake Titus, the man turned hard left into a narrow side street that was blocked by two vegetable carts parked side by side. He hesitated and then set off towards them but stopped again when it was clear he was trapped. He turned to face Titus and, panting, yanked down his hood and glared back at him. There were only a few strands of greasy black hair plastered to his forehead, damp with sweat. His cheeks were sunken, and his sharp eyes were too small for their dark sockets.

Titus was blowing harder than he had even at the peak of his training. Under any other circumstances, the contest would have been a complete mismatch. As it was, he could barely find the breath to speak.

"Just … give it up … you damn fool," he said drawing himself upright.

His quarry sneered and reached into his filthy cloak and produced a vicious looking knife. Titus checked his step and wiped his mouth. He dropped to a fighting stance with his cudgel raised above his shoulder. The knifeman registered Titus' cauliflower ears and calcified features, and his face twitched with uncertainty. Then he attacked, making sweeping arcs left and right with successive steps forwards, and the blade ripped through the air.

At the end of the backhand swipe, Titus brought his club crashing down on the knifeman's wrist. There was a crack of bone and the knife was dislodged, tumbling into the gutter. He shrieked and clutched his hand, taking his eyes of Titus, who stepped forwards and delivered a brutal hook that lifted his assailant off his feet and span him around. He was already unconscious as he bounced off the vegetable carts behind him and slumped to the floor.

Ludo had heard the sickening blow as he rounded the corner: Ambrosius was next, followed by Bulla, who looked ready to expire and sounded like a braying donkey. Ambrosius replaced his baton on his belt and slapped Titus on the back, waiting for his breath to return.

"Have you killed him?"

He approached the footpad who, to his surprise, was now snoring. Titus shrugged and retrieved the knife from the gutter.

"Quite pretty," he said to himself, wiping the dirt off it and pocketing it.

As Ambrosius bent over the unconscious man, he tried to quell the familiar surge of anger that made him dizzy with anticipation. It would be easy to wake him up and watch him gurgle and sputter as he drew a knife across his throat. Or to pound him repeatedly in the face as he asked the same question he always asked criminals he had just caught. Did you do it, you bastard? Did you kill my beautiful wife, the only person I truly loved? Just say the word!

"Tribune, what now?"

Ambrosius took a deep breath and stood, letting his mind clear. "Bulla, go and see if you can find whatever he threw away in that alley."

The watchman's chest was still heaving and he shot him a look of exasperation. He turned away, muttering Syrian curses under his breath.

"Titus, help me bind him up, then we'll bring him to and walk him in. Ludo?"

"Yes tribune?"

"On your way back, tell Bulla to bring the print and ear stud to the barracks."

"Right. And what about the body?"

Ambrosius considered the problem for a moment, caught between protocol and the situation he had created. "Have her wrapped up and carted to the Watch House's crypt. The dockside can be reopened when the search is done."

"The crypt?" Ludo raised his eyebrows. "And then?"

"And then it's over. You can resume your duties."

Ludo regarded him for a few moments before nodding and walking away.

"And Ludo?"

"Tribune?"

"My thanks. If there's any trouble, I'm taking it all. Understood?"

Ludo shrugged and walked on. "I saw nothing, I did nothing, Prefect. In fact, I wasn't even there..."

III

Emperor Septimius Severus' vast palace loomed before him, dominating the Palatine hill like a gleaming marble citadel. Its grand facade of narrow, soaring arches looked as though it had been designed for gods rather than men. But then modesty was not a characteristic of the Prefect of the Praetorian Guard. Though he was over fifty, Gaius Plautianus looked much younger, with thick black hair swept across a craggy brow, and piercing blue eyes that combined savage intelligence and depthless cruelty. His thick beard was shot through with flecks of grey and was cultivated to resemble that of classical busts of Hercules, and his impressive physique did not detract from the comparison. Not only did he live up to the very epitome of a member of the ancient aristocratic Fulvia clan, but as a former legionary commander, consular senator and current favourite of the Emperor, he had set daunting new standards.

His strides were confident and purposeful, and not without a certain swagger. His consular robe, clasped at the shoulder with a golden brooch and belted at the waist with a silver studded cingula, clung to his thick calves in the face of the brisk wind that had cleared the last of the fog from the city. Passers-by and idlers milling around the gates to the Circus Maximus cleared a path for the group, and their conversations dropped to a whisper as they watched them pass.

But the Prefect ignored them all as if they didn't exist. The conversation with his five Praetorian deputies was ribald and brash, and when the informer tried to keep pace with them and catch his attention Plautianus looked through him. The informer was forced to scurry ahead of the group and then trot backwards in an effort to catch his eye.

"Commander, sir? A word with you if I may?"

"Tertius," he said, employing his own term of address, meaning 'third', which he had never deigned to explain, "I see you bobbing up and down like a sewer rat. What do you want?"

"Just a private word … if you have the time?"

"Certainly. You have as long as it takes me to walk from here to there," he said without breaking stride, "which I make about thirty paces." The other Praetorians sneered at the informer, who was now jogging alongside the group and was becoming exhausted.

"I think … it may be more appropriate to talk … in private."

"Nonsense! I won't be seen plotting with the likes of you in front of these fine fellows! Out with it man, we're nearly there!"

The informer squirmed. "Well, it concerns my payment … which I haven't received."

"Vulcan's hairy arse! I've not even delivered the information yet, less still detained the seditious little shit!"

"No sir!" he replied, raising his hands, "You misunderstand me! I was referring to … the other matter? With the priest? In the College of Augurs?"

Plautianus shook his head. "That was second hand, second rate information. Don't get ideas above your station, you scoundrel! I use other informers you know. But as I'm in a generous mood today … what do you say, men: the spy offers up any other half-baked nugget to compensate and he gets his payment?"

"Commander, anything to move the little 'turd' from downwind. The stench is making my stomach turn!" The group roared with laughter at the pun.

The informer bared his teeth and forced a smile. "Yes, very droll Well did you know that the vigiles are dealing with a murder they failed to disclose to the City Prefect?"

"Good for them. Relevance to me?"

They were at the foot of the palace steps now, and two armed guards outside stepped aside for them. Tertius bounded up two at a time to get nearer to Plautianus.

"I think the victim," he hissed, "was the young mistress of the Emperor's son."

Plautianus called the group to a halt. He frowned at the informer and fixed his eyes upon him. His voice was low and bristled with menace. "Did you just accuse Caracalla, son of the Emperor, of having an affair, you poisonous little fucker?"

Tertius swallowed hard. "This is why I sought to speak to you in private, commander. I know that he is your son-in-law."

Plautianus' breathing had become ragged with barely concealed rage. "Go on."

"Her name is Terentia and she's the daughter …"

"Yes, yes I know whose damn daughter she is!" He took a deep breath, fighting against his anger, and smoothed back his hair. "And you say the fucking bucket carriers are dealing with it?"

Tertius nodded. After a long pause, the Prefect jabbed his finger at Tertius. "You wait outside for me here. Don't move and don't speak to anyone, understood?"

But before he could reply, the Prefect had swept past him and entered the palace.

IV

Emperor Septimius Severus' vast and opulent reception chamber was empty. But this did not concern Gaius Plautianus, who knew exactly where to find him. His footsteps rang out against the marble flagstones as he strode past the stone lions guarding the royal throne, which glimmered with ancient magnificence in the light cast by the giant candelabra. He threw aside the purple velvet curtains that concealed a private corridor leading to the Emperor's herb garden, the innermost of his inner sanctums, strictly out of bounds for all save his most favoured few. His Praetorian escort knew the drill well: they remained stood to attention in the main chamber, their eyes respectfully averted from the throne.

The corridor emerged at one end of a garden bordered on three sides by a portico and on the fourth by a colourful pavilion containing an aviary reputed to hold the finest collection of rare birds known to man. The scent of rosemary and mint, and the playful twitter of birds greeted Plautianus as he spotted the Emperor strolling deep in thought with his back to him.

"Imperator!" he saluted, his fist striking his chest with a heavy thud.

Septimius Severus waved away the formality without turning around. "Come, old friend. Walk with me."

When Plautianus drew level, the Emperor gave him a sad smile, gripping his arm. Though they shared the same Libyan heritage and were of a similar age, the heavy burden of overseeing the vast empire had taken its toll. The once thick curls of his hair and beard had thinned and greyed, and his swarthy face was a map of deep lines. But it was the stoop of his shoulders that was most telling: his head was permanently bowed in contemplation.

He stopped by one of the sections of herbs, whose tiny yellow buds were wilting, and clicked his tongue.

"Of all the hardy perennials to fail me, the fennel is dying. Doesn't like the cold," he said rubbing the crumbling leaves between his fingers. "Spring seems like an age away, doesn't it?"

"Yes sir," he replied: small talk was not his strength. "That it does."

They strolled on for a few more moments in silence.

"Matronalia festival in two days." Septimius' tone brightened. "I expect you have bought your wife a gift befitting her nobility?"

"I was never very good at the smaller touches. I …"

"Julia thrives. For over half my life she has been the cornerstone of all this," he continued, gesturing to the palace around him, "and so setting aside one day in the calendar by way of gratitude seems pitifully inadequate, doesn't it?"

Plautianus gave him a look: the Emperor was being more introspective than ever.

"And these incessant rumours … the soothsayers and doom-mongers are having a field day. This fog that comes and goes, they say, is a sign of the gods' displeasure, trying to smother the human folly they see beneath them. Or that the Northmen's own deities have sent it to conceal their armies that approach our city gates as we speak. But the frontier roads and borders are no more threatened now than at any point in the last decade: that much we do know." The Emperor stopped and turned to his Prefect. "No. The shadows are much closer to home than that, are they not Gaius?" An enigmatic smile crossed his face. "Well? Was this not the reason you requested my time: to nip another plot against my life in the bud?"

"You read my concerns too well, sir. I'm afraid I cannot make the information any more trifling than that." They carried on walking.

Septimius sighed. By now they were at the aviary. He picked up a handful of millet and poured it down a chute where it collected in a small bowl inside the cage. "And who, tell me, has been overheard whispering in dark corners of the senate house?"

"Senator Maracanthus, sir."

The Emperor whistled softly. "Senator Maracanthus! Poor old underappreciated Marcus Maracanthus. Did my overlooking you for the consulship really wound you so deeply? Revenge is so … futile and tasteless."

"Would you have me arrest him, sir?"

Septimius pursed his lips and retreated into his thoughts for a while. Plautianus often thought that at such moments he had slipped into a trance.

"Who else?"

"In fairness, no-one else seems to have entertained him sir."

"And the source of this information is?"

"A spy; a quadruplator to be exact."

"Such a wearisome, tawdry business. How reliable is he?"

"As reliable as they come, in my experience. I have a secretive network, as you know, and I have people watching over him too." He shifted the weight on his feet. "May I speak openly?"

"You may, as ever."

"I have always had my doubts about Maracanthus, with or without the input of informers."

"Oh? His record is impeccable, even though he is a new man."

"He is from Gades, and Spaniards are never to be trusted. They say Hannibal fathered enough love children in the region for their treacherous descendants to populate a small city!"

The Emperor's face cracked into a smile. "I hope your doubts are better founded than legionary tavern talk!"

Plautianus tapped the side of his head. "Of course! Circumstantial perhaps, but corroborated, nevertheless."

"You shall not have him arrested." Septimius was serious again.

"No?"

"No. With nothing more concrete than the hearsay of a spy, I wouldn't want to drag the whole wretched business through a trial. Make sure he goes missing on his way home from the senate or something, but keep it clean, understood? And if he requests his own honourable exit, do not deny him that small mercy."

"Yes sir. All understood."

"More feeble allegations of conspiracy, father?"

Septimius and Plautianus turned in surprise. They had not heard Caracalla enter the courtyard and had no idea for how long he had been stood listening with his hands clasped behind his back.

"Ah, my son. One day you may learn the value of the informer."

Plautianus regarded Caracalla with thinly veiled dislike. The young whelp was only seventeen but had developed an unsettling habit of appearing at uncomfortable moments and then just staring with those depthless brown eyes and the permanent frown that gave the impression of constant displeasure with life. Combining Moorish and Syrian heritage, in many respects he was a handsome boy; tall, slim, with unruly dark curls and the first wisp of a beard on his cheeks, but it was the strange manner about him that nullified his qualities. Plautianus was in no doubt that his daughter Fulvia Plautilla was not happy in her marriage to him, or indeed the reverse. But it was a politically crucial arrangement.

"Young master, and how are your studies progressing?"

"Tedious, but progressing. Father, I would like a word too." He flicked a contemptuous glance at Plautianus. "In private."

The Prefect bristled but Septimius let the disrespectful gesture pass. "Of course, but let me say something first. Don't think I didn't hear of the beating you gave to Uncolpius last night. The poor fellow is hobbling about the place black and blue! Slaves are an expensive business you know and are not, despite what others may say, to be treated like dogs."

"I agree," added Plautianus, "A delicate balancing act of cajoling, iron discipline and the faintest hope of manumission."

Caracalla smirked at him. "Not unlike how to treat over-opinionated wives then. I had accused him of stealing one of my ear studs and wanted to test his integrity. He passed, actually. But anyway, father?"

Plautianus clenched his jaw, gripped the Emperor's hand and took his leave, offering Caracalla a tight, sardonic smile as he passed him.

Caracalla watched him go. "I don't like him one bit. He thinks far too highly of himself and it's all gone to his head. Mother agrees."

Septimius wagged a finger at him. "Now you hold your tongue! He is a fine soldier and an experienced adviser, both of which talents your mother accepts. I do not employ him for his charming company. You ought to show him some old fashioned respect, like your brother Geta."

"Geta's a stammering fool. And he's studying in Athens, so he doesn't have to suffer the man like I do."

"What is it you wanted to speak about?"

Caracalla bowed his head. "I'm worried about Terentia. She was supposed to see me last night but failed to show. That never happens."

"The gods, will you stop mooning about after her! You are a responsible, married man and should be thinking every day about taking over this great empire after I die. You are too young for affairs with consul's daughters! And Terentius Piso is a trusted friend!" He softened his tone when he saw how close to tears his son was. "She will be fine, I'm sure of it."

"No. I had one of my dreams and it was very vivid. I think something dreadful has happened to her."

V

The quaestionarius wiped the blood-flecked sweat off his forehead with a rag, and hawked a ball of spittle into the corner of the dank, echoing cell.

"Old leather, tribune."

Ambrosius raised his eyebrow. "Meaning?"

"It's a phrase we interrogators use. It means I can go on lashing him for as long as you like. He'll mark but he won't tear."

Ambrosius nodded and turned to face the wretched looking prisoner. His arms were shackled above his head to manacles dangling from the ceiling and the filthy tunic that now clung in tatters to his body revealed here and there angry red welts from the whip. Though he shivered, he glared at Ambrosius with burning hatred. The watchman ignored the malevolence and looked him over. The heavy silence was punctuated by a hiss as a drop of water from the ceiling fell onto one of the pitch-burning torches fixed to the walls.

"Did you examine his body, as instructed?"

"I did, tribune. There's plenty old scarring there but nothing recent. I don't mind giving him a few different stripes, make it seem he's been scratched, if you like?"

Ambrosius laughed. "Not at the moment, Vitalis. Revive him and throw him back in his cell."

The interrogator grunted and upended a leather bucket containing ice cold water over the gasping prisoner. Just then, Titus thundered down the stone steps into the chamber carrying two cloth pallets.

"Tribune, look!" He thrust in front of him the initial copy of the boot print found at the dockside and then handed him a second print, pressed on a similarly prepared dustsheet. "I don't think he was there. The prisoner's hobnails don't have the same pattern, and they're worn out. And they're too small."

Ambrosius frowned. "Vitalis! Over here."

The granite faced interrogator lumbered over, whistling and trying to disguise the limp from the serious injury that had curtailed his days as a patrolling watchman. Although he had been a vigil for almost twenty years and his knowledge of the city streets was the equal of any man in any cohort, he was always deferential to men of much less service but higher rank.

"Yes tribune?"

"What was it he said about breaking into the dockside building?"

"Ah … because he lives on the street and he wanted somewhere warm to sleep. He carries the crowbar for that reason, and the knife for self-protection."

"But why that building?"

The quaestionarius counted the reasons on his thick fingers. "Because it was the first one he came to. He said he had no idea you'd all be in there, less still that someone'd been killed inside. And that, if he'd known, of course he would have chosen another one. That was pretty much all he had to say before he clammed up and I got out the lash. A very surly customer, all in all."

"One more thing. You've dealt with more dead bodies: how long before stiffness sets in?"

"Depends, tribune. Cold can slow it down but usually peaks after about twelve hours."

"Which means she would have been killed just before the first watch of the night?"

The gaoler thought about it. "Probably just before darkness fell, yes."

Ambrosius shook his head. "That's all, Vitalis. Make sure he's given bread and water and allowed to clean himself up a bit. And get the medic to have a look at his injuries. He'll stay here until the Prefect of the Watch makes a decision with him."

"Tribune."

"Oh, and Vitalis. Who's the optio in charge of the cells? You appear to be doing two jobs."

Vitalis looked away. "It's Statius. He's sick."

"Again?"

The interrogator nodded and walked off, whistling a different army march.

"So you don't reckon he had anything to do with it then?"

Ambrosius registered the fatigue and disappointment in the centurion's face. He gripped his shoulder and winked at him. "I don't think so, Titus. But an impressive chase for a washed-up old soldier nevertheless. Get one of our clerks to scratch up a quick libellus; I'll seal it and get it despatched. Then you can get some rest. You earned it."

VI

Incorporated into the original walls of the city, the Castra Praetoria dominated the north eastern skyline of Rome with a faceless, imperious disdain. So featureless to the outsider, the camp was a hive of power and ambition. It was because of its role in the assassination of his predecessor Pertinax that the Emperor had disbanded the original Praetorian Guard and replaced it with five thousand of his own trusted men from the legions that he had himself lead to victory against the Pannonians. As if their loyalty wasn't assured enough, he had already increased their pay by half. These elite soldiers shared the camp with nine divisions of Urban Cohorts, junior in status, under the command of the City Prefect.

As Gaius Plautianus strode to the main gate, the informer trailing in his wake, there was a flurry of activity atop the walls.

"Halt, state your business and the watchword," ordered the sentry, whose crestless helmet marked him out as an Urbanus.

Plautianus looked up at him and the sentry's eyes widened. "Humble apologies commander! Open the gates! Now!"

Plautianus shook his head and stalked inside once the gates had rumbled open. "Wait here," he bounded up the steps to the gatehouse and burst into the guardroom. The sentries inside jumped back in shock. "Well?"

The young soldiers looked to each other in bewilderment.

"Do you want to hear the damn watchword or not?"

"I … but I knew it was you, Prefect!"

"And what if it was someone who merely looked like me and told you the watchword was 'I'm going to come up there and put a fucking dent in your head and then piss all over you'? Would you have still let that person in just because you thought it was me?"

"No sir."

"I should fucking hope not!" he bellowed into his face.

The informer listened to the tirade and shifted in discomfort. He hated this camp. He hated being looked at as if he had just been scraped off the shoes of the guardsmen or cavalry who looked down at him as they passed by, or spat onto the floor of the parade square and ground it into the sand with their boots. He knew they all understood the nature of his business

31

and they resented the fuel it gave to the rumour and intrigue that always threatened to ignite the city into revolution. There was an abundance of precedents, particularly during an Emperor's twilight years, when the struggle to fill the vacuum of power could be at its most bloody. And it would be their own jobs and lives on the line.

Plautianus emerged from the sentry post stony-faced and the informer followed him down the main avenue of the camp, which divided the Urban Cohorts' and the Praetorian quarters. They passed Spartan, single storey barracks, otherwise featureless but for their small, grilled windows. However, on the other side of these, the informer knew, the buildings were more hospitable, with stuccoed porticoes, stables and paddocks, generous quarters for senior officers and corps staff and open air exercise palaestra. Riotous shouts emanated from one of these as they approached. Whilst passing the entrance, Plautianus stopped and, arms folded, watched the drills within. The informer noted his change in demeanour: it was well known that, unlike many predecessors, his ascension to the prefecture was through military rather than political success.

A detachment of Praetorians was practising the 'tortoise' formation. At the sound of a whistle, from a standing start each man dropped to a crouch, gripped the belt of the man in front with one hand and hefted his oblong shield above his back with the other. Meanwhile, another detachment of the guard was bombarding the formation with wooden bricks and stones, buckets of hot sand and colourful abuse. Once they had advanced the length of the palaestra, they broke formation and ran back to the start, whilst a gnarled old drill instructor barked insults at them, stamping on the back of those slacking in their sets of press-ups. The whole exercise was brutally exhausting: even in the bracing air, the men were drenched in sweat and their faces were contorted with pain.

But there was someone on the exercise ground not participating in these drills. Plautianus was about to move on when he caught sight of him, and a grin crossed his face. The informer peered around the lintel to see what he was looking at. The barrel-chested Deputy Prefect, Vibius Brutus, was throwing punches at a padded post with such reverberating force that they threatened to wrench it out of the ground. So engrossed was he in the exercise that he didn't hear his name being called, and it was only when he heard the loud whistle that he stopped and looked up. Though their heritage was different, a casual observer might assume they were brothers. They had similar physiques, though Brutus was a little shorter and broader.

Similar too was the look of restless energy in his narrow eyes. He sauntered over, wiping the sweat from his face with his leather wrist wraps. The two clasped hands.

"When you've finished beating up that twig, join us in my quarters. But have a wash first: you smell like an elephant." Plautianus punched him playfully in the chest.

"There's no-one left to fight me. And the post doesn't moan like a whore whenever I beat her!" he replied, ignoring the informer. "Give me a bit longer. Maybe you can even break open some wine, you old miser."

Plautianus grunted with satisfaction and continued to his quarters at the opposite end of the camp, above which fluttered two pennants, each depicting a red scorpion with its pincers raised. The soldiers guarding the entrance saluted and stepped aside. In the austere reception chamber were four stools and a table on which was an earthenware water pitcher, whilst a crucifix shaped wooden frame on the right supported the Prefect's bronze parade cuirass. The room beyond allowed more concessions to comfort, if not quite luxury. Oil lamps and candelabra dotted the perimeter, in the midst of which was a huge desk. A calfskin map of the fourteen regions of Rome occupied the better part of another wall, and a flattering marble bust of the Emperor, looking many years younger, dominated another. A heady smell of expensive leather, spices, wax, various oils and stale sweat emanated from the chamber.

"Sit," said Plautianus, pointing to one of the stools. "I want the City Prefect to witness what you have to say."

"I was hoping, commander, for a word in private."

Plautianus rounded on him. "What more do you want? Is this not private enough for you? I don't make a habit of allowing your type within these walls!" he said, lying. "This concerns him and he doesn't care for your profession any more than do I!" Plautianus went outside and issued curt orders to the sentries. "I intend to freshen up. Help yourself to some water. You'll be called when we are ready.

VII

Even as Ambrosius entered his courtyard, he had a vague sense of having missed something. The leaf-strewn square had seen better days, and the weathered stone Cupid bore a pitcher that had not spouted water for as long as he could remember. Nevertheless the tenants of the eight tenements counted themselves luckier than most, especially those like the tribune who had lived in the dangerous slums of the Subura district. An old woman, bent double, hobbled past him on her way out and he greeted her as he crossed the courtyard.

It hit him as soon as he opened the door. His young daughter Poppeia was scowling at him, hands on hips, dark eyes flashing with hurt. An image of her mother flitted before his tired eyes. He struck his forehead with the palm of his hand and hurried over to her. "Bona Dea, I'm sorry!" he protested, with outstretched arms. But she ducked under them.

"You promised me!" she shouted, tears welling in her eyes. "You promised you wouldn't forget again!"

"I … work …" But even as he started, he realised just how feeble was the excuse.

"It's always work with you! You never have time for anything else!"

Anna entered, her hands raised in a gesture of peace. "Hey, hey, little flower. Now what's all this fuss?" She shot Ambrosius a disapproving frown.

"Come on, let's go and pick up that dress. It's not too late!"

Poppeia burst into tears. "It is too late!" she said between sobs, "He said he would only keep it for the first hour. It's midday now! You forgot about it because you didn't like it, because it's not the sort of thing mummy would have worn!"

"He might still have it! And there's still today and tomorrow before Matronalia. That's plenty of time to find another!"

"You don't understand!" she said, balling her fists. "You never understand! I never ask you for anything! Just to show some interest in things I like!"

Ambrosius winced. Anna noticed and gave him a look.

It'll be alright.

"If you'd been around more, mummy would still be here!" She ran sobbing into her room, slamming the door behind her. The accusation, they all knew, was unfair but stung him nonetheless and he sagged against the door, backheeling it in frustration.

Anna hesitated for a moment and then took him by the arm, leading him to a table in an adjoining room that doubled as kitchen and bedroom. Her pallet was tucked alongside the brick oven, the warmest part of the draughty tenement, and a rare luxury in most blocks in Rome. She and Poppeia had been making bread, and the homely smell lingered. She picked off a morsel and offered him the rest. He shook his head and they sat in silence for a while.

"Well ... She's certainly her mother's daughter!"

Ambrosius looked away. Faint sounds of street life drifted through the room: an anvil being struck; raised voices: a hawker selling his wares, perhaps, or someone intoning one of the Imperial cults.

"She's still too young to control her heart with her head, Ambrosius. Give her time."

He said nothing.

Anna noticed again the worry lines around his eyes, deeper than usual. She shifted on her stool.

"Do you still pray twice daily to the household gods for revenge?"

Now he looked at her. His eyes were not friendly but she asked anyway.

"Does it help?"

He didn't reply.

"Or does it make you feel angry? Even more angry that they stay silent, or maybe even mock you, or maybe," she said raising a finger, "don't even exist. While you hope against hope that one dark night you will bump into whoever it was in some alleyway so you can finally have your revenge?"

His eyes were glaring now.

"But have you ever thought 'What if this never happens? Or what if he's already dead?' Well?" She paused. "You can look at me like that all you want, as long as you hear me. Because I worry about you. I worry that other lives – yours, Poppeia's – are slipping by whilst you pursue this ... this all-consuming hatred. Larissa is never coming back, Ambrosius, but you can still do something about Poppeia's pain. And your own."

She could see, as she had before, the fire in his eyes being dampened by the tears that were now gathering.

35

"When the bailiffs came knocking the very day after my … after Decimus' funeral, and looked right through me at the meagre possessions we had with nothing but money in their eyes, I prayed as well, just like you. I prayed that the Furies would pluck out their black hearts whilst Fortuna would smile on me every time I used to loop that old tray over my shoulders and go and sell whatever I could salvage from the rubbish tips, do you remember it?"

Despite himself, a weak smile tugged at his lips and he nodded. "But I needn't have prayed to the distant heavens because you and Larissa lived right next door to me and I agreed to move in after a bit of persuasion …"

"A lot of persuasion," he said quietly.

"Alright, a lot of persuasion. The point I'm making, Ambrosius, is that sometimes the answer to our prayers is close at hand, and it doesn't take the intervention of gods to point it out."

She poured them both a cup of water. "So I have a question for you."

He raised an eyebrow.

"Tell me one thing that Poppeia has done this week."

"What?"

"Seriously, just one thing."

He frowned at her. "I don't know. She's been to her lessons … she's … she's…" Her green eyes were intense and made him look away in shame. "Fine. I don't really know."

"I've not asked her but I'm sure Poppeia doesn't know anything about what you've done either, or how, or why, does she?"

"No," he said after a time. "Probably not."

"You lug your cares around with you and lock them away at the end of each day, and nobody but you knows about them! She's only a girl but she is growing up so quickly, Ambrosius!" Anna rapped the table with her knuckles for emphasis. "She needs you! Talk to her! Tell her how you feel and how much you, too, miss Larissa. Tell her how much she reminds you of her mother's best qualities and how deeply she is loved. I promise you she'll listen and she may even surprise you with what she understands."

A tear breached Ambrosius' eyelid and others threatened to follow. She reached across the table and grasped his hand.

"Go and get some sleep. I'll take Poppeia out and get her what she wants. And when we're back, perhaps you can speak to her then."

VIII

Under the gaze of the most powerful men in Rome, the informer Tertius squirmed on his seat: Fabius Clio, the City Prefect, Vibius Brutus, Deputy Praetorian Prefect and Gaius Plautianus, Praetorian Prefect and the most senior of the three. He had never seen Clio before but he knew that he must be a senator with rigorous legal training, because these were prerequisites for the City Prefect's job. He had a high-pitched voice, thinning fair hair brushed forwards to disguise its retreat, intelligent dark eyes and a pointed nose. The powerful physiques of the two Praetorians either side of him made him look like a slender child in comparison and, whilst they lolled on their chairs, Clio had propped his chin on his hands and was watching him like a hawk. Tertius cleared his throat.

"Exalted gentlemen, I know that you find aspects of my work distasteful," Plautianus threw back his head with laughter at that, "but … but the burden of relaying the truth is a heavy one, because if I knowingly relay false information or information that I do not believe to be true …"

"Yes, yes, spare us all that bullshit, will you. We're busy men, just get to the point," said Clio with a dismissive wave.

"Yes sir. I'm just saying I know the consequences of passing on false information. Just this morning, in the middle of the last watch, I was walking home, taking a shortcut along the docks when I came across a body. It was the body of a young girl, fourteen or fifteen at most, I would say, and quite well-to-do looking, if you understand me. Her stole was covered in blood. It was only when I moved aside some of her hair that I saw its source: a large dent in her skull. Very shortly after this, as I stood there wondering what to do next, I heard footsteps approaching and saw the glow of watchmen's torches. I panicked, because I would have been arrested for her murder, and so I hid on the roof of a disused building." The informer raised his hand to pre-empt the question on Brutus' lips. "Yes, yes, I know you might wonder why, with the vigiles on hand, I didn't just continue on my way home. Unfortunately, it's the nature of my work. I cannot make a living if I fail to contribute information of my own that might go towards the apprehension of a dangerous criminal at large."

"Mars' great hairy balls! Did you hear that? The man's heart is as pure as a Vestal Virgin's!" Brutus snorted at him. "And here's me thinking you were just a common little bounty hunter!"

"The gods! Will you please refrain from this oily self-indulgence and just stick to the facts!" added Clio, throwing up his hands in frustration.

Tertius swallowed hard and forced a smile. "Certainly. One of the others, whose name appeared to be Titus, a great oaf of a man, questioned the tribune, called Ambrosius, why he wasn't about to hand the matter straight over to the Urban Cohorts." Tertius noticed Brutus flinch with interest at the mention of one of the names. "The tribune said, and I'm talking verbatim here, that he should do but he wasn't going to, lest the girl end up thrown in a pit, like the body of every other victim they investigate." Tertius glanced at Clio in the hope of seeing him bristle at that insult, but his expression was inscrutable. "Well, Ambrosius then ordered the watchmen to rope off the area."

Tertius was about to continue but murmurs of interest made him stop his account.

"And I'm told by commander Plautianus that you were able to identify the body of this girl. Who was she?" asked Clio.

"Terentia, daughter of consul Terentius Piso."

"And you know this how?" he asked, frowning.

Tertius took a deep breath, steeling himself. "Because I have seen her cavorting in private with the Emperor's son. The affair is no secret within certain circles of informers."

"What?" Plautianus jumped to his feet, his face crimson. He reached for his sword, which he then remembered he had removed before visiting the Emperor. That moment of forgetfulness saved the informer's life. Vibius Brutus leapt off his chair.

"Easy, Gaius! We may need this little reptile alive! Relax man!" he protested, clamping Plautianus' arms by his side. "Calm yourself and sit! I know this is hard but we have to hear it!"

Plautianus sagged back, his body shaking with rage. "I will rip off your balls and feed them to you if you dare slander my daughter's marriage one more time!"

Tertius had cowered away. "Please commander! I appreciate there is never a good time to hear such a thing but I am certain of my facts! I went to some lengths to verify them! And as soon as I was sure I came straight to you. You may despise me and what I do but … surely you would rather hear it from me, like this, than overhear some drunk peasant in the street or some old gossip at the well?"

Plautianus glared back at him, clenching and unclenching his fists, but his ragged breathing began to subside. Clio massaged the bridge of his nose with his thumb and forefinger. "Leaving aside for now the sordid details, there are other questions to answer. Quite pertinent questions."

"I think I know this Titus fellow. If it's the same man, he was a champion boxer in the legions," said Brutus. "He continually refused to fight me, the miserable coward. Says his wife forbids it. Can you believe that?"

Plautianus shot him a reproving look. "You talk of boxing in the middle of this? Do you ever think of anything else, man? What about this tribune of The Watch: do you know anything useful about him? Who is he, anyhow? And what's his interest?"

Brutus shrugged his massive shoulders.

"I know who he is," said Clio, brushing a spot of lint from his red leather sandals. "I know him quite well in fact. His name is Ambrosius Milo. He was a carpenter somewhere in the north of the city but four or five years ago his wife was murdered. He became the worst sort of Subura drunkard and gambler for a while before he came to his senses and was taken on as a watchman. He has something about him alright: he became tribune in five years, when it takes most other men at least another decade." Even Brutus, ever reluctant to bestow praise on another man, especially a mere vigil, grunted in agreement. "He earned recognition for cleaning up the acts of one or two of the centuries he was attached to with reputations for being the rowdiest, most demoralised in the city. As a matter of fact I personally offered him promotion within one of my Urban Cohorts. He turned me down flat."

"Witless fool," rumbled Plautianus. "Why?"

"He was very bitter that we had no success in tracking down his wife's killer: he told me his young daughter could do a better job and that he was content where he was." Clio gave the smirking Brutus a withering look. "A fool indeed," he added pointedly.

"Well? Was there any progress made in identifying a killer?"

Clio shook his head. "We turned out the usual tavern roughs and street corner cut-throats, and our quaestionarii were kept busy for a while I remember, but nothing came of it. The guilds in the area were no help either. They got fed up with Ambrosius himself hassling them every day, and there were rumours he assaulted one of the local politicos, but nothing came of it."

"I like him already," muttered Brutus.

"She was killed near the Hill of Gardens and brigands sometimes flit in and out of the northern boundaries: it was probably one of them, or a damned Samnite, given the level of violence. But people have short memories in this city and before long, someone else above the level of the usual worthless peasant gets killed and we have to move on. There's only so much that can be done, you know that Prefect."

Plautianus made a non-committal murmur and shifted in his chair. "Anyway, the fact remains this whole mess needs clearing up and, whatever this watchman's reasons, he has made a grievous error of judgement. This was a consul's daughter, damn his arrogance! And you should be taking it personally, Clio. See to it that he makes a full report and a grovelling apology to you and then walks away from this matter. Immediately. Is that clear?"

"Perfectly clear, Prefect."

"And one more thing. Where in Hades is the body now?"

The informer Tertius, who had been trying to speak, raised his hand.

"What?"

"I hadn't managed to tell you everything."

"There's more?"

"Yes. The tribune and a few of his men broke into a building. He seemed to think the girl was killed inside rather than on the dockside."

"Well? Did they find anything?"

"I don't know. They would certainly have found me lying on a nearby roof though, so I had to leave at that point. But before this, I saw – not to say heard – the tribune breaking the girl's fingers and then take a knife to one of them."

Clio wrinkled his nose. "Are you quite sure?"

"Juno's tits! The man's a fucking lunatic!" Plautianus laughed without mirth. "Not being content with taking on something that is none of his business is one thing, but desecrating the body of a senator's daughter … it beggars belief! Deal with him, Clio, or else it'll be me that you have to face. And you," he said, turning to the informer, "if you have nothing else to offer, can go."

"Yes sir," he jumped up, grateful to be on his way, then hesitated.

"Well, can you not see yourself out?"

"Of course, commander. But there remains the question of my fees … if this is not an inappropriate time to raise the issue?"

Plautianus' voice was a low rumble. "Don't test my patience one second longer, you rodent. Bring me names, not tittle-tattle. Then you will be paid. Now get out!"

Tertius did not look back until he had left the camp.

IX

Dusk was falling as the senate broke for the day and a biting wind made the senators shudder as they filed out of the ancient building onto the wide steps to await their litter bearers. One or two of those whose attendants were late issued curses through chattering teeth as they watched their colleagues ease themselves into their own sedans and click their fingers through the thick curtains, to be swept away through the gloomy streets.

Marcus Maracanthus was one of the unlucky ones. As their numbers dwindled, the dark crept over the city and lights twinkled through the gaps in the shutters of the houses on the Palatine opposite, describing the contour of the hill. Soon, he and the elderly Praetor Lentulus Cato were the only two remaining on the steps, and their conversation died as they watched the onset of the moonless night. It occurred to Maracanthus that fate could not have provided him with a more appropriate figure than the hoary old conservative Cato to confide in. They were from vastly different backgrounds: Maracanthus the son of a Spanish ranch owner, Cato from a long and distinguished line of Roman statesmen stretching back beyond the turbulent years of the Gracchi.

No, he could bear it no more. He had only made arrangements to tell one person, an old and trusted friend, but what he really needed was the view of an experienced senator. But who could be trusted in these days of dangerous intrigue? Maracanthus turned to the elderly senator and was just about to speak when Cato was distracted by the noise of approaching footsteps.

"At last!" he rasped. "I'll have you flogged for this, useless fools!" He waved his walking stick at the four attendants who materialised from the darkness and were jogging over to the senate house, the sedan compartment bobbing up and down between them.

"Please accept our humble apologies, sir!" said the Moor as he lowered the litter to the floor. "We had to take diversion. There was trouble along Via Sallustiana. This was all my decision."

Maracanthus noticed that the strap securing the Moor's huge scimitar to his belt had been unfastened and the weapon had been exposed from underneath his cloak. But Cato waved him away. He turned back to Maracanthus as he eased himself onto the cushion.

"Will you not accept a lift, young Marcus? These great ogres can manage the both of us. In fact, I'd say they deserve it."

Maracanthus looked on, sorely tempted. The privacy of the litter would have provided a good opportunity for a quiet word but the frail old senator was shaking in the cold. "No, thank you all the same. Our houses couldn't be further apart. A safe journey home!"

Cato nodded and drew the curtain, and was whisked away towards his house on the Cispian Hill. Maracanthus watched him disappear and waited for a few more minutes. A dog howled somewhere in the distance and he thought he heard a quiet voice carried along the breeze. He wrapped his toga about his head and scratched his grey beard, wondering what had happened to his attendants. As a rule, he treated them well and they were reliable enough. Another dog barked, closer this time. The senator sighed and set off down the steps towards the Hill of Gardens.

As he passed the black outline of the newly constructed Arch of Septimius Severus on his left, he plunged into a darkness so profound it brushed against his skin and from which he knew he would not emerge until his feet struck the incline up Silversmiths' Rise. There were no houses along this stretch of road, only locked temples and civic buildings that had been boarded up for the night and which loomed over him from both sides of the narrow street. Nor did this part of the city, like much of the rest of it, have any torches affixed to the walls for the watchmen to attend to. He began to hum to himself to banish his misgivings. Yes, he would definitely raise the question to the aediles at the next meeting of the senate. Question to the house: why is the centre of Rome, one of the most dangerous, most densely populated cities in the world, so inadequately lit? And he would not let the usual tired excuse of expense decide the matter. Iron brackets, nails, pitch, wood, extra patrols … that would not scratch the surface of the obscene budgets routinely granted for even the most basic of public festivals.

The hairs on his nape tingled and the skin across his swarthy forehead tightened.

Was it a faint scuff of feet he heard ahead of him and to his left?

He stopped in his tracks and listened hard, trusting in his soldierly instincts. He had himself, more than once, led scouting parties deep into enemy territory in Pannonia, years ago. There had been few amongst his men with a more attuned sense of danger …

No, there was nothing waiting for him in the dark, only unseen leaves and twigs scraping across the ground. He felt his skin slacken.

He quickened his pace. After a few moments, his nerves began to hum and he froze to the spot. Something passed in front of the shadows a few yards ahead of him, blacker than the ambient darkness. He looked behind him, his mind racing. Fight or flight? The primeval animal instinct. In an instant, his mind was made up. He set off back down the street on legs that had become numb with fear, and his mind screamed at them to gather pace.

Another shadow hit him hard in his side, winding him as he clattered onto the street. He flung his arms about him in blind panic, catching his assailant in the midriff and making him grunt in pain. He felt powerful, furious hands grip his toga and an inhumanly solid blow to his head that - in the curious, omniscient sliver of a second before death - he knew could only come from a boxer's fist-plate.

X

The weak light offered by the candles dotted about the subterranean room cast giant shadows of the two men. Though there was no chance of their being disturbed or overheard, experience had taught them to exercise extreme caution at all times, and they spoke in hushed tones.

"We have … a problem," said the one with the bull neck and decaying yellow teeth.

"I assumed that was the reason you dragged me here in the dead of night," replied the other pulling his cloak tighter about him. "What?"

"It's the girl's body. Somehow, it's been found but it hasn't been handed over to the Urban Cohorts or the Praetorians. In fact," he said, rubbing his arm, "we're not entirely sure where it is."

"Not entirely sure?" his eyes narrowed. "Explain yourself."

"A patrol of watchmen found her. But for some reason, they didn't report it and it seems one of their tribunes has taken possession of it."

"And why would he want to do that?"

"I don't really know. It could be for any reason! I'm sure he doesn't know anything: how can he?"

"What did I tell you about disposing of her properly, you incompetent fool! On your life, you had better retrieve the little slut and close the matter once and for all. She jeopardised my position enough in life: I don't want even more grief now she is dead, do you hear?"

"Yes sir, I'll get straight on to it," he replied, scratching his forearm.

"What's the matter with you, you dolt?"

"She dug in her claws," he said, lifting up his sleeve, "see? Itches like hell."

He glanced at the three inflamed scratches on the soldier's thick forearm. "They're infected. Locate the body and deal with it. Do it unnoticed and the problem might work in our favour: the blame would fall squarely on the vigiles. They're under pressure as it is with their slow response to the Pincian fire and the funding from the tax on slave sales being threatened. One more foul up might finish them off. Don't let me down, or you'll end up the same way! Now, I'm going back home to sleep and I don't expect to be disturbed by anything less than good news." He swept out of the room without another word.

XI

As he did every time whilst doing the rounds of the Watch House, a rambling old dwelling bequeathed to the state years ago and converted as one of the outposts of Cohort IV, Ambrosius strolled past the dormitories and listened to the loud snores of the watchmen within. The foot patrols of the city were seldom uneventful and he appreciated the need to drain every last minute of sleep when the infrequent opportunity arose. By the end of Sebaciaria, a napping vigil would scarcely feel like he had rested his head on his pallet before the bugler would sound his watch and he would have to force his stinging eyelids apart and sit in the dark for a moment or two. The pattern was always the same: sleepy grumbling, groping about to locate a kit belt, a splash of water on the face, finding a spare torch or tallow candle (no easy feat when they were never replaced where they should be) and back out on patrols, all but dead on his feet.

Ambrosius tried to share the discomfort of it all whenever possible: the men expected it of any half-decent superior. On this occasion, however, he would not be walking the streets of his regio. He made his way down the steps to the labyrinthine crypt, where the sudden drop in temperature always made him shudder, even though he anticipated it.

Good for preserving bodies.

He approached the stone slab and steeled himself before pulling down the sailcloth that concealed the girl's body. Her long black hair had been oiled, combed and arranged to conceal her facial injuries; her eyes were closed and bronze coins had been placed over both lids to pay Charon the ferryman for her one way journey across the Styx. Her pale, waxy face was more serene than when she had been found, as if the final, terrifying moments of her life had been erased from her mind. The embalmers had worked their arcane skills well and, when the body was eventually reclaimed, her next of kin would be granted some consolation that due respect had been paid to their own flesh and blood. He felt a lump form in his throat. Who could do such a thing to a mere child?

His thoughts turned to his daughter Poppeia. The guilt was hard to bear and he had never succeeded in coming to terms with it. Twelve years old and he still couldn't quite let her in. How could he, when with every passing week she acquired another of her mother's characteristics?

Whenever he looked at her, his first thought was to seek traces of his wife in her speech, the way she moved or even ate, and not to appreciate her for the young woman she was becoming. He shook his head. She was young but not stupid. She knew what he was thinking and her feelings would one day harden into resentment.

No, he still had his beautiful daughter and that provided more than enough solace for any man to endure life's hardships. He would just have to try harder: there would be time to bridge the gap and heal any wounds. Which was more than this girl's father could say. Ludo, the centurion of the few watchmen on day duty, had surprised Ambrosius by his resourcefulness in making the necessary enquiries. He had provided Ambrosius with a statement from one potential witness, a resident of a tenement overlooking the docks, and a promise of another. He pulled the sheet back over the girl's head and returned to the study to look over the statement.

*

The second watch after midnight, Conticinium, was signalled by one of the cohort's buglers in the courtyard. As if on cue, Bulla and Titus trudged through the front gate. Bulla stopped to add a votive berry to the flame within the shrine dedicated to Cohort IV's Genius. Ambrosius was waiting for them in the porch to the building's main entrance with his hands on his hips and a grin on his face: it was not the first time he had noticed Titus avoiding the shrine but he chose to ignore it.

"You know, it's uncanny. But every time – to the very second, no less – that the end of a watch is announced and you two appear through the gate. Now it could be your well-developed sense of timing, built up over years of experience, which lets you plan a route bringing you back at the right moment. Or, and I think this more likely, you are both idle bastards and you hide round the corner until you hear it called."

Bulla and Titus smiled and unfastened their equipment belts, receiving his rare good humour without comment. Ambrosius slapped them both on the back as they passed him. "There's freshly made bread on the oven: help yourself. Neptune's shrivelled sack Bulla! Even on a cold February night you still sweat like a hog!"

"This is because every woman in the city wants me while their husbands are asleep. It's exhausting."

"That's right," added Titus, "and he's so fat because after every clumsy fumble, the women give him a honey cake. Right, Bulla?"

"This is not fat: this is the Syrian muscle! It's you Italians who are so skinny!"

Their insults faded as they retreated into the dormitory kitchen. Ambrosius shook his head at the unlikely pair and waited until the rest of the section had returned through the fog that was rolling in before returning to the study. Lulled by the constant drip from the outflow of the water clock, he fell asleep at his desk.

When the next section of watchmen had left the building and Bulla and Titus had tired of their good-natured bickering, they flopped onto their pallets in rooms on opposite sides of the corridor and waited for the pleasant waves of fatigue to crash down upon them. Bulla was on his back and snoring in seconds and Titus was on the verge of sleep when he heard what sounded like scuffling from somewhere within the building. He closed his eyes and listened hard. Damn rats.

Silence.

Within seconds, he, too, was snoring. Had he been awake for even a few moments longer, he would have heard the faint scraping and soft thud from within the crypt.

*

The middle of any watch was the quietest time in the Watch House. All those on duty were out in the dark streets and the rest were fast asleep. The few officers and staff were either in the cohort's main barracks or, like the tribune, busy in their offices.

Titus forced his eyelids apart and rubbed his face. He didn't have much time: maybe as long as it would take an average vigil to walk once around his region. He slipped a pair of leather soles over his sandals, retrieved an unlit torch and tiptoed down the corridor, listening hard as he approached Ambrosius' room. There was a flickering strip of light at the bottom of the door but he could hear snoring from within. Thanking his luck, he pulled up his hood, lit the torch from a lamp in the corridor and stepped into the chilly courtyard.

The sleeping city fascinated him. Even the rare moments of silence were pregnant with life, and there was a constant tension in the air that thrilled him. It was a deadly place, for sure, and even he would never step out unarmed. But, if he listened hard enough, he could also hear the very lifeblood of the city flowing through the narrow arteries of streets: the distant rattle of carts; rats, foxes and dogs scuffling and fighting in the shadows; foolhardy citizens – mostly drunk – staggering home and, occasionally, armed retinues hustling the wealthy and influential through the night on secretive missions. It was the wake of one of these that he was following now.

The guilt of what he had done weighed heavily upon him: even Lucia didn't know. But it had also brought him closer to people of the same mind that he was sure he wouldn't otherwise have even bumped into, never mind spoken to. Senators, knights, common soldiers, wealthy tradesmen … they were all involved now, all in terrible danger if they were discovered.

He pulled the cloak tighter about his broad shoulders and merged with the shadows underneath the overhanging balconies, away from the glow of the moon reflected by the slick cobbles of the street. The house he was making for was, from the outside, an anonymous adjunct to a row of shops, a candlemaker's and a workshop, marked only by a wooden door in a featureless whitewashed wall. He reached it now and, looking left and right, knocked twice, paused and knocked twice more. After a few moments, he heard padded footsteps and a keyhole shaped light appeared in the door as the wax bung was removed from within. He sensed rather than saw the eye weighing him up before the door was opened and he was ushered in. The steward didn't say a word as he smothered Titus' torch with a damp towel and led him across a small, lamp-lit atrium. He opened a door for Titus in the far wall and left him to descend the narrow steps alone. A single candle burned in a niche in the wall ahead, marking a turn in the echoing corridor.

He followed the faint hum of conversation, groping the shadows to avoid bumping his head. The corridor swept downwards: the air became instantly cooler and smelled of damp stone and fresh paint. Turning another corner, he could see the reflected light of candles twitching on the rough-hewn walls ahead. The whisper of conversation stopped and, when he entered the small room, the faces that turned to him were anxious and alert. He recognised the sharp-eyed senator with the distinctive birthmark on his cheek and assumed the four men ringing the walls were his retinue. One of them was partially obscuring a new fresco of a pious looking figure with a golden sun rising behind his head. He had seen before the tall man – a poet - with swept-back hair and grey eyes, but the short, bald man with a paunch was a newcomer, as was the man in a cook's apron with a young boy and a girl either side of him. His arms, protectively draped round his children's shoulders, were as thick as a blacksmith's.

"Welcome, brother," said the poet, offering Titus a firm handshake. "You're just in time."

"Good. We can start." The senator had a clipped accent and a brisk manner, and Titus sensed he was nervous. "Grumio?"

Grumio kissed his children's foreheads, whispered goodnight to them and ruffled their hair before one of the senator's attendants led them out of the room.

"The place of meeting had to be changed because there is some suspicion that they are on to us. I will have to make efforts to inform the others myself tomorrow."

"On to us?" The poet frowned. "Do we have another house to gather in? This is quite cramped. What about yours?"

"Not a chance!" he lowered his voice. "No. This will just have to do for now."

"And the fire a couple of days ago? In the Pincian district?" asked Grumio. "Any news?"

"Deliberate." They all looked at Titus. "I have friends in The Watch that helped out there. Some of them smelled naphtha."

"Not The Watch's finest hour, from what I hear. Very slow response."

The grey eyes bored into Titus and he wondered if he had lost someone close. "It broke out on a street that divides Regio VII from Regio VI. It wasn't clear whose fire it was, at first."

"Does that actually matter?"

"Regardless," asked the senator, sensing the straining atmosphere. "Did we lose anybody?"

"A few watchmen and a staff officer."

"You know what I mean."

Titus looked down. "Some brothers, yes."

There was a reflective silence. "But we must fight on," the senator retrieved a scroll and raised his defiant chin.

"Yes we must," said the grey eyed poet with an enigmatic smile. "To the very last."

XII

Ambrosius slept throughout the night and it was just as the day relief was arriving that the trouble broke. He was awoken by the cry of dismay from a familiar voice - Ludo - and the sound of hobnailed footsteps rushing to and fro past his door. He jerked upright and wiped the saliva from the corner of his mouth, just as the door to the study crashed open. Ludo was wearing a look of panic.

"Tribune, major problems! Where do I start?"

"What's happening? Why are they charging about like a herd of cattle out there?"

Ludo took a deep breath. "It's the girl's body."

"Yes?"

"It's gone missing. It's not in the crypt!"

"What?"

"It's gone, damn it! Vanished! Disappeared without a trace, the sailcloth with it ... how many more ways do you want me to put it?"

Ambrosius' stomach lurched. "Show me."

"There's nothing to show! I told you the room's empty, tribune!"

"It can't just vanish. It has to be taken by somebody. I want to know how!"

"Wait. That's not even the half of it tribune. Her parents are here! And her father's a senator; a former fucking consul no less!"

A relieved smile crossed Ambrosius' face. "Ah, you bastard! You had me there for a minute!"

"I assure you this isn't a joke, tribune." Ludo watched his smile fade. "We're all fucked. They're in the courtyard, with their attendants and a litter. He's got a golden seal on his finger the size of a bull's testicle, he's wearing a purple-banded toga. He's real, alright, and he's demanding to see you. Now."

"Does he know her body's missing?"

"No. Not yet. But he's becoming impatient. I was going to leave that happy task to you, you know, being the senior man and all."

"How considerate of you, Ludo." Ambrosius dropped onto his chair and buried his head in his hands. "No, I don't see another way around this. Get

51

one of my men to stall him; someone with a bit of presence. Use … I don't know … Stilicho the German. We're going to the crypt."

As the pair hurried down the corridor towards the cellar steps, Ambrosius issued curt orders to everyone they passed, including a confused Bulla.

"What's going on, tribune?"

"Later, man. Much later," he replied without looking back.

Ambrosius had been hoping to find some obvious explanation where the body had gone. But even as he approached the bare stone slab, such hopes evaporated.

"In the name of the gods!"

"I don't understand it! How can someone just stroll in from the streets, pass through two gates and ghost past the better part of thirty men without being seen?"

"Who raised the alarm, damn it?"

"Your quaestionarius, Vitalis. He was dealing with one of your men's prisoners when he said he heard one or two noises but thought nothing of it at the time because the old house is haunted and always creaks and groans under its own weight. It was a good few hours afterwards that he finally got round to checking. He's not in a good way, tribune. He feels very guilty for not somehow preventing it."

"It's not his fault," Ambrosius muttered. "I'll speak to him later." He threw his hands in the air and sighed. "Well, there's nothing else for it. I'll have to fall on my sword and tell the senator. Why did I not listen to you, eh, Ludo? Why didn't I just hand the whole shitty mess to the Cohorts?"

*

It was said at the time that of all Rome's outstanding architectural achievements, the finest was by far the oldest and the one least mentioned: it was also largely invisible. The Cloaca Maxima, 'the Great Sewer', was already over 800 years old and began life as an open drain for the local marshes. As the city grew and space became more precious, the drain was gradually built over and soon became lost under the gargantuan weight of the metropolis above it. The eleven aqueducts supplying the city channelled what water remained after supplying the private houses, fountains, baths and imperial palaces into the sewer, providing the means to continually sluice away the effluent of everyday life and keep the tunnels clear of obstruction.

And it was precisely this quality that the two small, slim men in hooded cloaks, their faces swathed in rags to protect against the evil stench, sought to exploit. The narrow maintenance gangway along which they were edging was in places coated in slimy lichen that glistened in the light cast by their torches. Several times they cursed in panic as they lost their footing and teetered on the edge of the gurgling black water that slid by a couple of feet beneath them. Though they had only covered one mile of sewer in two hours, their tunics clung to their sweating bodies, and the rags wrapped around their faces were hot and clammy, creating a sense of almost unbearable claustrophobia. They had been briefed that the tricky part was stealing the body from underneath the noses of the watchmen; the rest would be straightforward enough with a half-decent plan of the sewer network. In reality, the reverse was true. The pair, inveterate burglars and cut-purses, had been approached by an informer who had intimidated them with what he knew about them and had made them a good offer. They had both not cared much for the hint of blackmail but, lucrum gaudium! The joy of profit always won through.

Small and nimble, they had managed to remove the iron inspection cover from the sub-cellar floor, muffling the noise with the rags they now wore, and clamber up into the bowels of the townhouse. Using nothing more than the light from a storm candle, they had negotiated the confusing warren of corridors under the dormitory rooms to locate the crypt. In their panic to bind up the girl and spirit her away, one of them had dropped the body as he dragged her off the slab, and her head had struck the flagstones with a soft thump. They had frozen to the spot in anticipation of the rush of watchmen's feet that, to their surprise, did not arrive. They were out of the room and back down the ladder to the sewers in half the time it had taken to reach it.

But by now the thieves were at the point of exhaustion. Their arms ached from the weight of the body and their backs were sore from being forced to walk bent to one side to avoid striking their heads against the curved sewer walls. Even the torches they carried with their free hands were a dead weight.

"Fuck it," said one. "This is far enough. Even if someone did discover the route, they wouldn't bother tracking this distance. D'you get the two coins?"

The other nodded, too tired to speak. They lowered the body to the gangway and stretched their backs as best they could before picking her up by her head and feet and dumping her into the water. One of them cursed as the stinking splash-back drenched his cloak.

"The dirty little bitch!" He glared at his colleague, who was trying hard not to laugh. Then he, too, sniggered and the pair cracked up into gales of laughter.

"C'mon you bastard! Let's get out of this filth-hole. I've been needing a shit since we got down here." Their laughter travelled far along the silent, dank tunnels of the Cloaca Maxima.

XIII

In the courtyard, the senator ignored Ambrosius' proffered hand and stared back at him. He was tall and angular and his thinning white hair, sharp cheekbones and long nose reminded the tribune of a vulture. The mousy woman next to him, whose hood was pulled over her hair and who was sniffling into a scented handkerchief, was no beauty either. He saw no resemblance to the girl in either of them and he hoped that they had been mistaken.

"This is my first visit to any watchmen's barracks," he said, "and I pray to the gods it will be the last. I do not appreciate being made to wait out here in the cold with this monotoned idiot whilst you ineffectually try to hide the chaos I seem to have created with my simple request."

The tribune glanced at the browbeaten German vigil. "And what is your request?"

He clenched his jaw. "I am senator Publius Terentius Piso. I am reliably told my daughter is here. I would like to see her."

Ambrosius swallowed hard. Did he also expect her to be alive? "I think we should talk in my quarters. Please follow me, your attendants …"

"Can damn well wait out here! Dear?"

Once inside, Ambrosius offered the senator the chair on which he had been enjoying an untroubled sleep only minutes before and had another two brought into the office. Piso looked about the room with a frown and gave a contemptuous sniff when invited to sit.

"Well, where is she?"

"Let me first offer my condolences …"

But Piso waved his words away. At least he knows she's dead, Ambrosius thought.

"This is very difficult for both of us. We would just like to claim her body and be gone." The senator's voice caught in his throat.

"Then I'm sorry to be the bearer of dreadful news, senator. We did recover the … a young girl of about fourteen or fifteen years yesterday morning from the dockside. On my authority, she was brought here so that she could be identified. I ensured she was embalmed with respect and had already made some progress in tracing her final moments." He took a deep

55

breath, "But some time after Gallicinium her body was removed from the crypt. The alarm had just been raised when you arrived. We're doing everything we can to ensure ..."

"What?" The senator exchanged disbelieving looks with his wife, whose thin mouth dropped open.

"My beautiful daughter?" she murmured through trembling lips. "You have lost my beautiful girl? How can you lose ...? How... dare ... you ...! Then find her! Find her you horrid wretch!" She sprang from her chair and flew at the tribune, who stumbled back in shock. But Piso had anticipated her and with impressive reflexes for a man of his age, caught her by the shoulders and drew her close to him, struggling briefly with her until she gave up and sobbed. Piso held her tight by his side and glared at the tribune with eyes like glowing charcoals.

"Show me where you kept her!"

Ambrosius caught himself about to repeat Ludo's own words: but the room's empty. He nodded at the senator. "Of course."

As they descended into the basement, Ambrosius could feel Piso's eyes boring into the back of his head and he half expected to be pushed down the stairs. The few other watchmen they encountered instinctively fell silent as the stony-faced senator breezed past them, backing into doorways or stepping aside to let them by.

The crypt felt even colder and more forlorn this time, and he heard a gasp – or perhaps a sob – catch in the mother's throat when he gestured to the slab in the centre of the bare room. Piso strode over to it and hesitated, before turning to Ambrosius.

"Leave us."

The tribune nodded and backed out of the room.

At first, there was silence in the crypt. Then the heavy breathing began to transform into a howl. He heard hands being scraped across the stone and then a lowing, like cattle, of raw, heart-rending grief. Eventually, the moaning subsided and he heard the senator sniffing as he tried to bring his emotions under control.

"Watchman!"

Ambrosius stepped inside and Piso stalked over to him. "I hold you," he hissed, pointing a talon-like finger, "personally responsible. I have never, not in my whole life, heard of such staggering incompetence. My daughter is all we had. You have not heard the last of this! I curse you. You find my daughter so that she can have a proper burial or else, mark my words, your own will surely follow."

It appeared to Ambrosius that the senator wanted to say more and every tendon in his pained face twitched with emotion. But then he turned to his wife and whispered some soft words to her before leading her back towards the stairs, barging past the tribune. He heard a stiff 'get out of my way' from the corridor above before the senator's footsteps disappeared, leaving the room in an oppressive silence.

Ambrosius stood rooted to the spot, his mind a maelstrom of confusion, regret and exhaustion. Being abruptly awoken from deep slumber, the panic of Ludo and his frantic colleagues, the disappearance of the girl's body, the sudden arrival of her parents and their stormy departure ... Did all that really just happen in the space of five minutes? It dawned on Ambrosius that the gods had taken a sudden, unreasonable dislike to him. He trudged back towards his office with his mind spinning.

After a few moments there was a diffident knock on the door. Despite receiving no reply, Ludo peered round it.

"That sounded like it went well?"

The tribune tried to speak but then waved his unformed words away.

"Perhaps not a good time to tell you that her uncles are here too?"

Ambrosius gave him a hard look.

"No, they're not. Don't worry, I was just being ... ah ... no, poor timing. If you want to speak to me I'll be in the courtyard briefing my lads. I'll ... leave you be."

XIV

Sleep did not always come easily to Ambrosius during the day but when it did, it engulfed him violently. As he lay sprawled on the mattress, his head thrashing from side to side, visions of his wife Larissa fighting in vain for her life haunted him with frightening clarity.

He bolted upright, his eyes wide open, and wiped the sweat from his face. He looked about him. The empty room had a preternatural stillness about it. The door was open and was being nudged to and fro in the breeze that drifted in from some other part of the tenement. He fell back onto his elbows whilst his laboured breathing subsided and then dropped back onto the bed with a long, sad sigh.

*

Ambrosius' head had barely touched his pillow before the banging on the courtyard door. Both Anna and Poppeia were out for the morning so there was no chance of using them to stall his unwelcome visitor. Muttering curses under his breath, he stumbled off his bed, donned a tunic and unlatched the door.

A small, bald man with an officious air about him looked him up and down, one eyebrow raised. "You are Ambrosius, tribune of the Fourth Cohort?"

"Not if you're a peddler, no."

"Sadly for you I'm not. I have already wasted time calling upon you at your cohort's barracks. Your men sent me here."

"I never sleep there, if I can help it. I have a daughter, so I don't get much sleep as it is."

The visitor was unmoved. "I am an actarius of Junius Rufinus, Prefect of the Watch. I'm here to escort you to his headquarters immediately."

Ambrosius clenched his jaw and looked over the staff officer's shoulder. A couple of heavies were lolling against the rim of the fountain. "I outrank you. You call me 'sir'. And I know the way perfectly well."

"I think we both know that's not going to happen. Consider yourself under arrest. Sir."

Ambrosius barely resisted the urge to drive his fist into the actarius' nose. He slammed the door shut.

*

Though he had gargled, splashed water on his face and run a comb through his hair, Ambrosius still felt dreadful. His eyes were raw and burned with fatigue, and his tired mind did not feel fit for a searching discussion. By the time he had jostled his way through the crowded and noisy streets of the imperial marketplaces, his mood was murderous. On their way to headquarters, they watched a petty squabble between two mud-spattered cart drivers over right of way in a narrow street develop into blows. Neither man seemed aware that the city streets were out of bounds for carts during daylight hours and only became even more aerated by the wild gestures of other inconvenienced pedestrians. Under other circumstances Ambrosius might have intervened: as it was, he was tempted to join in.

Eventually, they turned into a wide side street that ended in a large gated archway flanked by lintels in the shape of Corinthian pillars in relief. The masonry was well worked but had begun to weather and chip in places, adding a faded splendour to the place. The actarius approached the door and rapped on the knocker and a small grille slid aside. A bored looking face gave a cursory inspection of the caller, before the grille slid shut and the main gate creaked open.

Ambrosius hadn't visited the vigiles' headquarters in more than a year and, had his state of mind been different, he might have been able to appreciate its impressive design. It was easy to forget that the place was also an active barracks, bustling with hidden activity: its administrative function aside, this was where Cohort I was based, though the ugly rows of dormitories were hidden from view behind the main headquarters. Two colonnaded ranges bordered the grassed courtyard whilst the main building opposite the entrance resembled a Greek temple.

The group cut across the courtyard and entered the main hall, where the air was cooler. Their steps rang out across the mosaic floor as they approached another staff officer sat at a desk by the door to the Prefect's office. He nodded at the tribune's escort who took his leave without another word.

"Tribune, you can go right in. The Prefect is expecting you."

Ambrosius smoothed down his hair and entered. Junius Rufinus had just finished dictating to a flustered looking commentariensis, and was in the process of sealing a document with hot red wax. He gestured Ambrosius to a seat without looking at him.

"No, Mancinus, that one … take that – the top one – to Priscus in the Basilica. Leave the other letter, yes? I'm not done with it."

"Sir."

"Good, that's all for now."

The tribune took a seat and looked around him at the organised chaos. Neither the room nor its owner had changed one bit since he had last seen him. Rufinus had greyed early in his twenties and his hair was now silver. His tanned face and piercing blue eyes gave him the appearance in this environment of a distinguished librarian, but the position of Prefect of The Watch was no place for a bookish man. The office was junior in status to that of the Urban and Praetorian Prefects, and its holder could therefore expect to be treated as such. Yet it was by some margin the busiest of the three posts due to the sheer daily volume of lower level criminal and civil proceedings that the Prefect and his deputy were expected to deal with. Rufinus blew on the wax, set the document aside and leant back in his chair.

"Water?"

"No, thank you."

"Yes, well I'm sorry I had to disturb you so soon after your night's work but it's in your interests to hear this from me sooner rather than later."

"Sounds important."

Rufinus cleared his throat. "I'll come straight to the point because I have a rather tedious hearing to preside over shortly regarding petty theft from the public baths. You are being sent to Ostia when the next detachment leaves for its four month tour of duty."

"Sir? I was there in December! I'm not due another tour this year!"

"Yes, I know that. But I imagine you'll know how hard I had to fight for you to retain your job at all. This was the only acceptable compromise."

"What? Acceptable? Why in Hades would I want to go back to that hole? Who wanted me out of my post?"

"I think it's best you don't ask too many questions, tribune. I think it's best I don't ask too many for that matter! So let me remind you what your role entails, just in case you had forgotten. One, extinguishing unsupervised fires in and around the city and punishing those responsible for them. Two, supervising patrols of your region to deter and catch thieves, cut-throats and beggars. Three, catching runaway slaves. Now, you tell me which of these functions includes investigating the murder of noblemen's daughters, desecrating their bodies and then losing them?"

Ambrosius nearly fell off his seat. "Desecrating the body? What on Gaia's earth …?"

"Yes, desecrating! I was informed that you broke the poor girl's fingers for Jupiter only knows what ghastly reason!"

"There was a reason! Who ..." Right then, somewhere within his subconscious, a small bell of alarm rang, warning him not to enquire how the Prefect had heard that detail. "I was making headway with it. I'd found where she was killed and ..."

Rufinus rolled his eyes. "That's not your damn job, Ambrosius! Leave that to the Urban Cohorts and the Praetorians! Has it not occurred to you that they, also, might have been making headway – more than you – if they had only been allowed the opportunity? They have access to the Emperor's own physician, the world renowned Galen, for goodness' sake! Who knows what he'd have been able to tell them? You have upset some powerful people, Ambrosius. I am protecting you from yourself by sending you to Ostia: hopefully all this will have blown over by the time you return."

"I didn't murder the girl, damn it sir! And you know I have little enough respect for the Urban Cohorts as it is, much good they did for me when Larissa was killed! That's why I wanted to do the right thing by the girl, don't you see? Can't you have a word with ... with, what's his name, Clio when he's calmed down? I can show you what I've already done – show him if necessary!"

Rufinus sighed. "My orders haven't come from Clio, Ambrosius. They're from higher than that. Much higher in fact. Believe it or not, I'm on your side. You're a good watchman and, truth be told, I was delighted when you turned down his offer to join their ranks, all those months ago. But you acted incorrectly here and leave me in a very difficult position. You should, at the very least, have come to me first. You can expect a visit at some point to that god-forsaken outpost you seem to so favour. Please don't create a scene: just give them what you've gathered so far and preserve your dignity. I'm sorry but you will be leaving for Ostia tomorrow. And you'd be well advised to do so both quickly and quietly!"

Ambrosius looked aghast. "Tomorrow? Not a chance. Tomorrow is Matronalia and I'll be in the city with my daughter come what may, even if that means walking away from the vigiles for good. I'm sorry too, Prefect."

"Damn it all, Ambrosius! Must you be so pig-headed? You are making life unreasonably difficult for me when it seems I'm your only ally here!" Rufinus banged his fist down on the table in frustration. "Fine, leave the day after tomorrow! But don't push my patience any further. That is all, tribune."

Ambrosius looked on in shock. He had expected censure when he was summoned, but enforced exile to the port of Ostia … Rufinus had already selected another document and was weighting the corners down with pebbles. This interview was over. He stood and headed for the door before pausing.

"What about the man I bound over yesterday morning?"

Rufinus looked up with a frown.

"The footpad that my centurion Titus chased down?"

"Ah yes," replied Rufinus with a dismissive wave, resuming his reading, "he was flogged and released."

*

Ambrosius felt light-headed as he made his way back across the courtyard, oblivious to the gentle heat of the sun on his back. He did not blame Rufinus, for whom he had a certain respect, and it was clear that the man's hand had been forced. Ambrosius did not doubt him when he said he had fought hard to seek any compromise at all. All the same, only a fool would trust every word of a man in Rufinus' position.

Desecrating her body …

He had reached the main gate now. A sentry appeared, heaved back the sliding bolt and then swivelled on his heels to pull back the gate, which shuddered in protest. Ambrosius looked on as Rufinus' words reverberated around his head.

You broke the poor girl's fingers …

How could he have learned that unless he was there? From Ludo? Titus or Bulla, or perhaps another watchman? Not a chance. He had seen how confused they had all been by the turn of events.

The orders are from higher than that. Much higher …

Ambrosius froze as he was crossing the threshold. The faint sense of unease he had been feeling since he had first laid eyes on the corpse exploded in his mind. The answer was as obvious as it was sinister.

He was being watched.

*

After Ambrosius had left, Rufinus rolled up the scroll in its leather cylinder, and peered out of his room.

"No more visitors today," he stated to the staff officer outside.

He returned to his desk and removed two more letters from the drawer, re-reading the one from the Praetorian Prefect, Gaius Plautianus.

"… the arrest of Tribune Ambrosius Milo for his extreme misconduct, following which the City Prefect and I agreed you could be trusted to exact your own punishment. Need I remind you of my efforts in securing your present role and of recent conversations re: promotion to a senior position within my Praetorian Guard? It would reflect badly on you if you failed to resolve this situation robustly and …"

He slapped the desk in frustration, took a deep breath and folded the letter back up.

Had he let Ambrosius off too easily?

He could well understand Plautianus' anger and the senator's profound hurt. The threat to his own career progression seemed trifling by comparison but Ambrosius' actions had been incredibly frustrating … The tone, however, of the second letter …

M Maracanthus to J Rufinus. Old friend, much affection!

Any danger of you becoming a generous man soon? Still waiting for dinner invitation over at your new place. When I heard from one of the Aediles that you had acquired your little plot on the coast all those months ago I honestly thought, evidently against my better judgment, that you would be laying on a celebratory feast fit for the Emperor! By the gods, I would give my right hand to get away from the stresses of the city for a few days. And a man in such a state of mind can only take so much cuckolding from his wife: you need to give your own household the level of attention you bring to the senate, she says! And the garden is an embarrassing ruin! I take her advice in good humour of course, and she sends her affections to you and yours. Write me back at your earliest convenience. Ever in friendship, MM.

Rufinus frowned at the letter, and turned it over. There was no other writing on it. Maracanthus was a taciturn, soldierly man of few words, not usually given to committing such meandering thoughts to paper. On instinct he unraveled it, scanning the parchment for clues. And there, at the bottom corner of the letter, his eyes settled upon three dots of ink, nondescript and innocuous to every man in the world other than himself.

His blood ran cold.

He retrieved a cylindrical case from one of the shelves, disguised with the irrelevant tag 'REGIO II: archived'. Glancing at the door again to assure himself it was shut, he tipped out the three sheets of papyrus contained within, selecting the one with three dots in its corner. The document was otherwise blank, save for the elongated holes cut out at random intervals. He placed this on top of Maracanthus' letter, holding it down at the corners with his table weights. It was exactly the same size as the letter beneath:

dangerover

heardplot

against

 Emperor by right hand man

need

advice

Rufinus' eyes widened in alarm. There was no doubt he had selected the right decoder page. And now that he looked at his old friend's handwriting, it did seem unusually cursive, with some of the sentences compressed or elongated as if to force the target words into the areas that the decoder would pick out. Whilst Rufinus was confident that no one else on earth would ever notice such small details, this in itself was out of character for the fastidious senator.

He rolled up the decoder pages and returned them to their shelves before hurrying to his door.

"Aelius," he asked, startling the officer. "The letters I received this morning, who delivered them?"

"Sir?"

"It's a simple enough question, is it not? Who delivered this morning's documents?"

Aelius shrugged. "The same freedman who usually does. I don't know his name … why do you …?"

"You'll have to find someone else to preside over this morning's hearing. I have an urgent matter to attend to."

"But … there's not time sir!"

"I don't care! Go and drag Balbus out of his pit if you have to, or postpone it or …" he gestured vaguely as he was already some way across the main hall, "I don't know, use your imagination!"

Aelius stood up to protest to the Prefect's retreating back and then slumped back down in frustration.

XV

As it stretched north to the city walls and beyond, the Via Lata, along which Rufinus now hurried, scythed past the famous Hill of Gardens. Here, on the southern slopes, the gardens of four of the most ancient aristocratic figureheads - Pompey, Sallust, Lucullus and Acilius - competed for the attentions of the Roman citizenry. In spring and summer, the hill was a riot of exotic hues of purple and pink, lush shades of green and dazzling yellows and oranges.

But on this crisp, late winter morning, the effect was muted. The hill could have been a raging inferno and still Rufinus would not have noticed. As he passed the crumbling ruins of the Fontinalis Gate, his head was bowed in contemplation, and he brushed off the attentions of the beggars and hawkers that congregated in the shadows of the Servian wall with a dismissive wave. In his opinion, Rome had never been so overcrowded with such useless levels of humanity. Crime and disorder were in some districts so rife that even a small band of armed men would only set foot in them for a tidy price. It was now a popular tavern pastime for some braggarts and local hardmen to bet on taking a walk through certain streets of the Subura at night and living to tell the tale. Some made substantial sums of money; others never emerged at the other end. And still the desperate and the needy came shuffling through the city gates from all parts of the empire in a misguided search for food and shelter and hope.

The only people in sight were slaves tending the gardens and a workman hammering away at a cartwheel in a workshop nestled within a cluster of buildings. The workman, a bearded man with forearms as thick as hams, glanced at him without interest as he threw down his hammer and wiped his brow. Rufinus veered off the path and bounded up some stone steps cut into the hillside that gave way to another path bordering a high stone wall.

At first, he didn't hear the sobbing above the soughing of the trees and the noise of his own laboured breathing. He straightened and pressed close to the wall. Rufinus knew that Maracanthus had no children and few slaves: there was therefore only one person it was likely to be. He made his way to the entrance.

Having rapped on the knocker for a second time and received no response, Rufinus turned his back to leave. But then he heard the door hatch being slid open and shut, and the bolt being withdrawn.

Maracanthus' lugubrious chief steward opened the door, looking worried. "Domina apologises but she is not receiving visitors at this time."

"And the master?"

The slave's face twitched. "Dominus has been … called away. For a while."

"I see. Might I ask where he is or how long he's likely to be?"

"You may sir, but I'm afraid I wasn't told. Now if you will please excuse me, I have a great many more duties to oversee than usual. I wish you a good day."

"Senator Maracanthus," said Rufinus, pushing back the door, "may be in grave danger. Go and tell your mistress who is calling. Now."

The slave made a face. "Wait here, please." He crossed the atrium, muttering under his breath. "Domina: Junius Rufus awaits."

"Rufinus!" he hissed, glaring at the slave's back. Rufinus looked around. The hall was simple, elegant and allowed a few concessions to the owner's Spanish heritage, notably the exquisite pair of rearing bulls flanking the pool in the middle of the chequerboard atrium. The walls were painted a rich, deep red, and two of them featured mythological frescoes. But there were no wax facemasks of illustrious ancestors to be seen: Maracanthus was a new man to the senatorial ranks. What was in evidence, however, was the sombre, empty mood that pervaded the place, and Rufinus began to wonder whether he was already too late.

Maracanthus' diminutive wife Martha appeared at the study door. She was wearing a plain stole and her long black hair was hung over her shoulder in an unfussy plait. She wrung her hands and, even though she had applied some make-up, had dark rings under her eyes.

"Would you care for something to drink, Junius?"

"No, thank you. I'm sorry to disturb you like this. Perhaps we may be able to talk somewhere private?"

Martha looked behind her. "That will be all Prolitho, thank you. Please, Junius. We can go to Marcus' study."

Rufinus followed her into a Spartan side room decorated only by a desk and a tapestry on the opposite wall. She sat a respectful distance away from him and clasped her trembling hands on her lap. Her voice cracked as she spoke.

"Prolitho says you might have some news?"

Rufinus scratched his head. "The slave said Marcus had been called away, but he wasn't very convincing. Martha, what in Hades is going on?"

Disappointment crossed her face like a cloud. "I was hoping you might be able to tell me. He hasn't been here for nearly two days, he's … missing, and four of his best slaves with him. I'm so worried something has happened to him. But Prolitho said you thought he was in danger. Why?"

"Possibly, but I don't know what to make of it. You will have seen him much more recently than me. I'm sorry, this must be terribly difficult. When exactly did you last see him?"

"Yesterday morning, before he left for the senate house. The four slaves I last saw when they went to collect him later that evening. But is he in danger?"

"I don't know. Potentially … It depends on exactly what he has heard, and who else knows."

"Possibly … potentially! Please don't play games with me! Tell me what you know!" Her lips began to quiver.

"Please Martha, bear with me. I just need to know what you do to make sense of it. I don't want to put you in any danger …"

"Tell me!"

"Fine." Rufinus cleared his throat and lowered his voice. "I received a letter from him this morning, an unusual one. It was encoded but I understood he had overheard a plot against the Emperor. It had been written quickly and said nothing more, which is why I am here. Now you perhaps see why I am being so discreet. Has he said anything to you, anything at all?"

Martha looked down. "No, not in so many words. But I know him too well. I knew there was something on his mind. A few days ago he came home late, looking grey, grey like ash. I smelled drink on him, which was not like him. When I asked what was wrong, he wouldn't speak and came straight into here, sitting where you are now. And when I persisted he became irritable, like it was a great effort to talk to me. He would only say that after the senate had disbanded for the day, he left with everyone else. But then he realised he had left some documents – nothing particularly important – in one of the private suites, so he went back to get them. He overheard an argument in an adjoining room. Nasty threats were being made, that's all he said about it. Then he retrieved his papers and left, though he couldn't be sure he'd not been seen." She sighed and picked at a loose thread in her stole. "He was very quiet in the days afterwards but I didn't press him. I think I was just relieved he hadn't taken a new lover! How stupid and selfish of me."

Both were quiet for a few moments. "What should I do, Junius? I've sent the whole household searching all over the city, but still there's no word! He has no other relatives in the city that I can ask. He always trusted you, can you help? What do you think has happened?" But before he could reply, she continued. "It may not mean much to you, but it's Matronalia tomorrow. War would break out and he would still never miss spending that day with me, buying me gifts and looking after me. He may occasionally forget other dates but never this!"

Rufinus chose his words carefully. There were only two scenarios, as he saw it, and he wasn't about to discuss the first. "He may have left the city for a few days and taken his slaves with him, to get help or seek advice. Even at the expense of being absent for Matronalia. He wouldn't have wanted you to be in any danger, which is probably why he didn't elaborate. You know the saying; ignorance is innocence."

"But you don't believe that do you?" She held him with her dark eyes. Tears welled in them. "You said he asked for your help? If that's true, why did he not wait here to confide in you?"

There seemed little merit in refuting the point: she was far too shrewd for that. "I promise you I will do anything I can to help. Meantime, you must try to remain calm and be positive. Marcus is a resourceful man." Rufinus rose from the seat and placed a hand on her shoulder. "And a word to the wise: call off your slaves. They'll end up drawing far too much attention to themselves. And to you."

When he was outside, Rufinus took a deep breath and tried to organise his thoughts. He could not remember the last time he had contemplated poking around in the murky waters he was now about to disturb.

Just try to remember the rules, you old fool, he muttered , or you'll end up the same way.

XVI

There was a knock on the tribune's door and Bulla entered without awaiting a reply. He was chewing a chicken leg and a greasy line of juice was trickling down his chin.

"A bit of common courtesy wouldn't go amiss."

"Yes, but there's a few Praetorians at the gate. I try and show them the contempt whenever I can get away with it. I even offered their Prefect a bite of my chicken. He told me to stick it up my arse. How ungrateful is that?"

"The Praetorian Prefect is here?"

"Looks like it. Has he come for to take you away, tribune?"

Ambrosius stroked his chin. Had Rufinus forewarned him or had he imagined it? He had been so tired he couldn't recall. "I wouldn't be surprised. Well they'll have to wait for their little moment of fun. Tell them to stand to in the courtyard. I have something to attend to: I'll be out shortly."

When he did go outside, he saw that Bulla was mistaken. It was the Prefect's deputy, though he wasn't the first person to confuse them. He had only met him once before and had taken an instant dislike to him then. Ambrosius didn't see that opinion being revised now, with Brutus sneering at him with his hands on his hips. Missing only his plumed helmet, he was wearing full parade order, medals included, and his pomaded beard and hair glistened an impressive shade of black. Ambrosius cast his eyes over the other visitors: he had chosen three of his burliest subordinates for his retinue. Ambrosius saluted him without any zeal: the gesture was not reciprocated, by any of them.

"I see you're not here on a social call, commander."

"Correct." He turned to his Praetorians. "You see, I told you these bucket carriers were smart!" They guffawed on cue. The grin faded from Brutus' face and he was all business. "Whatever it was you found when you were scratching about in Praetorian affairs, I want it handing over immediately, before you lose all trace of that too, by order of Prefect Gaius Plautianus. Is that clear, watchman?"

Interesting, thought Ambrosius. And your first slip-up. "Clear as glass, commander. Felt I had a point to make to the Urban Cohorts, who made

69

such a mess of finding anyone for my wife's murder." He scuffed the floor with his boot. "Figured I could prove myself better, that's all."

"Personal vengeance, eh?" Brutus sneered and thumbed towards his heart. "Gets you right here, doesn't it?"

Ambrosius tested his luck. "Though how you found out about our corpse so quickly makes me wonder ...?"

"Nothing escapes our attention, you should know that. A rat farts on the Aventine and I hear of it. Enough, anyway. Give us what we're here for."

"Of course. There's not much anyway. Follow me, please."

Titus and Vitalis were sluicing out the two holding cells in the crypt.

"Praetorians!" barked Ambrosius as the small party descended the stairs. The watchmen straightened.

"Well, well! If it isn't the scared rabbit Titus! How are you keeping, watchman?" Brutus' sneer was now a beam. Ambrosius looked at Titus glaring back at the Deputy Prefect in perfect surprise. He hadn't accounted for them knowing each other.

"So this is where you're keeping the great Titus, the faded legionary prize-fighter?" He turned to Ambrosius, punching Titus playfully in the stomach as he did so, testing his physique. "Scrubbing the shit and piss out of the cells! You are full of surprises, eh watchman? Is that how you keep him fit these days? An illiterate has-been he may be, but show him a little respect!"

The Praetorians roared with laughter. "So what do you say, old man? How about that match-up you've been avoiding all these years? You choose the rules and name the prize: can't say fairer than that."

Ambrosius looked on in dismay: he had never seen Titus so close to exploding. And he knew that if he did, all Hades would break loose and there would be bloodshed. Titus glared back at him, clenching his jaw. The atmosphere in the room became murderous. Nobody spoke. Only the torches hissed in their wall brackets.

"Cat got your tongue, eh? Or does your wife still forbid it?"

It was Vitalis who reacted. He lurched across and shoved Brutus in the chest. "Just back off, sir!"

Brutus barely moved.

The Praetorians' hands were on the pommels of their swords in a heartbeat though, to Ambrosius' great surprise, Brutus clicked his tongue in disapproval and they removed them.

The Prefect looked Vitalis up and down with an expression of mild amusement. "Impressive spirit, old man! Perhaps I should be challenging the quaestionarius here instead! Or is that how you became lame in the first place?"

"Commander, did your orders from the Prefect also include mocking my men and igniting a brawl? Somehow I think he might take exception to that," said Ambrosius between gritted teeth.

"No, you're quite right. Us fighting men, eh? Incorrigible." He readjusted his cuirass and straightened. "So then, just give us what you have."

"Titus, next door?"

Titus disappeared for a few moments. Ambrosius had visions of him pounding the walls with his bare fists in frustration. He returned with two wax tablets and the shoe-print.

"What's this?"

"Two witness testimonies on the tablets, both endorsed, and a boot-print lifted from the scene."

Brutus looked at the meagre evidence. "Is that it?"

Ambrosius nodded. "If more witnesses come forwards, we can send anything on to you."

"And what use, by Neptune's shrivelled sack, is this doodle of a peasant's sandal? Did your daughter paint that, watchman?"

"The outline of a sandal that the girl's killer was wearing as he stood in her blood, do you mean?"

The logic registered on Brutus' face and he grunted. "Not much use without the sandal though is it? And its owner. Or did you also plan to steal the shoes of every citizen in Rome, watchman?"

He smirked at his colleagues. Satisfied with his quip, he beckoned them to pick up the finds. Halfway up the stairs, he turned and wagged his finger at Ambrosius. The sneer was back. "And don't think you can go snooping around in serious business again! Stick to putting out burning loaves of bread and chasing slaves: understood, watchman? We have eyes and ears everywhere." With that, they all left.

"And there's your second slip of the tongue," said Ambrosius quietly.

"Come again, tribune?"

"The Deputy Prefect can't resist a good boast. I was told this morning by Junius Rufinus, that the orders to give up any evidence came from much higher than Fabius Clio, who would usually be expected to deal with a cold-blooded murder. So I assumed that the Emperor himself had stepped in at the request of his distraught former consul, Piso. That would have made sense. But not so. Instead, the Prefect Gaius Plautianus himself seems to be paying an unnatural interest in the girl's death. Why is that I wonder?"

"Right now, all I can think about is cracking his damn head off his shoulders." Titus' fists were clenching and unclenching.

There were cumbersome footsteps on the basement stairs. Bulla appeared, his eyes bulging.

"I've just seen the Praetorian jackals leaving with our murderer's boot-print. And the statements! Someone please to tell me what's going on?"

"They're welcome to them. The statements are useless: Ludo and his relief followed them up and they came to nothing. And as for the square of sail cloth," Ambrosius and Titus grinned at each other, "Brutus is now the proud owner of our dockside thief's sandal print. We've still got the original."

"Ha! Idiots! And the ear stud?"

"You don't ask, you don't get. You missed his little performance down here, Bulla. He got so caught up in strutting like a peacock, he forgot to follow through his task properly. Didn't cross his mind to search a single room, arrogant fool."

"So what now? Will you still try to avenge the girl?"

Ambrosius looked away. He had forgotten his own predicament for a moment. "That'll be difficult. I'm being sent to Ostia. I have to go immediately after Matronalia."

"Whose damned idea was that? Then we go too!"

"Rufinus. Says he's doing it in my own interests. He didn't say who forced his hand but I could make a few guesses. Thing is, he may have a point. Listen, you three, this is important. I need you to keep your eyes open here and be careful who you speak to. Either we've got a snitch, who helped spirit away the girl, or a spy is watching us very closely from outside. Maybe both. Brutus as good as said so before. They say Rome's a city of spies at the moment. I don't think that's just tavern gossip. There's no other way word could have got to him, Plautianus, the miserable senator Piso and Rufinus so rapidly if that wasn't the case. They even knew that I'd cracked her finger to get at the skin beneath her nail." That made them look uncomfortable, as Ambrosius knew it would. "I want to get the bastard that killed her, no doubt.

But I want to watch your backs too. I could do without anyone else disappearing from here in the middle of the night."

XVII

Junius Rufinus had not ventured into the mean streets of the Subura district for several years, and it soon became clear that it had not improved any in the meantime. He glanced about him, guided more by instinct than memory, as he turned off the Argiletum, an ancient road leading from the forum. The upper floors of the tenements looming over him were in places so close together that their occupants could reach out and steal the laundry from the lines that hung from the rickety balconies opposite. The light was dim and the narrow pavements were strewn with waste. An oppressive smell hung over the streets like a trapped pall of smoke. Hungry eyes watched the Prefect of The Watch as he passed by.

After only a few wrong turnings, he came to a familiar intersection, where the upper tiers of the buildings almost kissed. Rufinus gave a wry smile: the prostitutes working on opposite sides of the streets here could whisper and still hear each other, though their antics were somewhat louder. He stopped a few doors down. Above the tavern's entrance hung a battered sign with a faded, grotesque face upon it, and the word 'Gorgona'.

The moment he entered, the smell of stale sweat, dirty straw, potent wine and smoke from the sputtering lanterns pinned to the walls assaulted his nostrils. The place was as busy as ever, though a raucous group of young men celebrating some sort of party drowned out most other conversations. He pulled up a stool at the bar, giving himself a sidelong view of the saloon. The innkeeper appeared and appraised Rufinus with beady eyes.

"What'll you have?"

Rufinus glanced over the ceramic jugs on the bar counter. In the flickering light of the lanterns, he could see an oily film on the wine.

"What's in the middle?"

"Same that's in the other two: home brew," the innkeeper harrumphed. "Sorry; no Falernian here my friend!"

Rufinus shrugged, feeling more conspicuous by the second. He put a low value coin on the bar and accepted a cup from a mid-priced jug. To his faint annoyance, the innkeeper did not move and was watching him as he took a draught. The syrup-like wine burned his throat as it went down, leaving a bitter aftertaste. He wondered whether it had been diluted with any water at all.

"Bracing, isn't it? My father's vineyard. Has pepper in it too." The innkeeper grinned. "So, what brings a gent like you to an establishment like mine?"

The jeering from the party reached a shrieking crescendo. Rufinus looked over and caught a glimpse of a flushed woman with glossy black hair. She rose from the middle of the group and hitched up her stola, removing a tangled piece of straw from her mane. Lying on the floor was a groaning young man with reddened cheeks and tousled hair. His eyes were closed but he wore a wolfish grin. The woman spun around, making eye contact with Rufinus as she tucked away a pert breast. His eyes widened. Whilst not beautiful according to conservative Roman values, she had alluring green eyes, dusky skin and pouting lips that suited her luscious figure. He liked the way she stared at him brazenly, without shame. She blew away a stray lock from her face and stalked off towards the stairs without looking back.

"Aha!" The innkeeper winked and tapped the side of his nose. "I understand now. But don't be fooled by the light, my friend. She's not as young as she looks. Few of them ever are."

The barkeep moved away to serve other customers. Rufinus tutted and moved to a table in the far corner of the room. A toothless old man with a rheumy eye sat on an adjacent table nodded, and some of the other customers looked at him as he sidled past, but he avoided eye contact with them all. They were a rough looking lot but he didn't sense any hostility, so he settled back and observed the customers that came and went, making his wine last as long as possible.

XVIII

Dusk was falling and long shadows crept along the halls and chambers of the imperial palace. Slaves were doing the rounds, lighting the candelabra and oil lamps with tapers, refilling those that were empty from little clay flasks. The Emperor's household was nowhere to be seen, each member having taken to their own private quarters, and a hush had settled about the place.

Desperation and a gnawing sense of tragedy had deprived Caracalla of sleep for the past two nights. He had barely eaten, and the pallor of his face highlighted the dark bags under his eyes. He lay on his bed, tossing and turning, irritated by every ambient noise and distraction.

There was a meek knock on his door and Fulvia Plautilla entered. "Your sleeping draught, husband."

Caracalla rolled away from her. "Leave it on the dresser."

Fulvia lingered in the doorway. "We could at least speak to each other once in a while, and make this tedium bearable."

Caracalla frowned. He could not bear to look. Whenever he did, he wanted to superimpose Terentia's delicate face onto hers. He did not think she was a bad looking creature, but her face bore too many of her father's masculine features: her brows were a little heavy and her jaw too square for his liking. He had once conceded that her eyes were a striking shade of blue but that had been early in their arranged marriage.

"I'm not well. Please, just … leave me alone."

She opened her mouth, but then her eyes welled up and she hurried away, determined not to let him see her crying again. Caracalla tutted and sat upright. It was no use: drained though he was, he would get no rest this evening either. He retrieved a robe and went to find his father.

Even as he rounded the staircase and emerged onto a rug-covered hallway that led to his father's private rooms, he could hear the muffled conversation within. A familiar voice approached the door and it opened before he reached it. Caracalla found himself face to face with a grim Gaius Plautianus. The prefect muttered a perfunctory 'Master' and strode past him. Caracalla watched him go and entered the sombre room.

"What's going on? What was he doing here?"

"Sit down, Lucius dear," said his mother, Julia Domna.

"No, I don't want to. I just want to know … there's something happening. Is it my Terentia?"

She sighed. "Your wife, Lucius, is Fulvia. But, yes, I'm afraid this is about Terentia. Won't you sit down? I'd rather you did."

"Just spit it out mother!"

"Terentia is dead, Lucius. I'm so very sorry." She took a step towards him and then hesitated, as he stiffened.

"What?" he croaked.

The Emperor cleared his throat. "This is why the Prefect was here just now. He … there was a delay in confirming that it was her that had been found. Gaius will now have a meeting with her father and his Deputy Prefect to establish what happened …"

"What? What do you mean?" Caracalla's eyes darted in incomprehension between his parents. He swayed on the spot, feeling light-headed.

"She was found by some derelict buildings at the dockside. It appears that she… that she may have been killed there, but …"

Caracalla buckled at the knees and collapsed to the floor.

XIX

The lanterns in the Gorgona banished the gathering gloom outside and made Rufinus feel drowsy. He was now halfway through his second cup of wine and still he hadn't seen any of the signs he wanted. He knew he would have to leave soon otherwise he would be heading home in total darkness. It occurred to him that it was probably no bad thing he was already feeling a little drunk: nobody in their right mind would want to venture out around here after dusk.

The door opened again and a sandy haired man entered wearing a military issue cloak. After a quick look round, he went to the bar and sat where Rufinus had. Rufinus watched him as he ordered a drink, exchanging brief but friendly words with the barman. Though he was of ordinary height and build, he had a self-possessed, independent air about him. Rufinus tried to remember the criteria and the protocols. From what he had heard, there were still some codes that imperial agents wouldn't pick up on, jealously guarded like jewels. But that had been years ago: the language of the street was in a constant state of flux as a necessary matter of survival. He had been thinking about little else for the last hour but now his mind was hazy. Pick the wrong man and you'll either be fleeced or executed. Probably both.

The newcomer was neither a regular nor unfamiliar with his surroundings. He could see no rings on his finger. His money was ready to pay the innkeeper, with no fumbling inside a pouch to draw attention to easy pickings. He was armed, but discreetly: when he reached to the counter to sip his wine, there was a slight, but tell-tale shape at his hipline …

The gloom deepened outside and Rufinus was becoming edgy to leave. When the man next glanced around, Rufinus made brief eye contact with him and tapped the rim of his cup twice with his thumb. The man's eyes paused on him for the most fleeting of seconds before continuing a casual sweep of the room. He then turned back to the bar and had a brief conversation with the innkeeper. They shared a joke and he was served another cup of wine. Were they discussing how to trap the silver-haired man in the corner? More people entered the Gorgona and only two left. He began to tense whenever the door opened, his paranoia deepening with every second. How many would it take to bundle him away? Other customers began to eye the spare stool at Rufinus' side. He would have to give it up soon.

Five more minutes passed.

Ten, and dusk was turning to darkness outside. He began to think that maybe he had been mistaken. Either way, he had come no closer to establishing Marcus' whereabouts today. He would just have to take his chances and venture home.

As he was on the very point of leaving, the stranger sauntered over to him, carrying a small leather pouch.

"Knucklebones or dice, my friend? I have both."

Rufinus swallowed hard, his mind racing. "Dice then. If I throw any more Four Vultures I'll be broke."

The man fixed him with a brief, intense stare. Then he nodded and chuckled. "Then you share my bad luck. An evil throw for sure! Dice it is."

He took the spare stool and retrieved a wax tablet from a fold in his cloak. "We both keep score, yes?"

"Fairer that way. I must warn you I don't have much coin. So keep the odds low, yes?"

They shook hands. His grip was strong but not excessively so. "Name's Trystan."

Rufinus very much doubted it was. "Tiberius. Well met."

"Good. Odds low then. Drink for luck?"

Rufinus declined and scrutinized him as he emptied the dice onto the table. He had an easy, friendly manner but there was no doubt he could handle himself. Out of the corner of his eye, he looked about him. The approach had not stirred the slightest bit of attention: if anything, the volume of noise had risen and everyone was engrossed in their own conversations.

Trystan unclipped the tablet and scribbled on the wax surface with a pointed stylus. Then he nudged it towards Rufinus. Whilst Rufinus read it, Trystan kissed his fist and cast the dice on the table.

Was an aegent next you. Hedd to byd tyme. Wante?

"Damn! Hopeless!"

The poor spelling didn't surprise Rufinus - many commoners were illiterate – but the content spooked him. He had failed to register anything sinister about the old man who had been sat at the adjacent table. He erased the words with the flat end of the stylus and wrote:

Trace senator M. Maracanthus. Missing 2 days. Poss. of plot?

"A Venus and first blood's mine!" Then Rufinus threw the dice. His own score was no better. "See? That's why I don't ever have much coin!"

Rufinus watched Trystan's face as he glanced at the tablet. If he was surprised by the request, he didn't show it.

"Hard cheese, Tiberius. Though we only agreed an obol first up and if that breaks the bank, we have problems my friend!" He laughed. "No? Okay, give 'em here."

Trystan erased the words and added his own before throwing the dice:

Wyl inqyr on street reference bountyes. Plot?

And so the painstaking process went on as Rufinus disclosed more and more information whilst trying to gauge how trustworthy the man was.

After half an hour, Trystan agreed to meet Rufinus in the tavern for more dice in five days. There was no further discussion. Trystan simply erased the words, clipped the tablet and rose.

"Good game, Tiberius. I got lucky, I guess." They shook hands again. "Next time you'll do better I think! See you around. The wife'll kill me if I leave it any later."

When Trystan had left, Rufinus flopped back onto his stool, drained and light-headed. He regretted not taking water with the wine and pondered his next move. He looked at the people around him, wondering what it might be like to have their carefree lives. Even as a young man he had been unable to live in the louche way that many of his peers in the equestrian class were comfortable with. And yet had he, in devoting himself to his studies and his civic career at the expense of even the briefest phase of drinking and whoring, become more successful?

Rufinus shook his head. The exercise was destructive and made him feel melancholic. He squeezed his money pouch and felt just how much lighter it was. Although coins had been spent, it had nothing to do with a game of dice. He didn't begrudge the cost, though he couldn't help wondering if he would ever see any return. He reached down to tie up his sandals, steeling himself for the unpleasant journey home. When he looked back up, he caught sight of the woman he had seen when he entered. She was clearing away cups from the tables and creating quite a stir wherever she went. Rufinus could not help but stare. She sensed his attentions and turned to look at him, giving him a practiced smile. To his surprise, she did not immediately move on and he averted his eyes, conscious of his quickening pulse and flushing face. She approached him and picked up his cup.

"You like another?"

Rufinus swallowed hard. She had a strange accent that he couldn't place. "Not for me. I have to leave now."

"What? Are you mad?" she put her hand on her hip. "Do you have wife?"

"I beg your pardon?"

"You have no ring. No ring, no wife to complain you are late!"

He frowned at her. He wanted to tell her to mind her own business, but the unwavering gaze of her feline eyes, set beneath carefully plucked eyebrows and lashes blackened with Kohl, fixated him. Though he looked for it, there was nothing suggestive, teasing or chiding about her words. Her smile faded and then she shrugged and walked away.

XX

It was her very lack of reaction that was most disheartening. Ambrosius hadn't known what to expect when he told Poppeia the bare facts of his impending departure to Ostia but a frown and a shrug certainly wasn't it. Anna sensed the atmosphere thickening behind her as she prepared some food at the stove.

"Did you hear about Didius and his wife?"

"What?" He gave her an incredulous look. "No. Why, are they going to Ostia as well?"

She stopped stirring the pot and looked at him. "No, Ambrosius, they aren't."

"So why are we now talking about them?"

"I don't know … I'm just trying to change the subject; lighten the mood."

"Fine!" He threw his hands in the air and leant back in the chair. "What happened to them?"

"They were arrested."

He glanced at Poppeia and was disappointed to see that this news had her interested. "For what?"

"They left their house for a short while. A fire was still burning in the hearth."

"Well … that's what you get for being so careless and risking burning your tenement down. And half the city with it. Fires start every day in Rome like that: that's what the law's there to prevent."

Anna took the pan off the heat and set it down with a loud clang.

"Ambrosius! They left in a rush because their son was sick: they needed to find a doctor!"

"Sorry to hear that. But they could have still put their fire out with …"

"A bucket of water," she interjected sourly. "That's what the Watchmen that broke in helpfully told them when they got back."

Poppeia tutted and Ambrosius frowned at her. "People always have excuses. That's probably what I'd have said too."

"And must you always be so pig-headed?" She glanced at Poppeia and lowered her voice a shade. "Their son is very poorly: he's running a fever, they tried to do what was best for him, got hauled off by your friends and now they can't afford the fine on top of paying for some quack physician to tell them what they already knew. Can't you do anything about it before you go?"

"No," he sighed. "No I can't?"

"Why not? You're a tribune. You've known Didius for years!"

It struck Ambrosius that he had never seen Anna so animated before. She had a plain, thin face and straight dark hair that was almost always tied up and concealed by a white scarf. Practical and unfussy. But now her green eyes were wide and challenging. "Well?"

He picked an apple from the fruitbowl and span it by the stem. "Because I've not told you the half of why I have to leave."

"Go on."

"Look, I'm not going to Ostia again because I want to. I'm being forced to. And if I tell you the reason, you must keep it to yourselves, understood?"

"I'm not a baby," said Poppeia. "And you're only telling me this now because you feel guilty."

"Guilty?"

She rolled her eyes and looked around the room.

To Hades with it. You can have it straight, he thought. "I have to go because a little girl, not much older than you, has been murdered."

Poppeia snapped her head round. "Oh … who?"

"A senator's daughter. We found her yesterday, very early in the morning."

Anna put her fingers to her mouth. Nobody spoke for a few moments.

"But … so … what, I mean why …" Poppeia's voice trailed off.

"Why does that mean I have to go to Ostia?"

She nodded.

"This is why I wanted you to promise me you'll keep it just amongst us… yes? It's not supposed to be my job but I wanted to try to find who killed her, so Bulla and Titus and I took the body back to the crypt in the barracks …"

"The toad and the big ugly one?"

Ambrosius laughed, despite himself. "Yes, those two. We took the girl back there to be embalmed whilst we thought about what to do next, and how to get word out to find her parents. Meantime, Titus chased a man trying to break into the building she had been in just before she died but it wasn't the right man so he was released. Later that night someone stole her body from right underneath our noses." Poppeia gasped in shock but Anna was behind her stroking her hair. "And that's the problem."

"But … but I still don't understand why you have to go? You did nothing wrong. You wanted her to be safe!"

Ambrosius looked at her and felt a peculiar sadness pass. Did it have to take something so appalling to happen to someone else's daughter to draw paternal affection from his own?

"It's not quite that simple," he sighed. "There are other things happening that I don't yet understand. But I do know I've upset some very powerful people, and not just the girl's father so, even though I hate the idea with all my heart, maybe it's a good thing I have to leave for a short time. There's every chance there are informers watching everything we do. In fact, they may already be working as watchmen in my barracks."

"Do you mean, like, spies?"

"Exactly that."

Larissa, he knew, would have been horrified by the notion. Not so Poppeia, who was awestruck.

"Why do you think there are informers at work, Ambrosius?" Anna asked. Though her tone was level, he saw she was sceptical.

"The Watch Prefect, Junius Rufinus, summoned me yesterday. He said he was under orders in taking action against me but didn't tell me who gave them. But the point is he knew things about what we'd done that he couldn't possibly have known unless he was there. And how else could anyone have stolen a body from the building without knowing when was the right time to enter unless he was using his own eyes?"

"A vigil doesn't get paid much, Ambrosius. We all know they're as ready as any other man to turn a blind eye for the right price."

"Hey, enough of these slights against watchmen!" Ambrosius checked his rising irritation. "I had considered that but I think I now know where everyone was. Nobody else springs to mind. And even if that were the case, an informer or some kind of agent would still have to be involved to make the approach in the first place."

"Not unless it was a body snatcher acting on his own."

"What?" Ambrosius and Poppeia both wrinkled their noses.

"I've heard there are people who do such things for whatever reason. Don't ask me why …"

"I don't think that's likely. Not with my lot, anyhow."

"You don't look very convinced of that," said Anna, arching an eyebrow.

"You two are very stupid. It's obvious how they would've got to her and taken her away?"

"Oh really, clever clogs?" Ambrosius leaned back on his chair and folded his arms. "And why 'they' exactly?"

"One person couldn't carry her away, daddy."

"Ah, but she was very small, see. Hardly any bigger than you."

"Well, I'll tell you why," Poppeia tucked her hair over her ears and shuffled on her seat. Ambrosius felt a stab of yearning for Larissa: it was exactly as she did when settling into a discussion. "You probably wouldn't remember because you were always thinking about work," she said with a grin, "but you used to throw me over your shoulder before putting me to bed when I was little and groaned because I was getting heavy, saying 'Oof, you're a dead weight!' So that must mean that dead people weigh more than live ones."

Ambrosius pursed his lips and nodded at the logic. "Not sure about that: they're certainly more awkward to carry but I'll let you have that one. You may proceed, counsel."

"Well anyway, as I was saying, you're both being very stupid. You're missing something very obvious. I don't think anyone was paid to let someone inside or take her away or that someone came in the door or window when everyone was asleep, like a burglar. There's more than one way rainwater gets into a house."

"What, through the roof?" He winked at Anna. "Be a bit loud, wouldn't it, ripping all those heavy slates off?"

Poppeia rolled her eyes. "No, stupido. Through the floor!"

"Through the floor?"

But Ambrosius' tone wasn't mocking. He massaged the bridge of his nose and tried to envisage the layout of the rooms adjoining the crypt. He had only made a cursory search in the moments of blind panic after Ludo had reported the body missing but nothing had been obvious. Besides, that was Vitalis' domain and, truth be told, Ambrosius didn't care much for the dank underworld he inhabited.

Anna ruffled Poppeia's hair and resumed stirring the soup, then nearly threw the entire contents all over the stove as Ambrosius' fist clattered onto the table.

"You, my little beauty, are a genius!" He jumped up from the table and hurried round to give her a hug.

"Daddy, stop it you'll pull my hair out!"

Ambrosius planted a loud kiss on her forehead. "How do you fancy coming with me to do some investigation?"

"Yes! Can I?"

"Of course you can! Come on, go and get something warm on!"

Poppeia leapt up, returned the hug and then skipped away to the door.

"Er! I don't think so!" Anna had one hand on her hip and the other wielded a wooden spoon. "Sit yourselves right back down!"

Ambrosius slumped back onto his chair and Poppeia followed, tutting.

"If you think I'm letting you out at this time of night to go traipsing halfway across the city with empty stomachs you've got another thing coming! Are you both mad? Whatever little scheme you've just hatched can wait until morning!" She rapped Ambrosius on the head with a satisfying thunk.

XXI

The final preparations for the Matronalia festival began just after first light. The sacred grove on the Esquiline hill, in which nestled the temple of Juno Lucina, by then almost six hundred years old, was a hive of activity. Teams of slaves directed by garrulous freedmen set about clearing the temple steps of stray leaves and rubbish, whilst the more dexterous were fashioning garlands from sprigs of the ubiquitous Holm Oak trees to be hung from the temple's pillars.

Elsewhere a gang of slaves, helped by junior priests, was constructing temporary pens to shelter sacrificial lambs and cattle for their final feed, whilst others struggled to drag the reluctant beasts up the hill. Even at this early hour, enterprising vendors had set out their stalls to ensure the prime locations for selling spiced sausages, pies and sweetmeats to those watching or taking part in the procession to the temple. Ambrosius and Poppeia were oblivious to the preparations as they hurried to the Watch House. Despite the chilly start to the day, there was a festive atmosphere to the city's streets that was matched by Ambrosius' own optimism.

As they entered the courtyard, Ambrosius put his hand on Poppeia's shoulder, holding her back. Ludo was in a close discussion with two other men, and Ambrosius recognized one of them as an ambitious young officer on the Watch Prefect's staff, a cornicularius excused front line duties. He heard his name mentioned but they were speaking too quietly to pick up much else. The three threw back their heads with laughter at some shared joke before Ludo glanced towards the gate and did a double take. The two officers followed his gaze and their expressions changed. They made their excuses to Ludo and walked out of the courtyard, offering the faintest of nods to Ambrosius.

Ludo cleared his throat. "You're a good few hours early, tribune. Showing your daughter round?"

"Something like that. Friends of yours?"

"Oh, er, they were just making sure we'd got all our deployments right," he said, gesturing vaguely. "Some of the granary stocks are running a bit low: seems Balbus, Rufinus' deputy, is a bit concerned there might be a few break-ins."

"Right. Is Vitalis in?"

"Vitalis? Yeah, I assume so. What's this all …?"

Ambrosius took Poppeia by the hand and led her along the main corridor past the dormitory rooms.

"Daddy, I don't like him. He's sl–"

Ambrosius silenced her with a finger to his lips and a wink. They descended the short flight of steps leading to the basement and the crypt, where they encountered Vitalis wiping his hands on a rag as he talked to a few more watchmen.

"Tribune?" Vitalis glanced at Poppeia and smiled. "What are you doing here? Shouldn't you be asleep?"

"Probably. Gentlemen, haven't you got grainhouses to be guarding?"

The vigiles exchanged puzzled looks. "If you say so, tribune," said the eldest of them. He inclined his head to the stairs and they all took the hint and left.

"Vitalis, this is my daughter Poppeia, who has more brains than the whole of the cohort put together. So go on, my girl, tell us what you think!"

Poppeia gnawed her finger, suddenly shy in front of the grizzled gaoler.

"Don't worry," growled Vitalis, "Whatever you say'll be more intelligent than anything that lot could come up with."

Poppeia looked to Ambrosius.

"Go on, you're alright!" he said, glancing at Ludo, who was now on the stairs.

"Well … umm. I think that the little girl that … that the men that took her got in through the floor."

"How's that then, young miss …? I don't follow."

"Nor did I at first, but I think I might now. Come on; bring a couple of torches."

They followed Ambrosius deeper into the crypt and then into an adjoining room in which Terentia's embalmed body had once lain. "This is where we last saw her," he said to Poppeia who shivered. "Now then, Vitalis, where's the sewage outlet?"

"The sewage?" he replied, wrinkling his craggy face. "Well … alright, that's down another level. Back out, staircase to the left, down the hatch then follow your nose for a while."

"I thought so. So then, someone coming up from there wouldn't have to cross your path if you were in the cells?"

"No. No they wouldn't. But they'd have to be quiet as a mouse for me not to hear them, tribune."

"Let's give it a go shall we?"

The group had to jog to keep up with the excitable tribune. They reached the trapdoor and Vitalis helped Ambrosius drag it upright.

"Watch your footing down the steps. Very worn. They can get a bit …"

On the very first step he nearly stumbled headlong into the darkness and he swore at his carelessness, causing Vitalis to cover Poppeia's ears. "… a bit slippery."

The torches crackled as the flames encountered the dank air and the watchmen covered their noses with their sleeves as they descended. After a few minutes, they emerged at a stoop into a long corridor. The torchlight threw the darkness back no more than twenty feet and cast the faces of the watchmen in demonic contours. Drips of water echoed around the low, curved ceiling.

"All this time working here," said Ludo, "and I had no idea we were on top of foundations older than Caesar's gran!"

"Listen!"

From somewhere beneath them they heard the faint sound of rushing water. Poppeia felt conflicting and thrilling waves of emotion wash over her. Whilst she was in no doubt she would never in a hundred years want to be here alone, she felt secure in the presence of these tough men who were only there because of her idea: she couldn't wait to tell her friends.

Vitalis nodded. "The Cloaca Maxima. She's right under our feet. Straight on, tribune."

They pressed on, slower now, into the cloying darkness and, even with his limp, Vitalis was able to keep the pace. The sound of the water grew louder, and the stench less bearable, with every step.

"There should be an inspection cover a little further down, tribune."

They moved on into the stinking darkness. Poppeia squeezed Ambrosius' hand though refused to admit that she was finding it difficult to breathe.

Just when all save Vitalis thought they could bear no more, the light from Ambrosius' torch crept over a slight depression in the floor.

"And there it is," said Vitalis. "Is that what you were looking for, tribune?"

Ambrosius peered at it and felt a stab of disappointment. The circular cover was much smaller than he had hoped.

"So were ancient builders dwarves then, Vitalis?" asked Ludo.

The quaestionarius ignored him. "Doesn't look like this has been disturbed in hundreds of years, tribune."

Ambrosius took the torch, which was already beginning to dim. He murmured agreement and lowered it over the cover. "Take a closer look."

"I don't see anything," said Ludo. "What are you pointing at?"

"Look again, there, at the lichen and dirt: there's separation between the iron rim and the floor around it. If it hadn't been disturbed it would have grown right across it. It's been lifted up alright, and very recently I'd say."

"Well, if it had, it would have to be by a midget. There's no way any of us would fit down there!"

"I would."

The watchmen looked at Poppeia in surprise.

"No."

"But daddy!"

"Out of the question!"

Poppeia put her hands on her hips and scowled at Ambrosius.

"Why don't you give me a hand lifting this instead?" asked Vitalis, taking a grip of one of the grill bars. Grateful to be of some use, Poppeia bent down and tugged. It didn't move.

"You try twisting it, I'll pull it. On three. One, two ..."

The cover rasped as they dragged it away from the opening. Ambrosius thrust his torch into the darkness with a whoosh that drove the fetid smell upwards, making them all gag.

The torch illuminated the first few rungs of a badly corroded ladder.

"That's where your mice got in, Vitalis." muttered Ludo. "What now?"

Ambrosius scratched his head.

"I've seen all I need to see, thanks Vitalis."

"Are you not curious what's down there?" asked Ludo as Vitalis replaced the cover.

"Not really. Shit and water I imagine. And rats."

"Don't you think that's where the girl might be?"

"No. If someone went to those lengths to negotiate the sewers and sneak into the crypt to steal her body in the first place, they wouldn't just dump her down there afterwards. She could be anywhere in Rome by now. Anyway, no-one's going down there to have a look. I wanted to see whether my girl had a point. It's possible alright. Difficult but possible." He turned to Poppeia and pulled her close to him. "Let's go."

They retraced their steps, moving quicker now. The torch sputtered and faded but Ambrosius ignored it.

"You look thoughtful, tribune," said Vitalis.

"Well …" added Ludo, "care to let us in?"

They approached the spiral steps to the basement and bounded up them, grateful to be out of the bowels of the earth. Ambrosius replaced the trapdoor and tossed the guttering torch to Ludo, who caught it with a frown.

"Needs re-pitching. Both of you; watch everyone, trust no-one," his eyes paused upon Ludo for a brief moment. "Think on this for a moment: we find the girl at the dockside and bring her back here. We only have time to publish a single, vague notice in the forum. Yet that very night, or early the next morning, her body is stolen from underneath our noses. A few hours later, the girl's father, senator Piso, comes to collect her. A few hours after that, I'm summoned to see the Prefect of the Watch and questioned about what we did. That evening, we're paid a visit by Vibius Brutus, the Deputy Praetorian Prefect." He shifted the weight on his feet. "Don't you see? We keep getting caught on the hop and that's because we're up against some very powerful people. And to top it off, we've just seen for ourselves that the body was probably stolen by people coming in through the sewers. Through the damn sewers! Now who, I ask you, is able in the space of less than twelve watches to learn all that and then find the means to negotiate the Cloaca Maxima like Theseus did the Labyrinth?"

The question hung in the air.

"I'll tell you," he continued, jabbing his finger at the floor. "Someone with enough influence to beg, steal or borrow the original plans for both this stretch of the sewers and this damned building! Now that person is not someone you want to play pat-a-cake with."

"Alright, say the original plans did still exist, tribune," asked Vitalis. "Where?"

"Who knows? The Aediles are responsible for maintaining all public buildings. Where do they keep all their archives: the treasury? Some temple or basilica? The Records Office? That'd be my guess. You discover who removed those documents and you find the killer, or at least somebody closely connected. I'd put my life on it."

Ludo grinned. "Are you planning to raid the Tabularium?"

"I guarantee if one of us did gain access, that person would never again see the light of day. No, me and my daughter are going to enjoy

Matronalia." He looked at Ludo. "That's the only plan we have, isn't that right?"

Poppeia smiled and hugged her father again: they both knew there was no way it would be left at that.

XXII

The bar at the corner of Via Labicana and The Shrine of the Good
Goddess, near the Esquiline Hill, was doing a roaring trade with those
wanting to avoid the crowds attending the Matronalia, though there were
still a few men dressed as women even here, being the one day of the year
devoted to celebrating femininity.

Poppeia was munching on a warm pastry and being mothered by Anna
and Titus' effervescent wife Lucia, who were engaged in the endless task
of brushing the crumbs off her new green dress. Ambrosius thought it was
a hideous, shapeless garment and it was a sure sign of progress in their
relationship that he felt able give her his honest opinion, albeit a tempered
one. The fact that he knew Larissa would also have cringed at it he kept to
himself. Lucia and Anna could not have been more different in
temperament and yet, to Ambrosius' pleasant surprise, they were getting
along famously. Lucia was clucking at Poppeia like a brooding hen.

Every so often, the girls would lean in and Lucia would make some
comment or other, they would snigger and she would shoot Titus a
smouldering glance. Ambrosius could make out the odd word as he talked
to Titus and Bulla, but the heated wine had dulled their senses and they
were both oblivious to some of the lascivious comments that Lucia was
making. Not a conventional beauty, Lucia was certainly striking. She had a
full figure, black hair in ringlets as thick as rope and an enchanting smile.
Although watchmen could not legally marry until they retired, many did
anyway. Titus had been with Lucia for years and he wondered why they
had remained childless.

Bulla punched his arm, interrupting his thoughts.

"What's so funny?"

The Syrian looked at Titus and they both cracked up laughing. "Do you
not remember that, tribune?"

"Remember what, or are you on about the same thing again?"

"Hey, Anna! Have you heard the slave story?"

Anna shook her head. "Will I have to cover Poppeia's ears for this?"

"I've heard this one so many times," said Poppeia with her mouth full.
"It's boring."

Bulla's eyes bulged with enthusiasm. "Never! It happened a year or so ago. We were all out on patrol in the dark and the tribune was not had a good mood ..."

"Nothing new there then," said Anna.

"Well ... anyway ... as I say, he was having bad day when some snooty old dear comes run out into the street brandishing a big ladle, screaming at us like the Caledonian whore, 'Are you just going to stand there like idiots? My Herman's escaped again!' 'Alright, lady!' he says. 'Who's Herman?' 'He's a slave you fool!' she shouts, 'I've only got two! Go and find him this minute!' Then she chases for us down the street. By this time everyone is hanging out their shutters demanding to know what's going on and telling for us to shut up. I've never seen him so scared – he's got his hands in the air as we run away – and he shouts back at her, 'Calm down, will you, we didn't damn well let him out! I've never heard of Herman! I wouldn't know him if I fell over him!'" Bulla snorted like a donkey, spilling some of his wine. "So we run round the corner and he trips over the sack of rubbish on the pavement and goes flying. He's cursing like a good'un and then this bag of rubbish lets out groaning. It is happen he's just fell over Herman, who was hiding from the old witch!"

Lucia and Anna shrieked with laughter whilst Titus and Bulla doubled up again. "She gave poor old Herman the thrashing of his life!"

Anna dabbed the corner of her eyes. "You never told me about that!"

"Strange that." But even Ambrosius was grinning now.

They carried on talking, oblivious to the newcomers gathering in the street and the lengthening shadows.

"Looks like the secret's well and truly out about this place," said Anna.

A woman let out a piercing scream. There was a scuffle a few yards away and the crowd parted.

"Leave her alone!"

Titus, Bulla and Ambrosius broke away from the girls to see what has happening.

"Please be careful!" Lucia shouted after them.

"Give me your fucking ring, bitch!"

A young man and woman were at that moment being robbed by two men with cloaks pulled over their faces. One of them looked like he would wrench the girl's finger off as she fought back. Her partner, at that moment pinned to the wall, screamed and kicked out, catching her assailant in the shin. The one pinning his arms back stepped back and punched him hard in the stomach, making him sag to the floor.

Although people were shouting at them, nobody intervened.

"I got it! Get his purse and go!"

They both sprinted away down Via Labicana towards the eastern city gates, barging past an old man who tried to stop them, sending him sprawling.

Titus was already in pursuit, followed by Ambrosius and Bulla, who could only manage a half-drunk waddle. One of the robbers stumbled whilst the other broke clear, and Titus caught him by the hood after only twenty strides, yanking him downwards without stopping. He clattered to the floor where Ambrosius dropped on him. He grabbed a fistful of hair, tugged his head backwards and then drove it hard onto the cobbles. His body went limp.

Meanwhile, prolonged only because of the effects of the wine, the other pursuit was rapidly reaching its conclusion. The thief panicked and weaved across the street, risking a glance over his shoulder just as Titus slammed him between the shoulder blades with the flat of his massive hand. The hammer blow could be heard forty yards away by the onlookers at the bar. He gasped as the wind was driven from him and sprawled to the floor, skidding a short way along the cobbles.

Titus gripped him by the tunic and hauled him up, glaring at him.

"You just ruined my drink."

The robber, a rangy youth with a dirty face and wispy facial hair, looked petrified. His breath came in wheezing gasps. "Don't hurt me … I'm poor!"

Titus propelled him back towards the bar with great shoves and he staggered back towards his mate, who was being pinned to the wall by Ambrosius and Bulla. The crowd formed a crescent around them, now emboldened to shout threats and insults. When he reached them, Titus pushed him to the floor and put his hands on his hips.

"Where's that couple got to?"

"Here they are! Let 'em through!"

"Did you see that?" whispered another in awe. "That one can't 'alf run for the mountain he is!"

"Never seen them before …"

"I think they're legionaries. Or Praetorians."

"Nah, look at how pale they are. They're bucket carriers!"

The crowd parted for the distraught girl and her partner. The hapless young man was rubbing his stomach and trembling with delayed shock.

"Do 'im right in, lad!"

Ambrosius ignored the wag. "I take it you don't know these two, young man?"

He shook his head.

"What's your name?"

"Claudius Numitor, sir. This is my fiancée, Thea."

Ambrosius regarded them. They made a well-groomed pair, not the obvious type to attract trouble. They had the same flaxen hair, though his was curly and hers straight and fine, like silk.

"Don't owe anyone money do you?"

"No, sir!"

Ambrosius turned to the robbers, who were crouched against the wall of the bar, their chests heaving. One of them looked very groggy, and was already sporting a sizeable lump in the centre of his forehead.

Ambrosius stretched out his hand. "The ring and the money pouch. Give them to me."

The youth with the dirty face retrieved them and handed them over, though his wide eyes never left Titus. Ambrosius returned them, to profuse thanks.

"So, what to do with these thieving scum?" asked Bulla.

Ambrosius pursed his lips, keen to avoid wasting precious time presenting them to the Watch Prefect's deputy on his last day with Poppeia. He turned to the young couple. "Ever heard of the 'Twelve Tables'"

"Yeah, do it!" shouted someone in the crowd.

Confusion crossed Claudius' face. "Er, vaguely sir, from school. Ancient laws? I don't remember any of them." He glanced at Thea, who shook her head.

"We do. Titus, stand them up would you?"

Titus gripped them and shoved them against the wall. "Want me to hold 'em whilst he gets on with it?"

"Gets on with what?" asked the youth with the swollen forehead.

"Si membrum rupsit, ni cum eo pacit, talio esto," recited Ambrosius. "'If one has maimed another, and does not buy his peace, let there be retaliation.'"

"What?" he snorted. "I didn't maim him!"

"Well let's see shall we?" Ambrosius sneered at him. "Lift up your tunic, young man."

Claudius did as asked. His body was lithe and hairless, like a girl's, which only emphasised the reddening where he was punched.

"Looks like you maimed his skin to me, you little bastard. Right then, step forwards please. This may turn out to be your lucky day after all!"

Claudius hesitated.

"You can't do that!" The thief was squirming under Titus' iron grip. "You can't!"

Ambrosius stalked over to him and gripped his throat. His teeth were gritted and his nostrils flared in a rush of anger.

"Ambrosius …" said Anna, stepping forwards. "They're just kids."

"Rubbish, they're scum!" shouted someone in the crowd.

"'If one is slain whilst committing theft, he is rightly slain.'" Ambrosius' grip tightened. "Prefer this one?"

The youth managed to shake his head and Ambrosius let him drop, leaving him gasping for breath. Titus dragged him back up.

"Do it!" An image of Terentia's body flashed before his eyes, making him wince. And the bloodied, frenzied scene of her death. And Larissa, smiling at him. His beautiful, beloved Larissa … "Summary justice. Do it now."

"Sir, we have our possessions back! That's enough for us. But … thank you, all three of you."

"I'm not asking you, mister," Ambrosius' tone resonated with menace. He jabbed his finger at the robber's stomach. "Talio esto. He might have killed her, if things were different. Think on that."

Claudius noted the sudden change of mood and decided not to push it. He shuffled forwards, unable to look the robber in the face, who responded with a mocking smile. Seized by righteous anger, Claudius drew his fist back and aimed a punch at his stomach but it was a feeble, mal-coordinated effort. It occurred to him that he had never thrown his fists in anger and that he was quite unsuited for the purpose. The thief recoiled in Titus's grip but then the sneer returned.

Is that all you've got, girl?

"Go on lad, you can do better than that. Put your back into it," whispered Titus.

But far from satisfying him, the futility of his anger made him feel even more inadequate as a man. He had frozen to the spot when he was first attacked and now he had frozen again. On a whim, he tried a punch with his other hand but it was even less effective and it landed on the point of the thief's elbow. Pain lanced through his fist and he recoiled, clutching it. The robber let out a snigger and the sheer humiliation of it all made Claudius want to scurry away and cry.

"Step aside," said Ambrosius nudging past him. He threw a savage punch that landed flush in the thief's solar plexus, making him buck forwards in pain. He curled into a ball, pawing at the cobbles, gasping for breath.

"Bulla?"

Bulla stepped forwards and butted the other thief with a resounding clop. His head jerked backwards against the brick wall, the double impact knocking him out cold. Titus allowed him to slip through his hands to the floor, where he lay motionless.

"That'll do," said Ambrosius. He prodded the winded man with the tip of his sandal. "Get up and get out of here. Now."

For a moment, nobody said a word. Then the astonished onlookers began to melt away or resume their conversations. Thea and a sheepish Claudius skirted the thieves and walked away without a backward glance.

"Where did that come from?" asked Anna, her voice hoarse. "And in front of Poppeia!"

But, for the second time in as many days, her reaction surprised him. Averse to any violence, Larissa would have been horrified. Poppeia, by contrast, looked awestruck. She took Ambrosius' hand.

"Is it sore, daddy?

Ambrosius stroked her hair, touched by the simple gesture. "It's fine, my little flower. Everything's just fine."

"I think we'll make our way back and leave you boys to cool off," said Lucia. "Come back when you're ready and we'll have some food on the table before you go to work. Don't be long and don't drink too much. It's supposed to be our day, remember?" She winked at Titus, who beamed back at her.

With that they walked away, swinging Poppeia between them.

Ambrosius watched them go, turning away from Titus and Bulla so that they would not see the tears that had suddenly welled in his eyes, but it was in vain. They had seen the look on his face and were already wondering what to do about it.

"Right then Bulla," said Titus, rubbing his hands together, "one more round before we lose the tribune here to the fishmongers and the crab-flippers for a few months."

XXIII

That evening, two young men staggered into one of the taverns by the Colline Gate in the north of the city. They were drunk and disheveled.

The barkeep watched them enter, supporting each other as they flopped onto bar stools. One of them had a livid bruise the size of an egg in the middle of his forehead, though they both looked like they had been dragged round the city walls behind a chariot. He was in two minds about serving them but they appeared to be in no mood for trouble. They paid up front with a gold coin (which surprised him a little) and asked that he keep serving them until the value of the coin had been met. He duly served them the cheapest wine at a vintage price.

The barkeep paid them little further attention, other than refilling their cups, though he didn't care much for the throwaway comments of one of them, whom he distinctly heard saying that 'he was glad he hurt the spoilt little bitch'. But then, as every roadside tavern, bar and stabling post keeper in the empire knew, a man couldn't expect to serve strong drink to a rough and ready clientele and expect the conduct of a Vestal Virgin in return.

It was a busy evening because of the Matronalia. The main saloon was smoky, stale and buzzed with conversation amidst the triumphant and despairing shouts of the dice players. Nevertheless the barkeep was able to register the comings and goings of his customers, as was expected of him in the face of the whimsical and draconian edicts issued by the Emperor. He didn't pay much attention to the handsome but shifty looking character that worked his way around the room, eavesdropping on conversations and chipping in with cutting observations about politics, and so wasn't surprised when he saw him leave alone. He did recognise the odd over-painted whore that came and went, though as a rule it was easier for him to deter the attentions of the authorities if he forbade any open prostitution. He also noticed when the youth with the large bump on his forehead drained his cup, shook hands with his companion and left. All in all, however, it was business as usual.

And so it came as a shock when the armed guard of Praetorians burst in. It took a few seconds for their arrival to percolate through the room: there was the odd shriek from the working girls but then the room fell quiet. The owner's heart thudded against his ribs when the ranking Praetorian approached the bar with a scowl, and his mind raced through all of the possibilities: was the after-hours drinking becoming too obvious? Were the locals fed up with the brawling outside or the gambling getting out of hand?

"This one?" his voice sounded like he was swallowing gravel. He turned towards someone concealed in the shadows. "Right, you're coming with us, son."

He gripped the dirty faced youth and heaved him, open-mouthed, off the stool. He propelled him towards the entrance, where he was engulfed by the rest of the Praetorians, who couldn't resist roughing him up with a few cheap shots as they swarmed outside.

The Praetorian glared at the bar keeper as if daring him to challenge his actions. Then he looked around the room and the customers, to a person, averted their eyes. He looked back at the owner and grinned, revealing his decaying teeth, before slamming the door shut.

After a few moments, there was a ragged exhalation within the room.

"That'll be you next if you don't pay up soon!" announced one of the dice players, and there was a relieved gale of laughter.

The bar keeper sagged onto the counter, to the applause and cheers of some of his regulars.

"Not yet, caupo!" they shouted in unison. "Not this day!"

*

For the already bruised young thief, the journey through the heart of Rome in the city's only purpose-built horse-drawn cage was the single most terrifying event of his life. As the cartwheels bumped and shuddered over the cobbles, his eyes darted to and fro, registering through the iron bars the hulking forms of the Trajan Baths and the Colosseum for the last time in the fading light.

He had never had anything to do with the Praetorians in his life and their hostility towards him was visceral. Nor was his bewilderment eased by anything he said or asked of his contemptuous escort. Whenever he protested his innocence or tried talking to them, all he received in response was spittle or jabs with the scabbards of their swords, and then laughter and bursts of abuse. He soon gave up, resolving to make one last effort when he had arrived at his destination and to ignore their roughhouse banter and boasting. But even as the cage veered left, his heart sank further. He braced himself, praying that he would not experience the sensation of tipping backwards as the wagon descended into the forum and what lay at the end of it. He calculated the seconds it would take at the speed they were rolling along.

Thirty seconds … forty … he gasped for breath as he realised he had been holding it in. Fifty seconds … fifty five … surely he had passed the entrance by? He relaxed and looked on as happy couples and small groups of people strolled by, some looking the worse for wear after the day's excesses. All of them, however, paused to watch the unusual spectacle of the Praetorians escorting the wagon. He caught a few of their pitying or insulting words on the slight breeze, envying their freedom.

The cart lurched and he was thrown backwards against the wooden slats of his cage. His stomach swilled, and the Praetorians laughed at him as he retched.

"Travel sickness will soon be the least o'yer worries, boy!"

The rattle and clatter of wheels on cobbles changed to a smooth hiss as they skimmed over the dirt that covered the flagstones of the forum. He drew up his knees and watched in despair as the temples of Vesta, and Castor and Pollux swung into view, and he knew then with absolute certainty that he was heading towards the notorious Tullian Prison.

There was a short, sharp bark of command from someone at the front and the wagon halted. A heavy chain rattled behind him and a high-pitched grating suggested iron scraping against stone. He looked around him: to his left was the austere form of the senate house, locked up for the evening, and to his right the speakers' platform, bristling with the darkening beaks of enemy ships captured over five hundred years ago.

"Get him out, they're waiting."

A Praetorian opened the cage door with a key from a belt pouch, from which he also removed a leather thong. This he used to bind up the prisoner's hands in the praying position, so tightly that he felt his circulation being constricted. The soldier dragged him out with a grunt and he stumbled to his knees. He was now shivering uncontrollably and all feeling had drained from his legs.

"Come on, get up and stop fucking about. We've got some serious drinking to catch up with!"

There was a snort of laughter and he was shoved forwards again. The Tullian was a low, squat building that nestled by the eastern slope of the Capitoline, and everyone knew its history: not just any common criminal would find himself here. The prison had incarcerated the likes of famous heretics, whom Christians called 'Saint Paul' and 'Saint Peter', the Gallic warlord Vercingetorix and several members of the Catilinarian conspiracy. Everyone also knew that no prisoner who entered ever emerged alive.

"No! No, this can't be!" he dug in his heels. "There must be some mistake! There ..."

A stinging cuff round his head silenced him. His legs were kicked out and he was dragged towards the entrance.

"No! No! No!"

He was raving now, and began to thrash out at his captors. He caught one of them on the bridge of his nose and he grunted in surprise. Then he felt a heavy thud to the side of his head and darkness engulfed him.

*

When he jerked awake, he was shivering against a foul smelling bale of hay. His hands were bound and there was a dull throb in his head that pounded when he moved his eyes. The circular, unmortared walls of his cell were low and coated with slimy green lichen.

And he was not alone.

Sat opposite him on a crescent of stools was a selection of the most uncompromising looking men he had ever laid eyes on: except one. The man on the right, much slighter than the others, looked vaguely familiar. He had thick, pomaded hair that was swept to one side and small, beady eyes detracting from looks that might otherwise have been described as handsome.

When he tried to speak, sharp pain lanced his jaw, and he clutched it. There was drying blood on his fingers.

"He's round," said one of them, who picked up his stool and dropped it nearer to him.

"Are you hungry? Or thirsty?" his soft voice was at odds with his flinty, scarred face.

The prisoner glanced over the man's shoulder at the nobleman who was stroking his impressive beard and fixing him with an unwavering stare. He nodded. "Good. Gaoler, bring over that bowl would you? And the water."

The prisoner looked at the food: for a fleeting moment the aroma of stewed rabbit replaced the stench of the cell.

"Tastes even better than it looks, believe me," chuckled the quaestionarius with the soft voice. "You're welcome to it in a few minutes but you need to answer a few questions first. That way you can eat it before it gets cold, yes?"

The prisoner nodded again.

"Your name?"

"Mathias, sir"

"Mathias or Mathias-sir?"

"Just Mathias."

"Do you know why you're here, Mathias?"

"No," he croaked, "I've not done anything." It was agony to speak but co-operation seemed the only option.

"Ah, but you were clearly heard in the tavern to say that you … hang on a minute …" he opened up a wax tablet and put the stylus over his ear, "that you were 'glad you hurt the spoilt little bitch' and later 'shame really … wildcat … would have fucked like a Babylon whore for the right price,' Not really the words of an innocent man, no?"

"What?" Mathias looked aghast. "How …?"

"You see, it says so here. And that man's memory," he said, thumbing over his shoulder to the one with pomaded hair, "is quite astonishing."

The spitting of the torch flames filled the ensuing silence. His inquisitor's beetling eyebrows met in a frown.

"So you're denying ever saying those things?"

"No. No, he's right. I did say those … things." Mathias had noted the subtle change in mood and was desperate to appease him. He shivered. "Can I please have some of that stew?"

"Later. Do you know exactly who that 'spoilt little bitch' was?"

"Er, no sir. Look sir, I sleep most nights on the street. Sometimes I get by … Sometimes I have to do … whatever I can to eat. It's nothing personal though."

The men shuffled uncomfortably and he could sense by the thickening of the atmosphere that he had said the wrong thing. His inquisitor stared at him.

"'Nothing … personal' you say. What if I told you that the person you violated was a senator's daughter? What would you say about that?"

"Oh, the gods! No … I wouldn't do that if I knew, no!"

"A criminal with principles eh?" he looked across to the one scratching notes onto a wax tablet. "What did you mean when you called her a 'wildcat'?"

"It was just a throwaway comment, sir. She put up a struggle, that's all I meant." The throbbing in his jaw was becoming unbearable and his mouth felt strangely lopsided. "I'm not proud of what I do."

"Make a note of that, scribe!" He raised an eyebrow. "Mathias is 'not proud of what he does'. That may make all the difference later on. Did the girl scratch you?"

"What? I don't know … maybe."

"Take off your tunic."

"I can't, sir. My hands are still bound."

A look of impatience crossed the inquisitor's face.

"I … I think she may have caught my arm though, if that helps."

One of the guards stomped over and tugged up his sleeve. Mathias noticed the look he gave the inquisitor but didn't understand it.

"So then …" he retrieved the stylus from his ear and leant forwards to prod him, "we have some red marks down your forearm, take note of that also."

The prisoner glanced to the back of the cell where the bearded nobleman was now whispering to the man with pomaded hair and the Praetorian who had dragged him away from the tavern.

"You'll be pleased to hear I'm nearly done with you, Mathias. Then it just remains to decide upon a fitting form of punishment."

"Punishment?" his stomach twisted. "But I've already been punished, look!" He lifted his tunic up to reveal a bruise at the top of his belly.

That caught the inquisitor off guard. He frowned and peered at the welt. Murmurs filled the room.

"Who did this?"

Mathias sensed a last reprieve and leapt upon it. "I thought you already knew? After the … incident, I was chased and caught by some people. I thought they were soldiers. They mentioned the Twelve Tables and beat me, and my friend. I returned what I'd taken and they let me go!"

The nobleman at the back became agitated. He glared at the men next to him, hissed something then stalked over to Mathias.

"You, boy. I am Gaius Fulvius Plautianus, commander of the Praetorian Guard and if you care an ounce for your life you will answer me truthfully. Have you ever seen these people before?"

"I've never seen them before, sir. Any of them."

"Describe them."

"There were three of them. A squat, ugly one with bulging eyes; a great ox of a man and the tallest … he seemed to be giving the orders and he was the one who punished me. He had curly, greying hair and thick stubble, with bits of grey in that too." Mathias pointedly glanced at the bowl of stew and his stomach growled at him. There were less furls of steam coming from it now.

Plautianus looked to Tertius, who nodded. "Boy, look at me! If you sign an affidavit to that effect, you will have your food."

"Gladly! And then I can go?"

"Oh yes, you'll be gone alright. Scribe, I want a word with you and Secundus outside."

"Yes sir."

"You there, gaoler, stay here with him. Make sure he doesn't eat until after he has signed. The rest of you can follow me."

*

Once the cell door had been closed, Plautianus wheeled on Tertius. "Now, I don't know in what pond you've been ferreting about to drop that thing in there on my lap, then pissing up my leg like some kind of moronic, over eager puppy, but you're damn lucky I don't have you flogged for it! So …" he said, after a deep breath, "you'll have to earn your pay."

"Yes, I … of course, commander."

"Listen, all of you. The informer here has found me a murderer. A pretty wretched specimen, it has to be said, but there are certain parallels and he'll do. That wax tablet, let me see it."

Plautianus scrutinized every word before handing it back. "Good, and pad out the bit about those watchmen. Cut his binding and get him to put his mark at the bottom, then let him have the food. You there, I assume you can be trusted to give him the good news? But keep him sufficiently alive, understood?"

The quaestionarius nodded.

"Excellent," said the Prefect, rubbing his hands together, "it just remains for the rest of you to fetch the appropriate witnesses, on my authority, and then we're done. Get to it, gentlemen! Tempus fugit!"

Plautianus turned to the senior Praetorian. "Secundus, I think it's high time I paid the informer here and finally put a stop to his whining!"

Yet at that moment, on the verge of converting his long hours spent traipsing around the city, Tertius began to have doubts.

"What's wrong with you, you ungrateful wretch? Take a look," Plautianus opened the cell door with his boot, "you just did the empire a great service for once!"

Mathias was scratching his mark on the scribe's tablet with a crooked grin, and his knee was bouncing up and down in anticipation of eating the stew. When he received it, he shoveled it down, wincing with pain as he chewed.

"Name your price, Tertius."

"I'm not ... he's already ..."

"Ten thousand sesterces?" asked Plautianus.

"Ten thousand?" The sum left him open-mouthed.

"Eleven, then. Takes account of your expenses. That's my final offer!"

Tertius had never earned so much in all his years as an informer combined. He looked once more inside the cell, where Mathias had devoured the stew and was looking expectantly towards the door.

"Done," he said, and turned away.

"Excellent! We shall finish up here and then meet you upstairs. Afterwards, Secundus will see you get your money direct from the treasury. Here, use my seal." He removed a gold ring and gave it to the Praetorian. "Since this prisoner has harmed a senator's property, I only think it fitting that the state should recompense you for his capture. And that is what will go in the ledger."

"Thank you, commander."

"Good. Now wait upstairs."

Plautianus watched him trudge up the steps and tugged at his beard. "Secundus, I didn't like how that went one bit. It looked very much like the weasel is developing a conscience. A man who knows what he does is too dangerous to have just moping around. Wait for him to get his money and follow him. Then make him have an accident, but don't leave any trace!" He jabbed his finger at the Praetorian's chest. "Understand? And when you're done, divvy up half the money amongst yourselves – just half, mind - and I don't want to hear any more about it."

"Very kind, boss. Consider it done." He saluted and hurried up the stairs.

Plautianus entered the cell and set the tablet bearing the prisoner's confession down on a ledge at the back. Mathias' eyes followed him across the room.

"Prefect, sir? Can I go now?"

Plautianus glanced at the quaestionarius on his way out.

"Begin."

XXIV

Tertius cursed himself again. Even though he had agreed to come back for the other half of the money tomorrow, he was still hopelessly outweighed. Every pocket in his cloak was filled with silver, and he had even fashioned two slings from dustsheets in the treasury and stuffed these with coins too. It had seemed like a good piece of improvisation at the time, but now they chafed his skin and the coins jingled with each step, despite his efforts to muffle them with rags. Here and there he could make out the silhouettes of human forms concealed in the darkness, and sense the stares of hungry eyes watching him as he passed. He began to reason with himself to banish his fears.

Was he really so stupid, or had greed clouded his judgment? Or was it some other unfamiliar feeling that had pricked his conscience: pity? Whatever the truth of it, armed only with a small dagger, what he was doing was nothing short of suicide!

A figure staggered towards him and the hairs on his nape bristled. As he was close enough to make out his face, he also caught the reek of stale beer and oily fish from a cheap cookhouse. He squinted at the informer as he approached, as if he was having difficulty focusing. At the moment he drew level, he bumped into him. Tertius gasped in shock as he stumbled into a wall with a chink of coins, and he fumbled for his knife. The old drunkard cackled, winking and touching the side of his nose, before ambling away. Tertius took a deep breath whilst the pounding of his heart subsided and shifted the slings over each shoulder to ease the chafing. He set off again and tried to estimate how long it would take him to emerge from the slums. He guessed it would take another ten, fear-ridden minutes. The street now curved around a series of forbidding tenement blocks, restricting his view. He hesitated and considered turning back, then steeled himself to press on.

Two more figures approached.

They also looked somewhat unsteady on their feet but nothing so pronounced as the old drunk. The larger of the pair had pulled up the pointed hood of his cloak and looked from a distance like a priest from one of the Capitoline colleges. Tertius didn't like the look of them but didn't break stride. He had noted a cut-through ten yards ahead and decided that he would turn into it, hoping that the noise he made wouldn't betray his rich pickings. He glanced at the pair before ducking into the alley. They were in the middle of a conversation and weren't paying him any attention.

The cut-through was a long alleyway lit only at either end. He thought that turning back would make him look like a soft target and so pressed on, his ears straining at the silence. As he was half way, he stopped. The shadows to one side of him moved and a mound of discarded rags stirred into life. A bony hand emerged from the clothes and claw-like fingers opened.

"Spare a brass obol for an old war hero, stranger?" the voice croaked.

"Dis Pater!" hissed Tertius, stumbling into some rotting crates behind him. The beggar's arm darted out and gripped the hem of his tunic, tugging him down. Tertius yelped and groped for his dagger.

Two hooded figures entered the alleyway. Tertius spun around as he heard a stone being kicked behind him. Icy panic clawed at him. But then his fingers brushed the sheath of his dagger, which had been pushed towards the small of his back by the weight of the slings.

"Dis, help me!" he shrieked at them.

The cloaked figures sauntered towards him and reached into the folds of their cloaks. Tertius' quivering hands unclipped the sheath and he hacked at the arm still grasping his tunic. The beggar let out a hideous scream but did not let go. As the pair were no more than ten paces away, the beggar released his grip, whimpering in agony. Tertius turned to the two silent men.

"He tried to rob me!"

Their faces were concealed but he was sure one of them smiled. Tertius' heart pounded. He knew from painful experience that fighting was not his strength.

He ran.

He didn't look behind him but he knew they were after him. With each stride the weight of coins dragged him down and his legs turned to lead. He started emptying his pockets and, when he heard the steps gaining on him, he decided to lose the slings too. He frantically sawed away at the cloth with his knife, nicking his skin over and over as he scurried ahead in the darkness. The sling snapped loose and coins scattered everywhere, tinkling unseen on the cobbles, down his thighs and into his groin. As he attacked the second sling, he stumbled and the knife slipped from his grip. He was screaming now and tried tugging the sling over his elbow but somehow trapped his arm tight against his chest. The alleyway ended only a few paces away and he pumped his free arm for all it was worth, bracing himself for a hit from behind.

Something small thumped into his back and the heat of a thousand wasp stings lanced through him. He shrieked in agony and lost his footing, clattering onto the tip of his elbow. He squirmed on the greasy cobbles trying to free his arm from the sling and grope at the source of the spiteful pain with his other. He sensed rather than saw the shadows that loomed over him and could only make out a few muffled words of conversation, as if they were speaking through scarves wrapped about their faces.

"Go back ... last ... of them ..."

"... fucking job ... again."

And then Tertius felt a knee on his spine. The knife was tugged from his back: indescribable pain sucked the air from his lungs. He felt his hair being yanked backwards so tightly he thought he would be scalped. He recognised the voice that bade him 'a good night', but his last memory was the white hot pain that darted across his throat.

XXV

Plautianus barely recognised the prisoner when he returned to the cell a few hours later.

Mathias hung from manacles hooked from the low ceiling. His face was encrusted with dried blood and one of his eyes was pulped and closed. Through his swollen lips - and it appeared something of a miracle that he was alive at all - his every breath formed small bubbles of blood. When the interrogator had first lashed him, the pain and disbelief at his betrayal had been outrageous and his body had recoiled as if a shoal of electric eels had brushed against him. His initial instinct had been to fight and tense against every brutal blow in the belief that it would end and he would live to breathe fresh air again. But when he had felt his jaw crack and his ribs splinter, he abandoned himself to the realisation that resistance was excruciatingly futile, and every thud and spit of the whip thereafter became detached and distant. He cast his mind adrift and focused on an image of the skeletal ferryman Charon emerging in silence from banks of mist that hung over the River Styx.

For a moment, the Praetorian Prefect hesitated, doubting the wisdom in letting anybody else see the quaestionarius' handiwork, least of all the divine Emperor of Rome, the Emperor's son and the former consul Terentius Piso. The quaestionarius' bare chest was heaving like a race-winning thoroughbred's. The muscles on his rangy body stood taut and proud, and runnels of sweat and blood had stained his breeches. He discarded the whip and fist-plate onto the floor and gave a crisp salute as the group entered.

"Your majesties," he said in his soft voice.

Septimius Severus wrinkled his nose at the acrid tang inside the cell.

"Dismissed," he said with a flick of the wrist, not taking his eyes off the prisoner. The interrogator bowed, retrieved his towel and left the cell.

"This is the signed confession," said Plautianus, showing it to Terentius Piso. Though the senator's face was pale and drawn, his expression remained inscrutable as he opened the tablet and read its contents.

"So let justice be done," he whispered, giving the tablet to Caracalla.

Caracalla snatched it from him, his hands shaking as he devoured every word and his face trembled with pent-up emotion. He sniffed and wiped his nose with the back of his hand as tears breached his eyes and streamed down his cheeks, blurring his vision. The senator patted his shoulder and took the tablet from him, offering it to the Emperor who shook his head solemnly.

"And how was he found?" asked Severus.

"One of my informers tracked him, sir. He heard him boasting of his conquest in a tavern by the Viminal and, when we got him back here, the quaestionarius you have just seen did his work well, drawing out a confession. There are certain other signs as well, if I may?" Severus nodded and Plautianus tugged Mathias sleeve above his elbow, where there were faint red scratch marks. "What little we were able to salvage from the mess created by The Watch is that young Terentia put up a struggle befitting her proud status and bent her nails, which is consistent with these marks."

"And what progress have you made in tracking her body?" demanded Piso.

Plautianus looked to the floor. "I'm sorry, though we are still trying. I scarcely need remind you that it was not a grievous error made by the Praet …"

"I don't care whose mistake it was, Prefect. I want to know how you intend to punish the man responsible!"

"To be frank, my priority had been trying to rectify the problem rather than exact punishment, though if you think otherwise?"

"That is exactly what I think!" he snapped. "I have met the man myself, and his acolytes, and it is my opinion they are not fit to clean the streets, never mind protect them!"

"Reform of The Watch is something I want to propose in due course." He looked to Severus who paused for a few seconds before inclining his head in agreement.

Whilst Plautianus and Piso were talking, Caracalla approached Mathias, whose head had sagged towards the floor. He knelt before him.

"Look at me," he hissed.

Mathias was breathing, but only just.

"Look at me!" Caracalla gripped his chin and tilted it back.

Mathias' remaining eye opened a fraction.

"Tell me, tell me why!"

His throat gurgled and rasped as bright, painful lights danced through the slit of his eye. Nausea twisted his stomach and an icy chill begin to seep into his bones. Then the blur before him materialized into a face that was wrought with pain and bitterness.

"Not … me …"

"What? What are you saying?" Caracalla was shouting now, and the other men in the cell broke off their conversation.

"As … what … men …"

Mathias' whisper trailed away as a shiver rippled through him and he went limp, swaying slightly on the creaking manacles.

Plautianus swore and stalked over, upending a bucket of cold water over the prisoner's body, making Caracalla fall backwards on his haunches in avoiding the splash.

"What did you do to him?" demanded the Prefect. "What did he say?"

The note of anxiety in his question did not go unnoticed. Caracalla drew himself up, narrowing his eyes at Plautianus.

"Nothing, Prefect," he replied. "Nothing at all."

PART II

I

The deluge began with a distant flash of lightening that made the clouds glower an angry shade of purple and unleashed fat bulbs of rain that spattered and drummed on roof tiles with a force that threatened to crack them apart. Great sheets of water spilled from the choked gutters and drilled into the city streets below, turning them into treacherous, muddy streams. The storm would relent in less than an hour, when the awestruck citizens of the city port of Ostia would open their doors to slickened cobbles that had been scourged clean of filth and human waste, and air that was, for a few precious hours, sweet and pleasant to breathe.

Ambrosius' spirits sank as he watched the clouds skim the rooftops from the upper storey of the barracks. The twenty mile journey to Ostia had been dull and depressing, and every step that took him further from Poppeia and his home had posed a monumental challenge to his resolve. He dropped back onto his chair and took another long swig from the wine flagon by his feet.

Longinus, a vexillarius from Cohort IX who had been appointed his second in command for the detachment's tour, looked on and rubbed his bald pate as he did every time he was about to broach an uncomfortable subject.

"Begging your pardon tribune, but once this weather sorts itself out, there'll be a big queue of petitioners. Might be a good idea to keep a clear head."

"I'm aware of that Longinus, thank you. That's one of the reasons I'm trying to get drunk."

Longinus looked away in disgust. They had only relieved the outgoing detachment for two days and already vigiles of his own cohort were grumbling to him about the tribune and his quick temper. He doubted he would be able to fend them off for weeks, never mind months, before there would be open revolt in the barracks, and the situation was testing every shred of his diplomatic skills. He took a deep breath.

"Fine. I'll go and make preparations downstairs, in case you need me."

Ambrosius watched him go and shook his head. The man meant well but, despite his rank, was no leader. To Ambrosius, a leader who tried to be all things to all people was not a man to be trusted. He drained the wine pitcher and let out a satisfying belch then lolled his head back and closed his eyes. Within minutes he was asleep.

*

The inevitable knock on the barracks door came just twenty minutes after the storm passed. Longinus slid open the hatch and peered outside, wrinkling his nose. As before most salutationes of late, he was struck with conflicting emotions of revulsion, pity and shame in feeling both revulsion and pity. Unlike the vast majority of the plebs, he had long since become used to being treated as a respected citizen. But his childhood memories of scrabbling for his very existence on the streets still tweaked his conscience.

Longinus nodded towards the stairs that led to the officers' rooms on the upper floor, but his man was intercepted half way up by a stony-faced Ambrosius, who was brandishing another pitcher of wine.

"Yes, yes, I heard, damn it!"

With a sigh, Ambrosius trudged towards his chair in the courtyard of the barracks and dropped onto it, beckoning towards the door. Longinus positioned his bulky frame in the doorway to prevent a stampede and a waft of damp clothes and hair followed the knot of citizens as they filed inside. The first to approach Ambrosius was a small, paunchy man with rheumy eyes and a few strands of greasy hair parted to one side. He was wringing his hands.

"Ah, what a surprise to see you again. Remind me of your name?"

"Phocius sir."

"Phocius, how is it that you are always at the front of the queue? Do you camp overnight outside?"

"Thank you so much for your time, thank you. My wife is terribly unwell, sir, terribly. It gets more difficult to look after her with each passing day."

Ambrosius gave him a blank look.

"We live above the baths, you see? Very noisy and she can never sleep."

"Plug her ears then. Is that all you came for?"

"Is there nothing you can do to get the superintendent to keep the noise down?"

"What, in the public baths? Have you lost your mind man? No! There is nothing anyone can do. Why don't you just move?" Ambrosius was already looking towards the door.

"Well I had considered that. But it's the expense you see. We couldn't possibly find somewhere cheaper ..."

"Has it not occurred to you, you half-wit, that the location is why the rent is low?" Ambrosius scrutinized him. "Wait a minute, are you asking us for money?"

Phocius shuffled on his feet.

"I think I've heard enough. Off you go Phocius. Go and stuff your wife's ears with wax."

Phocius hovered for a moment before bowing and giving him a tight smile. "Thank you kindly, sir. You are a good man." But Ambrosius had already beckoned for the next citizen.

"Wait in line, won't you!" Longinus bellowed into the street. "If I see anyone pushing in, they'll go straight to the back!"

Ambrosius filled his cup and drained it. The inconvenient passing of the rain clouds had ruined his siesta and he was feeling quite drunk.

"Come on, Longinus. I haven't got all day!"

The next to enter was a shifty-eyed chancer. Astyanax was not his real name, but a Greek affectation he used on the rough streets by the harbour, meaning 'guardian of the city.' Ambrosius didn't fail to see the irony in it, given that Astyanax was a gullible fool who would struggle to defend his own chicken coup from an angry kitten. He groaned when he saw him.

"Make it quick, Astyanax. What is it?"

Even within the secure confines of the watchmen's barracks, the man saw fit to glance left and right with his narrow eyes before speaking. "Tribune," he whispered, "I am a marked man."

"Explain yourself in one sentence."

"I mean, I accepted a favour from a money lender on the Street of the Fullers and I've since learned that this man is a dangerous businessman ..."

"Then you are even more of an idiot than I imagined."

Astyanax raised his hands and quickened his speech. "But tribune, you are doubtless a man with contacts. I could guarantee you the support of my entire guild should you ever stand for election, if you could simply ... if you could make this man ... disappear, for a while. Perhaps."

Ambrosius glared at him. He felt his anger rise, accelerated by the wine. He rose from his seat, gripping the armrests. "You take me for a common cut-throat? Why should I involve myself in your grubby little affairs? Get out!"

Longinus spun around and strode over. "I'm sorry tribune! I swear I meant no offence!" He cringed when Longinus' meaty hand gripped him by the shoulder and propelled him towards the door. He could still be heard protesting his innocence even when he was sent stumbling onto the street. Ambrosius smoothed back his hair and composed himself, resuming his seat. Then he rose again.

"Longinus, I can't stand any more of this drivel today. I've got affairs of my own to think about. Take over here will you. One of your lot can stand by the door."

Longinus glanced at another watchman, who made a throttling gesture when he was sure Ambrosius wasn't looking. Then there was a scuffle by the door and raised voices.

"Out o'the way, gawd damn you!"

"Oi, watch it!"

"Let him past, curse you all!" shouted Longinus. "Move aside!"

A ruddy-faced market trader with a cloth cap wheeled a barrow of vegetables into the atrium, and his beady eyes scanned the room, settling upon Ambrosius.

"Tribune! You owe me for two weeks' deliveries, so you do! Your bleedin' predecessor ..."

"Damn my predecessor!" Ambrosius waved him away as he stomped up the stairs. "Deal with it, Longinus. I've had enough for today."

Back upstairs, Ambrosius flopped onto a pallet and tried to organize his thoughts. He looked around him for some wine, then thought better of it when the room started to spin. He groaned and closed his eyes.

*

Ambrosius' eyelids twitched. The sound of knocking interrupted his pleasant daydream. It repeated itself, louder this time, and his name was called. He jerked upright.

"Tribune Ambrosius, sir. Longinus sent me to get you."

117

Ambrosius rubbed his face and glowered at the nervous young watchman peering round the door. The fear in his eyes made Ambrosius' anger dissipate.

"I'm sorry tribune, I didn't realize you might be asleep!"

"It's alright, lad," he muttered, "what does he want?"

"There's someone downstairs he thinks you might want to see."

Ambrosius frowned.

"He's not one of the usual ones, sir."

*

Ambrosius splashed his face with cold water but his head still felt foggy as he shuffled across the landing. He descended the stairs like an old man, ignoring Longinus' reproving stare. All proceedings in the forecourt had stopped and some of the watchmen sniggered at their tribune's ineffectual efforts to disguise his state. Longinus cleared his throat and nodded towards a stranger in their midst. The man was taller than Ambrosius with receding hair that was greyer than his own. He had sad eyes set in a swarthy, weather-beaten face. Though he looked like a man who had asked for little from life and been given even less, there was a certain dignity in his bearing. He approached Ambrosius and shook his hand. The man's calloused grip made him wince.

"Sir, my name is Fabricius, from Calabria."

"Fabricius, welcome to Ostia. Please, sit. So," he asked, barely concealing a belch, "what dire event has forced you to leave such a pretty part of the world for this shit-hole?"

Fabricius' face remained set. "I believe I have been greatly wronged, tribune."

"Who here does not?"

The visitor said nothing. Ambrosius regarded him, wondering if he was being polite in ignoring the fumes of wine he breathed. "And who, might I ask, has wronged you?"

"The Praetorian Guard, sir."

"The Praetorians?" Ambrosius laughed, looking towards Longinus who shrugged his shoulders. "What, all of them? Very brave of you to complain to me then, isn't it? Or stupid."

"Brave, no. Stupid … possibly. I'd already been sent packing by your predecessor here a week ago. I was going to give up, but then I heard that a new detachment had taken over, so here I am trying again."

"Here you are. So, what is the complaint?"

"For what it's worth, I had been honourably discharged two years ago after twenty as a soldier. I wanted to exploit the Tiber trade route between here and Rome for a few years before retiring to Calabria. Nothing fancy, just onward importation from the port warehouses to the city. Small to medium cargoes, that's all. I got a good deal on an old merchant ship and managed to pay her off because things were going quite well and I was busy. I even considered investing in another and hiring a crew."

Fabricius' jaw set and he cracked his knuckles. "But about three weeks ago, I arrived at the docks at dawn, like usual, and noticed a few men loitering around my boat and others that were moored up. They wore the same cloaks and were all big, swarthy, nasty looking types. I wanted to ask them what they were up to but I know they'd have turned on me. They stared at me as I went about my business and eventually disappeared, though I didn't see where." Ambrosius glanced over the man's shoulder at the impatient faces by the door and felt a stab of resentment for them and their trifling problems.

"A few days later," he continued, "my boat disappeared. The only thing they left was this," he said, retrieving a tatty piece of parchment, "which had been nailed to my mooring post, and a pouch of silver coins tucked in a hollow behind it."

Ambrosius took it and flattened it against his lap:

NOTICE OF REQUISITION TO THE OWNER

BY ORDER OF HIS MAJESTY'S IMPERIAL PRAETORIAN GUARD, YOUR CRAFT HAS BEEN TAKEN IN CONNECTION WITH ONGOING OPERATIONS ALONG THE RIVER TIBER. IT WILL BE RETURNED TO YOU IN DUE COURSE.

Ambrosius ran his fingers over the cracked wax seal at the foot of the notice: it seemed authentic enough. "And how much was there in the pouch?"

"Ten silver, barely enough to cover me for a few days. I've been out of pocket for a week and there's been no sign of my boat. I know plenty of people by the docks and they've not seen or heard anything either. My livelihood has been destroyed, tribune."

"Longinus," said Ambrosius, wiping beads of perspiration from his forehead, "no more callers today. They can come back next week. Everyone, gather round."

Whilst Longinus coaxed the reluctant crowd away from the door, a small throng of watchmen assembled. "This is a genuine complaint raised by

Fabricius of Calabria. Who here, in the last couple of days or on previous tours here, has ever encountered a Praetorian?"

The watchmen looked at each other and shook their heads. "Nor I, tribune," said Longinus, "but then again I wouldn't go looking for one either." The other watchmen murmured in agreement.

"It may be too late for that. I want us all to question anyone that looks out of place or is paying undue attention to whatever we're doing. Is that clear?"

As he expected, there were several confused faces in the room. One of the watchmen spoke up.

"Tribune, what's all this about? This is Ostia: it can get a bit rough here but it's still a pretty dreary place compared to Rome."

"I agree, but those are my instructions." The room had started to spin and his stomach swilled. "Longinus?"

"Yes?"

"I want more of us out and about during the day. Eight extra pairs, three hour patrols then rotate: six on two off. I want four more upriver, same … same pattern. Once we have a description of the boat, they can start. Leaves us light during the night watches but …" he belched again and tasted bile. His forehead was now lathered in sweat, "I doubt there'll be fires tonight after that downpour, anyway. All understood?"

"Are you alright, tribune? You look terrible."

"A fever, that's all." Ambrosius caught one of the watchmen smirking at the back of the group.

"And one more task. You there," he said pointing to the young watchman who had woken him up, "fetch me a jug of water. Can you write?"

"Yes, tribune."

"Good. Then take notes here. Once we're done, that's your duty for today."

Whilst he was questioning Fabricius, Ambrosius could feel the colour draining from his face and, when it became clear that he was losing the battle to retain the contents of his stomach, he stopped. Even had he been sober, he doubted there was anything more to be learned. The boat was gone for as long as whoever had taken it saw fit and there were no loose ends to follow up. Under any other circumstances, Ambrosius would have ascribed the matter as just another example of imperial hubris but, after recent events, the apparently motiveless theft of a hard-working citizen's boat cast an altogether different light.

He looked at the notes in the tablet book but the effort of trying to refocus the blurred letters made his stomach lurch. He gripped the armrests and looked about him for a bucket.

"Tribune, do you think my boat was taken as the note says and that I'll get it back?"

Ambrosius shook his head. "Sorry. Twice over."

"What else should I do about it?"

"That seal," he said, pointing towards the note with a trembling finger, "is genuine. And the only higher power than the Praetorians is … is the Emperor himself so I suggest you write it off. Perhaps you should sub-contract your work to another boat owner, or start from scratch, or … something. I sympathise but that's little more use to you than a straw oven."

Fabricius looked at him for a few moments, his face inscrutable. "I thank you for your time, tribune Ambrosius." He rose. "And I hope your fever clears soon. I'm sure it'll leave you with no more than a hangover."

Ambrosius watched him go and then his stomach clenched. He reached the nearest latrine just in time.

II

She wanted me," announced Bulla. "This is three already and it's not even the fourth hour of the night yet."

"Bulla, the only woman we saw in that house was three feet tall, bared her teeth at you and looked just like the door keeper's mastiff. Or perhaps I just didn't see her even though I was there. Perhaps women only reveal themselves to you and are invisible to mortal watchmen like me."

"I'm not talk about the last house, blockhead! The one before that with the, you know," he made exaggerated shapes to imitate breasts, "fiery little red head!"

"Fine, I'll admit that the prostitute that answered spoke to you like you weren't asking her for her fiftieth tumble of the night, when she had a raging headache and you only had two obols in coin, but that's not to say she wanted you. Just leave it anyhow, will you, you're giving me a damn headache!"

Titus turned to Chest, one of a fresh batch of tirones that had just been distributed amongst the seven cohorts. He smiled but said nothing, having said little all evening as they patrolled the streets of the Aventine district. Titus weighed him up. He was a well-built young man and proud of his gymnasium-honed physique, which was the reason for his nickname. He came with a reputation as a ladies' man, and his hairless arms and long, wavy hair, cut so as to curl from the base of his helmet, reinforced the image. Titus hoped otherwise, but young Chest bore the hallmarks of a recruit who already seemed to regard himself highly. He had not impressed Bulla, who tended to be a hasty judge of character.

"You'll learn to ignore him," said Titus, "and just block out his endless blathering like you were deaf. No point arguing with him as I just did."

Chest smiled politely and adjusted the pole across his shoulder that bore at either end the two empty rope buckets.

"You want to make this call, Chest?" asked Titus.

The trio stopped at one of the doors of a series of tightly packed townhouses.

"Sure. Hold this would you?" he said, giving the pole to Bulla, who narrowed his eyes at him.

Titus winked at Bulla, trying hard not to crack a smile, whilst Chest rapped on the door. At first there was no response but then tired curses from an upper window broke the silence, prompting Bulla and Titus to take a discreet step backwards.

Chest looked up as shutters opened and a furious, matronly face appeared, then just as quickly withdrew.

"Watchmen of the Fourth Cohort, madam," announced Chest, hands on hips.

The woman reappeared and emptied a bucket of water over the unsuspecting watchman.

"Yes, I have my damn water ready in case of fire! I have another one here, if you'd like to see that too, no?" She shook her fist at him. "Well don't you disturb me at this hour again, you arrogant whelps!" She slammed the shutters, leaving Bulla and Titus roaring with laughter. Chest, drenched, held his pose for a few long moments, his mouth open in sheer astonishment.

"Well then young man, what did you do wrong there then?"

"The bitch!"

"I'll tell you what you did wrong, you weren't very observant!" said Titus, guiding him away from the door. "Look at the shape of the house: no courtyard. No courtyard means no night janitor with dog necessary to defend it, which means having to wake up the grumpy lady of the house instead. Which, in turn, means getting drenched. Don't worry, you'll learn what each house in your district is about soon enough!"

They resumed their patrol, allowing Chest to dry himself with one of Bulla's spare all-purpose cloths. The residential streets were quiet tonight and were well lit by the glow from a gibbous moon. The only signs of life came from the odd homeless beggar snoring inside a doorway or nocturnal animals that snuffled in and around the rubbish looking for bones and rotting food. Titus led them down to the Emporium near the banks of the Tiber where he lifted his helmet to rub his flattended hair. Then he retrieved a small flask from a pouch on his belt, which he promptly hid when he spotted the torches carried by another patrol of watchmen skirting the far side of the Emporium. He saluted them. They returned the gesture but didn't wander over and soon disappeared from view.

"Here," he said, offering the flask to the shivering Chest, "get some of this down you."

The recruit eyed him for a moment but then took a swig of the undiluted wine. He gasped at the strength of it and passed it on to Bulla.

"Warms you up a bit, no?"

"Mind if I have a bit more? I'm freezing."

Titus nodded at Bulla, who handed it back to him.

"Thanks," he said, wiping his mouth.

"See that stretch of wharves over there?" Titus pointed towards a string of run-down buildings that stretched north of the Emporium. "That's where we found the senator's daughter."

"You were involved with that?"

"Yeah ... er, both of us were. That's why our tribune got sent to Ostia."

"I heard about it when I was told which cohort I'd be attached to. Caused a bit of a stink didn't it?"

Titus laughed distantly and took a final swig of the spirit. "Could say that."

"I asked a few of the men about it but they clammed up pretty good."

Bulla and Titus looked at each other. "That's good to hear. It's still a bit raw, Chest. The Fourth's not had an easy time of it recently."

"Sorry."

"No matter. Now you know. It's different amongst just us three but you don't know in what trouble a loose tongue can get you. These days, especially."

The men were quiet again, consumed with their own thoughts and, across the city, there was an unnatural hush. The ungainly silhouette of a heron approached over the moonlit stretch of the Tiber that threaded between the wharves. It settled on a nearby rooftop, letting out a distinctive caw, and another bird with a flat, high-pitched call answered it. After a few moments, the heron cawed even louder and Chest looked around for a stone to throw at it. Just as he was taking aim, the bird set off in a great flurry. Another three trills sounded.

"Weird sounding bird."

Titus and Bulla froze.

"Is not a bird, you clot: is a damn whistle! Three for fire!"

The trio gathered up their equipment and set off in the direction they thought the noise had come from. They plunged into the confusing warren of streets south of the Aventine as more whistle peals reverberated off the closely packed walls, making them stop at each fork in the street.

doorway but the ferocious heat flayed his eyes and lungs, and he staggered back, cursing his rashness. He spotted Stilicho's rangy frame, leading the line of buckets.

"Split the line!" he yelled to him. "Source and doorway, here! Bulla, who was the last one out?"

On the opposite pavement, Bulla scanned the coughing, retching forms and dragged one of them up, a soot-blackened man of about fifty. Titus hurried across the street.

"Look at me! Why are they not using both staircases?"

"There's only one," he croaked, "the left, and it was on fire when I came down."

"No, there's two, one at either end of the corridor. Both lead to the street door."

The man shook his head. "The other rotted through weeks ago. Wasn't replaced."

Titus clenched his jaw. "Where's the landlord?"

"In there I hope." The man spat into the street.

Titus made a noise of exasperation and then looked round as a pair of carts, each being dragged by a unit of specialists, rumbled into view through the soot and flickering smoke.

"Over here, over here!" He walked past the huddled, blackened forms, peering closer at some of those partially obscured by blankets, but he recognized none of them. He turned back to the carts. On the back of one was a trusty Ctesibius water pump, a marvel of Greek technology, partially submerged inside a large vat. Titus barked orders at the men as they unloaded the equipment and set about assembling it with shaking hands.

"The siphon, bring it over here and get the rest of those people in another line! Stilicho, there's a street pump round that corner; that's your starting point once the house buckets are emptied, yes?"

"Yes boss!"

"And tell me that vat has some water in it?"

"Course it has, boss," the German gave him a toothy grin. "I'm senior aquarius remember!"

The watchman dragooned bystanders into a line to relay the buckets emerging from the houses into the vat, repositioning and urging them on when the effort dropped.

"Cushion, centurion?"

Titus had not seen it being dragged off the back off the second cart but it was just what he needed. He glanced up at the building: two children were hugging each other and shrieking at the garret window. It took him a few moments to realize that he had seen them before.

"We'll get you down! We'll get you down!" He frantically waved both arms at them but they didn't seem to recognize him and so he removed his helmet. "See! We'll get you!" The boy pointed him out to his sister and they renewed their screams.

"How many do we have?"

"Just this one."

Titus scratched the stubble of his chin. Other watchmen by the second cart were frantically assembling poles topped with grappling hooks but he doubted the building was structurally weak enough for them yet. "Right, dump it under the garret."

Cushion was a grand term to describe a six foot square dirty cloth bag stuffed with feathers, though it was a proven life saver, if used properly: Titus had seen what happened when more than one person at a time tried to jump on it.

After yelling last second alterations to a third watchman adjusting the direction of the nozzle with a forked pole, the pair on the siphon furiously worked the handle to drive water down each piston. Jets of water now pulsed from the spout to a height of ten or more yards.

"Come on, there's nothing to be afraid of!" shouted the watchmen by the cushion. "We've got you!"

The children shook their heads and were shaking. It was a jump of fifteen yards and Titus knew from experience that the cushion presented a very small target from that height.

"Come on! You'll have to hurry! It must be very hot up there!"

The vigil had patience but it wasn't working. Bulla had seen what was happening and hurried over.

"Get down from there before the fire monster turns you into the lump of coal!" he shook his fist at them. "Don't make me come up there and kick you out!"

The children screamed at him.

"What the fuck are you doing?" asked the incredulous vigil.

"Look out!"

The girl jumped first, pushed by her brother, landing on the cushion with a whump.

"Good girl! Good girl!" but when Bulla tried to pat her head, she ducked out of his reach and screamed.

"Subtle, Bulla," said Titus, "very subtle."

He shrugged as the boy followed his sister out, landing less cleanly but not hurting himself. Titus ran over to them and pulled them over the road. "You two! Do you remember me? Where's your mummy and daddy?"

They were both hyperventilating and staring through Titus, trembling like newborn lambs. He led them over to the others, where a kindly looking lady drew them in.

More carts rumbled towards the scene and there was, surprisingly, equipment from other regions: another pump bearing the stamp of Cohort V, based just beyond the Capena gate, one from Cohort III, and a third came from Titus' own Watch House with a set of kegs on the back. There were even medics wearing their distinctive white headbands and a tribune from Cohort VII across the Tiber, who assured Titus that their heavy equipment was at that very moment trundling its way across the Sublicius Bridge. Titus thanked him but they exchanged knowing looks: it would be too late for the people still trapped within.

Within twenty minutes of the blaze starting, there were three pumps and two lines of watchmen and citizens trying to beat it back with a constant flow of buckets of water. Only five more people had jumped onto the two cushions now at scene: those able to speak confirmed that there were still people on the first floor but couldn't say how many. Medics were dashing from person to person tending burns with salves made from crushed herbs, cleaning wounds or trying to revive the unresponsive with pungent compounds made from the leaves of Mentha Pulegium, more commonly used to bring round unconscious boxers. There were still several untreated, blackened and retching forms huddled together on the opposite pavement, alongside those already dead.

Smeared in grime, Chest came running over to Titus. His damp tunic was stuck to his body.

"Centurion," he panted, "done it. Way in to both buildings."

Titus slapped him on the shoulder.

There was a shriek from the crowd. A flurry of hands pointed to the block to the left of the inferno.

"It's spread! The gods, it's spreading!"

"Get a damn pump over! Get – me – that – pump!" Titus hollered at the nearest crew.

"Chest, Stilicho. Take whoever you need and get to work with those blankets. And be quick about it." Titus helped heave the siphon nearer to the threatened wall, and water sloshed over the planking. He cupped his hands around his mouth, "Work that bastard handle for all you're worth!"

The watchmen responded. Water exploded from the nozzle and drilled the scorched wall. The flames faltered and died, retreating back across the alleyway to a few exhausted cheers.

An unearthly groan emanated from the building, followed by a cracking that sounded like thunder. The upper left floor sagged upon itself with a great crump, expelling a scalding gale of dust and smoke. Chunks of masonry thumped to the floor and a lump of carbonated wood knocked a watchman near the front of the line senseless: his colleagues dropped their buckets to help drag him away.

"Break the line! Get back!" Titus gripped a pair of watchmen by their cloaks and pulled them back. "Grapple teams, ready?"

"Yes boss!"

"Focus on the left!"

Pairs of watchmen began to hack away at the weakened timbers and loose bricks with the long, unwieldy poles, heaving backwards when the hooks got a good purchase, gradually exposing the charred contents of the rooms. This macabre unveiling prompted fresh howls of anguish from the residents and, despite angry shouts to stay back, one or two risked their lives to dash across the street in hope of recovering blackened keepsakes.

A bulky figure caught Titus' eye, silhouetted against the night sky by the glow of the fire opposite. Chest was shuffling with difficulty over the rooftop to the left, hugging a keg tight against his body. The roof sloped more than Titus had guessed and, judging by how carefully Chest picked his footing, was also in a poor state of repair. Two other watchman followed him, carrying what looked like a furled-up sail between them.

"Did I say you could have a rest, ladies?" Titus shouted towards one of the siphon crews who were watching their colleagues. "Keep going!"

On the roof, Stilicho fumbled inside a belt pouch and retrieved a hammer and several square headed nails as thick as a man's thumb. The hammer rang out a tune that was at odds with the mayhem below, and a few bystanders now turned to watch, pointing and speculating about what was happening. When the blanket was secured to the roof, the watchmen spaced themselves out and – on the count of three – unfurled it over the side of the building. The dirty patchwork stretched only two thirds of the way down the side of the narrow alleyway but it was the best they could manage. Chest now uncorked the keg and poured the acetum vinegar mixture down the blanket, turning his head aside from the potent fumes. The onlookers on the street now saw a dark stain spreading down the blanket as it became soaked in the mildly flame retardant liquid.

Titus raised his thumb and the three watchmen on the roof assembzled their kit and hurried back down to resume their efforts. Once or twice, a flame licked across the alleyway and turned a bluish colour as it hit the acetum. The centurion noted this with satisfaction and handed out the last few grapple hooks, then joined in the efforts to demolish the building, bit by bit, before the fire overwhelmed the crude barrier and spread. Despite the constant rain of bricks and wood onto the street, people were still making sallies towards the crumbling walls, imploring the watchmen to work faster or find their missing loved ones. Titus' patience began to crack.

"Bulla, you say you're good with women: get them away from here!" he shouted over his shoulder. "They can gather in the Field of Mars or the forum for now, or the barracks' courtyards at a push. Chest, Stilicho … you help him. Give yourselves a breather."

The men gave him disappointed looks but were far too exhausted to argue, and set about herding the crowd together. This proved to be almost as arduous a task as dealing with the fire, because many were unwilling to tear themselves away. Some even fought with them, until they were dragged off by other onlookers or friends, and in the end it took the efforts of nine watchmen to persuade them to leave. Bulla resorted to tired shoves to get people on their way, his own patience and nerves already shredded.

One man in particular drew his attention.

He was tall and wore a cowl that covered the top half of his face but exposed his jaw line, along which ran a carefully trimmed beard. He was munching an apple and observing the fire and the frantic action with a cool detachment.

"Come on people, please, leave the area, you too mister," said Bulla as he leaned on him to coax him along.

Despite Bulla's considerable bulk, he did not even sway an inch, like a statue carved from Parian marble. The man stopped as he was about to take a bite from his apple and turned his shadowed face to look at Bulla as if he was a fly that had done him the indignity of landing on his arm. Then he shrugged and sauntered away, leaving Bulla scratching his head before resuming the exasperating task of clearing the street.

Another great section of the upper story collapsed with an impressive rush of smoke and debris, dragging the garret with it. The watchmen greeted the sight with another cheer. And still the water pumps and buckets kept up the relentless barrage of water, until they threatened to bleed the cisterns dry before the flames were brought under control.

III

"You have a visitor sir."

"Send him away," said Gaius Plautianus without looking up.

The Praetorian shuffled uncomfortably on his feet. "Begging your pardon, he says it's important, commander."

"Who does not?" Plautianus shot him a look. "Other people's important is my trifling, so get rid of him, d'you hear? I leave for the senate shortly."

The guard held up his hands. "I understand, commander, but the visitor says you'll want to hear this before you go to the senate."

Plautianus glared at him and then tossed the scroll he was reading onto his desk. "Tell him to be quick."

The guard disappeared and there was a brief conversation outside the Prefect's door. When the visitor entered and saluted him, Plautianus straightened in his chair.

"Primus? I wasn't expecting you. What is it?"

The man removed his cowl, revealing long, brown hair, through which he ran his fingers.

"Prefect," he said coolly.

"Well? I was on my way to address two hundred dry old men, Primus, impatient men. I'm told you have something to tell me. What is it?"

"No, I won't take any water, thank you."

"Come on man, don't play about!" Plautianus rose and readjusted his toga. "This isn't the time!"

Primus regarded him with his wintry grey eyes. He enjoyed watching people squirm before him, even those as powerful as the Praetorian Prefect. His very presence, he had known since he was young, had an unsettling effect on people, and when he had allied this to rigorous training in all the dark arts of his trade, he knew that the differences between him and ordinary people had become so pronounced that there was little point in pretending otherwise.

"I'll get to the point then. Do you still intend to take over command of The Watch?"

"Have you heard otherwise?"

Primus shrugged.

"I don't presume to comment on any aspects of your," the Prefect waved his hand vaguely, "your … line of work, as I wouldn't expect comment from you on the demands of running the Praetorian Guard! So present me with facts, if you have any, and I shall pay you. Leave me to worry about what to do with them! That's the problem with the bureaucracy behind this damned imperial administration: too many small minded people with too many opinions above their station!" Plautianus slammed his hand down on his desk, drawing a raised eyebrow from Primus.

"You should exercise more caution commander! The walls have ears."

Plautianus glowered at him. "Get to the point of what brings you here. Don't test my patience."

"I have some good news and some less than good news. Which would you like to hear first?"

"What? Is this some kind of prank to you? Get to the point!"

"As you wish. I have another senator for you to feed to your ever-hungry lions."

"Come on, who?"

Primus picked at a bit of apple lodged in his teeth. "Aulus Vedetius."

"Vedetius? That young peacock with the blotch on his cheek? What is he, a quaestor? An aedile?"

Primus shrugged.

"He'll keep; he's a nobody from Gaul," Plautianus tutted. "What else do you have?"

"I have no further examples for you to use against the vigiles. In fact, what I witnessed last night does you no favours whatsoever."

"What is that supposed to mean?"

"Sadly another house church of Christians went up in flames last night. Near the Aventine this time."

"And?"

"Quite an impressive response. They saved dozens, with help from other watchmen from all over the south of the city. And they brought the block down before the flames spread. I hear they're quite the heroes in the area this morning. If I were a betting man, I'd say this will have already reached the ears of some of your dry old senators. A prudent man might think twice before launching an assault on The Watch so soon after this."

"Some fucking timing, you damned idiot!"

"Your orders, Prefect, didn't specify a day or an hour."

"Did anybody see you?"

"Of course not."

Plautianus made a noise of exasperation and sagged onto his desk. "Is that all you came to tell me? You have nothing else?"

Primus shrugged again. "Not without lying."

"Then bring me plausible lies, damn you!"

"They tire me, and I lack your powers of imagination."

Plautianus jabbed his finger at him. "Watch your mouth, informer. I could make you disappear without a trace if I chose to."

"I don't doubt it, commander. But you don't hold all the dice, remember?"

The Prefect glared at him and then strode towards the door.

IV

The wooden creak of Gaius Plautianus' bench as he sat back down was the only sound to break the stunned silence inside the chamber. The Praetorian Prefect surveyed the hoary old senators through the gauze of dust motes illumined by the sunlight streaming through the high grilles, and tried to keep all traces of the contempt he felt for them from his face.

"This is a naked grab for power!"

Lentulus Cato sprang up. His jowls trembled with outrage, momentarily disguising the slight shaking of his body that no physician had been able to arrest.

The silence within the senate house deepened. The oldest man amongst them had dared voice the dangerous opinion that many now felt. But he didn't care. For generations, his conservative forebears had spoken out in this very chamber. Despite the inherent dangers of bruising imperial egos, none had ever been silenced for it. He wasn't about to become the first.

"What motive, what other possible reason does the Prefect have for wanting to turn one of the few remaining public offices into his own personal army?" There were a few tentative murmurs now, but Cato waved them away with his bony hands. "Who is this wolf in sheep's clothing, that presumes to dispense with one of the crucial reforms brought in by the divine Augustus, one of the greatest Caesars that the world has ever seen, that has been saving untold lives, protecting countless properties and keeping the streets safer for over two hundred years? Well, commander? You grace us with your presence for the first time in Jupiter only knows how long, and this is the reason? Shame on you!"

The chamber erupted with cheering and foot stamping, but Cato ignored it, squinting as he scanned the rows of seats for Marcus Maracanthus. It was unlike him to miss such a momentous session, and he would surely have been one of the first to speak out now, but he was nowhere to be seen. Malicious rumours had been circulating for a few days that he had taken a new lover, a Syrian freedwoman, and eloped with her. Cato had left a few senators with their ears ringing whenever they had even entertained the gossip. He tutted and lowered himself to his seat. On the front row, Plautianus' face had turned a shade of crimson. From his chair in the middle of the house, the cadaverous presiding magistrate banged his staff onto the marble floor three times and the raucous noise began to die away to the cries of 'Order! Order in the senate!'

Another senator rose, cutting a gaunt figure amongst the rows of senators.

The staff rang out again on the floor.

"Senator Pubius Terentius Piso!"

The room became quiet again: nobody had expected him to be present so soon after the loss of his daughter.

"Perhaps, colleagues, I might be the first to disagree." His usually resonant voice was tremulous. "I speak as only one who has experienced the sudden loss of a child can, with one wish in mind. That nobody in this chamber ever has to wake before first light or lay down to sleep at the last to the constant whisper of a beloved daughter's absence. I care little enough about my future now to share this one truth with you. I have lost my faith in the gods. I am no longer a religious man and, forthwith, will be stepping down from the College of Pontiffs." There was a sharp intake of breath from the floor: Piso was notorious for his piety. "Little enough good daily worship and sacrifice brought me! Yes, gentlemen, you may look at me like that, as if I have lost my mind! I have not. But I still believe this. If there is something practical, something sensible, however unorthodox, that can be done to prevent this from ever happening to anyone again, we should not stop striving until we can make it a reality.

"The litany of incompetence after the disappearance of my Terentia … no – tell it straight - that followed her cold-blooded murder … was staggering. A bungled, unauthorised investigation by people barely competent enough to read and write was followed by the loss of her body. Yes, gentlemen, the actual loss of her body! Tell me, how does anyone lose a body?" Piso raised his hands as disbelieving murmurs filled the room. "Not only did we have to contend with the unfathomable sorrow of her death, but we also have to accept we will not be able to give her a proper burial." Tears filled his eyes now and he dabbed them with a linen cloth before composing himself.

"So now, her restless soul wanders the city seeking justice and repose. Would you deny her the single consolation that this will never happen again only because of politics? I thank senator Cato for his history lesson: two hundred years ago the divine Augustus did indeed create The Watch in response to the needs of the time. Who could deny that the needs have changed again? The stench of this city's rotting core fills all of our nostrils.

The overcrowded slums are more lawless than ever, and beggars and cut-throats roam the streets with impunity." There were a few mutters of hear, hear and I agree. "So I say this: we must do whatever is necessary to cure this illness. Like most of you, I don't like the idea of giving one man such a powerful mandate: the precedents are not always good. But I am prepared to make an exception."

He turned to Plautianus and pointed at him. "We have not always seen eye to eye, Prefect, but I respect your military credentials. If you truly think you can make a difference, I would charge you with eliminating this sickness infesting our city. Don't let us down." He looked around the room. "If there is a better man for the job, I suggest he stand up and be counted now. It concerns me not who it is: I care only about what he can do!"

Solemn voices of consent echoed around the chamber. From his seat on the front row, the Praetorian Prefect himself now rose and cleared his throat.

"I think …"

The magistrate banged his staff on the floor and coughed politely. "It is customary to wait until invited to speak, commander."

Amidst ripples of laughter, Plautianus' face became thunderous.

"Senator Gaius Fulvius Plautianus!" The magistrate gave him a tight smile.

Plautianus waited for the noise to subside and tried to keep his temper in check. "I thank senator Piso for his kind words. I also welcome any contributions about how to deal with the crisis we face over the future of The Watch …"

"Crisis, Prefect? What crisis?"

There was a collective intake of breath. Plautianus was so surprised by Cato's brazen interruption that he momentarily couldn't speak, and the old senator rose again, batting away the hand of the man next to him.

"A matter of hours ago, colleagues, it came to my attention that multiple cohorts of vigiles displayed extremes of courage and resourcefulness in extinguishing and destroying a blazing tenement block in the Aventine district …"

"Hear hear, I also heard this, bravo!" shouted Aulus Vedetius.

"… and nobody present could doubt that without their intervention countless more lives would have been lost. And I am told that the fire was about to spread before the flames were beaten back. This is not the first time, Prefect, this is not the first time," he said, raising his voice above the chatter of support, "that The Watch has distinguished itself in this manner. So I respectfully repeat, what crisis is there to fix?"

The incipient noise of support faded as the senators saw the look on Plautianus' face. His beard bristled and the veins around his thick neck stood proud.

"Are you deaf as well as blind, Cato?" He checked his tone in the face of a few disapproving jeers. "I too heard of the fire and I join those in commending the watchmen's efforts. Nobody here doubts their potential but fires aren't what the average person on the street cares about, senator. People aren't asking 'how can I get home to my family today without being burned alive?' They're asking 'how can I get home to see my son, daughter, wife or mother without being beaten and robbed'. Violent crime is rampant and The Watch isn't up to dealing with it. The farce after the shocking murder that senator Piso has mentioned should not have happened. It should have been brought to the attention of the Urban Cohorts and the Praetorians, and it was not. Days passed and the affair turned into a shambles. By stark contrast, within just two days of taking over my men had arrested and secured a signed confession from a villain who boasted of what he had done and bore the marks that proved it. That man is now dead and senator Piso and his family may mourn their loss in private."

Cato was on his feet in a flash. "Was that man executed after a trial?"

"No, senator, he was not. He died in the Tullian prison, where he belonged."

"How very convenient!"

"Convenient? Convenient for whom? Senator Piso, who may now grieve in private? I'm not sure I understand your point."

"That wretched dictator Sulla had much the same attitude, Prefect!" raged Cato, his voice trembling at top pitch. "Do you also have a list of proscriptions that you will one day nail to the senate house door? Is my name on your list?"

"If such a list existed, senator, rest assured yours would feature prominently."

The presiding magistrate watched the exchange with a look of horror on his face, and his staff hovered above the floor. The atmosphere was charged: nobody wanted to see a senator argue himself into a nasty accident but the spectacle was irresistible, like a close gladiatorial duel.

"I wonder what the Emperor Septimius Severus thinks of your breathtaking arrogance?"

Plautianus shrugged and produced a wax tablet from his toga. "Since you mention it, the Emperor was present in the gaol. He approved of course. As did Senator Piso and the Emperor's son, master Caracalla."

A hush descended and all eyes turned to Caracalla, who had been sitting lost in his thoughts at the end of the front row. At the mention of his name, he looked up, his face a sickly mask, dark crescents ringing his eyes. He met the stares without interest and focused once more on a milky swirl on the marble floor.

"To kill off any doubts within this room, perhaps I ought to read the confession," Plautianus approached the magistrate and unclipped the tablet. The old senator took it and scrutinized it, grateful for the restoration of order. After a few moments he nodded and returned it.

"... marked, as just verified, by the criminal in question: one Mathias of Rome. I warn you in advance, colleagues, the contents are not pleasant." He cleared his throat and was about to speak when there was a slight commotion on one of the front benches. Senator Piso stood, deathly pale, and sidled towards the end of his row. When he was clear, he turned to Plautianus and raised his chin.

"You will forgive me, Prefect, colleagues, but I don't think I would be able to hear this for a second time. Good day."

Sympathetic words of support followed him as he left the chamber, head bowed and shoulders hunched.

Plautianus shook his head sadly. "I'm not sure I'd have been able to make it here at all in his position. Senators, I was going to skate over the sensitive parts of this disgusting document, but I feel it only right to read it in full now he is out of earshot." From the corner of his eye he saw Caracalla become rigid with tension.

"With your permission?" he turned to the magistrate.

"Proceed when you are ready, Prefect."

"March first, consulship of Caracalla and Geta.

My name is Mathias, of the Viminal district of Rome, son of unknown mother and father. I make this statement following my arrest today by the Praetorian Guard when I was in a local tavern with my friend. I am a pauper and live on the street, and have to make money to survive however I can. Mostly, it is not my own for I have no profession. I am not proud of what I do. It was only after I was arrested and taken to the Tullian that I was told that the girl I attacked and robbed was the daughter of a senator. I admit I told my friend in the tavern that I was 'glad I hurt the spoilt little bitch' and that she was a 'wildcat' and that ..."

The uproar drowned out his voice and he stopped, glancing at Caracalla. Unnoticed by the other senators, he was sat with his hands on his knees, his fingers balled into trembling fists. He glared at Plautianus with undying hatred as the Prefect waited for the noise to die down.

"... and that 'for the right price she would have howled like a Babylonian she-wolf' ..."

The noise that erupted in the chamber following this could be heard across the forum and it took a few minutes before Plautianus was again able to proceed.

"... I was drunk and was not thinking about what I was saying. By the gods, I would not have touched her had I known she was the daughter of a senator of Rome ..."

"You should have had him torn to pieces Prefect!"

More howls.

"Order! Order in the senate!"

"Please, senators, please allow me to get to the end ..." he said, raising his arms, "Thank you ...

"After I attacked the senator's daughter but before I was arrested by the Praetorians, I was chased and caught by some people. I thought at first that they were soldiers. I would describe them ... well, suffice it to say on his description alone, we know exactly who he was talking about ... and I was later told that they were watchmen. They had been drinking. They then beat me ... quoting the Twelve Tables, and then let me go ..."

"They let the bastard go?" shouted a senator on the back benches. "A damned disgrace!"

"I want to say that I am very sorry about what happened and ... on it goes. Colleagues, I will not bother with the snivelling apology at the bottom," Plautianus' eyes roved the room and settled for a moment on Aulus Vedetius, "though it is available for your inspection, should you be interested."

The chamber fell silent, and the flames of the oil lamps dotted around the room flickered in the slight breeze, though it was not this that made Vedetius shudder. Plautianus clipped the tablet and took his seat. One or two groans greeted the elder statesman as he rose this time.

"Senator Lentulus Cato!"

"A stinging indictment on this city's rabble for sure. However," he coughed, "I'm sure I echo some of the confusion in this room about two things within that affidavit. Firstly, though the prisoner admits attacking a girl, at no point does he mention actually killing her. Secondly, the timings trouble me. You say the vigiles made a shambles of the investigation for a few days, lost the body and so on, before the Praetorians took over. But here we have them chasing the culprit, presumably having first identified him, beating him and then, mindful of the gravity of the crime, releasing him! I might understand this if they had merely caught a thief with his hands in someone's pockets in the forum, but not even the most ignorant blockhead would let a murderer go free." He smiled coldly at Plautianus. "Are you quite sure that the right man died in the Tullian prison?"

"Damn your self-righteousness, senator Cato! The statement is quite clear and I for one am glad he suffered!"

"Hear, hear!"

The dissenter was a junior senator, a quaestor, keen to make the right noises in front of his peers. But Plautianus was glad for the interruption: he had identified the flaw in the chronology whilst he had been in the cell listening to Mathias and had hoped the question would not be asked. He narrowed his eyes at Cato as he stood again.

"Senator Gaius Plautianus!"

"The statement also fails to mention that the prisoner was inhaling and exhaling throughout, but that doesn't mean to say he wasn't breathing, senator Cato!"

A few guffaws followed his response.

"I didn't think I would have to remind someone of your experience how these things work, however ... this affidavit is no different to other legal documents you all know. It contains the relevant facts only. As to your first point, let's not play with semantics: the creature admitted to a violent attack. Whether or not he intended to kill her or even knew that he had killed her when he had finished is a matter of conjecture. Several eminent people, myself included, witnessed scratch marks on his arm. One of the few things we did manage to establish from the vigiles was that she had defended herself so valiantly that her nails had bent. Feel free to cross-examine the Emperor himself on this point if you wish!"

"Hear, hear!"

"As to timings, exactly what the vigiles were up to is anyone's guess. I would personally like a separate enquiry. But I will add this: if only they were under Praetorian command! Then I would be only too happy to speak on their behalf!"

Plautianus sat down to foot stamping and applause. Cato knew his questions had been deftly swerved but he also knew that the balance of support had tipped away. Just as he was about to concede the floor, he glimpsed the forlorn figure of Caracalla, conspicuous amongst the excitable senators all around him. A thought occurred to him and he stood again.

"Senator Lentulus Cato!"

"Oh dear! Not ready to accept defeat yet, Cato?"

He waited for the laughter following the quaestor's quip to fade. "I note … I note that the Emperor's young son Caracalla has kept his counsel throughout this exchange, yet we are told he was present before the prisoner Mathias died. Before I yield the floor, doubtless to the satisfaction of those within this chamber, I would be interested to hear his views on the issue of the prisoner's last words. Young master … If you would care to indulge us?"

Cato was careful to be as bright as he could with his tone: Caracalla had already established a reputation for his moodiness and acerbic tongue. Expectant eyes settled upon him.

Caracalla looked like he had been jolted out of a bad dream and rose slowly.

"Senator Lucius Septimius Bassianus Caracalla!"

He surveyed the packed rows until his gaze came to rest upon Plautianus. Their eyes locked in mutual dislike for a few heavy moments

"Yes, I was present. No, I would not care to indulge any of you."

He swept his robe about him and strode out of the chamber, with the weight of the senators' stares pressing his back. Several of them turned to Cato with quizzical frowns, though he kept his own face expressionless.

When the heavy doors had closed behind him, uneasy murmurs filled the chamber. The presiding magistrate rose.

"The senate will break for refreshments." And thank the gods for that, he muttered to himself.

143

V

Junius Rufinus took a deep breath outside the Gorgona and looked up and down the street. Nobody seemed to be paying him any attention but then, he thought to himself, would he even know if they were?

The same barkeeper was drying tankards behind the counter and gave him a sullen nod as he entered. Whether or not he recognised him, there was no cheery greeting this time. He ordered a cup of diluted wine and a plate of cold meats and went to sit in the same alcove at the back. There were a few inveterate drinkers and gamblers bent double over a game involving a chequer board and counters, and they spoke in hushed tones. The only other person inside was a foppish looking man with a stylishly trimmed beard, contemplating a wax tablet and drumming one end of a stylus against his lips. Rufinus took him to be a hard-up poet. They had a reputation for frequenting dingy drinking holes in the name of seeking inspiration and yet somehow only finding prostitutes and strong beer.

To avoid the same treacherous journey home through the dark streets of the Subura, he had arranged to meet Trystan in the early afternoon, and the difference in atmosphere within the tavern was remarkable. The relative peace settled his nerves and he soon began to relax, assisted by the wine that the moody barkeep had set before him. His stomach growled and he wondered if his food had been forgotten. Moments later, however, his question was answered.

Like the Gorgona at this hour, the same woman now bringing him his food also appeared different. She wore a faded cream stola that made her look more demure and, as she set down the platter, he noticed for the first time the faint lines around her eyes. She glanced at him as he thanked her and then did a double take.

"I didn't take you for hardened drinker," she said, wiping the table down with a rag.

"You're right. I'm not."

"You have no place better to go?"

"Doesn't look like it does it?" He winced at his curtness that, try as he might, he seemed unable to lose in polite conversation. He tried again as she was about to move away. "Interesting accent you have. Where are you from?"

"I was born on the banks of Yam Ha-Melach," her tone suggested she had been asked many times, "though your dry language calls it Dead Sea. Do you know where that is?"

Rufinus frowned. "Of course I know where it is. I've swam in it."

"Really?"

"Yes, many years ago."

A dark look passed her face. "With Roman army then. You fought against my people?"

From across the room, the poet glanced up at her. She ignored him but Rufinus lowered his voice self-consciously. "No, not exactly. I served on the procurator's staff."

She gave a little derisive laugh. "Even worse! You sat at desk and watched other people do it!"

Rufinus turned his attention to his platter of meats. "Thank you. This looks fine."

She scowled at him and then huffed and moved away. He watched her bustle about the room. He had limited experience with women but was in no doubt that by any standards she was a prickly creature. He picked at the dried beef and pickled artichokes, and let his thoughts return to Maracanthus. Martha's nerves, he knew, would be allowing her no rest and he felt desperately sorry for her.

The tavern door opened but it wasn't Trystan. A short but stocky man with a flushed face and thick stubble entered and looked about him before walking, unsteadily, to the bar.

He asked himself the same question: if there was no news from the informer, what was the next step? The decent thing, he knew well enough, would be to go and see her regardless. At least he could say he had tried. The newcomer swaggered over to Rufinus.

"Someone sat there?" he said, indicating the stool next to him.

Rufinus pointedly looked about him at the saloon that was almost full of unoccupied stools.

"No, help yourself."

He stared at Rufinus and then yanked it away with a grunt, before dropping it next to the bar tender from the Dead Sea. She gave him a disapproving glance, tutted and carried on scrubbing a table top. When her back was turned, he forced his hand up her stola and groped her buttocks.

"Give me a quick fuck for a coin, Zeli. You know you'll like it."

"Get away from me, you pig!"

"Now don't be like that!" He forced his hand round to her thigh.

She slapped him hard about the cheeks and everybody in the bar, even the regular gamblers, stopped what they were doing and looked up. The man grabbed her hand and tried to pull her down onto his lap.

"She says no," said Rufinus through gritted teeth.

The man let go of her hand and glared at the Watch Prefect, looking him up and down. "Who asked you, peasant?"

Rufinus swallowed hard. He felt his stomach rise.

"Well? You interfering fucker! What's your problem?" he sprang from his seat and stalked over to him.

Feeling trapped in the alcove, Rufinus got up and stepped out of it. The man was about his height but was younger and much more solidly built. He also did not look like he was a novice when it came to bar brawls.

"Oi, settle it outside!" shouted the bar keeper. The street door opened and Trystan walked in, reading the situation instantly. He hovered by the entrance, the pouch of dice and knucklebones in his hand. Rufinus cursed his bad luck.

"Look, I meant no offence!" he said with his hands up, but the man wasn't listening. He clenched his fists and approached, sensing an easy victim in the greying man before him.

But appearances were deceptive.

Rufinus had never been a strong man but the Prefect of The Watch was at least expected to be familiar with the sort of roughhouse defensive techniques that his men practised. They were founded upon surprise and efficiency, and over the years Rufinus had paid more than a passing interest in them. He kept his hands up but his fingers were rigid, waiting for the drunk to step into range. As soon as he was close enough to smell the stale wine on his breath, Rufinus speared his fingers into the man's Adam's apple. He clutched at his throat, sputtering for breath, and his eyes bulged in astonishment. Rufinus drove the flat of his boot at his knee. The joint made a resounding crack and he dropped instantly, banging the back of his head on a table as he went down.

Everyone in the tavern froze in disbelief, though Trystan gave him a reappraising look. Rufinus hesitated then gripped the stricken man by the scruff of his tunic. He dragged him towards the bemused Trystan, leaving a wide furrow of dirty straw in his wake.

"Really, I'm terribly sorry! He … well, left me with little choice …"

"You can't leave him in here!" said the bar keeper. "Prop him up outside or something!"

"Right, fine," he looked up at Trystan. "If you wouldn't mind?"

Trystan shrugged and helped drag him outside, causing people passing by to tut and sidestep them on the narrow pavement. They positioned him so that his back was leaning against the wall and Rufinus checked to see if he was breathing. His face had turned purple but his chest was still rising and falling.

"Blind drunk!" he pronounced for the benefit of people in the street, and he certainly looked it as his head lolled onto his chest. Rufinus slapped his cheeks and turned to Trystan.

"Let's walk."

"Probably best."

They strolled in silence for a few minutes until they ducked into the steep backstreets, alive with grubby children throwing stones at half-broken jugs, labourers making deliveries, beggars and the elderly, who did little else but sit in their doorways and gaze at passersby.

"The less I know about most of the people I deal with," said Trystan, "the better. You, however … I'm not so sure: not after that little show."

Rufinus had to stop to let a child with a filthy face and runny nose dash past him. "I'd rather keep it that way. Hard to trust anyone these days."

"Fine. I respect that."

"I'm interested in what you may have though."

"Of course … business … d'you have the balance?"

Rufinus palmed him a small pouch of coins, which Trystan squeezed, testing the density of its contents.

"Good. An honest client." he smiled sadly. "Not many of those left in this city." Trystan took Rufinus' hand, replaced the money pouch and closed his fingers around it. "I kept my side of the bargain but I'm sorry to tell you there's not much out there, my friend, or at least not enough for those extra coins."

Rufinus stopped in his tracks and looked at the pouch in surprise. "Nothing at all?"

"Nothing of any substance, apart from the odd rumour."

"Such as?"

"Such as your senator having an intense affair with a near Eastern courtesan and leaving Rome, Italy even, with her."

"What?" scoffed Rufinus. "Marcus Maracanthus? No chance. His was one of the few marriages in the senate actually based on affection." They carried on walking. "You could have reported that back to me and settled your task. Why didn't you?"

"True enough. But I disregarded it soon as I heard it."

"Why? I assume you know nothing about the man, so how can you make that judgment?"

"Oh don't get me wrong, Tiberius. I wasn't making a moral judgment. My only code is if you want good referrals you give good information. But beyond that? When you do what I do, you have to leave your morals at the door. Besides, a wealthy senator having a piece of a pretty slave girl, or boy, or a whore would hardly be anything new, would it?"

"It would be with him!"

"Look, I don't really care one way or the other." Trystan lowered his voice. "I was merely saying that the rumour didn't come from a reliable source. It was forum tittle-tattle, if you see what I mean; lowest grade information. When I started making discreet enquiries with my better-placed sources, the sort of people you really don't want to be bartering gossip with, they were pretty quick to say they knew nothing. And that, in itself, may actually tell you more than words."

"What's that supposed to mean?"

"That they're scared, or covering up, I don't know. But I took it as a warning and backed off. You soon know when you've got all you're going to get out of someone, believe me."

Rufinus scratched his head. "Poses more questions than it answers, doesn't it?"

Trystan shrugged. "Way it goes."

They were approaching the main thoroughfare of Via Tiburtina now and Rufinus sensed that the informer was keen to be on his way. "Was there anything else? Anything else at all that I can go and tell his wife? I ought to tell you he's a close friend of mine, on top of everything else."

"There is nothing concrete, my friend. Depends what sort of a light you want to put on it, and on how realistic she's prepared to be, doesn't it? I heard nothing to say for certain either way but ..." he blew the air out of his cheeks, "you must know the signs aren't good."

Rufinus looked away. The pale orb of the sun was now obscured by clouds and there was moisture in the air.

"Doesn't have any business that takes him to Ostia, or family you know of over there, does he?"

"Ostia? No, not that I know about. Why do you ask?"

"Well, nothing relevant then. Just that I got wind of a contract that's been secured over there."

"Contract? What sort of contract? Trade? What's the relevance?"

"You could say that." Trystan looked amused. "You genuinely have no idea what I'm talking about, do you?"

"I don't think I do."

Trystan leaned towards him conspiratorially. "I mean 'termination of life'. There was a very secretive tender put out. High risk but big reward. Not really my sort of thing but I was offered it only because of various favours I'm owed. Now I'm telling you, just in case your friend had any reason to be over there, but now I see that he doesn't."

Rufinus raised his eyebrows. He was not so naïve to think that this sort of thing didn't go on, but to hear it expressed so matter-of-factly alarmed him. "Why did you even think it might have anything to do with Marcus?"

"No, bit of a stab in the dark I grant you. Just trying to be helpful, Tiberius, tell you everything I heard. Mention was made of a ranking public official, who's obviously been ruffling some feathers over there. These sorts of jobs are quite rare: often tendered by very wealthy, powerful people who want to be able to wash their hands of it in case … You alright?"

A look of abject horror had seized Rufinus' face. "Damn the gods to hell!"

"What? What's wrong with you man?"

Rufinus gripped him by the sleeve. "Tell me what you know!"

Trystan removed his hand. "Damn you, I just have! That's it!" he said through gritted teeth. "What the fuck's the matter with you?"

"Who do you think they were talking about, these contacts of yours? A senator? A local politician? An officer of the vigiles?"

"I don't know. A 'public official' was all I heard. It could be any of those. What do you care anyway?"

"My name's Junius Rufinus. I'm the Prefect of The Watch, and I just sent my best tribune there. He'd upset some people alright; powerful people! I want you to get it called off: you have to!"

149

Trystan recoiled. "Oh no! No way, and I don't care who you are! I told you I turned the job down flat and it went elsewhere, don't ask who because I don't know!"

"Who else then? Who do I speak to, or pay off?"

"You must have lost your mind," he said, shaking his head. "First, trust me, you couldn't afford to, second … these aren't some builders that you just hire and fire if they do a bad job, my friend. We're talking serious, dangerous individuals that would not appreciate anybody interfering in their business. You'd end up with your throat cut before you even got a sniff of who they were. You must be a man with half a brain, if you are who you say you are. Think about it."

Trystan looked agitated now. He nodded at Rufinus and walked away. The Watch Prefect stood rooted to the spot for a moment and then jogged after him, catching him by the arm. Trystan spun around, glaring at him.

"Please! Listen, you have to help me here. I came to you to save one good person and find out today I might have lost two! Double … treble the money …"

Trystan's eyes narrowed and he raised his finger inches from Rufinus' face. His sudden change of demeanour was alarming. "No, you listen to me! I owe you nothing! I've risked too much already. Never contact me again, you understand?"

His face softened when he saw the hopeless look in Rufinus' eyes. He knew how that felt. "Look, you want a last piece of advice from me? Get your man out of there. Do it now and Fortuna may yet smile on him. That's all you can do."

With that, he swiveled on his heels and walked away without looking back. Rufinus watched him go and ran his hands through his hair, tugging at it in desperation.

Why me? Why now? He wanted to scream out in frustration …

He glared at the children that had stopped throwing stones at broken pots and were regarding him with some curiosity. He kicked at a shard that had landed in front of him and stalked away, bitterly cursing the cruel gods.

VI

The light was already beginning to fail by the time Rufinus reached the Ostian Gate and low, grey clouds were snuffing out what remained of the day. There had also been a light drizzle since his meeting with Trystan, and the moisture had by now soaked through his clothes, making him shiver. All in all, he felt in a very bleak mood indeed, which the persistent beggars huddling outside the archway did nothing to alleviate. When he dismissed them with a stern Gallic curse, he was not surprised to hear some of them switch their pleas to that language: it was reputed that some of the older vagrants here were able to beg in eight different tongues.

The last time he had visited this place had been six years ago, at the height of spring and in the company of a wealthy and not unattractive widow. How different had his mood been then as they left for the countryside! The dalliance hadn't lasted through summer, though they had remained on reasonable terms. She had remarried less than a year later, leaving Rufinus to rue, not for the first time, what might have been.

The building he was looking for was one of the first to have been built when the city had finally burst at the seams and spilled outside the Servian walls ringing its ancient core. Tucked behind a grassy verge fronted by a row of crumbling tombs, he located the stable block more by instinct than memory.

And it had fallen on hard times since.

It was a long, low structure with a sloping roof of dirty red slates, some of which were missing or broken, and walls that were in need of repointing. He remembered that there was a fenced paddock at the back, bordered by Poplar trees, where Drusilla had selected a white Iberian horse. He wondered if it was still alive as he approached the entrance shed and encountered the familiar smell of dung, damp hay and fodder. Though a small bell over the door had tinkled when he entered, nobody came to the counter and he drummed his fingers on it. On the wall behind the counter hung various shapes and sizes of harnesses and bits, which at least gave him confidence that the stable was still functioning. After a full two minutes nobody had appeared. He tutted and called out, but there was no response.

Slapping his hand on the counter, he walked back out of the shed and looked around. Though traffic was beginning to back up outside the gates in readiness for admission to the heart of the city after dark, there was no interest in the stables.

Shit, shit! He hissed, as panic began to gnaw at his resolve. He had visions of assassins surrounding Ambrosius' quarters, unsheathing their knives at that very moment. He couldn't help but wonder: was that how Marcus Maracanthus had met his grizzly end?

Where was the damned owner?

He took a deep breath and composed himself. Where else nearby was likely to be open or able to provide him with what he needed? He could think of no other stabling posts, although he was sure he must have been passed scores of them in his time without even realizing it.

"Can I help you?"

Rufinus span around. The appearance of the fellow before him did not suit the effeminate voice. Although he was ruddy cheeked and looked like a Satyr, his tattooed forearms were as thick as a child's legs and he bore a weighty farrier's hammer. Rufinus recognised him, but nothing about the stable owner's expression suggested the same of him.

"Well? You were impatient enough to take me from what I was doing."

"Yes, yes I'm sorry. I'm … it's just that I'm in a terrible rush …"

"Aren't all city folk these days?"

"Quite. Look, I hope you can help. I've been here before and hired a fine horse but I need something delivering urgently … I'm not a good enough rider to get it done on time … even if I did use the mount I rode last time …"

"Let me stop you there, sir. I'm afraid there's no chance of that. I used to employ the odd dispatch rider but I let the last one go a few years back. Not enough business to justify having them just hanging about. I'm sorry, you may want to try …"

Rufinus dropped the pouch of silver coins with a loud thud onto the counter.

"It's a very important message, you see," he added.

The owner cleared his throat, not taking his eyes off the pouch. "I'm still not sure I could get hold of a good rider at this hour …"

"Papa, is everything alright?" The young voice came from somewhere within the stables.

"Your son?"

He nodded. "All's fine, just get on with re-shoeing her will you!"

"Okay," came the disappointed reply after a few moments.

"He was a very fine young horseman for his age, if I remember rightly?"

The owner's eyes narrowed at Rufinus. "He's not yet a man and it's getting dark."

"Half the sum again if you can guarantee delivery by return," said Rufinus, nudging the pouch across the counter.

The owner tutted. It was clear he wanted to tell his wearisome customer in no uncertain terms where to go, but times were hard.

"Look, it's only to Ostia. We both know it's a straight run. And the person I need the letter delivering to is a good, honest man. He'd look after him and ride back with him, if it made you feel any better. But that would depend on getting there quickly."

The owner glared back at Rufinus.

"I really would be most grateful," he said, showing him the leather scroll case.

"How would you guarantee me the rest of the coin?"

"I didn't just dig that up, if that's what you mean."

He tutted again and opened the pouch, testing the coins to his satisfaction. "Give me that. Mothax, come here a minute," he snatched the case from Rufinus' hand, "I may have a job for you!"

"Thank you."

"This better be nothing more than you say it is. I mean that!"

After a few moments, Mothax entered the shed. Rufinus only vaguely remembered the skinny youth who had brushed down Drusilla's Iberian but the young man before him had grown beyond recognition. In fact, other than his beady eyes, Rufinus would not have believed he was related to the owner at all. He was already much taller than his father, lacked any of his bulk and had proud shoulders and unkempt fair hair that curled over his neck. He exuded youthful energy and Rufinus felt his prospects surge.

"Father?" he said, appraising Rufinus with a friendly smile.

"Right, this … gentleman … wants a letter taking urgently to Ostia. I did tell him we don't do that sort of thing anymore, and it's up to you if you want to go, because I certainly won't force you, but … well, it's your choice," he said, his eyes falling once more on the money pouch.

Mothax's eyes lit up. "Ostia? Can I? I'll take Bellerophon: he's desperate for a run out!"

His father sighed. "Up to you, though I'm not done with Iphigenia's shoes yet, so you can't take her."

"Excellent! Young Mothax, you won't remember me but I certainly remember you showing my friend a fine white Iberian six or seven years back. And a good deal of promise you had then!"

Mothax's smile faded a touch. "Penelope. She went lame."

"Ah, shame. Anyway, I'd like you to deliver that letter to the tribune of The Watch in Ostia, there's only one barracks there, you can't miss it, his name is Ambrosius …"

"Whoa, hang on a minute!" interjected the owner. "You said there'd be no danger. Sounds like a bloody queer business to me! Who are you anyway?"

"Father!"

"No, it's fine. It's a personal matter, urgent family business. Very urgent. The fact that he's a night watchman is by the by. That just happens to be where he is, unfortunately, else I wouldn't be here."

"Answer my question!"

Rufinus sighed. "Look, my name's Junius Rufinus. I'm Prefect of the Watch."

"Wow!" said Mothax.

"Like hell you are."

Rufinus rapped his finger on the counter in mounting exasperation. "The seal on that scroll. Take a look at it."

The owner tipped the scroll out of the case and scrutinised it. A clear imprint of Stata Mater, the goddess of fire prevention, in the red wax disc. He frowned.

"So why can't you just get one of your own to deliver it, if it's so urgent?"

Rufinus laughed. "Do you ever see mounted watchmen? My lot would be a liability on a horse! I need a proper rider, not a keen amateur." He changed his tone. "Look, I don't mean to be rude, but I came here in genuine haste on a very personal matter. If you don't think you can help, I can take my business elsewhere. I simply came here because I've been before and you're already on the road." He reached out for the scroll.

The owner hesitated only for a second. "No, no. It's fine. Had to make sure, that's all. And he's my only boy," he said patting Mothax on the back.

"Good, then I'll give him brief directions."

154

When he was finished and Rufinus had got Mothax to repeat his instructions, he was led to the stables behind the shed. The state of the fence bordering the paddock went some way to explaining the look in the owner's eyes when he laid eyes on the silver coins. He closed his eyes as they crossed the grass and remembered the look of glee on Drusilla's face when she first rode the Iberian.

Happier times.

He opened them again and shivered at the drizzle and the light wind that made the pointed tops of the Poplars bend in unison.

"Here he is!" announced Mothax.

In contrast to the state of the building, the horses were in fine shape. Bellerophon's nostrils flared and he tossed back his glossy black mane

"Very impressive. He'll be there in no time."

Father and son exchanged a few words about when he had last been fed and watered, which roadside posts and taverns to avoid and the like. It was obvious to Rufinus that Mothax was barely listening as he secured Bellerophon's bridle and reins, and whispered reassuring words to him. The stallion's ears twitched and his head bobbed up and down as its withers were stroked.

They led Bellerophon out of the stables and onto the gravel path that led through the tombs and merged with the main road. Rufinus made final arrangements about the balance of payment and shook hands on the deal as Mothax mounted up. They both watched him, consumed by different thoughts, as he broke from a canter into a gallop against the flow of carts and wagons that were backing up down Via Ostiensis, his fair hair streaming behind him and Bellerophon obedient to every flick of the reins.

VII

The city walls were an invisible speck on the purple horizon by the time Mothax realised he was lost.

He had followed the gentle south western sweep of Via Ostienses for half an hour before youthful impatience had got the better of him and he had left the main road to avoid running headlong into any more lumbering wagons. There had been angry words the last time but Mothax's complaints about the recklessness of an unlit cart had fallen on deaf ears. An argument with a single driver was one thing, but the three heavies that had emerged from under the tarpaulin were a different proposition altogether, and he had left the road along the cinder path that had at the time appeared to run parallel with the main road.

But in the scanty light cast by the torch he had thrust in front of him as he rode, he could recognize no familiar landmarks now. The silence of the late evening was unearthly, unlike anything he had ever experienced before, and the sounds of Bellerophon's hooves, his heavy breathing and the slight rip of the flames through the cool night air all seemed distorted to him. The sky was shrouded with clouds and there was not a star to be seen, and he couldn't shake the nagging suspicion that he had somehow begun to drift north westerly. Only once in the distance had he seen a flicker of light – barely more than a pinprick – that suggested he was not entirely alone, but that had gone as quickly as it had appeared. He assumed that it had been a shepherd lighting a fire for another night with his flock.

The faint line of the horizon suggested that the track forked, still some way ahead. The light he had seen had been on higher ground, hinting that there were low hills to his left, which he was keen to avoid in the dark even though his instincts told him that this would be where he would eventually rejoin the main road. And, if this assumption was correct, that would mean that the mighty River Tiber would be somewhere to his right. Whilst he knew that the river discharged itself in Ostia, hitting one of its banks would not necessarily be a good thing: the river meandered aimlessly at some points, almost doubling back on itself. And because he would not know exactly which part of the river he had encountered, he would not know in which direction he was heading.

All of these thoughts entered his mind as he approached the fork in the path and he slowed Bellerophon. As if sensing his rider's uncertainty, Mothax had noticed that the stallion had been a little hesitant in plunging into the shadows, and Mothax had to stroke his neck and encourage him onwards. He screwed up his eyes and tried to read the lie of the land: he was sure that he could make out a slight valley scything through the undulating landscape: a well-used shortcut perhaps? On impulse, and against his initial thoughts, he swung his mount to the left and dug in his heels. Bellerophon flared his nostrils and redoubled his pace.

It was not long before Mothax began to question his decision. The track had narrowed and he could feel the black forms of Holm Oak trees massing either side of him, enveloping him and his little pocket of light in impenetrable shadow. Moreover, the ground was poor, with sudden dips and rises, and was strewn with sharp stones, making him fear for Bellerophon's footing. He swore aloud and slowed him to a gentler gallop. At the periphery of his torchlight, he fancied he saw movement in the bushes ahead of him and to his left. He scanned the shadows but could see nothing. When he was almost level with the bushes, he caught another glimpse of furtive movement, a bulky shape lurching towards the track.

What he experienced next was both sudden and intensely painful. Bellerophon sensed danger and tried to leap but his front legs were too late in clearing the rope pulled taught between trees on opposite sides of the track. He clattered to the ground with a terrified whinny and Mothax was thrown clear over his head, landing on his shoulder with a resounding crack, the torch skittering away a few yards ahead of him. His vision clouded as bolts of pain seared through him and he wanted to shriek in agony, but was unable to summon any voice. The shadows of three figures passed over him.

"A fucking messenger … that all?"

"I don't see nobody else passing by … shit place to lay up …"

Their voices were gruff. The stockier one had a grey beard and sly eyes. Mothax felt his back being kicked hard but the thud was strangely detached. He willed himself to feel for the dagger in his belt but even his good arm would not respond.

"Just take the damn bag off him will you … stop fucking about."

He felt the leather straps being dragged from his shoulder and the pockets to his cloak being rummaged through. His vision faded once again and he became light-headed.

"Anything valuable?"

The brigand with the beard, a former soldier, broke open the seal to Rufinus' scroll:

JR to AM. Greetings ... in your strongest interests to return to Rome ...

He grunted at it and frowned: what followed did not make any sense, as if it were written in some kind of code.

He lost interest in it, tore it up and tossed it over his shoulder. He slipped the small purse he had taken into his own pocket and drew out his knife.

"Now open up your mouth, pretty boy."

Mothax tried to resist but the strength had evaporated from his body and it was all he could do to remain conscious. The brigand wrenched open his mouth, peering into it like a dentist. The stench of rancid fruit and stale beer washed over Mothax and he retched.

"Well?"

"Not even a gold tooth!"

"Just put him out of his misery."

"What about the horse?"

"What about it? Look at it; it's lame. Leave it."

"Well, put that poor fucker out of its misery then!"

"What? You having a laugh aren't you? I'm not killing a horse. Bad luck ain't it? Let the hawks and rats have it."

Mothax's vision clouded once more and a sudden chill drifted through him. The bearded brigand gripped the messenger's face, watching in curiosity as his eyelids fluttered.

"Nighty night, son," he muttered, drawing his blade across Mothax's throat.

The trio dragged his bloodied and limp body to the side of the path and threw it into the bushes. The smaller of the trio had a pronounced swagger as they disappeared back into the woodland.

"A waste of good stallion that, Saturninus. Would have fetched a fair price at the market!"

"Next time, cut a little slack in the rope then! You're only meant to unseat the rider you daft little prick," answered the one with the beard, slapping him on the back.

VIII

"It's not that my men don't like you," said Longinus, "it's just that … well, they're just not used to your style, I suppose."

He and Ambrosius walked on in strained silence. He had not been looking forwards to broaching the issue with the tribune, who did not have a reputation for tact in difficult conversations, but he could not put it off any more: his men would lose all respect for him. Over the past few days, Ambrosius had taken to lengthy walks by himself along the banks of the river, and Longinus had resolved to talk to him then.

"I'm not here to make friends, Longinus. You probably know it wasn't my choice to come here. I'd already done my tour. Why do you care so much what people think anyway?"

The vexillarius shrugged, though he had often wondered himself. "It's a question of motivation. Once a horse is dead, why keep flogging it?"

Ambrosius snorted. "What? The job is the same whoever's in charge! Has been since The Watch began – they all know that. If he doesn't like it, a vigil should just find something else to do with his time. I just don't see your point, man!"

"Maybe that's the problem!" he blurted out in exasperation. "With respect, you don't seem to see anybody else's point of view, tribune! Of course you're right; they all know what they're signing up for the minute they swear the oath, or at least damn well should do, but what's so wrong with going a bit easier on them every now and again? The gods know it's a thankless and dangerous enough job as it is!"

His terse words hung in the cold air. For a moment he wondered if he might have overstepped the mark and braced himself for a curt reply, but Ambrosius was deep in thought. They had passed under the old Sullan walls and the Tiber flowed to their left, its surface pale and sluggish in the light cast by the few storm lamps that hung from the cabins and wharfs on the opposite bank.

Ambrosius sighed, in no mood for a searching discussion. "Perhaps you're right, Longinus, and your cohort just happens to be in my firing line. I've nothing personal against any of them. So you can go away and tell them that if it makes you feel any more loved in their eyes."

"That's not what I've been getting at, tribune."

159

"I wasn't being serious. Don't take yourself so seriously! Here, have a drink."

Longinus frowned at the stoppered flask that Ambrosius produced from his cloak.

"Go on man, take some!"

Longinus took a sip and screwed up his face, spitting it out. "Damn it, what in hell is in there?"

Ambrosius chuckled at him and took a generous mouthful, gasping at its potency. "I picked it up from some shady little man in the Square of the Corporations the other day. Claims he gets it from somewhere down the coast but I think he brews it himself. It's made from fermented grape skins apparently."

"Why d'you drink that poison? It's vile."

"You'd need it if you got out more. Keeps you warm on the coldest of nights, I tell you."

The sudden noise of banging and muffled voices carried on the breeze stopped them in their tracks, and they hunkered down. The noise continued but it was too faint for them to make out what it was.

"Probably just …"

"Shh …!" hissed Ambrosius.

Still crouching, he beckoned Longinus to follow him to the next willow tree. There they listened intently but the conversation was too indistinct. Ambrosius pointed to the scrub bushes further along, where the thick screen of willows broke. Longinus shook his head.

"Too exposed!" he whispered.

Ambrosius attuned himself to the noises again, peering around the gnarled trunk. There were two or three lights ahead that went out at regular intervals, as if something was passing over them and obscuring the flames. Whatever was going on, they were now of the same mind: there was something not quite right about it. It was close to midnight, if not later, and the noises were all muffled.

Ambrosius jabbed his finger at the floor to indicate that Longinus was to stay and shuffled away into the dim light of the clearing. Longinus tugged his sleeve and shook his head, pointing back over his shoulder but Ambrosius frowned at him and carried on.

The noises stopped.

Ambrosius froze, no more than ten paces from the bushes. There were urgent whispers. Ambrosius' mind raced: should he press on or chance it and hurry back? He scurried towards the concealment, his thighs now on fire from crouching.

From somewhere in front and to his right, a dog barked. Ambrosius tensed, thinking his scent might have betrayed him, but the barking seemed to satisfy the people ahead and the banging resumed. This time, however, there was also the clatter of metal. On his hands and knees now, Ambrosius crawled around the bushes and peered through a break in the foliage.

What he saw in the pool of lamplight astonished him.

He squinted through the foliage, trying to make sense of it.

There were five of them - big, swarthy men - and he now understood why he hadn't been able to understand what they were saying. It wasn't that he and Longinus hadn't heard them properly: it was because they weren't speaking Latin, or any other strain of Italian language. Where they were from he could only guess: they were darker than most Romans without quite resembling the poor African wretches in the city's slave markets.

Of greater interest to Ambrosius, however, were the contents of the crates they were loading up and nailing shut with leather-muffled hammers: he had not seen such a fearsome collection of weaponry in all his life. One of the foreigners, his face concealed in the cowl of his cloak, was at that moment wrapping a spiked mace in an oilcloth. Another was gathering up a number of glinting scimitars and other swords into a much larger blanket. Though Ambrosius knew they were extremely heavy, these brutes were handling them as if they were made out of flimsy wood.

Even as the tribune was pondering how the weapons had got there, he noticed a deep wheel rut at the edge of the clearing that lead off into the darkness He assumed they had been dumped there from an ox cart, perhaps concealed under farm produce or tarpaulins. He watched them nail the lid onto the sixth crate and heave it on top of the others by means of rope handles at either end. There were a few rough slaps on shoulders and grunts of satisfaction, and then they stretched their backs or lolled about on the crates as if waiting for someone.

Ambrosius felt a deal more vulnerable. Whilst they were engrossed in their business, they had ignored what was going on around them. But now, as their conversation dried up, they had started paying casual attention to their surrounds. As he considered his next move, Ambrosius' thoughts were interrupted by one of the strangers making straight for the scrub in which he was crouching.

Damn it, you fool!

The tribune's pulse quickened and he reached for his knife. His eyes darted about for somewhere to retreat but he could see nothing, and he knew the sudden movements would give him away in an instant. Instead, he curled up into a tight ball, tucking his hands into his stomach. He took a deep breath and held it, not even daring to exhale.

The foreigner was on the other side of the bush now, whistling to himself. Ambrosius heard the soft clink of his belt buckle being unfastened and the ruffle of his cloak and tunic being lifted. There was a short silence and then a gush of fluid on foliage as he relieved himself. Ambrosius could feel the heat of it and braced himself as the odd drop spattered into his hair.

Hurry up and just fuck off, for Jupiter's sake!

But the stream seemed to go on forever and he struggled to contain his breath. Just then, one of the others in the group barked something out. The foreigner swore and finished up what he was doing before turning away and jogging back to join them. Ambrosius exhaled raggedly.

But a new noise drifted across to him.

A gentle sploshing of water.

He uncurled himself and craned his neck round to see what was happening. The strangers were stood by the river bank, one of them pointing across it. A hulking shape materialized out of the gloom, drifting towards an old jetty he could now see in the light of a storm lantern affixed to the vessel's bows. As it approached, he could hear the soft thump of oars manoeuvring her into place. Its bows touched the rotting planks of the jetty with the softest of dunks and there was a short flurry of activity on the bank as a boarding ramp was set up.

More barks of command and the men began to load the crates with minimal fuss. As he observed them, several thoughts entered Ambrosius' mind. Firstly, these men, whoever they were, were well drilled. Secondly, the ship he was looking at was possibly the very merchant vessel that Fabricius, the stony faced caller to the vigils' barracks, had had 'requisitioned'. The people he had described loitering round his ship were very similar. One thing was for sure, however, they were not Praetorian Guards, as the note nailed to the mooring post had said. So who were they? Mercenaries? He doubted they were some sort of covert river patrol. Pirates roaming the Middle Sea were one thing, but on the River Tiber?

As he looked on, the final crate was loaded, the gangplank hauled over the side and the lamps were snuffed out. Within a few minutes, the foreigners had boxed up and loaded enough weaponry to equip a small private army and now they were melting back into the blackness of the night as if they had never been there at all. Ambrosius waited until they had gone before scurrying back to an open-mouthed Longinus, whose bald pate looked like a small moon in the half light. Ambrosius flopped onto the grass next to him.

"What? Why are you grinning like an idiot?"

"Your head. Just as well you didn't follow me: I didn't realize how it glowed in the dark."

"Never mind that, what in the name of the gods was that all about?"

"Don't know, but one of them nearly pissed all over me."

Longinus' face cracked into a broad smile and they both burst into relieved gales of laughter.

Ambrosius produced his flask and took a hearty draft of the grappa, offering it to the vexillarius. This time he swallowed some without complaint, though his expression looked as though he was chewing stinging nettles, making Ambrosius laugh again.

"I honestly thought you'd had it," said Longinus, wiping his mouth. "That fellow was a mountain."

"Fortunately I couldn't see him. I was looking intently at the back of my eyelids."

"So what were they talking about?"

"Don't know: they weren't speaking Latin."

"Eh? What then, Greek?"

Ambrosius stood up and dusted himself off. "No, not Greek either. I have no idea what language it was. Anyhow, I'm heading back to think about it over some wine. Coming?"

Longinus nodded and Ambrosius hauled him up.

IX

Muttering to himself about the stupidity of trudging around the darkening city alone, Junius Rufinus struck the main road skirting the Circus Maximus and Forum before retracing the same steps he had taken a few days before, on the eve of Matronalia. Preoccupied by his thoughts and oblivious to his surroundings, he made the job of the assassin, who had been tracking him from a distance since he had passed him in an alleyway off the Vicus Longus, that much easier.

Only at one point did Rufinus hesitate on the path that wound around the Hill of Gardens and look behind him. Not seeing anything in the soughing trees, he frowned and continued on his way. Once outside the door, he composed himself and rapped on the knocker.

It took several minutes – and Rufinus becoming very cold – before the hatch was slid aside and the door opened, but mere seconds to read the atmosphere within. The building felt devoid of warmth, hope and, other than a solemn faced Prolitho, uninhabited.

The chief steward hardly registered Rufinus on the doorstep, as if he were an expected but unwelcome guest. A twitch of the head was the Watch Prefect's only invitation inside. Prolitho closed the door behind him and disappeared without a word into one of the rooms adjoining the atrium, leaving Rufinus to shiver at the feeling that he had entered a mausoleum. Few lamps had been lit and the place was silent. Then he noticed the wooden chests stacked in the corner of the hall. He walked over to them and lifted one of the heavy lids a few inches: it was full of women's clothes and accessories.

"I'm leaving Rome, Junius."

Rufinus turned on his heels. It scarcely seemed possible given her diminutive stature, but Martha had become even thinner in the past few days. In the dim light of an oil lamp, her face was taut and pale.

"Martha, I … where will you go?"

"I have friends in Luca. I'll stay there for a few days on my way back to Spain."

Even though he was only a few paces away, Rufinus could barely hear her, so soft were her words, as if merely uttering them was physically painful.

"Do you not think that might be premature? Marcus may yet …"

She winced and held up a frail hand to silence him. "No … please. He is gone forever, we both know that. But these rumours … these poisonous things people are saying are just too much …"

"So you have already heard."

She rounded on him. "You don't believe any of it, do you? It doesn't make any sense!"

"Martha, I'm afraid I've discovered nothing at all. I did as I promised and the only thing I got in response was that somebody had circulated malicious rumours about him. Even the informer I paid disbelieved them. But …" Rufinus threw his hands into the air, "well, I really don't know what else to say. I'm so sorry, so very sorry."

Martha nodded but then her face creased and she looked away, though there were no tears: she doubted it would be physically possible for any more tears to fall. Prolitho appeared in the study doorway. To Rufinus' surprise, he approached her and embraced her without hesitation, pulling her head to his chest. Far from recoiling at the touch of the slave, Martha sagged against him and began to sob as he cradled her. Rufinus' eyes locked with Prolitho's, who gave him the most brazen glare. He looked away in disgust and cleared his throat. "If there's anything you require of me Martha … you know where to find me."

But Martha had fallen asleep.

"I'll see myself out." He flicked a contemptuous glance at Prolitho and stalked across the atrium without looking back.

When he was out of sight of the house and had found the path, he slapped the nearest tree trunk in exasperation.

What had the world come to?

He sucked in a deep lungful of night air, both grateful to be back outside and regretting ever having returned, and trudged back down the path in hope of some company in the Gorgona.

*

Though the barkeeper scowled at him as he entered, he made no comment about the fight earlier in the day. Nor was there any sign of the drunken man himself. Rufinus took the fact that he wasn't still slumped against the wall outside as a good sign.

He ordered a cup of heated wine and sat alone with his back to a wall besides a group of regulars, the seat in the alcove having been taken by someone else. Anonymous and inconspicuous in the smoky tavern, he relaxed and mulled over what had happened, troubled only by the reality that he would prefer to share his thoughts with someone else.

The first cup slipped down so easily he ordered another. For the first time in his life he decided to abandon himself entirely to wherever drink might take him. Tomorrow, he declared to himself, would look after itself. Perhaps he'd also make greater efforts to contact some older friends. They'd certainly be interested in this day's bizarre events. The more of the spicy wine he drank, the more reflective he became, and the words of the informer Trystan came back to him:

My sources had been quick to say they knew nothing ...

A very secretive tender ... high risk but high reward ...

Termination of life ...

All around him, the din and cheering of the drinkers merged into one sound, like the crash of waves from afar, and he felt his eyelids grow heavy.

Termination of life ...

Get your man out of there ...

He didn't know for how long he had nodded off, but his head jerked upright and it took him a second or two to realize where he was. He felt instinctively for his small pouch of coins: it was still tucked into his tunic pocket.

All around him, the drinking, the gambling, the boasting continued unabated and he took another deep swig of his wine before his eyelids grew heavy again.

This time, he had a vision of the slave Prolitho glaring at him as he embraced Martha, either too upset or too far besides herself to resist. The power of the human touch, thought Rufinus, whatever the propriety ...

It was the hand on his own shoulder that made him wake with a start.

"I'm sorry!" she chuckled. "I thought I'd wake you before you started snoring!"

She had changed since the afternoon and, judging by the smell of crocus oil, bathed too. She had donned a slender silver necklace, her glossy black hair was tied high in a clasp and gone was the shapeless dress, replaced by a low-cut stole that had the same effect on her chest as a corset, leaving little to the imagination.

"Your cup is empty. Maybe you would like another?"

Rufinus nodded and she whisked away the cup with a smile. He rubbed his face and sucked in a lungful of smoky air to try and wake himself up.

He ran his hands over his money pouch, and looked around him, struck by the unchanging nature of the inn: once people entered, they were in no hurry to leave. The same people were stood or sat exactly where they were when he arrived. The poet with the foppish hair and thin beard was a newcomer. He was sat in deep discussion with an old timer, his wax tablet lying unopened on the table in front of him: Rufinus doubted any more odes would be composed tonight.

The barmaid returned with another cup of heated wine and Rufinus reached for his pocket.

"No," she said, raising her hand, "You have this one free for helping me before. He is such pig of a man."

"Thank you. And say nothing of it. It was no way to treat a lady."

She inclined her head in agreement but didn't move away.

"So … why you so tired?"

Rufinus laughed without mirth. "How long have you got?"

To his surprise, she tucked her long stole under her knees and sat next to him on the low bench. The fresh scent of her hair permeated the stale odour of the saloon.

"Well?"

"Well, firstly, I don't even know your name?"

"Zelika. And yours?"

Rufinus was still aware enough to correct himself. "Tiberius," he said offering his hand. Her skin was not as soft as he expected it would be.

"What? Why are you smiling at me?"

She looked away coyly. "You are very strange man, Tiberius."

"Strange? Why strange?"

"You are, how do you say in your dry language, very 'old fashioned' man, calling me a 'lady' and shaking my hand, when you know what I do here. But you surprised me very much by what you did earlier today. Was very brave."

"'Old fashioned' eh? Well … I certainly feel quite old today."

"Tiberius, what you do for your living?"

Rufinus looked away. "Bits and pieces for the imperial administration. Nothing very exciting."

"I see." She gave him an astute look. "And this why you so sleepy?"

"Not exactly. A long day spent running around out of concern for my friends."

"Oh? Tell me."

167

He weighed her up. She had no great guile about her: feminine charm she possessed in spade-loads, intelligence even, but nothing sinister. He cleared his throat, "Since you ask. What what would you as a woman think in these circumstances?" And with that, he let her have a fluent account of the issues troubling his mind, albeit in an account stripped bare of any sensitive references to political assassination or intrigue and pausing only to drink his wine and clarify certain points for her. Even without the high-level minutiae, it still sounded like a plausible tale of deception and excitement.

When he was finished, Zelika's eyes glittered. "Ahora Mazda! I understand why you so shattered now! But tell me, while you run about Rome for other people, what of your own life at home? Do you have wife and children?"

A look of sadness passed across his face. "My wife died in childbirth, ten years ago; the baby with her."

She covered her mouth with her hands. "I'm so sorry, Tiberius. I should not have asked."

There was a short, sharp whistle from the bar and they both looked round. The unhappy bar keep was looking at her, his hands raised in exasperation.

"I have to work. He is annoyed. I bring you another drink, yes?"

Rufinus nodded after a time. "Why not?"

She bustled away and Rufinus watched her go, feeling a little depressed at the memory of his wife Cornelia. Despite the tendency of time to recast memories in a fond and happier light, and his acknowledgement that his time with her was not always so rosy, he missed her with a dull ache in his heart. He missed her confidence and pragmatism and the warmth of her presence at night.

His attention was drawn to someone he could see looking at him out of the corner of his eye.

The poet.

Their eyes met and they both nodded and looked away self-consciously. But this time Rufinus registered something unexpected. As the poet raised his cup to his lips, his cloak momentarily exposed a large scar across his thick upper arm. The man was, perhaps, not so much of a dandy as his hair suggested.

Not your typical latter-day Catullus …

168

Zelika passed his table bearing a wooden tray of drinks. She deposited a cup of wine in front of him with a wink and then, on her way back to the bar, also dropped a small tablet onto the table. Rufinus paused as he was about to take a sip, frowning at it. He had not expected to be charged for these last two refills.

He put down his cup and unclipped the tablet.

Meet me upstairs after I leave room.

He felt his stomach flutter and he looked up. Her back was turned as she wiped down a table with a rag.

Had she deposited it on the wrong table?

He willed her to turn around but it was as if she was ignoring him. He muttered to himself about behaving like a schoolboy and sat back to enjoy his wine, feeling quite drunk now. He glanced around him: nobody on any other table seemed to be expecting a bill.

An odd turn of events in a day I'd rather forget, he thought.

Rufinus drained his cup and considered leaving, keen to start a new day afresh, content at least that he had done all he could for his old friend. He hoped that Maracanthus had foxed them all and was yet lying low somewhere. No, tomorrow he would return to the office and get his teeth into whatever more workaday tasks awaited him.

As he rose, feeling unsteady on his feet, he saw Zelika glancing at him. She was making for a door from which he had seen food being delivered. He watched her disappear through it and procrastinated for a few moments. On a whim, he followed. There was a door to his left, underneath the rickety staircase, and another further along to his right. He opened the first and his eyes adjusted to the gloom within. It contained nothing but a wooden palette and a wardrobe, so he closed it. The door further along was locked and, as he tugged at the handle, a cook in the kitchens ahead looked at him in between strikes of his cleaver against a chopping board.

"Hey, Grumio!" came a call from the kitchen. "Need a hand!"

The cook frowned at Rufinus and disappeared. The Watch Prefect decided against forcing it and took the stairs, his heart now racing with a childish sense of anticipation.

The dingy landing on this floor presented another three doors, all closed, and at the end the staircase continued above him to another floor. The door facing Rufinus had 'III' scratched onto it. As he was about to open it, he heard the alternate moaning and grunts of a sexual encounter within and so left it alone. He pressed his ear against the door of IV and could just about discern the murmur of conversation. He frowned and moved on to V.

Silence.

He entered. The room was a Spartan affair: there were battered shutters in the middle of the far wall, and pushed against the wall to the right was a bed flanked by tables with large candles burning on them. Zelika was sat facing him on the bed.

She rose when he entered the room and brushed suggestively past him to close the door. Then she was stood in front of him and without a word, she reached behind her and unfastened her stole, letting it slip to the floor.

Rufinus' eyes widened. He had not seen a naked woman for so long, and now here was one offering herself to him. He took in her figure in the candlelight. She was more voluptuous that he had imagined, with generous hips and a soft belly. Her breasts, released from the confines of her tight stole, now looked ponderous and heavy. His eyes settled on a pendant that glinted in the smooth scoop of flesh between them. She caught the look of surprise on his face.

"Is that a Chi-Ro symbol? The gods! You're a Christian, aren't you?"

"Yes, I am. And a proud one. Well?" she curled a lock of hair round her finger. "I saw the way you were looking at me. You can have me if you like. Or are you going to inform on me?"

Giddy with anticipation, he approached her and cupped her chin, kissing her softly on the forehead. When she did not resist, he pressed his lips against hers. She responded with equal vigour and tugged at his clothing. Rufinus guided her back to the bed without taking his lips off her face and neck.

*

When he was spent, he remained on top of her and quickly fell asleep, his arms wrapped around her. She listened, and when his breathing deepened and his body was limp, she slipped with some difficulty from underneath him, taking care not to wake him. Picking up her stole, she dressed in silence, pausing to look at him for a second before closing the door behind her. She glanced left and right before emptying the contents of the leather pouch into the palm of her hand, and smiled as she closed her small fist around the coins.

X

The following morning, there was a scuffle in the forum.

Whilst this was a common enough occurrence, its source was unusual. A brief note mentioning a late addition to the afternoon's contio had been pinned by other agenda notices on the board near the speaker's rostrum, and was causing quite a stir. "Totally unprecendented!" one man had exclaimed, shaking his head. "Revolutionary!"

"What?" asked a passerby wearing a turban. "What is it saying?"

"Think of the power they'd have!"

"Who?"

"About bloody time!" said another, turning to him. "This city's going to the dogs: too many damn foreigners: city's not big enough!"

The Indian frowned at him for a moment whilst the insult registered, then pounced. A few punches were thrown before the more sensible elements of the crowd intervened and separated the hotheads. Whilst the incident was soon forgotten, rumour of the notice spread quickly.

Anna and Poppeia were struggling through the chattering crowds inside Trajan's Market with cloth bundles of food tucked under their arms. Anna had to duck under a wicker birdcage suspended from a gaudy canopy and then sidestep a man bearing a tray of polenta cakes.

"I don't see why we can't just do the shopping somewhere else, 'Tellia," said Poppeia, wrinkling her nose. "And it smells so bad in here."

"Blood sausages! Finest blood sausages!"

"Because you can haggle easier here, that's why. Lots of competition."

"Damson plums! Fresh from Syria! Damson plums are here!"

"Gourds, buckets and candles! A scented candle for a classy lady like you, yes you madam!"

Poppeia tutted as the plum seller's tray poked her in the back and she glared at him.

"Ha! The bucket carriers selling off their stuff already, are they?" said a stallholder across the way. "Vote's not for another nine days!"

"They ought to appoint me as agent. Could shift 'alf their stock in that time!"

"Poppeia!" Anna took her by the hand and cut across the flow of passersby, drawing a number of disapproving tuts. "What did you say?"

The stallholder was now talking to two other men. She tapped him on the shoulder. "What was that?"

They broke off their conversation and looked her up and down. "What was what?"

"What you said about the Watchmen. Why would they want to sell their equipment?"

The stallholder took another bite out of his apple and gave his friends a smirk. "I didn't think that lot were allowed to marry."

"'That lot' aren't. They're too busy doing their jobs," she met each of the leering pairs of eyes in turn.

The stallholder shrugged and turned aside as he spat out some pips. "There's a notice just gone up in the forum. A vote on the Praetorians disbanding The Watch and doing the job theirselves, or somat."

Anna's eyes rounded and she hustled Poppeia away. The food under her arms now felt expensively heavy.

"Do you think daddy will have any job when he gets back from Ostia?"

"I'm sure he will," she replied quietly. "I'm sure everything will be just fine."

At the same time, an imperial litter was skirting the fish market, just north of the forum. The young nobleman inside moved the nosegay for a moment as he watched the animated crowds.

"Stop!" The sedan bearers responded to the hand thrust between the curtains and they set it down. "Jupiter, the stench is unbearable! You, find out why the mob is so excited. Take your tablet and stylus."

"Yes, Your Highness."

Uncolpius, Caracalla's personal attendant, brushed aside the curtains and hurried over to the noticeboard. As he was transcribing it, he saw another slave doing likewise. He was also clad in a shapeless blue tunic, with a wooden tag hanging around his neck that read 'I belong to senator Lentulus Cato.' The slaves nodded and smiled with the same foreboding as they scratched the words into their tablets.

When he returned, Caracalla snatched the tablet from him and absorbed its contents in silence. Uncolpius began to feel uncomfortable. It seemed to him that, especially of late, Caracalla was capable of just two emotions: mild contempt and vitriolic anger. And now it was the latter that threatened to explode. It was common knowledge amongst the gossiping household slaves that he was dealing with his tragic news very badly: some claimed to have overheard him sobbing throughout the night whilst tip-toeing past his door, whilst others recounted with some relish the flights of rage that left priceless crockery and vases smashed to bits throughout the private suites of the palace.

Caracalla rapped the rim of the tablet against his knuckles and glared at Uncolpius.

"You are certain that you have transcribed every word of this … this treason correctly?"

"Yes, Your Highness."

Caracalla pursed his lips. He removed another tablet from Uncolpius' bag and began writing a short note. Then he stopped, flipped the stylus over and smoothed the wax with the flat end, erasing the words, his hands shaking.

He thrust his hand through the curtain and clicked his fingers.

"Back home, now!"

The litter bearers took the strain and set off in rare haste back to the palace.

*

Caracalla bounded out of the litter before it had even been set down properly and stalked through the corridors of the palace. The Praetorian Guards posted outside the reception chamber jerked into life as he approached.

"Sorry, Your Highness, your father has …!"

He strode past them and they dared not lay a hand on him. He shoved the double doors to the opulent state room and they clattered back against the walls, startling his father and the delegation within. The room became very still.

"I hope," said the Emperor gravely, "that the reason for such a disgraceful entry is nothing less than a matter of life and death."

"Young highness," muttered his guest.

Caracalla ignored him. "Father, are you aware of this latest treachery?"

"All I can see is a disrespectful young fool brandishing a tablet."

"On which is written another naked attempt to whisk the throne from underneath you!"

Severus scalded Caracalla with his stare.

"Damn the gods father! Do you not care a fig for this flagrant abuse of power by Plautianus? Any of it?" Tears of frustration now threatened to spill down his cheeks and his lips trembled. "Do you not care at all?"

"We are all aware of the proposal – I am sorry, Critias, for this inexcusable interruption. This is the honourable Procurator of Judaea and these patient men are his legates. They have travelled thousands of miles to be here. He was in the middle of relaying to me events in his province, events which are fomenting unrest and heresy throughout the Levant and beyond. Followers of a long dead Jew, a mere peasant and a sorcerer no less, who it seems are bent on destroying the infrastructure of the entire Roman order. The Procurator tells me of riots and sedition, and of images of the Roman gods being defaced with impunity." Severus' eyes blazed with indignation and he leveled a finger at his son. "You, on the other hand, entirely lacking in any courtesy or intelligence, it seems, burst in and presume to interrupt us with your trivial notions about the night watchmen. So, you tell me, where should my concerns lie?"

Caracalla was stunned into silence. He looked from one impassive face to the other, finding no trace of sympathy in any of them. Crushed by embarrassment, he span on his heels and raced back through the doors.

The two Praetorians watched him dash away, tears streaming down his crimson cheeks, in total astonishment. They exchanged worried looks: he would not be the only one who would be feeling the wrath of the Emperor before the day was out.

XI

The Deputy Watch Prefect Balbus knocked at the door to Rufinus' office, his chubby face furrowed with concern. He flinched when he entered and saw Rufinus with his face over a bowl of hot water and a towel draped over his head.

"Great Jupiter! Are you alright Junius?"

Rufinus raised his hand.

"I assume you've heard news of today's contio? I'd scarcely believe it had I not seen it myself."

"Eh?"

"You've not heard, have you?"

Rufinus whipped the towel away. His eyes were bloodshot and there were dark rings underneath them. "Prefect, you look awful!"

"I feel it. What are you on about, Balbus?"

He took a deep breath. "There's to be a motion that control of The Watch is to be taken over by the Praetorian Guard. With immediate effect."

Rufinus frowned. "What rubbish. Where did you get that from?"

"It's on the agenda for this afternoon, Junius: it's been published in the forum."

It took a long moment for the information to penetrate Rufinus' wine-fuddled mind but when it did, there was a cruel inevitability about it. He sank back in his chair and rubbed his sweat-beaded face.

"It's just one damn thing after another, isn't it?"

"Is it? You don't seem so shocked, Junius. It's a thunderbolt out of the blue to me! What are we to do about it?"

"There's nothing we can do, is there?" he snapped. "If they want it badly enough, the Praetorians can damn well have what they want, can't they?"

His expression softened when he saw the look on Balbus's face. "Look, I'll explain later but take my word for it that there's more to this than meets the eye, though I don't know what exactly. You're going to have to preside over the hearings this morning, alright?"

Balbus blanched, as he always did at the prospect of hard work.

"Suck it in, man. You've been doing it long enough." Rufinus stood, and his limbs felt very heavy. "I'm going to clear my head at the baths and then make a few visits. And if I'm not here by this evening, you'd better prepare a search party."

And he wasn't joking.

*

It was approaching midday as Rufinus entered the gates to the Watch House of Cohort IV, for the first time in more than a year, to the best of his recollection. His extended trip to the baths had served two purposes: to purge himself of the strong wine (and acute embarrassment in being fleeced by Zelika) and also to allow more time for Ambrosius to have returned to Rome.

But even as he approached the main entrance, his grave sense of misgiving returned. A vigil he had never seen before, with a muscular physique and long hair, was on his way out.

"Good morning, where's your tribune?"

The watchman gave him a blank look. "Eh?"

"Your tribune, where is he?"

"Don't have one today," he said with a shrug, "Titus is in charge."

"And you are?"

The watchman looked him up and down. "Who's asking?"

"I'm Junius Rufinus, Prefect of The Watch, damn your insolence!"

The smirk fell away. "Sorry, sir! Titus is just inside, room on the right. Sorry, I just didn't recognize ..."

Rufinus brushed past him and entered. His first impression had been of the age of the building, of how low the red ceilings were and how the plasterwork curled and crumbled in places. It had not improved any.

The door to the right was open and inside a cramped study were two tired-looking watchmen whose faces were familiar to him. Both were heavily set, though the physique of the one with bulging eyes and Eastern features was more influenced by food than exercise. They broke off their conversation and looked at him in surprise for a moment, then jumped to their feet.

"Prefect!"

"You are Titus?"

"Yes sir. And this is Bulla."

"And your tribune, where is he?"

"Our replacement Fronto, d'you mean sir? He was recalled yesterday to deal with some problems in his own region. I'm looking after things for now."

176

Rufinus' heart sank. "Alright, I'll have a staff officer sent over to help. At ease, sit down both of you."

Bulla and Titus exchanged looks whilst Rufinus perched on the desk.

"Right, I'll get straight to the point. I need to know when you last saw or heard from Ambrosius Milo."

Titus blew the air out of his cheeks. "That must have been … when did we deal with those two robbers, Bulla? Ah, it was the evening of Matronalia." Bulla nodded in agreement.

Rufinus' pessimistic thoughts were interrupted by colourful swearing from down the corridor. Ludo's handsome face appeared at the door. "What's going on in here then, old hags' meeting?" He flinched at the sight of Rufinus. "Prefect! Wasn't expecting to see you here!"

"Yes, alright. Come in and shut the door would you? I was asking these men when they had last seen Ambrosius. It was five days ago. Have you seen or heard from him more recently than this?"

"No, sir. Afraid not. Is this about the damned contio today? Are you here to appoint a temporary replacement?"

"Oi! You back down!" growled Titus, "Worry about your own damn century!"

Rufinus gave a weary sigh. "No I'm not here to formally appoint a replacement. Quite the opposite."

"Oh," said Ludo sheepishly. "Is the tribune in some kind of trouble?"

"Sit down, please: it's exhausting me just looking at you!"

Ludo dropped onto the last vacant chair.

"Ready, centurion? Right, what I have to say is as important as it is secretive. I cannot emphasise enough the dangers of anything I say in this room getting out." He dropped his voice and looked at each of them in turn. "Is that clear?"

They all nodded.

"Good. I assume, centurion, that your blue language out there concerns the future of The Watch, correct? Fine. For the benefit of Bulla and Titus, there is to be a debate in the forum later this afternoon about the Praetorian Guard assuming all responsibility for The Watch with immediate effect. I happen to – please," he said, raising his hand, "let me finish because I'm extremely pressed for time. I happen to know that the senator proposing the motion is Rabirius Felix. He is one of the consul's lap dogs and it therefore follows that this has already been discussed and agreed in principle in a recent session of the senate. And regardless of what the plebs really thinks that motion will go before a full assembly and it will pass, either through bribery or trickery or both. That, alone, would be depressing enough news but I am now convinced of a deeper motive and an even greater danger."

Rufinus described everything he knew from opening the letter from Maracanthus to his first conversation with Martha and both meetings with the informer Trystan. He explained that the letter he had dispatched to Ostia had been partially coded in great haste but in the most simple of keys, which Ambrosius would have had little difficulty in identifying. In that letter, Rufinus said, he had stated that the tribune should leave Ostia 'without any further delay for his own and his daughter's safety' and 'leave word of his safe arrival at my office, irrespective of the hour.' It took him several minutes to relay everything, though he had reduced them to a shocked silence within seconds.

"I mentioned the safety of Ambrosius' daughter," he added, "only to increase his motivation to leave Ostia at once. There is no specific threat against her. But knowing the man as I do, he would have been beside himself with worry and would have gladly run the twenty odd miles home. It concerns me very much that there has been no word."

The watchmen absorbed his words in grim silence.

"What of the stable owner, sir? Did the boy return? We don't even know for sure your message was delivered."

"I thought of that. I went there this morning before I came here, but there was no sign of either of them. I take your point, though I don't think we can afford to wait on him."

"What about Anna or his girl: has anybody spoken to them? He worries about them. Maybe he's just not got round to you yet, Prefect."

"You're right, Bulla, that is a possibility, albeit a slim one. I didn't want to scare them unnecessarily but … well, we all know what Ambrosius is like. He would want to know exactly why he had been recalled and what the threat was. There's no way he'd let it lie."

Ludo clicked his fingers excitably. "Damn it, I almost forgot! On the morning before he left, Ambrosius came charging in here with his daughter. They raced downstairs to the cellar and he showed her where the senator's daughter had been embalmed. He said - what's her name - Poppeia had told him how she thought the body might've gone missing and he wanted to see for himself. So off we go even deeper underground and Vitalis the gaoler located for us a rusty old inspection cover. It didn't seem feasible at first, or afterwards, if I'm honest, but sure enough it lead straight to the sewers. The opening is very small but a child might be able to fit through, and that's where he reckoned the body had been spirited away."

Bulla and Titus looked at each other in surprise. "Why didn't you tell us about this?"

"Dunno, really," he said with a shrug, "must have slipped my mind."

"Well that's very interesting, centurion, but what's your point?"

"The point he made, sir, was that only someone with an intimate knowledge of the ancient sewer network would have been able to work out how to plan such a raid. That sort of knowledge would either have died with the original builders or been stored in the Tabularium, the Records Office."

Bulla looked from one person to another. "So what is the problem? Are we all stupid or something? We just go to the Records Office, no? Find out for ourselves!"

"Actually … yeah," said Ludo, scratching his head, "I didn't really think to ask him that. It's a public building, isn't it?"

A wry smile crossed Rufinus' lips and he shook his head sadly. "It was a public building. But since the imperial mint was connected to it, general access was shut down immediately. All that money … too much of a risk, they said."

"Even for you?" asked Bulla.

"Even for me."

A depressing sense of helplessness flooded the room.

"I didn't know that about the mint," said Ludo glumly. "So who can get in?"

"I don't really know … the Emperor; select senators; the Praetorian Prefect; the City Prefect, I imagine. One or two others, perhaps."

More silence. From the courtyard, there came the faint hum of conversation and laughter.

"Damn Praetorian dogs!" shouted Bulla, slapping his knee and jumping up. "Why can't you just go straight to the Emperor, sir, and let him know what sort of the snake works for him?"

Rufinus beckoned him to sit down. "Already considered and rejected, Bulla. Circumstantial evidence at very best. Where's the hard proof? I'd have nothing to show him other than a letter I could have written myself and the words of an informer, who would be an unknown quantity to the

Emperor, even if I could find him again and get him to testify with my own life intact. Besides, these aren't just commoners that I'd be accusing: they're his trusted bodyguard, hand-picked, I don't doubt. I'd be thrown in the Tullian myself!"

Bulla tutted and threw up his hands in frustration. After a few moments there was more laughter from the courtyard. "I take it the men are unaware of the contio?"

Ludo shook his head. "Only just found out myself, sir. Hadn't got round to telling them yet."

"Well then … I'll leave you men be. As I say, this discussion stays in this room, for now at least. I'm going to head back to the stables and see if there's been any word. Keep me informed if anything occurs. Gentlemen." He rose and headed towards the door.

"There is one possibility," said Titus, who had been pensive throughout.

"Go on."

"It's a bit risky, because it would alert them about what you've just been discussing …"

"Let us hear it then, Socrates!" said Bulla impatiently. "Don't keep us all waiting!"

Titus took a deep breath. "When that Deputy Prefect, Brutus, came stomping in here, demanding to take away what we'd found by the docks, he repeated an offer I've never really forgotten …"

"That fight?" snorted Bulla. "Forget about it! You're wife kill you before he did!"

"That'll do," he muttered. "I think I'll tell him he can have his fight, but only on condition that he can prove Ambrosius' safety."

"I've plainly missed something here," said Rufinus, "and that all sounds very noble, Titus. But it also sounds flawed in quite a big way. I don't really know Brutus but he seems very tight with the Praetorian Prefect, as you'd expect being his deputy. Supposing Plautianus is up to something, it'd be reasonable to assume Brutus would be knee deep in it as well, wouldn't it? He was the one who dispatched him to these barracks, wasn't he?"

"I think so too, and that's why it seems like a good plan. Whatever his answer, it shows what their position is because it puts him on the spot, doesn't it?"

Bulla made a face. "How?"

"Like this: if he can bring Ambrosius back to Rome, he gets his match and we get our friend back in one piece. And it also says that Brutus isn't involved, because there's no way he'd risk angering Plautianus by messing up his plans just for a boxing match. But if he says no, he can't, then I'd ask him why and he'd probably begin to squirm because he'd be going back on his boasts that he could beat me, which would be a massive loss of honour for him. I think that would prove that he and the rest of the Praetorians are all plotting something."

"And what then? So we'd have more circumstantial proof, still no Ambrosius, and we'd also have the Praetorians on our tails for sniffing about in their business."

"We're hardly in a garden of roses now though, are we sir?" observed a glum Ludo. "If we do nothing, The Watch will cease to exist anyway. Ambrosius with it!"

"Yeah, and he will cease to exist if Ambrosius is brought back here!" Bulla thumbed towards Titus. "Say he does agree to the match, he'd want to destroy you, my friend. Or he take the fight, beat you up and then claim, after all, he don't know where Ambrosius was. What do you think about that? When was last the time you trained hard? When was last the time you even …?"

"Pack it in will you? I'd make sure he allowed some time for training: that'd be part of the bargain. He couldn't fail to agree to that."

"I see your thinking, Titus, but it seems like an unnecessary risk to me," said Ludo, shaking his head. "I'm not a bad horseman: I could ride hard and get word to him, no bother."

"I like your spirit but I'll not allow it."

"Why not, sir?"

Rufinus couldn't help but smile at Ludo's wounded look. "Because recently people have a sinister tendency to go missing and never reappear. I don't doubt your skills on horseback but, no offence, I doubt there are many cavalry officers in the Roman army that could handle a stallion better than the young stable hand I paid, yet he's not returned either. I pray to the gods he is unharmed but I have a very bad feeling that he's been intercepted by the same powers that removed Senator Maracanthus from sight, and quite probably Senator Piso's daughter, and which also threaten one of our own. So, no," he said with a shake of the head, "I'll not just go on sending men blind into such danger. I've paid a heavy enough price as it is."

Rufinus turned to Titus. "I don't see any better options than your brave suggestion, Titus, though I leave the final decision to you. If there's any man likely to be able to ensure the tribune's safe return, it'd be the Deputy Praetorian Prefect, though there's no way I'd ever make anyone feel guilty about deciding not to go toe to toe with that brute. I know nothing of boxing, but by the looks of him he knows his business very well. I'll not be back at headquarters for another couple of hours. I suggest you don't rush your decision in the meantime. And who knows?" he said as he was on his way out, "Perhaps Ambrosius will have returned by then and this will all be by the by. Good day gentlemen."

The three watchmen stood and then slumped back down when he had left.

Bulla screwed up his face. "Were you being serious?"

"Deadly."

Bulla laughed bitterly. "Then you'd better no to tell Lucia. And now might be the time to get down on your hands and knees and pray like hell to the gods that you knock him over quickly, because I think you will have your contest. Our tribune is not fool: I bet my good looks he still lives!"

XII

It was the tenth hour of the day by the time Rufinus trudged back into headquarters and closed the door behind him. Though the daylight was fading, he didn't bother lighting any oil lamps, preferring to brood in the twilight of his office. It seemed that the more time and effort he invested in trying to bottom out his problems, the less progress he made. Moreover, Plautianus' offer of promotion within the Praetorian Guard – an offer he was once so delighted to receive – was looking more like a poisoned chalice by the hour. On which note, he was also developing a worrying appetite for the grog that the Gorgona served, though there was no way he wanted to return there tonight and he buried his head in his hands when he remembered the pretty sum of money that Zelika had stolen from him.

There was a knock on his door and, before he could answer, Balbus poked his head round it and threw question after excitable question at the Prefect about the afternoon's contio which, he pointedly remarked, he had been unable to attend due to the workload he had. Balbus remained oblivious to Rufinus' defeated look and curt replies until his enthusiasm gradually faded and he took the hint, leaving him alone once more.

It was not long, however, before there was another knock. Rufinus considered ignoring it before it was repeated and he invited he caller to enter.

A bulky shape filled the doorway.

"No sign, Titus?"

"None. What about the stables: anybody there?"

"No. The place was boarded up."

They were both silent as the inevitability of the situation settled upon them.

"I'm going to speak to Brutus then," said Titus quietly.

"You're quite sure? You don't have to, you know."

He chuckled. "Perhaps I've been looking for a good enough excuse all along. There's none better than this. What happened at the contio?"

Rufinus leant back in his chair. "There were a few heated protests in the crowd about the overbearing power of the Praetorians, and I did hear someone praise what you and your men did at the Aventine the other night but … all in all it was a pretty muted affair. It looks like the good people of

Rome have short memories and empty pockets. I saw some of the senator's flunkies mingling in the crowds, dropping a few sesterces and the odd reassuring word here and there, and that was that; straight onto the next item. The assembly meets in nine days and there'll be a formal vote then."

"And that will be that …"

"So it seems."

From the hall outside came the shout of a slave calling the hour of the watch as he went about lighting the lamps.

"Mind if I ask you what came of the fire in the Aventine, sir? It was definitely started on purpose; a fire inside, the door barricaded from the outside … And word is that the other big one on the Pincian was started with naphtha."

"I made all that known to the City Prefect, Titus. It's in his hands now but he's already got a lot to deal with." Even in the gloaming, Rufinus could see the look of disappointment on the centurion's face. "There have, of course, been other fires between those two. Smaller, perhaps, yet you mention those specifically."

Titus froze.

"Rumour has it the buildings on the Pincian and Aventine contained devotees of the cross." Rufinus gave him a shrewd look. "Have you heard anything similar?"

Titus' mouth moved but no words emerged.

"Titus, I have spent some time in The Levant and I know something of this religion. You have nothing to fear from me but …" he raised his hand to pre-empt the interruption, "but the Emperor and his son see it as a grave threat to the Roman Order. They do not tolerate threats lightly and they are answerable only to the gods: their gods. Be careful and trust no-one, am I clear?"

The centurion was about to object but sagged in the face of Rufinus' intense stare. "Very clear, Prefect."

There were a few moments of silent understanding before Titus patted the doorframe. "Well, I'll be on my way."

Rufinus got up and walked round his desk to shake his hand. It felt like a slab of warm granite. "Fortuna smile on your bravery. And, if the fight comes to pass, what is it the drill instructors say? Stick and move?"

"Yes, that's it," Titus smiled. "I'll make sure you get word of what happens, sir. Best if I'm not seen moving to and fro here."

"Yes, probably best."

With that, Titus left and Rufinus watched his bulky shape stride into the shadows across the hall, struck by the notion that he would be just one more person to disappear without a trace.

XIII

Dusk had settled over the city by the time Titus approached the imposing gates of the Castra Praetoria.

"State your name and your business!" shouted the sentry atop the walls.

Titus looked up. Two burly looking fellows in crestless helmets marking them out as soldiers of some Urban Cohort or other were staring at him.

"My name is Titus, centurion of the Fourth Cohort of The Watch. I need to speak to the Deputy Prefect, in private, immediately."

"Concerning?"

No business of yours was what he wanted to say. "Mark my words, he'll know! I'm only armed with a sheath knife," he announced, removing the leather scabbard and tossing it onto the floor, "for my own protection around the city."

"Stand by." Titus caught the note of disappointment in the sentry's voice: he assumed the man took great pleasure in dismissing people summarily.

The gates grated into motion and two soldiers approached him, weighing up the threat such a solidly built stranger posed.

"Raise your arms, watchman," said one of them, backheeling the knife away from Titus' reach.

Titus did as he was asked, letting the disrespectful term of address pass: he was not on his own territory now. The second Urbanus searched him and then nodded at his colleague.

"Right, follow us. I can't guarantee you any of his time, mind. He's very busy."

"I'll take my chances."

The gates closed behind them and the soldiers walked abreast of Titus along the avenue that led to the centre of the camp. Though he had never been inside before, he knew what the layout would be: the Praetorian base was planned like every other fortified camp he had experienced whilst in the army. And, like in other camps, the bearing of the soldiers inside changed whenever there was a stranger in their midst. Backs straighter, chests out, more swagger … it just wouldn't do to look sloppy in front of civilians.

He glanced in envy at the exercise ground as they passed by. Though formal duties were over for the day, a few die-hard fanatics were still working up a sweat with sprint-jogs and weight training. He knew the type well: he had been one himself. And if events were to turn out that way, he would need access to just such facilities.

The Urbani approached the Principia, a squat, Spartan building in the middle of the central avenue with two pennants above the entrance, decorated with red scorpions, pincers up and barbed tails ready to strike. Titus' heart began to pound and he silently cursed his stupidity. The whole plan depended on getting an audience with Brutus and Brutus alone and yet, here he was, approaching the headquarters he shared with the Prefect himself. Chances were, they'd be having a meeting in the same damn room. There was no way someone as experienced as Plautianus would see a watchman striding towards his headquarters, asking for an audience with his second-in-command, and not think anything of it. He glanced over his shoulder. There was no way out of this now: he was committed.

They halted in front of the Principia.

"Wait here please."

One of the Urbani stepped inside and, after a few minutes, there came the low murmur of conversation. He looked about him at the familiar sights of a camp and caught the unmistakable whiff of grilled meat from a nearby cookhouse. He began to hum an old marching ditty that came back to him, trying to ignore the churning of his stomach. His escort ignored him, staring straight ahead.

"How many years in you got?" asked Titus.

No reply.

"Me, I did my sixteen. Boy soldier, lied about my age."

Titus caught the soldier giving him a sidelong glance. He knew when his size intimidated someone, even an armed soldier. Silence was merely one natural response.

The second Urbanus emerged from the headquarters and beckoned Titus inside, inviting him to sit in an ante-room outside a central chamber which, by the looks of the decorative cuirass outside, belonged to the Praetorian Prefect himself. Not a good sign.

Titus was brought a cup of water. "He's busy at the moment. Wait here and he'll send someone for you."

The soldiers left him alone in the dim reception room, though he guessed they would be stood outside in case Titus had other ideas. As the minutes stretched away, Titus tried to rehearse the likely scenarios in his mind: what had seemed like a clever plan back at the Watch House now looked feeble. Who was to say that Brutus himself hadn't realized what Titus' unexpected visit would herald and that he wasn't formulating plans behind the closed door, with or without Plautianus? And he knew he would have to be on his guard for any trickery. Brutus was likely to be a very persuasive and convincing customer even if he knew that Ambrosius had been eliminated. He would take nothing less than a cast-iron guarantee if the bout was to go ahead.

His thoughts were interrupted by voices approaching the door. The first to appear was a Praetorian whom he didn't recognize; Brutus followed him, his bulky shoulders blocking the light from within. Both men were laughing at some shared joke.

"The gods bless you, commander. And the Greens!"

More laughter and then the Praetorian walked past Titus without looking at him. Brutus remained in the doorway with his hands on his hips. His broad grin reminded Titus of a jackal's.

"Well, well, I'd not have believed it had I not seen it with my own eyes! Come to apply to join us have we, watchman?"

"No. Just for a word in private, Deputy Prefect."

"Acting Prefect, for now. But of course. Where have my manners gone?"

Titus entered his quarters. Other than the cedarwood shrine to his left and the Zebra skin rug in the centre of the room, there were no concessions to comfort at all.

"Take a seat, watchman."

Brutus showed him to a chair and sat on the other side of an oak table, cluttered with parchments and writing implements. Titus noticed the rawhide hand wraps hanging from a hook on the wall to the right. Brutus caught him looking at them and his eyes lit up.

"Aha!" he said, wagging his finger at him. "I understand now! Wine?"

Titus shook his head. "I have a proposition you might like to hear."

"Go on," said Brutus, leaning back and locking his hands behind his head, making the muscles on his arms stretch his tunic sleeves.

"I might agree to a match-up if certain conditions can be met and guaranteed."

He gave a mocking laugh. "Such as?"

"We're concerned about the safety of our tribune, Ambrosius. You've met him …"

Brutus grunted.

"Our Prefect, Junius Rufinus, sent him to Ostia, but we think he may be in great danger and we need to get him away and back to his family. We think you might be able to help."

"We? Who's 'we' exactly?"

"Me, his family, his friends."

Brutus frowned at him. "So why don't you just send your watchmen friends to go and get him?"

Titus sensed the moment had arrived. He scrutinized his face for any trace of subterfuge but found none.

"Well, why come all the way here to bother me? What's your game eh, watchman?"

"Because, Dep … Acting Prefect, I'm convinced his own colleagues are the source of the threat. I don't know who amongst them I can trust."

Brutus was staring at him and Titus felt ice tricking down his spine: it was as though the man was reading his thoughts. Then the Praetorian's face cracked into a wide grin and he chuckled. "Oh dear, oh dear! Is he back on the sauce again? Racking up some bad debts, is he? Come on, he's a big boy now, why don't you just let him learn his lesson and take a good spanking like a man?"

"A soldier's loyalty may not mean much to you but not everyone is the same."

The grin on Brutus' face faded and Titus thought he may have overstepped the mark. "Look, if you don't think you can help then, fine, I'll think of something else. I'm only here because you said I should name my price. This is it."

Brutus held his gaze. There could be no mistaking what the man's sport was. His ears were swollen and his nose was flat and bent. Titus also noticed faint streaks of scar tissue and calcification above his eyebrows. Champion though he was, he had clearly shipped plenty of telling blows in his time.

"Now now, watchman. No need to be so testy. What exactly do you want for your price?"

"We want him back in Rome, if he still lives. Immediately. And I'd need time to train: I'm out of shape."

Brutus passed his eyes over Titus' physique but his expression didn't change.

"And that's it?"

"That's it."

Brutus stroked his beard. "And what does your Watch Prefect think of all this?"

"He knows I'm here. If anything, he regrets having sent him in the first place."

"So why did he not come here himself and ask me?"

Titus shrugged. "He has nothing to offer, I suppose."

Brutus harrumphed and rose from his desk. He ambled over to the toughened leather wraps and ran his finger down them. "The decision to exile him to Ostia for a while wasn't only Rufinus', you know." He turned to Titus. "Gaius Plautianus himself had a hand in that. In fact, he thought he was getting off lightly. Senator Piso was putting pressure on him for the death penalty, did you know that?"

Titus raised his eyebrows.

"No, I thought not," he said with a satisfied sneer. "Fortunately for your friend, the Prefect moderated Piso's anger and reached a compromise. Quite why he'd want to do that I don't know: your tribune's life means nothing to him either way. Let it not be said Gaius Plautianus is not a reasonable man! So," he said, returning to his seat, "if I was to agree to send some of my men to go and … and chaperone your man away, I'd be putting my own position at considerable risk. If the debt collectors and pimps hadn't got to him first, that is."

Titus sensed the faintest trace of apprehension in Brutus' manner. He had failed to consider the nature of the relationship between the Prefect and his deputy and now it posed a potential obstacle to his plans.

"You're very fortunate," he continued, "that Gaius isn't here now, come to think of it. I imagine he'd know what you wanted the second he laid eyes on you."

"Oh? And where is he?"

"He's taken leave."

"Hence your temporary promotion."

"Yes, hence my temporary promotion."

"So where's he gone?"

"Back to his estates in Libya I suppose," he answered crisply, "Why does that matter to you?"

"Because he needn't know Ambrosius would be back, if he was out of the country."

"Oh, he's no fool, watchman. He'd know soon enough, and in any event he'll be back for the vote on the future of The Watch." The sneer was back.

"And I dare say you'll be amongst the first in the queue to cast your token."

Titus ignored the taunt. "So then, what do you say to my offer?"

Brutus' dark eyes were fixing him again, reading his thoughts. "I say I'm interested, in principle. But you'd have to hear some of my conditions first."

"Which are?"

"If Ambrosius was found and returned, he would have to keep a low profile. There could be no guarantee he would be able to stay in Rome, but at least you would have your assurance he was safe. Also, if there was to be a match-up, it would have to be before the Prefect returned."

"What?" Titus was incredulous. "That would leave me with a week to prepare. Impossible!"

"Running the Praetorian Guard is not something you do half-heartedly. If Gaius was to return and see that things had been neglected whilst I was training for a boxing match-up, I'd not be able to explain it away easily. As I said, I'd be risking my own position in more ways than one."

Titus looked at the floor. "I've not fought in years. I'd need weeks – months – to come up to scratch."

"Those are my terms," said Brutus, leaning back in his chair. "You came to me, remember. What are you afraid of? Your wife?"

"Don't push me, Brutus. Or you'll have your match-up sooner than you anticipated."

Brutus threw back his head and laughed. "There you go, you see! That's the spirit that earned you sixty-one victories and no losses!"

"How did you know that?"

"Oh I've paid more interest in your career than you think, watchman! Your reputation in the barracks and drinking dives of the empire precedes you. And whenever I floored whichever gallant fool bragged his way into fighting me, I could never sit back and enjoy the moment. There'd always be someone whispering in my ear that I could never be called truly great until I'd cut you down to size!" Brutus paused to enjoy the look of surprise on Titus' face. "If I was to put you on the sand, I'd take your tally and have a century's worth of victories myself, more or less. That would be unprecedented. Maybe then those damned whispers would stop!"

"With only a week to prepare, you'd be taking the tally of a has-been. That's what they'd be saying."

But Brutus' smile did not waver. "I don't think so, watchman, nor do you. The reputations of some champions are immune to such technicalities. Was the great Milo of Croton ever called a pushover just because of his age?" He wagged his finger at Titus over the desk. "And don't you be getting any ideas about taking an easy kneel, either. That just wouldn't wash with me!"

Despite himself, Titus felt the old rush of blood. At that moment, he wanted nothing more than to wipe the conceited grin off Brutus' face and he caught himself picturing the man's weaknesses as he came up to the mark.

"Fine, I'll do it." The words were out of his mouth before he could prevent them. "If we fight Sardinian rules: two pauses apiece. I'll need a breather."

Brutus considered the amendment for a moment. "You drive a hard bargain, watchman. Thirty seconds, no more." He leaned over to shake hands on the deal. Titus extended his hand then withdrew it. "And Ambrosius back safe in Rome?"

Brutus rolled his eyes. "Done, damn you!"

Then they shook.

"Saturn Day, seven days from now. Fifth hour here in the palaestra," stated Brutus, rising from his seat. "Follow me, watchman."

They left Brutus' quarters. Dark had fallen and the camp was now illuminated by torches affixed to wooden stakes. Outside the main entrance, the two Urbani had been replaced by a tall, bearded Praetorian.

"Gabinius, fetch me an officer from the stables and have a half squadron prepare their mounts. And be quick about it."

The Praetorian saluted and loped off round the corner. "You see, I'm a man of my word," he said, turning to Titus. "Begin your training tomorrow. And if your friend lives, you'll know about it soon enough."

Titus nodded and walked away, his head awash with misgivings.

"And watchman? Aren't you forgetting something?"

He turned back, frowning. Did the braggart expect him to salute as well?

Brutus retrieved the sheath knife from a pocket of his tunic and tossed it to the ground in front of him.

"Very pretty. But, I ask myself, would a young Titus have needed it?" With that, Brutus disappeared back inside his quarters, whistling a lighthearted victory ditty.

XIV

Ambrosius lay on his back, listening to the wind howling through the narrow streets outside. One of the watchmen had failed to secure a shutter to the dormitory rooms below and, to his growing annoyance, throughout the last half hour it had been clattering against the wall.

He tutted and turned onto his side, covering his head with the pillow. Lately it seemed that everything had been conspiring to deprive him of sleep and he wondered whether Longinus had a point when he told him that the tribune's fractious temper had been causing such discontent. Maybe excessive drinking and lack of sleep had been making him unusually tetchy after all.

Bang!

"Dormant bastards!" he growled under the pillow.

For the past two nights, moreover, the encounter with the mysterious smugglers, if such they were, had been troubling him more than he cared admit. Several times he had felt close to identifying an explanation for what he and Longinus had seen, something blindingly obvious, but then the answer evaporated before his very eyes. One thing, however, was clear to him: Longinus, affable enough though he was, was either a man of limited intellect or willfully oblivious to anything that might compromise popularity with his men. He was now happy, on reflection, that the mercenaries were indeed engaged in covert river operations, and that was that.

Bang! Bang!

Ambrosius flung off his blanket and stalked over to his shutters, opening them wide. His face was lashed with the invisible spray carried on the bracing wind, and the shock of it made him take a breath.

No doubts the wily bastards out there will be huddled round a brazier somewhere supping warm wine with anything but patrolling the streets in mind.

In the pale glow from the light tower in the distant harbour at Portus he could see dark clouds scudding across the sea. Directly below him at street level, the shutter was flapping in the eddying wind.

Why in Hades didn't the dozy so-and-so's just shut the damn thing?

193

He contemplated going outside with a hammer and blasting a nail through the wood into the wall, amused by the prospect of rudely awakening the other watchmen in the process.

Bang!

The noise made him jump, but then a furtive movement in the street to his right caught his eye.

A scavenging dog or fox?

But it had appeared too large as it flitted past his peripheral vision …

He leaned further out of the window, wrapping his night clothes tighter about his body, and peered into the darkness below. His vision of the pavement adjacent to the wall of the building was impaired by a ridge of brickwork that separated the floors, and it was in any event so poorly lit down there that he could see nothing. Minutes passed and he strained his ears but soon gave up in the face of the mournful howl of the wind and the clatter of the loose shutter. He leaned back inside and, with difficulty, managed to latch his own back into place before he returned to the bed, more awake than before. He located a rag in one of the dresser tables and tore small strips off, rolling them in his fingers to form makeshift ear bungs.

But it wasn't enough. Though the noise of the wind and the shutters was muffled, his mind was too alert. Tossing and turning in frustration, he helped himself to a few good drafts of the wine in the earthenware jug by his bedside. There was nothing quite like the warming effect of an undiluted red on his spirits and he soon began to feel less tense.

He wondered what Poppeia and Anna had been doing that day, and memories of Larissa soon drifted into his mind, frustratingly indistinct. From nowhere, he had a vague recollection of a lesson he had been taught long ago, about why it was so important for every generation of reluctant schoolboy to keep the stories of great heroes like Achilles and Hector alive, otherwise their glory might one day be forgotten altogether. Was it possible that one day he would be unable to recall how Larissa looked? Or the inflections of her voice? Or her long hair that was so black it had a blue lustre when the sun struck it? He felt a dull ache deep within. She had drawn her last breath fifty nine months ago: another heaven and another earth must pass before her like would ever exist again; and another man.

He felt his eyes stinging and took another long swig from the jug.

Nearly forty years old and all alone.

He recalled when he had last lain with a woman. It had been months ago and, though she had been keen to see him again, he didn't share her enthusiasm.

He tried to think of something else and began to doze. Troubling visions swirled in his head: the senator's daughter, looking waxy and serene on the cold crypt slab …

You broke the dead girl's fingers …

Desecrating her body …

The orders are from higher than that …

*

Crouched in the street below, the assassin raised his cowled head and reflected on his current position. Whilst it had not been his intention to wake anybody on his reconnoitre, his mistake had worked out well. Whilst waiting in line for an audience with the tribune a few days back, he had been able to get a good feel for the layout of the place and had decided that the larger rooms beyond the courtyard had belonged to the officers, where his lucrative target would be. Since then, his contract had been confirmed (verbally, as always) and the evening's storm had provided him with a perfect opportunity to clarify the tribune's whereabouts with minimal risk of being caught: the streets were deserted.

He had just now managed to get a handhold of the window ledge and raise the ground floor shutter's inner latch with a slender iron rod, and the howling of the wind had disguised any noise he may have made. So far so good. But then, in trying to haul himself up to peer into the room, a sudden gust of wind had snatched the shutter from his free hand and it had slammed hard into the wall, making a fearful noise. He had dropped from the ledge and melted back into the shadows, though initially no-one had poked their head out to investigate the noise. After long minutes, he was confident that nobody had been woken and emerged to complete his task, just as the shutters to the floor above were thrown open and there, as Fortuna would have it, was the target himself, his profile framed by the weak light from the harbour tower. He had darted back into the shadows and for a few uncomfortable moments thought he may have been seen, but he could tell by the delay in the shutters being re-closed that he was safe.

So then, a direct in-out entry and attack, like a burglar, was now tricky given the position of his room, a setback, since once the target was dead in his own room, an assassin was free to search it at leisure to remove acceptable evidence of the completed job. Which left the question of how to progress the contract? He closed his eyes and recalled the interior of the barracks again, running his thumbnail along the line of his thin beard in contemplation. Although he found his mind was at its sharpest in the cold, this storm was a little too bracing for his liking. He recalled the steady stream of jobs he had in the sweltering hills of Greece and Asia Minor when he was still a young frumentarius, a spy attached to a legion but notionally in charge of prospecting corn supplies. Tracking down Christian agitators had been his bread and water, and word of his successes – some of them touched by genius - eventually found its way to the ears of the commander of the Pannonian forces, now the Praetorian Prefect. A little reminder of those climates wouldn't go amiss now.

And then a plan occurred to him. He backed around the corner of the building and took another look at the front door.

*

Ambrosius was now asleep. In his dreams he was a young watchman again, groping his way blind down the narrow streets of Rome. Forgotten voices tormented him as he struggled to locate the origin of a distant but urgent banging, as if someone was trapped inside a burning house. The noise was so soft at first that it echoed the hammering of his own heart. He stopped and tried to strain all his senses, in vain, and panic set in. But as it grew louder, instinct began to take over, even though the streets were a labyrinth to him.

Bang! Bang!

And another voice. A faint, plaintive cry masked by the hammering.

A woman's voice, repeating the same word.

He stumbled onwards, picking up the pace. He began to thrash on the bed, the sheets twisting and rucking.

A name. His name. Larissa's voice.

Ambrosius! Ambrosius!

A sudden warning so close he could feel the breath of each syllable against his ear.

A shadowy figure was leaning over him.

He bolted upright, eyes rounded, heart pounding.

The room was lit by the dying light of his lamp but he was alone. He pulled the rags from his ear and tumbled out of bed, turning up the wick. He dressed hurriedly and rummaged about in his battered travelling chest for his weapon, an old cavalry sword, a spatha, from Germany that he had picked up from an occasional stallholder in Trajan's market. He held it up in the lamplight. The sword had a bone handle and pommel and was an attractive piece, though it had not come with a scabbard and the blade was a little blunt in places.

He stepped onto the walkway ringing the courtyard and, hearing nothing, hurried downstairs. If the watchmen didn't much like him before, he knew they would hate him now.

*

The assassin backed off across the street, assessing the possible escape routes around him. Provided that he chose his moment well, his new plan looked like a decent option, though it would require diverting a few of the Prefect's men from their own assignment. He permitted himself a smile: on balance their task was considerably more demanding than his own, savage, uncouth brutes that they were. In just a few hours, he would be watching them at work again. His own role was easy: he doubted he'd even need to get his blade wet.

Satisfied with his night's work, he plunged back into the unlit side-streets.

XV

As dawn broke over Ostia, the market trader scratched his head and looked from the bag of silver coins to the backs of the burly figures wheeling two barrows of produce away from his stall. When the group had rounded the corner to the Street of The Round Temple, the tall man with grey eyes bent to a bow-legged stoop.

"The gawds bless you, guv'na! That's more than enough, so it is! You give my best to the chief now. Bring the barrers back when you done!"

The mercenaries burst into laughter.

"Whatcha gigglin' at, ya bog trotting brute? These are the best bleedin' cabbages 'n' turnips in Italy, gawd rest my soul!"

The eldest grunted with laughter and punched his cousin in the arm. "He's talking about you!"

They stopped at an alleyway and – when there was a sufficient gap between passers-by - the one named Primus put two fingers in his mouth and whistled. A few moments later, another two Libyans emerged from it carrying two heavy bundles that clattered with each laboured step.

"Come on now, clear those bleedin' veg from the barrers! Go on, look lively!"

"What's gotten into him?" whispered the youngest, in Berber.

"You just keep your mouth shut and let him do the talking. He's good!"

When the produce was piled back on top, they set off again and a few minutes later rounded the curved walls of the city's theatre. The handcarts rattled over the cobblestones and, as the watchmen's barracks swung into view, Primus gave the men behind him a sharp glance: all joking was over.

"Keep the noise down. Muffle the blades with the veg, yes?"

The men murmured understanding and pulled on their cloth caps, their eyes focused on the building at the end of the street.

XVI

As the mercenaries and the assassin approached the barracks, the mutterings within began afresh.

"They're hardly likely to try it on in fucking daylight, are they? Why can't we just stand down and get some kip?"

"What? You sound like you believe him! He's been drinking again, you dolt: nobody's interested in this armpit of a town! He's lost his marbles, I tell you!"

"And that damn shutter was probably just not shut properly. You were the last to touch it, Gavius, you half-wit!"

Those vigiles who had initially thought themselves lucky to have been out of the night's rotation – all twenty two of them - and who had managed to get some rest had been rudely awakened after midnight by the tribune banging on their door. Half-drunk with sleep, they had stumbled about in the dark making murderous threats under their breath. All of the available lamps and candles had been lit and, in grudgingly slow time, they had stood to attention as the tribune inspected the motley arsenal of mattocks, daggers, cudgels and stool legs.

Ambrosius had stopped in front of a young watchman from Neapolis, the detachment's joker. He was stood with his chest out and chin raised and carried the stray tabby that the men had adopted in the crook of his arm.

"And what the fuck are you playing at?"

"She was the only weapon I could find in the dark, sir. She's got a right nasty streak though!"

Several of the men were unable to repress their sniggers. Ambrosius had cuffed him about the side of his head, making the alarmed cat jump out of the watchman's hands and scurry away.

"Is this child one of yours, Longinus?"

That had wiped the smirks off their faces. Longinus had squirmed at the compromising situation and had mumbled an apology, but his reaction had only sent Ambrosius' opinion of him further south.

The patrols had trudged back inside and, once they were all back, Ambrosius had given them a précis of the situation: there were to be no more patrols that night; an attack, whether en masse or alone, was likely; they should exercise extreme caution; the smugglers he and Longinus had seen had been heavily armed, and so forth. Longinus himself, he noted, was reticent in stepping forwards to verify anything: having lost face with both camps following the earlier exchange, he could only manage a non-committal murmur. The watchmen had been forced to remain awake throughout the remainder of the night listening to the storm subside, sullenly munching bread and dried fruit and, as it turned out, defending themselves only against their own boredom and hunger.

And so the sudden commotion and terrific chorus of whinnying caught them all by surprise.

*

The Praetorian cavalry that drew up outside the barrack gates only numbered ten men and eleven mounts, five short of the half squadron that Brutus had tasked but, as an instant deterrent, it was perfect. They had ridden since before daybreak, completing the twenty mile journey in just under two hours, with one stop for rest. Even at this early hour, the poorer citizens of Ostia were out in numbers sufficient for the mercenaries to mingle without looking conspicuous.

Or at least, not to the eyes of the average passer-by.

But a battle experienced unit of elite Praetorian cavalry was not comprised of average men. As the squadron galloped in under the arch of the southern gate and swung right, the attention of the Decurion was drawn to the four strongly built men at the end of the street who were at that moment pushing two handcarts through the oblivious bystanders towards the barracks gates. At the sound of the horses' hooves, the two carts disappeared from view left and right. The Decurion squeezed his stallion's flanks with his ankles and the mount quickened his pace.

The Decurion dismounted and removed his helmet, rubbing the sweat from his hair and staring intently down the street.

"Something wrong, sir?"

"Those fellows with the farm carts, did you see them?"

"I did, sir. Aren't they a week early for a market day? Or a couple late. Strange ways they have over here."

The Decurion grunted in agreement.

"Want me to take a couple of lads and have a look, see what they're up to?"

The officer considered it for a moment then shook his head. "Let's just get this out of the way, shall we?"

The rest of the Praetorians dismounted and lead the horses to an ancient trough opposite the entrance, whilst two of the guards remained with them to organise watering and feeding them. The horses threw back their heads, snorting and whinnying in anticipation of some much needed rest whilst the Decurion rapped on the front gates. At first there was no answer and so he tried again, louder this time. After a long pause, the gates creaked open and he jumped back in alarm.

Scores of night watchmen, all armed, all looking fractious and tired, were crammed inside the atrium, staring back at the Praetorian as though they would tear him apart in a heartbeat. Dozens more watchmen rushed round either side of the barracks and fanned out around the astonished cavalrymen.

"What in Hades …?" yelled the Decurion, drawing his sword and dropping into a fighting stance. The other Praetorians formed up around him, their swords rasping from their scabbards.

"You treacherous bastards!"

For one terrible moment, a massacre looked imminent. Then one of the watchmen stepped forwards and the Decurion focused upon him, frowning at the strange shaped blade he was wielding.

"Drop – your – weapons!" shouted Ambrosius, "Drop them all now!"

"You must be the tribune."

Ambrosius faced the Decurion. He was a lantern-jawed sort with thick black hair and a purple silk neckerchief, the dashing type that well-born ladies would swoon over at society dinner parties. Though his voice didn't show it, Ambrosius could see that there was apprehension in his eyes.

"That being so, I have a message for you."

"Then deliver it."

"It's in my pouch," he said. "If we dropped our swords, it would be your great dishonour to run us through with yours."

"So try me."

The Decurion dropped his blade, easing the pouch over his shoulder without taking his eyes off the watchman. He tossed it towards him. Ambrosius retrieved it and removed the scroll cylinder, pausing as his fingers folded around the cap. He looked at the Decurion and gave it a slight shake.

"It contains no asp, or any other species of snake for that matter, I assure you," said the Praetorian. "I wouldn't ride twenty miles with one of them by my chest for all the wine in Greece."

The tension eased slightly but Ambrosius was oblivious as he read the contents of the letter over and over.

"I don't mean to hurry you tribune, but my horses need food and water. We rode here hard. Might I assume the danger of an ambush has passed?"

Ambrosius looked up at him. "This letter mentions a great friend of mine, Titus, by name. Did you see him yourself? I need assurances that this wasn't written with him under duress."

"I'm afraid I can't give you any. When Acting Prefect Vibius Brutus briefed me, he was alone. He merely said that a watchman by that name had struck a bargain with him, part of which involved delivering this to you in person, as a matter of great urgency. That's all I know."

"A bargain? What sort of bargain?"

"Again, I don't know. He didn't tell me and I didn't presume to ask."

Ambrosius scrutinised the letter for anything suspicious. The seal was genuine enough, although it was a different design to the one Fabricius had shown him.

"My horses, tribune? They need our attention."

The Decurion's voice cut through his thoughts. Ambrosius weighed him up: he didn't seem to care a fig about anything other than his mounts.

"We use donkeys to pull our water pumps in Ostia. There's fodder in their stables if that's any use."

"I'm sure it will be fine."

"Good. Your men can sheathe their blades and go where they please. You and I, meantime, will take a walk."

The Decurion gave Ambrosius a haughty look. "Very well. The mounts need some rest before we head back. Lead on, tribune."

Ambrosius tasked Longinus to look after the Praetorian cavalrymen and give them supervised access to the barracks, though they declined, still bristling from the nature of their greeting. Then he led the Decurion through the barracks to the colonnaded exercise yard. The Praetorian sluiced water over his face and neck from a rainwater basin.

"Quite a shock you gave us out there," he said, ringing out his neckerchief, "Were you expecting trouble?"

"I was, though the men were skeptical. And the timing of your visit makes me wonder what the hell is going on."

"Sorry?"

Ambrosius slipped a small knife from a sheath concealed under his sleeve and had it up against the Praetorian's throat before he could react.

202

He covered his mouth with the palm of his left hand and pushed him against a pillar.

"I'm quite tired and can't be sure my hand won't slip if you don't tell me the truth, you understand?"

The Decurion's eyes were wide with alarm. He managed a nod.

"Good. I'm sent here at a moment's notice to keep me out of harm's way because of what I know. Last night I saw a prowler in the shadows outside my window and I have no doubts he wasn't just waiting to congratulate me on my good work here. Then, you lot arrive with a letter you claim to be from my friend asking me to leave the safety of this place to come back to Rome, alone, with you dashing young Praetorians. So, when I release my hand, you will not shout for help but you will tell me why I would want to put myself in your hands where I can be knocked off and disappear without a trace on the way home."

Ambrosius eased the pressure from over his mouth.

"You're a raving lunatic, tribune! I don't know what in Hades you're talking about and, frankly, I don't care …"

"You're raising your voice!"

"Look, I was given the note to deliver here first thing in the morning! We even set out before dawn to be sure. I don't question the Prefect's orders, or those of his deputy. But if we were here to kill you, we wouldn't just roll up at your doorstep and tether up the damn horses, would we?"

"I said it's the return journey that bothers me!"

"I don't have any other instructions, for Jupiter's sake! And I don't give a rat's arse where you ride, or how. Ride way ahead of us if you prefer, I don't care, so long as you don't harm the horse we have for you. I just have to be able to prove you got back safely: that's all!"

Ambrosius glared at him. He passed the blade in front of his eyes before re-sheathing it and then stepped back from the pillar. The Decurion recovered his composure and straightened his clothes. "You're deranged, tribune, you know that? I ought to have you flogged back in Rome for assaulting a Praetorian officer on state duties!"

Ambrosius ignored him. He had not slept properly in days and waves of fatigue washed over him.

"We head back for Rome shortly," said the Praetorian. "I suggest you get your belongings together. I know nothing of your problems here but, from what we saw outside your barracks, this is no place for you."

"What?"

"There were four men pushing handcarts towards the entrance, big men. They were trying to blend in but I know a soldier's walk when I see one. And the marketplace is the other end of town. Do you usually get food delivered to your door here?"

Ambrosius stared at him with renewed confusion. He wanted to press the Decurion more but was still wary about showing his hand. He nodded. "We do, and I sign it off. I'll join you out front shortly."

The Decurion watched the haggard watchman trudge off towards the main building and smoothed back his hair.

"Damn peasant," he muttered, when he was out of earshot.

XVII

Bulla gave Vitalis the quaestionarius a look of dismay: Titus' training was not going well.

The three had been in the central palaestra of the sprawling Baths of Trajan since the late morning, when the courtyard had been much less busy than it was now. As the day wore on, the volume of bodies grunting, sweating and posing in the sun had cramped the available space to the point where there was scarcely enough room for Titus to draw back his fists without risking elbowing somebody in the face. And now his two colleagues were sat on a stone bench in the shaded colonnade, watching runnels of sweat streaming down the watchman's body as he threw booming punches at a padded post.

"He looks like he's about to pass out!" said the Syrian, his eyes bulging with concern. "Shall I call time and give him the breather?"

Vitalis frowned, and glanced at Bulla's belly. "Passing out would be good. Shows he's training hard."

"Good if he ever come round again," muttered Bulla.

Vitalis rose from the bench and whistled between his fingers. "Now twenty clap-ups before you have water."

Titus nodded, his chest heaving. He lowered himself to the floor and managed eleven push-ups before his arms gave out on him and he lay sprawled on the floor.

"Come on you great oaf! Don't just lie there!"

Vitalis glared at Bulla, "He needs encouragement not insults! Go fill up the pitcher!"

Bulla tutted and sauntered over to the well on the other side of the courtyard, self-consciously sucking in his belly as he walked past a group of well-toned young wrestlers. When he returned, Titus was slumped on the bench. Vitalis allowed Titus a few mouthfuls of water and poured more over his neck and shoulders.

"You're looking alright, Titus: there are just a few more cobwebs to shift, that's all," he said brightly. "But you'd expect that after six years."

Titus didn't answer. His mind was distant as he watched the younger boxers and wrestlers go about their routines. Whilst he still fancied he could spot their strengths and weaknesses, it had not struck him until today that his body might actually no longer be able to exploit them.

As they sat in companionable silence, a young man with long blond locks and a weightlifter's physique walked over to the post and started throwing huge, showy punches at it.

"Oi, hang on! We use that, clear off!" Bulla was on his feet.

The boxer ignored him and threw a crisp combination at the post before leaping back, avoiding an imaginary counter.

"What, are you deaf or something? We've been using all morning; we need it!"

"Go and call him off, Vitalis, before he gets himself a pasting," said Titus, leaning back against the wall and enjoying the effects of the cool breeze.

Vitalis limped over to Bulla. The boxer was grinning at Bulla. "Go stuff your mouth with cake, fatty." He resumed his exercise.

Bulla stood glowering for a few moments with his hands on his hips. Then he approached the post and, risking being knocked senseless, interposed himself between it and the boxer.

"Bulla, just leave it …" growled Vitalis.

The smile on the boxer's face had gone and he looked Vitalis up and down. "You should listen to the old cripple."

"Fuck you!"

The boxer shoved Bulla with both hands and he stumbled back, wheezing in pain as he struck the compacted sand. He stalked over and hovered above him, his fist clenched.

"Get up, you maggot!"

"Just back off, coward!" roared Vitalis.

By now, the commotion had reached the attention of the other athletes and some of the bystanders in the colonnades, who stopped what they were doing.

"Fight! Fight!"

"Go on, Davus! Don't let him speak to you like that!"

"Ah, just leave it out will you! It's a damn mismatch, just grow up!"

Titus twitched awake and saw what was happening. He swore and hurried over. "What's your problem, you damn fool?" he said helping Bulla up. "Go throw your weight around with someone who can fight back!"

"Fool? I'm a fucking fool, am I?" The boxer shoved Titus in the back, making him fall to his hands and knees. "Come on then, big man!"

A ripple of excitement passed through the crowd.

Titus looked up in surprise and his eyes met Vitalis'. The tough old gaoler exchanged a look with him that was impossible to mistake.

Smash him!

Titus drew himself up, feeling all the old juices of battle coursing through his veins. He cracked his knuckles and crouched into a fighting stance. The young boxer's face twitched with fleeting doubt but then, with all the swagger of impetuous youth, he bounced on the balls of his feet, rolled his neck and loosened his arms, and then began to circle Titus, who watched him behind his guard and felt a stab of disappointment.

Predictable. Circle left, out of a right hander's range.

Titus twisted awkwardly, as if the young man was disorientating him, keeping the movement of his feet in the periphery of his vision. The only question was whether he would lead with his left or right when …

The youth sprang forwards and threw a right hook with terrific speed. Titus caught it late with the back of his left and only just managed to glance it above his ear, where it scored a stinging cut.

The onlookers hollered with delight at the sight of first blood, sensing that they were watching a lion about to take down a bull. Encouraged by the wound, the youth now bobbed left and right and threw a flashing jab that Titus avoided by twisting his shoulder away but he blocked the predictable follow-up right cross flush in his palm. The youth sprang back and feinted with his head, then threw a stopped left hook, trying to coax Titus' guard away from his chin.

And with that, Titus had seen all he needed to see.

He dropped his guard a couple of inches to entice him, making sure he had sight of the youth's footwork. A second later and he saw his calves tense, signalling a mighty left hook.

But Titus had read him well. The youth had a common habit of tilting his head back whilst punching. As the youth's feet adjusted, Titus dropped his weight onto his left foot and threw a ferocious right hand over the top. His fist slammed square into his opponent's exposed mouth with a familiar pop of dislocated jaw and teeth. In a heartbeat, the power of the youth's hook withered and Titus felt it flop harmlessly against the back of his head.

He thudded onto the sand, where he lay motionless, blood oozing from his mouth.

The bystanders were stunned into silence for a moment before the cheers and shouting and applause began. Some of them hurled abuse at the stricken boxer, now that he was unable to hear or respond, but another athlete challenged them and they backed off, and he went to fetch a jug of water to revive him.

Titus ignored the astonished stares and turned his back on the courtyard.

"A pretty good day's work all in all, I think," said Vitalis, patting Titus on the back, though Bulla was unable to resist turning and spitting towards the youth, who was at that moment being drenched with cold water.

"Good enough I suppose," said Titus, removing his wraps with his teeth.

"Still need to work on your reactions though. Bit on the slow side."

Titus frowned at the quaestionarius, who winked back at him.

"You didn't need to step in anyway!" insisted Bulla, "I had him! Why you both look at me like that? I've taken on bigger men than that!"

XVIII

Ambrosius passed the journey back from Ostia in a surreal state of mind that swung between exhaustion and joy at the prospect of seeing Poppeia.

And fear of the unknown.

The Decurion had been cool towards him since the incident in the barracks. Ambrosius kept a watchful eye on him and his cavalrymen as he rode a short distance behind them but sensed no trap. They had even let him keep his sword, which struck him as a remarkably sporting gesture if they were planning to turn on him on some quiet stretch of the road. Still Ambrosius could not shake the unease that jarred him awake every time his eyelids became heavy and he lolled towards the mane of his horse, and he tried instead to focus his attention on the countryside, bathed for the first time he could remember this year in warm sunshine.

It was mid-morning as the riders came upon a roadside stabling house. They tied their horses up at the rear of the ramshackle building, alongside a small pen containing some snuffling pigs and a goat.

The scowling innkeeper watched the men enter as he leaned against the counter, weighing them up for signs of likely trouble. He decided they looked too travel worn and approached the Decurion once they had all taken seats either side of a long bench. Ambrosius sat apart from them and looked on as they ordered plates of meat, cheese and onions. Though he was keen to press on and had no place amongst the Praetorians, his stomach had been growling at him all morning. Very soon, the detached buzz of conversation, the warmth inside the tavern and his lack of sleep conspired to make his head droop and he could resist no longer. He folded his arms on the table and laid his head upon them.

He was soundly asleep when the noise of the wooden plate and cup set before him made wake with a start, and he looked about him in a moment of confusion. The Decurion took a seat opposite him.

"Here, take your food and drink. Looks like you need it."

The watchman rubbed his face and gave him a look.

"There's nothing wrong with it, for Jupiter's sake!" The Decurion took a small onion from the plate and ate it whole. "See?" he said with his mouth full.

Ambrosius tucked in.

"I have some additional instructions for you," he said, waving away the watchman's frown. "Look, your constant suspicion irritates me, and the back of my head is still burning from the stares you've been focusing upon it since we left."

Ambrosius shrugged. "What instructions? And why didn't you say anything in Ostia?"

"Because I didn't. I was told to say that you should keep a low profile in Rome and that you might yet be recalled to Ostia. And before you go asking me 'why' when I've finished, don't bother, because I don't know. And, no, I wasn't told what would happen to you if you disregarded the instructions. That's all."

The Praetorian got up to rejoin his men but Ambrosius gripped him by the wrist.

"Is my daughter safe?"

He glared at Ambrosius' hand and then looked him in the eyes. "I don't know, tribune. But you'll find out for yourself, soon enough."

Ambrosius stared at him for a few moments then nodded and released his grip.

*

The innkeeper watched the Praetorians mount up and pass by. He walked over to the counter and opened the hidden drawer by the serving hatch, wiping his hands on his apron in satisfaction as he looked at the small windfall he had just made. He closed the drawer again and walked back to the window in hope of seeing any more groups of customers. He would need to slaughter another pig if so. The group prior to the last lot – crude, hulking, swarthy fellows that they were – had damn nearly devoured everything he could lay his hands on. He was only glad that they had been in a hurry and paid up when they did: wild horses wouldn't have been able to drag them out otherwise.

He chuckled and went out into the rear yard to dig another hole for his latest stash of coins.

*

It was after midday when Ambrosius noticed one of the Praetorians pointing at something in the distance. There was now a dark smudge on the horizon from which wispy tendrils of smoke drifted to the sky.

The Decurion issued a few curt orders and the horses picked up the pace. Up to this point, the squadron had ridden in a casual, easy manner but now they assumed formation and the riders straightened their backs: the traffic on the road would be likely to increase and it just wouldn't do for the elite unit to appear slovenly.

Thirty minutes later the riders were trotting past roadside tombs as they approached the Ostian Gate, and Ambrosius was whispering quiet prayers of thanks for his unexpected deliverance. The escort drew to a halt.

"This is where we leave you, tribune," said the Decurion. "And remember the instructions."

Ambrosius thanked him: the man had been as good as his word. He dug in his heels and clopped towards the gate without turning back, his thoughts focused on getting to Poppeia as quickly as possible. He hoped their relationship had not been set back by his absence.

Then he heard a flurry of hooves behind him and, in an instant, he was surrounded by the Praetorians. Ambrosius looked about him in fear.

So this was where the treacherous dogs were to attack!

"Not so fast, tribune."

Ambrosius' hand gripped the pommel of his sword: he would be sure to skewer the pretty boy officer before his own blood was spilt.

"That's not your horse."

*

Ambrosius tore up the stairs and banged on his front door, cursing and fumbling for the key when there was no answer.

"Poppeia! Poppeia …? Anna …?"

The tenement was silent, cool and in good order, and there was no sign of a hurried departure. He composed himself but then caught a whiff of stale sweat and realised what a dishevelled state he was in. He whipped off his tunic and went to the kitchen, where there was a pail of freshly drawn water, which he heaved onto the balcony and stripped himself to wash. The courtyard was empty, though he caught the occasional glimpse of passersby in the street beyond the gate. It felt like all of the occupants had been evacuated, and he frowned at the unnatural silence.

He dried off and went back inside to find a fresh tunic. There was a neatly folded pile sat on his dresser that he hadn't left himself, and he ran his fingers over them as if to touch the absent hand that had put them there. For no obvious reason, he felt his eyes suddenly fill with tears.

What the hell is wrong with me? Get a grip, man!

A key rattled in the front door. Ambrosius stumbled as he ran towards it and yanked it open, making Anna scream in shock, dropping the large watermelon she was carrying.

211

"Anna!"

He drew her close to him and squeezed her, smothering her forehead in kisses.

"I'm so glad you're fine! Let me look at you!"

She readjusted her headscarf and looked at him in astonishment. "Why … I mean, what are you doing here? You gave me the fright of my life, you fool!" She drummed her fists against his chest but could not suppress a happy smile. "Have you been drinking or something?"

"No, no, I haven't. Long story," he said, walking past her and peering over the stairs. "Where's Poppeia?" He gripped her shoulders. "Is she safe?"

"Ow, you're hurting me Ambrosius!" She yelped, shrugging him off. "Of course she is! She's at her lessons! She'll probably be back soon. What on earth's gotten into you?"

"Thank the gods! Thank the gods for that! I'm going to get her, I'll be back …"

"Not in this state you won't! Take a look at yourself! And you made me drop the melon: that cost two asses that did!"

Ambrosius picked it up. "It's fine, look. A bit squished down here, that's all …"

But then the tears returned and his exhausted mind could not stop them. He turned his head away in shame.

"Hey, hey! What's wrong Ambrosius?"

He brushed her hands away and entered the kitchen, flopping onto a stool and holding his head in his hands. Undeterred, Anna followed him inside and drew up a stool next to him, rubbing his back. "It's ok, it's only a big piece of fruit!"

Ambrosius laughed, despite himself. "I'm sorry, I'm just tired, that's all."

Anna squeezed his hand. "Don't apologise. It's good to have you back, and Poppeia will be so happy to see you!"

He looked at her with swimming eyes, an unfamiliar emotion quickening his pulse.

"And you?" he asked, squeezing her hand.

"Me? Well, I …"

There was more activity outside the door. It opened and Poppeia entered, freezing when she saw Ambrosius. Behind her was a man he had never seen before. He had a kindly face and tousled, wavy grey hair. His smile faded when he saw Ambrosius.

There was an uncomfortable pause for a few moments before Poppeia shrieked with delight and ran into Ambrosius' arms. He gathered her up and swung her around, kissing her cheeks.

"Daddy! Daddy! Daddy!"

"My little flower! I've missed you so much!"

But even in this sweet moment another emotion nipped at his happiness. Through the blurry film of fresh tears he glimpsed Anna speaking with the stranger by the door as if they were old friends.

"How long are you home for, daddy? You're not leaving again soon are you?"

"No, my love, I'm not going anywhere soon," he said as he nuzzled her hair and caught a glimpse of Anna laughing, "I won't ever leave you again like I did."

XIX

By early evening, an uncomfortable silence had settled in every room of the tenement. Ambrosius found himself unable to make eye contact with Anna and felt unbidden emotions frothing in his stomach.

"So, did you both have a nice afternoon on the Janiculum?"

He nodded and took another slice out of the pear with his knife.

"Well? What did you do?"

"Watched the watermills grinding corn; watched the birds; had a walk. Just the usual."

Anna rolled her eyes and put down the stirring spoon. "Will you tell me what's wrong now? Honestly, your mood changes like the weather. You looked so happy before and now look at you!"

Ambrosius looked over his shoulder to make sure Poppeia wasn't listening. "Want to tell me who that man was?"

"What? What man?"

"The one that seemed so disappointed to see me here when he dropped Poppeia off. After all," he said, gritting his teeth, "it's only my fucking house!"

"I don't like the way you're speaking to me, Ambrosius."

"And I don't like the way a perfect stranger is left to walk my only child back to my house as soon as my back's turned!" He banged his hand on the table. "What in Hades were you thinking, woman? Have you been fucking him here too?"

His anger left her open-mouthed. "I can't believe you're treating me like this!"

"Well? Who is he, damnit?"

"He's my friend's father."

Ambrosius turned on his stool. "Poppeia! I thought you were having a nap!"

"I was, daddy. You woke me up."

Anna walked over to her and kissed her forehead. "Go back to sleep Poppeia. Your daddy's just tired and grouchy, that's all."

Poppeia rubbed her eyes and gave Ambrosius a disappointed look that stung him. She went back into her room.

"Happy now, you big bully?"

Anna bustled past Ambrosius towards the door, leaving him on his own. He closed his eyes and cursed, feeling the anger drain from him. This was not the homecoming he had imagined. He followed Anna onto the balcony and she turned her back to him, though he could see by the rise and fall of her shoulders that she was crying.

He put his arm around her shoulders but she brushed it off. "Anna, look I'm sorry. I just …"

"Just leave it will you? I didn't deserve that! As if I'd leave Poppeia on her own with any old stranger. Just leave me alone."

"But I don't know who he is."

"He's just a friend, okay? He's just a friend, and you have no right to speak to me like you did. I try so hard for you both and all I get is … is abuse! Well I don't have to take it from you, or anyone else!" She turned from him and went back inside. Ambrosius tugged his hair in frustration before stomping down the staircase to find Titus.

*

Ambrosius sprinkled some seeds into the flame within the shrine and whispered a quick prayer for Anna and Poppeia, then surveyed the quiet courtyard. In the distance he could discern sounds of people shouting. He entered the Watch House and went into his office. Titus did a double take, sprang from his seat and embraced him.

"The gods favour you, Ambrosius! I see you're still very much alive!"

"So don't get too comfortable in my seat, you old villain!"

They looked at each other fondly for a moment and Ambrosius thought he caught a fleeting shadow pass over Titus' eyes.

"Some wine?"

"Why not?"

They clinked cups and sat down. "Quiet round here. What's going on? Where's Bulla"

"Ah, some fight got out of hand in one of the Aventine guilds and I had to send most of them out. Bulla's getting too fat, so he's out on the streets with a torch with the rest of them!"

"And the Urban Cohorts?"

"I sent a messenger, one of the staff officers, who thought the task was beneath him. No response yet though, lazy bastards."

Ambrosius smiled. "Don't hold your breath."

"Well then. Don't look so happy to be out of Ostia, tribune! I thought you'd be grinning like an idiot! Something wrong?"

Ambrosius looked away. "A few problems at home, that's all."

Titus raised an eyebrow.

"Just had an argument with Anna and Poppeia overheard."

"Aha! Finally admitting that you're fond of Anna, eh?"

"I don't know … maybe. She looked shocked but at least a little happy I was back. But then, when I was speaking to her, some man I don't know dropped Poppeia off, looking disappointed to see me. Wanted to swing for him, I tell you."

"Jealous?"

"Perhaps a little."

Titus chuckled. "I wouldn't be. Sure there's nothing in it; she's a good woman. And next time you speak to her, take a deep breath first!"

"Anyway, care to tell me why a posse of Praetorians came banging on my door this morning? They said you'd been to see the Deputy Prefect! What in hell is going on?"

Titus refilled both cups and relayed to Ambrosius all that had happened in his short absence, starting with the imminent vote on The Watch and Rufinus' grave worries. Ambrosius was astonished when he learned of Rufinus' flirtation with the murky underworld of informers and no less so when he described his meeting with Brutus and the terms of the consequent match-up.

"And you risked all of this for me?"

Titus shrugged modestly. "You and the rest of us, tribune. There's much at stake."

"The Watch being disbanded; I can't believe it!" Ambrosius was silent again for a minute. "I have to get that fight called off. It's not worth it, Titus. I'm not worth it!"

"Not a chance. It's set in stone. Don't even think about interfering now: you're supposed to be lying low, remember? And besides, training's going well."

Ambrosius caught the flicker of doubt in Titus' eyes again. He looked away under Ambrosius' scrutiny but he didn't press him. It was enough that they both knew that to be a lie. He leaned back in his chair with a sigh. "The least I can do is to come back and free you up so you can train. And get some rest. For as long as it's left at least, this job'll grant you none of that, I can tell you."

"So I'm learning. No, I'm fine here: good thinking time. You should go. Go and spend some time smoothing things over with Poppeia and Anna."

Ambrosius thought about it. "Perhaps you're right. I'll be back tomorrow then." He rose and offered his hand to Titus. Titus ignored it, got up himself and embraced him again.

"It's good to have you back. Go. Go and win her over with your delicate charm!"

They both laughed at that. Ambrosius winked at him and left Titus on his own again.

When he had gone, Titus took out a wax tablet and drummed the metal stylus on the case, deep in thought. He unclipped it and tried to write 'tribune safe, fight on', but the simple task defeated him and he shook his head: the lines scratched on the wax were meaningless.

Rufinus could never promote a big, dumb illiterate like him but he could be an influential leader in other respects.

He went into the hallway and whistled through his fingers.

"Oi, codicillarii! Scribes! Don't even pretend to be awake! Urgent message needs dictating. Now!"

*

When Ambrosius climbed the stairs to his tenement, cradling some Winter Violets he had plucked from outside a senator's house on the Aventine, his stomach twinged with misgiving. He knew by the silence that something was wrong. When he opened the door, the light was dim and the atmosphere heavy. Anna was sat with her back to the door by the stove and she stiffened when it was opened.

"Hello," she said quietly.

"Hi." He approached her and set the violets down on the table. "I got these for you. I'm sorry I shouted at you earlier. You're right, you didn't deserve it. You've never …"

"I'm leaving, Ambrosius."

The finality of her tone stopped him dead. "You're leaving? Why …? You can't!"

"Really? Or what, you'll shout again?"

"No! I mean … where are you going? For how long?"

"I'm going to stay with my cousin, at least for a few days."

"Metella? But you hate her!"

She didn't answer. The implication that even staying there would be preferable made Ambrosius' stomach swill.

"Please! Don't go! At least stay here tonight and think about it!"

217

"I have thought about it and my mind's made up. I know things aren't easy for you but I can't stay here feeling like this, feeling so horribly disrespected! You really don't know how it is to lodge in somebody else's house, with somebody else's child, in somebody else's shadow, do you? When the very least you have to call your own is your self-respect! And you crushed it, Ambrosius, so I have to go."

Her outburst stunned him. He had no inkling that she had been feeling such turmoil. He reached out for her but she shook her head and rose from the table. And it was only then that he saw the pathetic bundle of belongings she had packed together.

"But ... what about Poppeia?"

A look of sadness crossed her face and she looked away. "I've already spoken to her and she understands. She's your daughter Ambrosius. She needs you, not me. I'm sorry."

She picked up her bundle and walked out of the door. Ambrosius turned but didn't follow her, though his every impulse was to do so. For a few long minutes after she had gone, he stood rooted to the floorboards, staring at the closed door.

Life is a lonely journey, his father once told him, and you should be grateful for anyone that accompanies you even part of the way. He had not, in truth, ever felt close to his father, a distant and aloof figure. But as he stood on the same spot and felt the familiar, oppressive silence settle on his shoulders, as it had on that fateful evening five years previously, he couldn't help but agree with the old man.

XX

Three days later, a dusty messenger stumbled off his horse and approached the encampment he had seen shimmering from a distance in the heat haze. His mount's eyes were dilated and dried froth streaked its cheeks. The rider was in little better shape himself on account of the hard ride across the sandy plains of Libya. His lips were dry and cracked, and his face was sunburnt in places. He drained the last few drops of water from his gourd and staggered over to the guard stood by the stockade encircling the tents.

The guard looked him up and down in consternation. "Wait here," he said rushing towards the larger tent.

A short time later, he hurried back to the messenger. "I'll deal with your horse: the Prefect will see you now."

When he entered the tent, a small throng of hard, swarthy faces stared back at him as their conversation petered out. The meeting looked like a gathering of Berber nomads, but the messenger was too far gone to care.

"Get this man some water," said Gaius Plautianus, removing the linen veil wrapped around his face. "Sit. You have a message for me?"

The messenger nodded wearily and removed the bag from round his neck.

"Come on, give it to me," he said, snatching it from him. His face darkened as he read the contents, and the other men gave each other knowing glances.

"Damn the gods," he muttered, rising from his seat. "I'll need a few minutes."

He pushed open the flaps to another section of the tent. The messenger was given a water pitcher and glugged a few mouthfuls as the men in the tent stared at him.

"What is it said?" asked one of them. His Latin was atrocious.

"How do I know? I just deliver the fucking things."

"Good answer."

The messenger deflected their attention by looking round him at the tent. It was typical of many he had seen in the nomadic settlements he had ridden through and the air was surprisingly cool inside. A few minutes later, the Prefect emerged though the flaps bearing another scroll.

219

"You may rest in one of the spare tents in the camp tonight and will want for nothing while you are here. But tomorrow you will return with this message." But when the messenger reached out for it, Plautianus withheld it. "And let me tell you this will be the single most important thing you will do in your life. You must not fail, which is why I will arrange for an armed guard to accompany you. And should you be overcome by some reckless curiosity, you will not understand what is contained within because it is encoded. Understood?"

"Yes sir."

"Good. Now you will leave us."

PART III

"There's death in every window as you pass along at night: you may well be deemed a fool ... if you go out to dinner without having made a will. Your drunken bully ... however hot with wine and youth he may be, avoids the one whose scarlet robe and long retinue of attendants, with brass lamps in their hands, order him keep his distance. But to me, escorted home only by the scant light of a candle, whose wick I husband with due care, he pays no respect ... and, having been pounded to jelly, pray to be allowed to return home wih a few teeth in my head!"
Juvenal, SATIRES, III

I

She was exactly where the informer thought she'd be: flirting with the drunks in the main room of the Gorgona. He took his seat in the dingy candlelight at the back, sipping his wine and watching her work the tavern. Fair enough, he thought, she's good. But with looks and a body like that, a complete fool could still make money.

He winked at her as she passed by, and she smiled back, glancing at his full tankard. He considered his options. However he carried it out, there were certain things he couldn't avoid. Under no circumstances could he be seen taking her upstairs, in case it all went wrong. He would need to make her comfortable with him, without drawing attention to himself, so that she would be more likely to open up to him. That was the hard part, eased slightly by the fact that he had no friends here and nobody knew his real name. This meant there was little chance of being compromised.

He noticed the way she would take away customers' empty cups and refill them without being asked. Nobody objected, of course, when she smiled so sweetly at them. An idea occurred to him. He drained his beer and pushed it away from him. Then he removed a small wax tablet from his pocket and opened it up, doodling and waiting.

Out of the corner of his eye, he could see a foppish young man with long hair talking animatedly to her. He didn't look like a typical resident of the Subura and he presumed he had come out with his friends touring the

221

drinking dens of the slums, looking for some easy love. Which suited him just fine. He resumed doodling.

Minutes later, she approached the informer's table. She bent down to retrieve his tankard, displaying her ample cleavage.

"Ah ah, naughty!" he smiled and gently took her wrist. "There's still a bit left in there!"

She looked into the empty vessel. "There isn't, but no matter, I can fill it up."

He liked her accent: quite seductive; Eastern, unless he was much mistaken. He withdrew his hand, allowing his fingers to brush her skin just for a fleeting moment. "Well, even so … a poor poet has to keep a clear head and a few coins in his pouch."

"You are poet?"

"A poor poet, but yes." Another smile, shy this time.

"Oh," she bit her lip and tapped the case with a painted nail, "in that case, I bring you another drink and you pay by writing me ode, yes?" She winked and took away his tankard. He opened up the tablet. *So far so good*, was all he wrote.

On her way back, the fop beckoned her over. She nodded but raised the tankard in the informer's direction, and he promptly dropped his metal stylus to the floor. When the customer glanced over, all he caught was a glimpse of the unremarkable crown of the informer's head. He saw her feet approaching and sat upright.

"Thank you! You're too kind."

"Did you write anything nice?"

"Oh, I'm getting the inspiration. You have a lovely musical voice, by the way. And unusually green eyes. Where are you from?"

She tucked a lock of hair over her ear. "Thank you too. My name is Zelika and I was born in Samaria, on banks of Dead Sea."

"That would explain it then. Good health!" he raised the tankard, glancing at the wax tablet. *You can go away now!*

Zelika lingered for a second and then swivelled away, wondering if she was losing her touch. As she passed, the fop put his hand around her waist and whispered something to her, a lascivious grin on his face. There followed what looked to the informer like a brief negotiation. Zelika raised her eyebrows and then nodded.

So he's a rich boy, he thought. Good for him.

She disappeared through a back door whilst her next customer clinked tankards with his friends, looking pleased with himself.

The informer primed himself, draining his drink and waiting for his target to do likewise. Moments later, the man gave his friends the thumbs up and headed for the door. He followed at a short distance, the tankard now in his pocket. He had seen several other customers coming and going through this door, so he knew he wouldn't look suspicious.

He entered a short corridor. Kitchens straight ahead, stairs to his left leading to the first floor landing. The man with long black hair was half way up them.

"Excuse me," said the informer brightly. "You left this."

The fop turned and looked at the man following him up the stairs with something apparently in his closed fingers. Distracted by the extended hand, he didn't see the other wrap around his neck and wrench it to the side with a powerful heave. The informer heard the satisfying crack and caught the body as it fell backwards. Pausing to ensure nobody else was nearby, he draped the body around his shoulders and climbed the rest of the stairs. He propped his victim against the landing banisters and removed the tankard from his own pocket. He inserted the dead man's fingers through the handle and turned his head so that it lolled over his chest.

The informer cast his eyes along the bottom of the three doors along the corridor. He crept past them, grimacing as one of the planks creaked underfoot. A dim light flickered underneath the door of only one, the furthest. Taking a gamble, he rapped quietly on the door. Soft footsteps approached from within. When the door opened, he was relieved to see Zelika, wearing only a diaphanous stole. She looked confused at seeing the poet instead of the fop but not in any way scared.

"Terribly sorry," he said, pointing to the form slumped by the banisters, "I had to help him up the stairs. He's dead drunk."

She glanced down the corridor, frowning. His ruse had only bought a second or two, but it was all he needed. Lightening quick, his hands were round her throat, shoving her back inside the room. He kicked the door shut with his heel. A look of pure terror filled her eyes.

"Don't even try to scream, my little Eastern princess. Calm down and you may come out of this unharmed, understood?" He relaxed his grip so that she could breathe.

223

"I'm pushed for time and will need to be quick. You may have guessed I am not, in fact, a poet. That is all you need to know about me. Better for you if you don't delay me further, right?"

She gasped, sucking in air, stupefied by what was happening.

"Question: the grey haired man, the loner, Junius Rufinus. I believe you know him. Tell me something interesting about him."

She shook her head. "I … I know no-one by that name! I swear it!" The grip around her throat tightened as the informer considered the possibility of him having given a false name, not unusual with public figures wanting to escape the infamy of cavorting with prostitutes and actors.

"I refer to the heroic old man who dealt so neatly with your over-amorous customer the other day. I recommend you don't play with my patience, lady."

"Ah … please! He's … he paid me and has … had me several times. He drinks a lot, keeps to himself, but … but … he said he was on procurator's staff! Yes! Ah …! What is it? You are scaring me! What you want to know?"

"You were doing better there. Continue."

"Please!" she panted, "You can have me for free … however you want …"

"Stick to the point, whore." The grip tightened again. "Do you know what the loner really does? I do."

"Ah! You are hurting me! Iesu, help me! He is administrator … a friend! He has missing friend! And … but he doesn't know where he is I think … it worries him. He … yes! He sent horse to Ostia to … to help other friend! Yes, I remember now!"

"Interesting. Tell me about these friends and why he sent a horse?"

"I can't! He didn't say … I …"

"Just one horse or a small squadron of them?"

"I don't … he just didn't …"

"Who told him to send the horse?"

"I don't know! I don't remember, I swear! Please! You are hurting me! I can't … breathe!" She started sobbing and, because he suspected she was telling the truth, he slackened his grip.

"This is important: what other little secrets has Rufinus told you while he's cosied up alongside you? His weakness for grieving widows?"

By a tremendous effort of will, she stopped hyperventilating. "I think you … you don't understand! He is … he is like closed book! Are you going to

224

kill me? Please ...! Ah! No secrets ... none at all, we are not like that. He takes me after I take his money. Then ... then he goes to sleep. Please let me go!"

"All in good time. Question: what do you know about his connections to the senate?"

"Nothing! I swear it! Politics is so boring ... I know nothing about! Please, let me go ...!"

Again, the informer suspected she was telling the truth. His questions had elicited enough of interest about Rufinus to confirm certain links but nothing more, and her voice was beginning to rise. Disappointment settled upon him. He had let Plautianus down in Ostia and his follow-up letter and instructions had been clear: no loose ends, no surprises. She was a loose end. Rufinus, the interfering Watch Prefect ... he appeared to be full of surprises. Both had to go.

He looked at her gaping, terror-stricken eyes.

Pretty, very pretty. But business and pleasure never mix well in this profession.

He wound her silver chain round his finger until the Chi-Ro amulet emerged from between her breasts.

"Hello, what have we here?" he asked, feigning surprise. "Another fish worshipper? Another rat from the catacombs? You are full of surprises aren't you? Now this just won't do."

Her fearful eyes hardened slightly. "You Romans ... so full of hate for what you don't understand."

He pressed his thumbs deeper into her throat.

"Maybe you can ask your maker to explain for me."

She gurgled and struggled, trying to rake him with her long nails. But her efforts weakened and were easily deflected by his elbows. He felt her body go limp. He grunted and let her down before opening the door and peering round it. All was quiet. Avoiding the creaking plank this time, he dragged the body of his first victim inside the room and removed a small dagger from another of his own pockets. He punctured the man's corpse twice above the heart before scattering a couple of coins on the floor. Finally, he pressed the handle of the dagger into Zelika's palm and closed her fingers around it, arranging both bodies to look like a brief but violent struggle had taken place. Satisfied, he closed the door, walked back downstairs and out of the tavern.

He took out a comb and, as he brushed back his hair, reconsidered two questions that bothered him.

Who sent the damn horses to Ostia? Why?

He would be sure to ask Rufinus before the man's suicide. A depressing, dishonourable business, having your career whisked away from you.

II

The day of the fight broke sunny and warm; exactly the sort of conditions Titus had hoped to avoid. He had awoken early and slipped out of bed, after kissing Lucia's forehead. She murmured softly but didn't wake up. His equipment had already been prepared and he left his tenement to go for a walk around the parks of the Pincian Hill to clear his head. He knew one or two presbyters that might have been able to offer him a blessing but didn't think it safe to visit them. It occurred to him that perhaps the enemies of The Faith were getting their way in making it so difficult and dangerous to observe it. Did this mean that Christianity was too frail? For the first time in many weeks, he experienced the faintest sliver of doubt. What if he was to receive such a beating that he died: would he still reach the Underworld? Would Lucia?

His lack of preparation troubled him by day and haunted him at night, and he found himself frequently pinching the spare flesh around his waistline and prodding the muscles of his arms. They had once been unyielding, like filled sandbags, but now … he had pushed himself hard over the last week and it had undoubtedly helped, but he knew it had barely scratched the surface of what needed to be done.

So preoccupied was he that he lost track of time and when he looked up at the path of the sun, he realised he risked being late. He had set out with every intention of going back home to say goodbye to Lucia but, when the time came, he just wasn't able, though he couldn't quite say why. Was it the shame of a broken promise, another lie to deepen the secretive life he was leading as a Christian? Or was it something he had once heard a man in the legions say: that in every parting there is a foretaste of death?

Shortly after he had arrived at the agreed meeting point by the Porta Viminalis, Bulla, Vitalis the gaoler and Chest joined him. Titus was a little surprised at seeing the tiro Chest but it soon became clear the new recruit to the vigiles knew his boxing, and he talked more about it in the time they waited for Ambrosius than the sum total of his conversation since his arrival in the ranks.

As the minutes passed, Titus kept glancing at the sun. Just as he was about to leave without him, Ambrosius hurried around the corner, looking

227

pale and unshaven. "I'm sorry old friend. Had to get one of the neighbours to look after Poppeia."

Titus nodded and they all set off. Bulla rolled his eyes when Chest began another recollection of one of the Pankrateion contests he had seen when he was growing up.

"You know, I think I preferred it when you said nothing!" Chest ignored him and carried on.

"So, how are you feeling?" asked Ambrosius quietly.

"Good thanks," he lied.

"Did you tell Lucia?"

"I did, I couldn't keep it from her."

"And?"

"She got very tearful."

"At least she wasn't angry."

"I'd have preferred angry, Ambrosius. That would've been much easier to take."

Ambrosius considered the remark but wasn't sure he agreed. He hadn't seen or heard from Anna for the last few days and had thought a good deal about how she might have been feeling and how selfish he had been. It was all about communication, he now realised, at which men were not naturally gifted, for all the good this lesson had done him.

After a few minutes, the walls of the Praetorian Camp loomed into view and the conversation petered out. Even Chest became thoughtful. When the duty sentry saw them outside the gate, he didn't bother challenging them and barked out the order to have the gates opened.

The expectant atmosphere within the camp was so thick that the five watchmen felt as if they had walked into a warm gust of wind. Whatever notions Titus had had that the contest would be a private matter between two fighters, he now saw, had been naive in the extreme. On reflection, the writing had been on the wall when Brutus had complained that, despite his prowess, he had never received the adulation he deserved. Word of the contest had evidently been circulating within the camp for the whole week, started, Titus didn't doubt, by Brutus himself within minutes of having shaken hands on it.

As the five made their way down the central avenue, there was a buzz of conversation, and Praetorian and Urban soldiers alike stopped whatever they were doing to point and comment at them, laugh or stare as they passed by. Titus kept his eyes fixed ahead and tried to keep his thoughts as clear as possible. It was enough for him that he knew the contest he faced would have been his toughest even when he was at his peak.

A barrel chested Praetorian in full parade order stepped out of the principia building ahead of them and approached, grinning broadly. When he drew close, the level of noise from the soldiers lining the avenue faded.

"So," he looked at each of the watchmen in turn, "which of you is the great fighter Titus? You?" he asked, pointing a meaty finger at Bulla. There were howls of laughter from the soldiers and Bulla glared back at him. There was something instantly odious about the man that his voice, which sounded as if there was gravel trapped in his throat, did nothing to alleviate. The Praetorian acknowledged the laughter and his grin became even wider to reveal his yellowing teeth.

"Forgive me, a little joke at your expense. Come; let me show you to the circle!"

They followed him to the exercise ground and the soldiers that were training within stopped and stared as they entered the courtyard. The vigiles couldn't help but be impressed by the facilities within: there were several padded boxing posts, complete sets of stone weights, stone plunge pools and even a well at the far end of the complex. They crossed the grass and approached an arch set into the curtain wall at one end of the palaestra that led through to a smaller courtyard. The square was bordered on its other three sides by sloping roofs supported by Doric columns that provided shaded viewing galleries. At the centre of the courtyard, was a circular pit of damp, compacted sand.

"You will have noticed," continued the Praetorian, "that there are more soldiers who want to watch this contest than there is space in the galleries, so we had to run a ballot for places. We did consider erecting scaffolding for extra seats and some bright spark even suggested digging a circle out of the grass in the palaestra, where there's a bit more room. Would you believe, he almost got his way! I put a stop to those plans myself because there's always the possibility of the fight being over quickly," he gave them his chilly grin, "and what a waste of good grass that'd be."

Ambrosius had heard enough. "So, what's your big job here today? Did you rake the sand?"

"No," the smile didn't even twitch. "I'm the referee."

Horns blared, making the watchmen start, followed by a deafening cheer from the centre of the camp.

"That'll be Brutus. You know, I've seen who knows how many of his fights, and I still don't think he knows what he's truly capable of. So good luck, watchman," sneered the Praetorian, "you'll certainly need it." He ambled away to speak to some of his colleagues.

"Come on," said Ambrosius, "we'll get set up in here. Don't pay any attention to anything: it's all just hot air."

But it was easier said than done. Having saluted Brutus' appearance from his quarters, the buglers now broke into a jaunty, martial tune that whipped up the atmosphere in the camp. Titus stood mesmerised by the archway in anticipation of his opponent's arrival.

It was Chest who stepped forwards to shake him out of his reverie.

"Centurion ... centurion! Limber up! Here, get rid of your tunic!"

Titus turned away and stripped down to his loincloth.

"Good, right, give me your hands ... relax ... no, let them go limp... now, throw out some jabs."

It was clear that Chest had at least a passing familiarity with the routines, and he was the only one of the four strong enough to manipulate Titus' mighty arms in the right way. He pushed and pulled Titus' fists like pistons and then shook them, as if trying to create waves in a piece of string, to get the blood flowing freely in his veins.

Titus moved away to shadow box as the buglers reached a stopped crescendo.

"Centurion, quickly, take these ear bungs and don't turn to face whatever comes through that entrance! Keep loose, don't overdo it. You're looking good!"

Brutus appeared in the palaestra, flanked by some of the burliest looking men in the whole camp, whose tunics stretched taut around their shoulders and arms. They struggled to restrain some of the over-zealous soldiers wanting to slap their champion's back or shake his hand.

The Prefect wore a scarlet Praetorian commander's robe and a triumphant smile that grew even further when his eyes locked on Titus limbering up through the arch, scarcely able to believe that, at last, his time had come.

Look at me, watchman! He whispered. Look up and see what's coming for you!

But Titus resisted, showing him his back and walking away to gather his thoughts.

Brutus' smile faded as he entered the courtyard.

"Watchman! Hey, watchman! Are these the only supporters you could scrape together? Did your wife scare the others away?"

Brutus shared the laughter of his attendants but not one of the vigiles acknowledged him. His entourage now took up positions by the archway to turn away those soldiers who were not lucky enough to have drawn a scratched token from the baskets a few hours before. As the galleries began to fill and some of the more nimble soldiers in the camp managed to scale the palaestra's perimeter walls to get a view of the action, Brutus could resist no longer. He sauntered over and Ambrosius feigned a double take, as if it were the first time he had seen him that day. He made a show of removing the cloth bungs from his ears and tapping his friends on the shoulder.

"You can take them out now – the racket's stopped. Sorry, commander, didn't hear you coming. What do you want?"

Brutus glowered at him.

"If you still wanted to pull out, watchman, now would be the time," he said, looking around at the soldiers still streaming into the courtyard, "though I couldn't guarantee you'd get out in one piece."

"Then I'd better take my chances in here."

The two fighters stared at each other for a few moments before Brutus smirked and turned away.

"Well done, Chest," said Vitalis, "I think you burst his bubble there."

Chest grinned and helped Titus bind the rawhide straps around his wrists and knuckles, and Titus permitted himself a furtive glance at Brutus opposite, beyond the circle of sand. His own trainers were engaging in some gamesmanship, pointing in his direction and whispering something. Now that he had stripped down, the differences in physique between the two were stark. Even beneath the thick coating of hair, the definition of the Praetorian's muscles was impressive. More doubts crept into Titus' mind, of the sort he had not entertained since his very first bout, when he was little more than a rangy youth.

"Ambrosius, my cloak."

He retrieved a small oilskin bundle and palmed it to Ambrosius.

"What's this?"

"If something happens, promise me you'll give this to Lucia."

The tribune looked at it with a frown. "What? You can give it to her yours …"

Titus hissed. "Promise me!"

231

Ambrosius nodded and pocketed it. By now, the galleries had filled and Brutus' men had managed, not without difficulty, to rope off the arch to the large palaestra, preventing anyone else from gaining entry. The watchmen gazed around them at the multitude of hot-blooded soldiers now hurling insults at them or yelling 'Prae-tor-iani! Prae-tor-iani!' Even Titus, who had fought inside the camps of rival legions, had never experienced such a hostile environment.

The referee summoned both fighters to the centre of the circle. "Alright, you've both agreed the rules: two breaks each and no more, d'you hear watchman! No biting, no gouging, blows below neck also permitted but above groin, no head-butting. Clear? Good. Final instructions from the side then come out fighting."

Titus returned to Ambrosius, Bulla and Chest, whose own stomachs were now churning in earnest.

"The gods are smiling on you, Titus," said Ambrosius, looking him in the eye. "Whatever happens I'll not forget what you did for me. So do what you've got to do, old friend. There's not a fighter or a man like you in the whole empire."

Titus winked at him: he only needed one God to be smiling on him.

"Go and wipe that smirk off the hairy pig's face!" hissed Bulla, his eyes wild with hatred.

"And remember," added Vitalis, "that you've got much more experience than him. He'll make mistakes. Just be patient."

"Here, open up," said Chest, stuffing the inside of Titus' lips with protective mastic gum. "Keep your laughing gear closed; let it settle! Good luck, centurion."

A whistle blew. Titus turned in time to see Brutus thundering towards him and sidestepped out of his path. The sand felt sticky beneath his boots and it took him a few moments to get used to it and the dimensions of the circle, all the while keeping his eyes on Brutus who needed no such adjustment and was at that moment trying to back him up against the edge.

Brutus launched an assault, completely surprising Titus by his speed. He unleashed a wild left which slammed into Titus' armpit as he covered his head and a chopping right that whistled past his skull but tagged his ear, drawing blood and making it burn and hum with pain. Titus swayed, too late, as Brutus dropped on his left foot to load an uppercut that drove Brutus' own hand onto his forehead. His vision blackened for a second and he staggered to one side, trying to clear his head. The crowd roared as they saw that he had been hurt in the very first salvo.

"Finish him! Finish him!"

"He's out on his feet!"

Titus straightened and backpedalled from danger as Brutus moved in. He swore at his slow reactions and sucked air through his teeth until the buzzing in his skull subsided. But Brutus had the scent of an early kill and charged him: he braced himself just in time. The two met like bulls tussling for a fattened mate, colliding with such resounding force that those watching drew breath in response. Then they set at each other and the crunch of rawhide on muscle and bone was like the incessant hammering at a shipyard. The attack by Brutus appeared to be part of no plan. It was as if he had been seized by an uncontrollable animal impulse, driven on by the bloodcurdling yells from the galleries.

The pair threw punches at will until they stepped apart at the same time, sweat running freely down both faces, their chests heaving. Titus glanced down and saw droplets of blood streaming from his own face but he worked his jaw and, though painful, knew it wasn't broken. Brutus circled Titus now, waiting for his breath to return before pouncing again. Titus pre-empted him, raising his guard and advancing, pawing at the air just ahead of Brutus' face, trying to disrupt his rhythm.

He stepped in and threw a Herculean right cross that would have stunned an ox, impressing himself by the speed of his arm. Brutus slipped the punch and dropped his weight onto his left foot, unleashing a shot to the watchman's exposed right flank, like an athlete hurling a discus. The force of the blow blasted the air from his lungs with an audible boom and he crumpled to the floor, gasping for air. He managed to stumble onto one knee, his eyes, wide with pain and surprise, searching for the referee.

But the Praetorian was stood with his arms folded outside the circle.

"He's taken a knee! Step in you damn fool!" yelled Ambrosius, cupping his hands around his mouth.

"You fucking cheat! Step back! Step back!"

Brutus hesitated and looked over to the referee. But seeing no signal, he now straightened and prepared to deliver the knockout blow.

"Step back, you cheating bastard!" Chest and Vitalis were screaming at Brutus, but he didn't take any notice. They hovered over the circle's edge, on the very point of entering themselves, thus forfeiting the contest, before Bulla pointed to the referee.

233

"Stop!"

The referee took a few reluctant steps forward and ushered Brutus away to his trainers, where he disdainfully waved away the offer of water. Chest hurried onto the sand with a pitcher. He poured some water down Titus' back and over his face, clearing the blood and sweat from his eyes.

"A lucky shot," wheezed Titus through the Mastic, desperately trying not to rub his side.

"No, you gifted it! You're better than that! How's it feeling?"

"Don't touch it!"

"Wasn't going to; they're watching you like a hawk. Ribs?"

"One or two I think."

"You should protect them better then. Want a mouthful of water?"

Titus nodded and tipped back his head.

"Time!"

"Fuck off! I only counted twenty!" shouted Bulla.

The referee smiled at him.

"Keep him away a bit longer; you've not given yourself time to spot his weaknesses yet! Good luck." Chest slapped him between the shoulder blades and stepped back out of the circle.

Brutus came charging once more, fired by the shouts of his men, wanting to finish the job with a spectacular knock out. Sluggish to get to his feet, Titus didn't have time to slip away and covered up as the blows rained upon his body and his arms, swaying to absorb the shots and disrupt their pattern.

"Fight, you coward!" hissed Brutus through gritted teeth. "You're no champion!"

A particularly heavy swipe penetrated Titus' defence and widened the cut inside his ear, stinging him venomously and sending rivulets of blood down his neck. Bright lights danced before his eyes and he felt the strength drain from his knees. He lunged forwards and drove Brutus away before he could land an even more telling blow. As the Praetorian chopped downwards to clear his opponent's hands, he momentarily exposed his face and Titus looped his left fist over to land a satisfying blow to his chin. Brutus grunted with surprise and stepped backwards, raising his guard. Titus responded by unleashing a fierce body shot of his own. It caught him below the ribs, narrowly missing his kidney. Brutus staggered back in agony and Titus tried to take advantage with an energy sapping flurry of follow up punches, urged on by the watchmen bellowing encouragement from the sides.

But Brutus was astonishingly resilient. He tangled up Titus' flailing arms by catching them in his armpits and wrestled with him until his own breath returned. With a roar, he lifted Titus onto the tips of his toes and hurled him aside as if he was no heavier than a child.

"Bru-tus! Bru-tus! Bru-tus!" chanted the crowd in admiration.

Spurred on, Brutus advanced once again, his teeth clenched in a rictus-like smile to show he wasn't hurt. Titus stepped back in dismay. His favoured shot to the body, which had felled dozens of previous opponents, had been soaked up with little to show for it.

And Titus was tiring already.

The effort required to get back onto his feet and grapple with Brutus had depleted his reserves. He stepped left and then sprang to the right as Brutus closed in on him, trying to buy precious extra seconds to fill his lungs and watch Brutus for any weaknesses.

The Praetorian launched another assault and they clashed near the edge of the circle. Blows rained on Titus from all angles and he covered up, waiting and waiting for a small gap to open up, a brief pause in the sandstorm. But there was none. Brutus was outstandingly fit and Titus was fading fast. The hard edge of the rawhide carried a spiteful sting and he felt his resilience crumbling, like mud brick walls in the face of a siege engine. As Titus struggled to find a gap, he glimpsed Ambrosius and the three watchmen. Bulla had his face in his hands, Vitalis was clenching his jaw and even Chest was quiet.

Titus dropped to his knee.

To his surprise, Brutus' punches fell away at once and he stepped back. Somewhere amidst the roar of the crowd he thought he heard Brutus panting. He glanced up, gritting his teeth as waves of agony rippled through him.

The look on Brutus' face was one of confusion.

How can you take that punishment?

"Stop!" announced the referee, unable to avoid the call this time.

Ambrosius, Chest and Bulla hurried over with the water, Vitalis lumbering just behind them. The flow of it over his face and neck felt wonderful.

"What are you doing? You're a sitting target! He's killing you!"

235

"Titus," said Ambrosius quietly, "turn it in. You've proved your point, you've still got heart and they've had their spectacle. Please. End it now and you can walk away with your head held high. Do it for us."

Titus' flanks heaved like a horse at the end of a chariot race. His body reverberated with the pain of the blows it had soaked up and he wanted nothing more than to raise his finger and end the experience then and there.

But part of him – some stubborn, faint streak of pride and belief – would not allow it. He looked over once more at Brutus and his trainers. They were watching him intently, anticipating the end and the wild celebration that would follow.

Coward! He had called him. *You're no champion!* He had said.

Those taunts were less bearable than all the punches he had taken combined.

"No," he growled, "It's not over yet."

"Titus, for our sake!"

"Time!"

He staggered to his feet and the crowd responded with a roar of delight. Their spectacle had an extended finish.

"Titus!"

But Titus wasn't listening. He was watching Brutus, whom he had seen flinch with surprise as he rose from his knee.

"Go, Ambrosius. I'm fine!"

The vigiles looked at each other in dismay.

"Get out of the circle, watchmen!" barked the referee.

Brutus moved in for the kill. Tiring or not, he was unlike any other fighter Titus had ever seen. His relentlessness was savage, bestial even and, despite his heavy physique, he was still extremely quick. As Titus backpedalled, he tried to clear his mind. Brutus threw a swinging right which he managed to slip under and move away, too tired and poorly balanced to counter. Titus ran his eyes over the Praetorian's stance and technique.

Both were solid, though he was prone to wildness.

Dizzy with exhaustion, he somehow avoided another couple of punches as his mind raced. He recalled what he had been told by wrestlers who would look for traces of a limp, poorly knit bones or tell-tale scars to exploit. Yet even as he scanned his opponent whilst trying to avoid him he could see none of these.

236

Brutus stalked Titus to the edge of the circle and forced him to respond. He threw a left jab and right hook that Titus could only deflect inches from his temple. The rawhide raked his forehead and opened a nasty gash across his eyelid, virtually tearing it away. Blood seeped from it and dripped into his eye, forcing him to blink furiously to clear his vision. Brutus dug at the watchman's damaged ribcage and pain lanced through his side, making him nearly faint. Titus doubled up in agony, using his own weight to force his opponent away before Brutus stepped in to end it all. This created enough distance for him to drill his own left square into Brutus stomach. It was a reflex shot – barely at half strength – and yet it merely bounced off his skin. Titus caught a fleeting glimpse of the musculature of Brutus' clenched torso before he felt a numbing hammer blow on his shoulder blade. He tried to remain on his feet but the force of it boomed around his spine and he tucked in his right shoulder and rolled away, to the derisive hoots of the crowd.

The unorthodox manoeuvre, however, bought him some crucial seconds. He got to his feet and wiped the blood away from his face, shaking his head to clear the sand and sweat, but this only dislodged a flap of skin from his eyelid, obscuring his vision. The fleeting image of Brutus' body had taught him all he needed to know.

A thick plate of muscle around his stomach.

No point wasting any more energy attacking it.

The memory of their meeting came back to him. There was a surprising amount of scar tissue around his eyes …

Brutus moved in. Titus' legs were turning into jelly and he couldn't suck in enough air to compensate. His head pounded, his vision was blurred and he could only imagine how battered he looked, gasping for breath, pain stabbing every part of his torso and face, blood flowing freely down his chin and neck. He decided to turn it to his advantage and dropped his guard slightly. Brutus crabbed forwards, setting himself for another all-in assault. As his feet twisted on the sand, Titus dropped his right knee almost to the floor and, mustering the last dregs of his energy, threw an overhand right.

It was an all or nothing moment. The danger was that his punch would sail wide and expose him to what would surely be a final, painful barrage.

But his timing was perfect.

His fist slammed into the bridge of Brutus' nose as he lunged forwards and it he felt it crumple, releasing a jet of blood down his chest, as if expelled by a set of bellows. Brutus stumbled onwards like a wounded stag, clattering into Titus. Down they went onto the compacted sand with a shuddering bump, and for a moment it looked as if neither of them would rise. But Brutus was an altogether sturdier opponent than the youth Titus had defeated in the Baths of Trajan and he was still conscious. Awestruck, the crowd was silent at the sight of the battered fighters grunting and heaving, one trying to get back to his feet, the other to shove away the heavy body sprawled on top of him. With an almighty effort, Titus pushed Brutus aside and rolled away. He staggered to his feet, wiping away the blood from his face.

There was a respectful ripple of applause, above which the four watchmen could be heard yelling in excitement.

"You've got him, Titus! You've nailed him!"

"Stay down, you bastard!"

Brutus rolled onto his front and Titus' heart sank as the felled boxer gamely scrabbled to his feet with all the unsteadiness of a newborn lamb. But no sooner had he stood, he dropped to one knee.

"Stop!" This time the referee had no hesitation in calling a halt.

"Twenty seconds, remember!"

Bulla's quip drew one or two sniggers from the galleries, though a brief scuffle near the back cut them short. Whilst Titus staggered over to the watchmen and had the blood and dirt cleaned from his face, Brutus' own men had hurried onto the sand and were assessing his shattered nose. They poured water over his head and down his back and exchanged quick, anxious words.

"Is twenty, call time damn you!"

But the referee ignored Bulla's yelling, his gaze fixed on the activity around Brutus.

An anxious murmur rose from the spectators as the referee walked over to Brutus, who was still on one knee.

"Thirty, you good-for-nothing cheating fucker! Time! Call time you damn cheat!"

"Prefect," he said, "I'm going to have to count you out unless you get to your feet."

He looked at the two hulking soldiers attending to him. They both shook their heads gravely.

"No, I'm not done!" he croaked, spitting blood. "Give me it, Julius! Give me your damn caestus! That's an order!"

The referee looked doubtfully at him. With reluctance, he slipped his hand into his pocket and removed the studded iron fist-plate. Brutus slipped it over the wraps covering his knuckles and then struggled to his feet.

"Do it!"

"Time!"

The referee's announcement met with howls of disapproval and protest from the watchmen, but the Praetorian kept his gaze averted. Muted cheers greeted the revival of the Prefect but, to the astonishment of the watchmen, there were even a few boos from an agitated section across the courtyard.

Ambrosius had been watching the exchange between referee and fighter. Whilst he had not been able to see or hear exactly what had taken place, he sensed by the reaction of the onlookers that something untoward had happened.

"Something's up. Just look out," was all he managed to say to Titus, but he could not be sure he had heard him over Chest's instructions.

Titus stretched out his bruised arms and raised them wearily in anticipation of Brutus' onslaught. To his surprise, however, none came. The spring had deserted his steps and it was on unsteady feet that he met Titus in the middle of the circle. Titus switched to the offensive, feigning left and right shots, gauging the other man's responsiveness. He threw a stopped jab, ducked under the expected counter that never came and threw a right cross. Brutus pawed it away with his left and swayed back groggily to watch it sail past his pulped nose.

Sensing a knockdown, Titus held ground and steadied himself for a left hook, swaying to his right to widen his punching arc. It was in that split second that he registered the iron plate on Brutus' cocked right fist. Its presence mesmerized him. Time took on a surreal quality as the fist slammed into his exposed temple.

The crunch of iron on bone was sickening. A dazzling, heavenly light exploded before Titus' eyes and then there was only a profound darkness. The slow, almost graceful, spectacle of his mighty body folding at the knees and toppling to the side was played out in a stunned silence. And even when the watchman lay motionless on the sand, the only sound that could be heard in the crowded courtyard was Brutus' ragged breathing. He slipped the caestus off his fist and tossed it behind him, then stood there uncertainly looking from the stricken boxer to the shocked faces in the gallery. The referee unfolded his arms and, when it became clear that Titus wasn't going to rise, strolled over to Brutus, gripping his wrist and raising it above his head. And yet even in this, his greatest victory, the rush of joy and adulation still eluded him.

"Bru-tus! Bru-tus!" came a few curiously half-hearted chants.

Ambrosius, Chest, Vitalis and Bulla rushed onto the sand. The tribune raised Titus' bloodied head and slapped his cheeks.

"Titus! Titus! Open your eyes! Open them, damnit!"

"Here," said Chest, handing him another pitcher of water, "use this!"

Ambrosius upended the water over his face. The blood and sand cleared sufficiently to reveal the multitude of bruises and deep cuts inflicted upon him, but Titus' battered eyelids remained resolutely closed.

"Give me the mentha!"

With trembling hands, Chest rummaged around inside the sack he had liberated from the baths.

"Hurry up man!"

"Here!"

Ambrosius pulled off the stopper to the vial and shoved the compound of ground leaves under Titus' nose, himself recoiling at the pungent whiff. There was no response. He looked in desperation at Brutus and the referee.

"Well don't just stand there! Get a fucking medic!"

"It's no use, watchman. He's dead."

Ambrosius scrambled to his feet and confronted the Praetorian. "Do it now!"

Under any other circumstances, the soldier would have laughed and beaten him, but there was something about the wild fury in the watchman's eyes.

"Medic here at once!"

"Is he breathing?" asked Vitalis.

Ambrosius bent down and placed his ear close to Titus' nose, straining beyond hope to hear some faint sound. There was none. He clenched his fists and pounded them into the sand, bellowing like a wounded bull. An elderly medic with a cloth band tied around his head hurried over. Ambrosius moved aside to let him work.

The physician unbound the rawhide straps from the watchman's limp hands and felt for a pulse at both wrists, then his neck.

"Chest ... does not rise or fall ... the neck ... no pulse, wrists ... no pulse. And ... oh my ... such a brutal, pointless sport," he tutted and looked up at Ambrosius, "his skull is badly fractured, here. I'm sorry, young man, but Death claimed him before he even touched the floor."

He stood up gingerly on joints that clicked. "I can clean him up before you take him. And I'm sure the Acting Prefect could lend you a cart ..."

But Ambrosius wasn't listening. He looked at his hands that had begun to shake and felt a chill numbness creep through him.

This isn't happening. This can't be happening ...

He dropped to his knees and gripped Titus' limp hand.

"I'm sorry, old friend. I'm so sorry!"

The Praetorian referee gave Brutus a look and shrugged his shoulders. "I'll be going to my townhouse." Then he sauntered away.

"Commander," said one of the attendants, "your injury."

Brutus glanced down at the dark stain in the sand formed by the blood that had been trickling down his face. He wiped it away. "To Hades with my injury. This man fought with courage: he deserves our respect. Find him a bier and place yourselves at their disposal." He turned to Ambrosius. "I'm sorry, watchman. Whatever this was about, don't let it be in vain."

Brutus lingered for a moment longer, then walked away, ignoring the hum of speculation that rose from the galleries, who showed no less appetite to remain than they had to watch the contest in the first instance.

Ambrosius fell back on his haunches, tears stinging his eyes. He looked at Bulla, who was sat cross legged, his eyes gaping in shock at his best friend's lifeless body. The tribune shuffled over to him and put a comforting arm around his shoulder. It occurred to him that he had never seen Bulla crying before. The Syrian, as he never tired of reminding anyone who appeared to be listening, had been born a slave, was beaten regularly by his cruel master, had watched both parents die in front of him, had been freed in the only stroke of luck his life had experienced and had spent his youth stealing to stay alive. Yet he had never cried. His proudest moment in life, he had said, was being allowed to claim free public grain as a citizen. But there were some things that were too much even for him. Tears gathered in his eyelids and spilled down his cheeks, and his body shook with emotion, but still he did not take his eyes off Titus, as if at any moment he might awake and trade insults.

Ambrosius had to look away, feeling himself on the brink of losing control of his own emotions. Some part of him was still aware enough of the tiro Chest standing by, and of a whole courtyard of morbidly fascinated soldiers. He took a deep breath. No, he would somehow put a lid on it and do his grieving in private. His eyes passed over Brutus who, despite his great size and his victory, cut a strangely dejected figure, as he stood to one side, pressing a rag against his nose. Only the Praetorian who had presided over the contest seemed unfazed by the outcome, and Ambrosius cursed him bitterly as he swaggered out of the courtyard.

He would never know whether it was chance alone or the will of the gods that made his eyes track back along the sand. Either way, it was not a conscious act. Amidst the confusion of footprints, churned up and spattered with blood, was one that caught and held his attention. Numbed by grief, his mind did not immediately register how or why he knew the distinctive pattern.

Three columns of five studs, one extra at the big toe.

The indelible image of the print in the young girl's blood flashed before his eyes. He scrambled to his feet, startling Bulla, Vitalis and Chest, and stooped over the sand, examining it with a burning intensity. The ferocious contest and the flurry of activity after it had left such a proliferation of impressions on the damp sand that it seemed impossible to distinguish any of them. He pulled at his hair in panic and turned this way and that, tying his mind in knots.

How many Praetorians had been in the circle? Just Brutus' retinue? Damn it, Ambrosius, think man!

"What's wrong, tribune?" asked Chest.

"Nothing … don't move …"

Bulla looked up at him with a frown.

Ambrosius became aware that people were looking at him and he patted himself down, feigning a look of relief as if he had located something in his pocket.

"Bulla, look to your left. Look what my right foot is next to."

The Syrian turned round.

"Is next to sand."

"It's what's on it, Bulla," he said through gritted teeth.

Bulla sullenly got to his feet, glancing down at the sand next to the tribune's foot.

"So what, is just …"

"Recognise it now? Don't stand there looking like that, we're being watched!"

"But … I can't see where it goes!"

"Chest, Vitalis, pack up the equipment and stay with Titus. Don't look at what we're doing."

Ambrosius knelt over Titus' body and choked back the tears. He retrieved a coin and placed it on his undamaged eyelid, whispering a prayer of safe deliverance to Charon the Ferryman.

"Bulla," he said, standing up again, "walk out of the circle a couple of paces to my left, bow your head in grief and meet me over there. You know what we're looking for."

Bulla nodded and did as he was asked. Feeling like a very poor actor, Ambrosius ambled away, looking lost in thought, whereas his mind was scrutinizing the sand and his heart was pounding against his ribs. But he was unable to distinguish any more of the same footprints: the sand was just too disturbed. He moved away from the centre towards where Brutus was removing his wraps. It was then that he picked up the pattern again, indistinct at first where another pair of feet had trodden over them, and heading directly towards the Acting Prefect.

Surely not?

He needed to see the soles of his shoes.

"Lost something, watchman?"

Ambrosius swallowed hard, trying to keep the resentment from his voice. "An amulet he used to carry with him. It's not in his pocket."

"If it turns up I'll send it on." Brutus remained still, putting his hands on his hips. Ambrosius tried a different tack. He lifted his shoe up and inspected the sole, then did the same with the other.

"What in Hades are you doing?"

"Seeing if I've stepped on it, what else?"

"It's that important is it?"

"Very."

Brutus harrumphed and lifted his sandal. Ambrosius only caught a fleeting glimpse of the pattern of hobnails but it was enough. The irony was not lost on him that the grave cost of proving he was not the young girl's killer had been the death of his own friend.

Ambrosius nodded. "Can we expect a bier to have the body removed?"

"You heard me yourself, watchman," he said tossing the bloodied rag onto the floor, "it will be done."

With that, Brutus walked away. Even as Ambrosius turned back to look for Bulla, he caught sight of the prints heading away from Brutus towards the arch to the larger courtyard. His eyes widened in sudden understanding.

He'd already left.

He hurried over to Bulla.

"So? Was it?"

"No. The Praetorian referee."

He spat onto the floor. "The bastard!"

"You three stay with Titus. I'm following him."

"Eh?"

"Just do it, man. I'll see you back at the Watch House. I don't want any of this to have been in vain. And one more thing …"

"What?"

"Get a message to Junius Rufinus as soon as you can. He needs to meet us this evening, first watch of the night, without fail. Can you do that?"

Bulla nodded.

"Thanks, old friend. And once everything is settled, we'll drink to his spirit tonight," said Ambrosius, gripping Bulla by the shoulder. "What Titus did will not be forgotten, I swear on it."

The Syrian looked away, his eyes glistening.

Ambrosius glanced over Bulla's shoulder and instantly regretted it. It was an image that would brand his mind forever. The afternoon sun dipping towards the colonnaded gallery; the animated mass of soldiers in the background; the absolute stillness of his great friend lying broken at the centre of the sandy arena, and the raw recruit, not dissimilar in physique, standing over him like a sentinel, looking expectantly towards his tribune.

He closed his eyes in a vain effort to expunge the image and wheeled away.

III

Situated nearly sixty miles south of Rome, Tarracina was a pretty coastal town with a busy port that moored ships seeking to take advantage of the cheaper harbour dues from around the empire. They bore cargoes of oil, wine, glass, marble, wool, timber and precious minerals.

And so the mid-sized merchant ship that docked in the warmth of the late afternoon drew no special attention as it was tied up and its quiet, efficient crew unloaded the unmarked crates onto mule-drawn wagons, paid the taxes without fuss at the old counting house and left the docks. It was only when they were clear of the town and the sun was dipping towards the Cypress lined hills that they branched off the main road and resumed talking amongst themselves. Anyone listening would not have understood them, unless they were acquainted with the Berber language. The track was flanked by Poplar trees that screened it and the modest villa at its end from view. Once the crates had been stored alongside the stockpile already assembled inside the villa's granary warehouse, the fifteen big men fed and watered the mules and went inside.

IV

Were it not for the Praetorian's throwaway comment that he was 'going to his townhouse', Ambrosius would have given up waiting for him. As it was, although he had failed to catch sight of him again as he had left the palaestra, he felt sure that he would notice him on the way out of the camp on the grounds that he would have had to change out of his parade uniform first.

By keeping his mind active with such calculations as he leaned against the counter of the corner bar by the Viminal Gate, he was barely able to keep thoughts of recent traumatic events at bay. But as he waited, fragments of conversation or images would breach his defences and make his eyes brim with tears.

What if I had never entertained the idea of taking the body of the senator's daughter to the crypt? Would Titus still be alive? Would Anna still be living in my house?

He gritted his teeth and steeled himself to change the topic of his mental conversation, taking another swig of wine and focusing his attention on the gates to the Praetorian camp, eighty or so yards distant. A minute later, the gates creaked open and he braced himself, only to see a couple of soldiers emerge laughing and joking. An evening's leave, perhaps? He relaxed again as the gates were closed.

Just supposing he was to see the murderous Praetorian leave the camp, what then?

He had made no firm plans, other than to follow him to find out where he lived. His impulsive nature would make him want to confront the man and force him to confess but he knew there would only be one, painful, outcome to that.

His thoughts were interrupted by the gates yawning open again, and his body tensed. The bier bearing Titus' shrouded bulk, borne on the shoulders of four sizeable Praetorians, emerged across the threshold, closely followed by Bulla, Vitalis and Chest. Ambrosius felt his throat constrict and he throttled the wooden drinking cup as he reined in his tears. The small procession turned left towards the gates in the old Servian wall, heading straight towards Ambrosius, presenting him with a cruel dilemma: to

246

follow the procession and pay his respects to his friend or to await the man he had been hunting for the past two weeks?

Caught in the midst of uncertainty he stood rooted to the spot. He was on the point of retreating around the building line when he glimpsed another figure leaving the camp gates just before they closed. There was no mistaking the stocky figure of the Praetorian as he jogged out of the gates, plainly attired now. If Ambrosius thought his own absence from his friend's procession was disrespectful then what the Praetorian did next was astonishingly so. In an effort to get ahead of the bier-bearers on the narrow expanse of cobbles, he came up the side and cut across them, compounding the gesture by looking back with a now familiar sneer. This alone was enough to set Ambrosius' mind in stone. He ducked around the corner of the bar and waited for his quarry to pass. Instead of turning right towards the Viminal Gate, he carried on, in the direction of the next gate along, the Porta Esquilina.

Ambrosius put his cup on the counter and fell in behind him, no more than twenty paces ahead of the procession. He sensed the watchmen's quizzical stares boring into his back, praying they would stay silent.

No call came and, after a few minutes, the procession turned right towards the heart of the city. Ambrosius glanced over his shoulder and saw the heads of Bulla and Chest hanging low. He slowed his pace and mingled with the oblivious throngs of people enjoying the warmest afternoon of the year to date, though his eyes were set on the Praetorian like a hawk's on a rabbit. Even as he watched him swagger down the street, his contempt for him deepened. Anyone in his path would be barged aside without so much as a backwards glance, though none dared challenge him: Ambrosius could envisage him baring his decaying teeth at them in his wintry grin if they did.

The Praetorian crossed Via Tiburtina, which entered the city via the Esquiline Gate, and continued heading south, still following the line of the Servian wall. They passed the gateposts of the barracks of Cohort II and a series of tenement blocks above busy street-level shops. Ambrosius panicked when he temporarily lost sight of the Praetorian and, scanning the multitude of heads stretching into the distance, nearly bumped into him. He had stopped at one of several stalls that were selling hot fava beans wrapped in vine leaves. Ambrosius ducked down and adjusted the strapping to his sandals, allowing the Praetorian a thirty yard head-start.

They were now approaching the soaring arch of the Porta Caelimontana, stacked on top of which was part of the support structure of a branch aqueduct of the Aqua Claudia. He glanced up at the kink in the towering Servian wall.

When his eyes dropped, the Praetorian had gone.

Ambrosius peered ahead, not believing his eyes, and then broke into a jog.

Scores of people going about their business; an elderly lady yawning at the roadside; Children playing. No soldiers.

He turned to the right, where he had a fleeting glimpse of the Praetorian disappearing into a building beyond the gate. Ambrosius followed cautiously and walked past two modest houses on the right, not daring to stop. There was no way of telling which of these he had entered: both of them presented faceless exteriors.

He continued down the street before dropping onto a stone bench that gave him a view of the houses. He wiped the sweat from his forehead and looked around. The area was quite wealthy and he knew anecdotally that it was popular with the families of Jewish merchants, who tended to keep to themselves. One or two of them passed him, bearded and wearing small cloth caps, and they stared at him as they went. It seemed like a strange district for the Praetorian to have chosen to live.

Thirty minutes later there had been no activity. He began to feel both tired and conspicuous. Poppeia was still in the care of neighbours and he had not himself slept since the previous day. Tonight, he knew, would be a long, eventful watch and he was in dire need of some rest. Reluctantly, he got up to make his way home and did not look back. He had not gone further than ten paces before a street door opened a short distance behind him and the Praetorian slipped out of it.

V

"So let me summarise, Ambrosius, just so I can be sure. You propose to bluff your way into the house of a respected Praetorian captain, rummage about inside his private rooms and then scurry away with a pair of his sandals so you can prove that he murdered the senator's daughter? Sweet Juno, if you didn't look so serious I'd say you'd just lifted the idea straight from one of Plautus' comedies!" Though Junius Rufinus laughed, he did not look amused.

"I'm being serious. We have a right to enter under certain circumstances," he replied, omitting that he had not even identified the exact address.

"Let me put it this way, tribune," said Rufinus, "I will not be seeking authorization from the City Prefect, Fabius Clio, for supervised access to the Records Office just so that you can fish about in the dark, desperately hoping to find a document with Plautianus' name on it. And be sure I am certainly not endorsing your other plan either. You won't thank me for reminding you, but that gallant man lying on the slab down there," he said, jabbing his finger to the floor, "risked everything just to guarantee your safety. And he was not the only one. I gather you had your warning, good and clear, that you should keep your head down whilst you are back in Rome. And yet here you are asking to lead a suicidal operation to stir up trouble with the very people that drove you to Ostia in the first place!"

"You needn't make me feel guilty for being alive, Prefect." Ambrosius bristled with indignation. "I know the cost only too well. Suppose we do find what we're looking for? What then? You'd have the proof you need to get that lazy fool Clio off his couch and finally do some good!"

"What proof? A dead body? Now that would be fairly damning proof! A confession, signed and sealed by the murderer's own signet ring perhaps? No, neither of the above, gentlemen of the jury: a pair of sandals!" He threw his hands into the air in exasperation. "Look, I know you have your own reasons for doubting Clio's ability after what happened to your wife. But let me assure you of one thing: that man possesses a mind as sharp as an eagle's beak."

"We both know what their significance is! And there may be other things in that house that are important. That and a name from the Records Office would be enough to go to the Emperor himself with!"

"Have you lost your mind, Ambrosius? A wretched pair of sandals wouldn't even get me five seconds of his time! I say it again, tribune: Plautianus and his kind are not the sort of men you can just accuse lightly! They're men respected by the whole imperial administration, with their loyalty proven over and over again. That's all the Emperor sees or cares to see, even if it's not the whole truth or even a scrap of the truth! And I'm not mocking you. If I don't test you in this way, Ambrosius, then who will?" Rufinus softened his tone. "Look, that's a very mild version of what you could expect! Just suppose you did find these damn sandals, and let's even say they were caked in blood, what do you think someone even sharper than Clio would say in his defence? That you stole his shoes, which were already bloody from the boxing contest, and then made your own impression on that bit of rag to which you attach such significance! Who is to say otherwise? And once the court had dismissed the evidence, Ambrosius, you would be a dead man."

Ambrosius took a deep breath to quell the anger building inside him. "Well the future's pretty bleak for all of us, isn't it? And I don't see anybody else trying to change it," he added, looking pointedly at Rufinus.

The Prefect met his eyes for a moment and then turned away, shaking his head. "You have heard my thoughts, tribune. The gods be with you, in success or failure."

When he had gone, Ambrosius sagged onto his desk for a few moments and rubbed his eyes. They were bloodshot and burned with fatigue and sorrow. Wanting nothing more than just to close them for several hours, he went over to the basin in the corner of the room and splashed his face and neck. Then he went outside.

The forty watchmen packed into the courtyard turned to face him and their conversation faded to an expectant silence. The unheralded sight of Titus' body being carried through that very courtyard and being laid down on the crypt slab by the four Praetorian pall bearers had stunned them. Many of them had only just awoken from the previous night's patrols and were still groggy when they heard the commotion. And now here they were a few hours later, stood to attention in anticipation of a special duty. They had all seen the Prefect of The Watch leave, looking distracted and irritable, and had been speculating why. Ambrosius noticed Ludo's face

250

amongst them. His century was not on night duty this month but, to his credit, he had pledged his help.

"Men of The Watch. Centurion Titus is dead. He died as he lived, with great bravery." Murmurs of agreement rolled through the courtyard. "Today has been one of the saddest in living memory. And you have just now seen our Watch Prefect leave this building, so I know you'll be wondering what the night has in store for us. We will drink to Titus' memory, but there is still work to be done and, out of respect for him, we will do it well." He struggled to keep his voice from cracking. "So then, a small detachment of four volunteers will accompany me to the barracks of Cohort V, near the Caelian hill, where I will be asking the tribune for his assistance. Once I have received that," he said, skating over his own doubts about the probability of actually getting any help, "I'll explain the plan in greater detail. Six more volunteers will shed their belt kits and helmets and be excused night patrols. The task for these six is not as straightforward as it sounds: they will split into two groups and pay casual attention to any comings and goings from the Praetorian Camp without drawing attention to themselves. They will then report back to me towards the end of the watch. Is that clear?"

The men exchanged a few quizzical looks but asked no questions.

"Volunteers?"

Forty hands were raised in the blink of an eye. "Good. Ludo … Bulla … Chest … are you sure you're up to this? I wouldn't hold it against you if you passed."

"We're with you, tribune."

Bulla did not respond. Nor did he need to. There was a cold look in his eyes that Ambrosius had never seen before.

"Fine. You too, Stilicho," said Ambrosius, pointing to the sizeable German. He suspected he would need every bit of muscle he could cram into his team.

"And Paulus: pick five others, put away your belts and do your best to look like anyone other than watchmen, understood? Good."

There were a few murmurs of disappointment from the thirty one other men who had not been selected. "As for the rest of you," Ambrosius continued, "you may consider yourselves reserves. Do not stray too far from this building and keep your own eyes and ears open for anything unusual. And if you hear our whistles then you better fly like Cupid with his arse on fire to help us out, do I make myself clear?"

The men nodded. "Demetri … where's Demetri? Congratulations man; you've just been promoted for an hour. Good luck one and all. Let's go."

Within minutes, the two units had left the barracks; one heading east to the Caelian hill and the other north east towards the Praetorian Camp. The full moon hung low in the night sky and cast the grimy cobbled streets in a sickly glow. Even though there was nothing unusual about the sight of five vigiles on the streets at this hour, he could not shake the feeling that they were being watched. And not just by the beggars and thieves that they could sense eyeing them from the concealment of the shadowy rookeries they passed.

After ten minutes, they crossed the Street of The Public Baths and entered the region patrolled by Cohort V. They could see by the way the house lamps reared ahead of them that they were at the lower slopes of the Caelian and Ambrosius made a quick calculation: the easier approach to the barracks was from the north but this took them close to the house of the Praetorian captain and he did not want to take on the risk of being challenged at this stage. He took a circuitous route south of the barracks, trying in the weak light cast by his torch to negotiate the tangle of streets using nothing more than vague memories of the place. The men on Sebaciaria duties had not done their job well here, he noted.

There were few words exchanged on the way: Bulla himself had been silent. Eventually he located the street he was looking for and came up against a long wall at the top of a crossroads. The only windows were on the second floor and they were small and grilled. There appeared to be no entrance on this side of the complex.

"Shit," muttered Ambrosius.

"Who are you lot?"

They turned to face two watchmen stepping out of the shadows with their hands on their cudgels.

"Tribune, Cohort IV. I need to see …"

"What's the watchword?"

"The watchword is don't fuck me about, I'm here to see tribune Scaurus. So show us the way in."

The two vigiles looked doubtfully at each other. One of them nudged the other, nodding towards the silver brooch of office that he had spotted underneath Ambrosius' cloak. He stepped aside.

"Good enough, I suppose. Follow us."

He led them around the line of the building to the front gates and banged on them with the back of his fist. Moments later, they creaked open and the five entered. The townhouse in which Ambrosius and his men worked could have fitted snugly into one corner of these barracks. Two colonnaded wings flanked a grassy courtyard and the range at the back was dominated by a grey two storey block, flanking which were stone sheds for the cohort's pumps and wagons. They made straight for the central building and were stopped by a trio of officious staff officers. As Ambrosius explained why they were there, his patience fraying by the second, a booming voice cut across the reception chamber. Ambrosius glanced towards a closed door.

"By Jupiter why don't you just show him in!"

Ambrosius smiled tightly at the staff officers as he entered.

Tribune Scaurus was stood at the opposite end of the room with his hands behind his back. He raised his bushy white eyebrows upon seeing Ambrosius and strode across the room to embrace him.

"Ambrosius Milo, you old villain! Let me look at you!"

Scaurus had snowy white hair that contrasted with his ruddy features. Jowly skin now covered what had once been a craggy, handsome face. He had been a blustering, quick tempered soldier in his youth but now, whilst the spirit remained, age, wine and rich food had taken their toll on his body. Five years previously, Scaurus had been the one to break the crippling news to him that Larissa's broken body had been discovered near the Hill of Gardens. Though his life had spiraled out of control for a time thereafter, he had never forgotten his kindly, gentle manner, and the genuine concern he had shown.

Be bold, young man, he had told him, gripping him by the shoulders. As great as your feeling of desolation is, your daughter's feeling of abandonment will be even greater. Be strong for her. You will mend and Vengeance will come, one day.

Ambrosius had credited those words with being his salvation, or at least one of its building blocks. As he rose from the depths of despair and gradually scraped his life back together, the words came back to him, resonating with purpose. Scaurus was one of the first people he went to see. Though he only gone with the intention of thanking him, he emerged knowing that he would become a night watchman. Scaurus, for his part, had not seemed at all taken aback by his visit: he said he had only been surprised he had not come sooner.

Scaurus shook hands with Ludo, Bulla, Chest and Stilicho and showed them all to seats, lowering himself onto one with a grimace.

"So then," he rumbled, looking from face to face, "I take it by the sorry looks of you all this isn't merely a social visit?"

"I'm afraid not, Scaurus. We're here to ask for a favour."

"Oh?" he said, his eyebrows rising like the wings of an owl.

"I need a few of your men. And a bit of local knowledge …"

Ambrosius explained his plan, which was also the first time his own watchmen had heard it. When it came to mentioning the bloodied footprint, he unraveled with a flourish the sailcloth he had brought along. It didn't receive the enthusiasm that Ambrosius had hoped for – Scaurus frowned at it as if expecting something to emerge from underneath it – but he didn't interrupt him. When he had finished, Scaurus was silent.

"Well?" asked Ambrosius, "What do you think?"

Scaurus cleared his throat. "I think it stinks. It's desperate, sounds like it was conceived whilst you were sat on the latrine and, what's more, it's damned dangerous, if you want my honest opinion." He watched Ambrosius sag with disappointment. "It's just the sort of job I'd have rolled my own sleeves up for, back in the day, but I'm afraid I won't be joining you myself on this one. How many do you need? Five more?"

Ambrosius blinked in surprise. Even Bulla managed to raise a fleeting smile. "Five would be good."

"Can't help you with the exact house for that damned Praetorian reptile, mind. Didn't even know we had one scurrying about on our ground, truth be told. Sorry. Tesserarius!" he bellowed. "Need you here this instant!"

One of the staff officers entered and took instructions from Scaurus. Whatever his personal thoughts were about the task, to his credit, the officer did not let show. He merely nodded, and left the room.

Just ten minutes later, there was a knock on the door and five more watchmen, fully kitted out, shuffled inside. Ambrosius explained the task and was relieved that they didn't ask too many questions. When they were done, Scaurus rose and shook hands with them all, offering encouragement and repeating, with patent regret, that he wished he had looked after himself better so that he could have joined them. Then he led them towards the gates and waved them out.

Still troubled by the sensation that they were being watched, Ambrosius insisted on hushed voices as they descended into a maze of tightly packed shop fronts and first floor balcony beams, near invisible in the dark, which occasionally clipped the tops of their helmets. Before long, Scaurus' men brought them through a dark alleyway to the junction with a wider street. The youngest amongst them, a lean looking character with a shaved head and pockmarked skin named Valens, called the group to a halt.

"This street," he whispered, "is the one you must have walked down after you'd followed him, tribune. Right is the Porta Caelimontana, left the Temple of Claudius and the Colosseum. The house we're interested in is down there at the other end, near the gate."

"Understood."

"And opposite is another alleyway. It leads to another street parallel to this one. That would take you to the back of those shops and houses, in case anyone tried to escape."

"They'd have to climb like a gecko to get over the back walls, mind," said another of Scaurus' men. He had long ginger hair and a beard and did not look or sound at all like an Italian. Ambrosius couldn't pronounce his name when he had first heard it and so called him 'Red'. "Very high, those walls."

"Keep out prying eyes."

"Or interfering watchmen," said Ludo.

"So then, Ludo, take Viator and Pollo here from the Fifth: you cover the back of those houses. The rest of us will go in by the front."

"Which one at the front?" asked Stilicho. "I thought you didn't know, tribune."

"I don't. Red here is going to knock on the second door from the gate, aren't you Red?"

"Whatever you say, tribune. Second door is good," he replied with a crooked grin.

"Any more questions?"

"Yes," said Pollo quietly. "Say the Praetorian does get spooked and somehow gets over the back walls, what then?"

"What would you normally do if you saw someone jump over the back wall of a house during the night?"

"I'd stop him, probably."

"No, you'd stop him definitely. And if he put up a fight, you'd stick him until he was twitching."

"Right."

"Any more stupid questions?"

There were none. The flames hissed gently through the tallow on the torches, reminding them all that time was limited.

"Good luck."

They all left the cover of the alleyway and split according to their instructions. Ambrosius felt the familiar surge of fear and exhilaration. As the seven watchmen approached the front door, Ambrosius felt his pulse quicken and his heart pound against his ribs. He wondered if Larissa might somehow be watching him and whether she might approve of what they were about to do. No doubts she would have rolled her eyes and smiled at him as she did whenever he mentioned one of his whimsical plans. Unbidden, an image of her vainly trying to fight off her unknown attacker entered his mind, spoiling the moment. He shook his head to clear it.

I won't fail.

This can't fail.

"Tribune?"

Red was poised at the front door, alongside Hesper, another of Scaurus' cohort. Ambrosius looked up at the featureless, white-washed wall. The shutters were closed and there were no signs of life. He cupped his ear to the door and nodded. He could feel the other watchmen around him tense.

Red rapped on the ram's head knocker three times and they all waited.

No response.

A minute passed and Red reached for the knocker again but a sharp click of the tongue from Ambrosius made him freeze. Padded footsteps approached the door and a grill slid open. A pair of beady eyes glared at the watchmen and there were muttered curses. The door opened slightly and a slant eyed janitor stood at the threshold, looking at them suspiciously.

"Yes?"

"Watchmen of the Fifth Cohort."

"I can see that," he snapped. "What do you want?"

Red cleared his throat. "We believe you have unsupervised fires within these premises."

"Rubbish. We have one and it's perfectly well supervised. By me. Now if that's all I'd like to get some sleep."

"And if it's all the same with you, we'd like to be sure," he replied firmly.

"How dare you impose yourselves like this! You should be more mindful of whose house …"

Good, thought Ambrosius. *Right choice ...*

"And you should be more mindful who you refuse entry to!" hissed Ambrosius, stepping past Red. "I'm the tribune of this cohort and by order of the Divine Emperor himself you will grant us access to this property!"

The startled doorkeeper took one look at Ambrosius' blazing eyes and hesitated.

"I have my own key anyway," said Ambrosius, raising a crowbar, "so I suggest you co-operate with my men. And perhaps then I'll forget your insolence."

The janitor procrastinated for a few moments before unbolting the door. Ambrosius hooked the crowbar back onto his belt and stepped past him into the dimly lit atrium. He looked up and flinched.

The two black soldiers, dressed in outlandish sets of armour, loomed out of the darkness in front of him. His hand fumbled for his cudgel but the soldiers didn't advance. As Ambrosius' eyes adjusted to the gloom, it became clear that his nerves were playing tricks on him. The armour contained no soldiers. They were trophies, stripped from foreign enemies, burnished and hung on man sized wooden pegs, conspicuous displays of military valour that now guarded the threshold with an imposing silence. The other watchmen, forced to an abrupt halt by the tribune, backed up against each other. The janitor scowled at the clumsy entrance, saying nothing.

Ambrosius allowed his pulse to settle as he entered and took stock of the surroundings. A few candles dotted around the small hallway illuminated the floor's two-toned mosaic. To the left was a doorkeeper's cubby hole, to the right a small shrine to the household lares and above the lintel of the door was a sign:

ANY SLAVE SEEN LEAVING THE HOUSE WITHOUT HIS MASTER'S PERMISSION WILL RECEIVE FIFTY LASHES.

There was a flight of stairs flush against the left wall and a darkened suite of rooms directly opposite. Set against the wall on the right were two doors: one was slightly ajar and he could just about make out the outline of stone steps descending to what he presumed were slaves' quarters. The second door was closed. There was a faint musty smell about the place that seemed oddly familiar.

"Hesper," he said, pointing to both eyes and then to the janitor, as he closed the door behind them.

The watchman nodded.

"Janitor, who else is here?"

He shot Ambrosius a haughty look. "Myself, a few slaves."

"And where's the master of the house?"

"Not here."

"Well, where is he?"

He shrugged. Ambrosius stalked over to him and prodded him hard in the chest, backing him against his cubby hole. "Maybe I didn't make myself clear before. I'm losing patience with you, you little maggot. You'd better talk or you'll be slung in a cell with just rats for company, got it?"

Ambrosius saw the flicker of fear in his eyes.

"I'll try again. Who is the master and where is he?"

"Julius Pennus, tribune, is a captain of the Praetorian Guard. He is not here now: he left earlier today. He didn't tell me where he was going, but why should he? Which is more the pity, because I'm sure he would've liked to meet you." His lip curled into a sly grin.

"Oh believe me, not as much as I'd have liked to meet him," said Ambrosius, feeling his bile rising. "Valens, Stilicho; upstairs. Red, Chest; downstairs. Bulla and I will check this floor."

"Err," said the janitor, "I thought it was our fire that you were interested in? The stove is in the kitchen, through that door. There's no need to send your men where they have no rights to go."

"I assume you have a hypocaust system?"

"But I only light it an hour before dawn. I've not even gathered the wood yet!"

"And upstairs, I'd like to ensure you have adequate fire prevention measures."

"This is ridiculous! What are you up to? I'll have the Praetorian Prefect made aware of what you're doing: it's a disgrace!"

Ambrosius clapped his hands, "Chop, chop, gentlemen! The janitor is quite right, we mustn't delay," the watchmen saluted and set about their tasks. "And what is it you do all day, anyway, sat in that box of yours? Must get awfully boring, no?"

"What …? You seem to think this intrusion is funny?"

Ambrosius rounded on him. "Funny, you say? Some of these watchmen were cited in the senate just the other week for their bravery in dealing with a major fire in the Aventine district. In showing a complete disregard for their own safety, they saved the lives of scores of men and women.

Now what do you have to say to that, eh? Nothing. So why not shut that cakehole of yours and let us do our jobs."

With theatrical brio, Ambrosius swiveled on the spot and beckoned Bulla to commence searching rooms on the ground floor, leaving Hesper to keep a close eye on the janitor.

"Nice going," whispered Bulla.

They entered a Spartan study. Quickly and quietly, they sifted through the Praetorian's correspondence. Citations, requisition documents, complaints, transfer requests … all of the usual paperwork associated with the military and nothing besides.

Ambrosius frowned as he unrolled one document after another and set it aside. "Doesn't it seem odd," he whispered, "that there's nothing, not a single tablet or scroll, which has anything remotely personal on it?"

"What do you mean?" asked Bulla.

"Well, even supposing this man has no friends, which is not that unlikely, you'd have thought he'd still write something with his own thoughts to somebody, given his rank. But there's nothing. No personal letters, no plans that don't involve the Guard, no family documents, wills, anything like that."

"Maybe they're somewhere else."

From the atrium, they caught the janitor's high pitched voice. Another complaint.

"This is getting us nowhere, Bulla. Let's just focus on finding those damned sandals before Hesper snaps that wretch's neck."

They worked through the study to the cluttered, dingy room beyond, which had no discernable function other than storage. To the right was a small room into which Bulla thrust his torch. The flame crackled in the dry air, casting flickering shadows inside a tiny kitchen. The usual range of utensils hung from a wooden rack above a brick oven and stove, on top of which was a layer of smouldering charcoal.

Bulla withdrew the torch. Ahead, a set of double doors opened to a small courtyard, containing what looked like a plum tree, surrounded by overgrown grass and weeds. The effect of the cool breeze against Ambrosius' face had a calming effect, making him forget for one pleasant moment the predicament he was in.

Forced entry to a Praetorian captain's townhouse, quoting non-existent complaints.

Citing the Divine Emperor's authority on false grounds.

Reading private documents.

Threatening a janitor who was merely doing his duty.

Retribution would be swift and painful. And all for a pair of shoes, Ambrosius laughed at himself. Would that be what was written as his epitaph?

He had to find some good evidence, and quickly.

Bulla returned from his short lap around the peristyle garden, shaking his head. "No more rooms. No storage. Nothing."

Panic gnawed at his nerves. There was every chance Pennus was still wearing the shoes he came back with earlier in the day. What then?

Ambrosius thought of the watchmen on the other side of the wall waiting in hope, ignorantly redundant. They went back inside the house and closed the doors behind them.

"There's no more rooms?"

"Not here."

They retraced their steps to the atrium. Chest and Red were already there. "No fires to report, tribune."

"Well of course there aren't," said the janitor, folding his arms, "unless you climb through the under-floor heating ducts and wait for a few hours!"

Ambrosius ignored the remark and tried to think. He glanced to his left. "What's behind this door?"

"I'll show you, shall I?" The smug look was back. He retrieved a key from the iron ring on his belt and unlocked it. "Have a good look, tribune."

Ambrosius tugged open the door and was assaulted by an invisible cloud of mouldy smelling dust, forcing him to step back and cough. The room was nothing more than a store cupboard for old blankets, clothes and wooden bric-a-brac that the Praetorian had collected on his travels. He shut it quickly, expelling another musty waft.

"See?"

That was one step too far for Bulla. Not having slept for over thirty hours, and in a day in which he had witnessed his best friend die in a brutal boxing match, his livelihood being threatened and his respected tribune insulted by a slave, his temper snapped and he rushed the janitor, his fist cocked. Red caught him just in time, shepherding him away, trembling with rage.

"Easy does it, Bulla. He's not worth it."

"Ha, you've really done it now! Wait 'til the master hears about all this!"

Just then, Valens and Stilicho came down the stairs. Ambrosius' heart sank when he saw that they were empty-handed.

"No water buckets up there, tribune."

They gave him a look: I'm sorry, tribune, we tried.

"Happy now? Worth all that, was it?"

"It is an offence not to have water buckets at the ready in this city, slave," said Ambrosius without any conviction, "so in that sense, yes, it was. We'll be round again; have it put right." He knew full well they wouldn't.

The janitor harrumphed and jingled his keys.

Time was up. They had to leave.

They fell in behind the tribune and headed for the door. For Ambrosius, this was more than just a set-back. He had not only staked his reputation on the whole enterprise; he had taken a very grave gamble with his own life. From now on, he would have to think twice before stepping round every street corner.

Just as he reached the threshold, he dropped his torch. It crackled and spat against the tesserae of the floor.

"Careful, damn you! That floor cost thousands."

"You fool," said Ambrosius, retrieving the torch, "stone isn't combustible."

The janitor tutted and opened the door to hasten them out, slamming it shut behind them.

Outside, Ambrosius gave a shrill whistle. A minute or so later, Ludo, Viator and Pollo came jogging down the narrow cut-through to rejoin them.

"Well," asked Ludo, "anything?"

Ambrosius didn't reply but strode off towards the alleyway from which they had first emerged, leaving Ludo to exchange looks with the other watchmen, who shook their heads sadly. Once they were out of direct sight of the house, Ambrosius called them to a halt.

"Not enough," he said to Ludo, rubbing his fingers by the light of his torch. "See? Grains of sand."

"Shows he was there though."

"Nobody's disputing that."

"So he left wearing the same pair of shoes, tribune," observed Chest. "Bastard slipped away before us."

"We could lie in wait for him?" said Red.

Ambrosius was beginning to like the flame-haired watchman's optimism. He wished he had joined Cohort IV. "No, though it does have a certain appeal. We've had our chance here, I'm afraid: we wouldn't even reach the front door next time. Come on, lead the way back to your barracks."

The watchmen were quiet on the walk back, passing only the odd comment about the footwear that they had found: similar size cut, totally different pattern of hobnails. They now retreated into their own thoughts. A motion had already been passed in the senate and now looked certain to be approved in the heavily-bribed assembly too. Praetorian and Urban Cohorts would soon be taking over their roles. The threat of poverty and hunger were forming like storm clouds above them.

Once they had reached the barracks the men of Cohorts IV and V shook hands and wished each other luck before going their separate ways, a gesture that seemed only too symbolic to them.

VI

Junius Rufinus sighed, ordered another cup of spiced wine and did not feel guilty about it. From being virtually teetotal, he had in the last couple of weeks come to rely upon the loosening effect of the grog served in the Gorgona. He looked about him at the clientele and realised that he had come to a similar conclusion about this, too. The gamblers, coffin makers, crooks and prostitutes within were merely a part of the furniture and did him no harm, at least not within these walls.

It was quieter tonight, subdued almost, though it was as warm and smoky as ever. He recognised one of the barmaids – a sharp-tongued Sicilian with a pinched face and too much make-up – but she was in no mood to talk. And there was even a rather rough looking fellow collecting cups and scowling at everyone who entered. Rufinus was certain that his function was more than merely tidying up. For the next five minutes, he tried to catch the eye of the Sicilian: no mean feat when the tankard-gatherer was casting his beady eye over all of the customers.

Eventually he took his opportunity and the barmaid came over.

"Another?"

Rufinus nodded. "One more thing," he said, touching her wrist before she left, making her start, "where's Zelika?"

She gave him a suspicious look. "Who's asking?"

"What?"

"Well?"

"A friend," he said, after a time.

She scrutinized him and her face softened. "Thought I've seen you before. You've obviously not heard, have you?"

"Heard what?"

"She was … she's … dead."

The wine turned to acid in his stomach. Dead?

"I'm sorry, sweetie. I see that's a shock to you too."

"How?"

She looked around her again. "Stabbed by a punter. Dispute over money, they say. Dangerous times, these. I didn't know her that well but she seemed nice enough. One on the house?"

But Rufinus didn't hear her. He shut his eyes and let his head sag against the wall.

"I'll leave you be sweetie. Call me over if you want another."

Of the maelstrom of thoughts and feelings that showered him, one echoed over and over inside his mind.

Guilt.

Instinct was both a blessing and a curse to him. Whilst it defined him as a person and distinguished him as an advocate and a strategist, it also jaundiced his view of people and life in general. But it also kept him alive. In possession of only the briefest of facts, he knew, he just knew, that her death had something to do with him. A whore and, it turned out, a thief, she had in recent troubled days been the closest approximation to a confidante, if hardly a friend. And now she was gone. That couldn't possibly be a co-incidence.

Numb with shock, he got up and left the tavern.

*

A few minutes later, the door opened and a tall man entered. He lowered the hood to his cloak and ran his fingers through his long hair, looking about him. He went to the bar and ordered wine then took it back to a spare table, drumming his fingers on a wax tablet as he waited to get the attention of a barmaid. He ignored the glare of a sizeable man with shaved hair stood by the counter and eventually a whore with a sour face passed his table.

"Excuse me."

She turned to look at him. "Yes?"

"I'm supposed to be meeting a friend for dice but," he gave her a sheepish smile and tested the blade in his pocket, "well, I'm late and I owe him money. You might have seen him: grey haired man, tanned face, doesn't look much like a gambler ...?"

She held his gaze. A handsome man for sure, but those grey eyes ...

"Sorry; not seen anyone like that tonight. Another drink?"

*

Ambrosius and the four watchmen trudged through the front gate of the townhouse, and he pointedly avoided the shrine as he entered the building. Piety would have been a hollow gesture at that moment.

There remained the matter of contacting Titus' funeral guild to arrange his cremation. He hoped he had been up-to-date with his payments: though he hated himself for it, he didn't feel like he had the emotional energy to

264

deal with that on top of everything else. Seeing his old friend in eternal repose would finish him off altogether. The macabre notion struck him that he might even be a little envious of his deep sleep. He smiled to himself: Titus would have laughed at that thought.

He opened the door to the study and flinched at the figure sat at his desk.

"I'm sorry, Ambrosius. I didn't mean to startle you."

Junius Rufinus looked how Ambrosius himself felt.

"Sir? Wasn't expecting to see you here?"

"No, quite. Can't say I envisioned it either. Come in, take a seat: it is your room after all."

Ambrosius drew up a stool and rubbed his face.

"Planning to use that, were you?" asked Rufinus, pointing to a wine pitcher. "Early drink to Titus' spirit?"

Rufinus poured them both a cup. "To Titus, dis manibus."

"Dis manibus, to the sacred dead."

They chinked cups and Ambrosius looked on in surprise as the Watch Prefect drained his in one.

"Feeling thirsty, sir? Another?"

"Not for me." He cleared his throat. "So then. How did you fare?"

Ambrosius sighed. "I had no difficulty getting help from tribune Scaurus at the Caelian."

"Scaurus," chuckled Rufinus, shaking his head.

"In short, I failed. He lent me some men and we got inside the property after a bit of a stand-off with the janitor and divided up to search the house but the Praetorian – he's called Julius Pennus apparently – wasn't there. He must've left without changing because I noticed some sand on the threshold. The janitor was full of himself: no doubt he'll be making trouble for me as I speak."

"You must be used to that by now."

"I suppose so. Not sure I'll be able to get out of this one without a scrape though."

Rufinus smiled and swirled his wine dregs broodingly as the quiet drip of the water clock punctuated the silence.

"Something troubling you? I mean, apart from the obvious?"

"I'll be going to speak to Fabius Clio in the morning. Seems you've been more attuned to the danger this city's in than I gave you credit for, Ambrosius."

"What? Are you saying … even without the sandals?"

265

"Yes, I am. As you know, I don't share quite the same enthusiasm as you for the significance of those damn shoes, but I do want to see who's put their name to all this … chaos. Enough is enough, and this is the last chance. In fact, I think it's been our only solid chance all along and it was you who spotted it. There's every chance, of course, that they've covered their tracks here, too. But … well, regardless of what comes of it, I ought to thank you. After all, nobody else will."

For a few moments, Ambrosius was speechless. He had never seen Rufinus so introspective before, and he wondered what was driving it.

"It was actually my daughter."

"Sorry?"

"My daughter, Poppeia. I assumed one of Gaius Plautianus' henchmen had taken the senator's daughter, either by impersonating a watchman or some other way. Truth be told, I didn't know how they'd got in. Knowing nothing of the building, she was the one who suggested they'd come in through the ground."

"Smart girl."

"Smarter than her father!"

Rufinus was distant again and retreated into his own thoughts. In the corridor, the flautist sounded the wake-up call for the first watch after midnight, Inclinatio, and the bugler responded in the courtyard, recalling those on the streets.

"I happen to know that Clio will be in the Basilica Aemilia throughout the second hour of the morning: I'd like you to accompany me, Ambrosius. Perhaps we can both prevail upon him whilst he's not in the Praetorian Camp, where chances are we'd be observed."

"Of course."

Rufinus drummed his fingers on the arm rest and then rose abruptly. "Finish up here, drink to Titus' spirit, then go home and get some rest. Tomorrow will be a trying day, one way and another."

"No, I have too much to do here."

"That's an order, tribune. I need your mind fresh tomorrow. Go and see your daughter. This place won't go to the dogs without you." Rufinus smiled briefly and then left Ambrosius alone to ponder the endless succession of twists and turns that defined his life.

VII

The hike through the seething city streets had left the three men lathered in sweat, irritable and, above all, hungry. Despite what they had been told and the preparations that had been made, the sheer mass of humanity, the extraordinary smells, the quirky mixture of imposing marble and gaudily painted slum were overwhelming. The directions they had been given had seemed so precise at the time: in reality, they were hopelessly vague. And now it was way after midnight.

Enter by Porta Appia. Straight on, Via Appia.

First street on right after shrine to Minerva.

Battered green door and lion head knocker.

Key behind loose brick at ankle height marked 'II'.

But there were numerous street-side shrines and, although they knew who Minerva was, one faded and worn sculpture looked very much like every other. And which virtue was she supposed to be representing? War? Wisdom? Art?

And who was to say which branch following the right turn were they supposed to take? For Roman roads forked at infuriatingly illogical points, and each street would open up more options, which increased exponentially the further you went.

As for a battered green door ... how battered, exactly, and what shade of green?

And so the mercenary that eventually identified the right address – entirely by chance – almost bellowed in triumph when he slid out a brick that had no mortar keeping it in place and grasped the elusive key.

They entered and checked each room, peeling away the dust sheets and tip-toeing up the creaking stairs. But the Prefect had been as good as his word. The place was empty and, compared to some of the streets and houses they had passed, exceeded their expectations. Basic but discreet, quiet and, best of all, stocked with food and weapons.

There was even a small amphora of wine with a tag around its neck, and another small scroll, also written in Berber. The soldier ripped it off and then his face cracked into a smile. He showed it to the others and they roared with appreciation.

In case you should even think about going to a tavern ...

Another soldier, the youngest of them, read the scroll and frowned. The others noticed his expression and their grins faded. The eldest snatched it out of his hands.

"What is the problem?"

"These directions to the walls of the Emperor's palace. Getting to this house was difficult enough, and these are three times longer. We should walk the way first. Tonight"

The eldest noticed the worry in the youngster's clear blue eyes. He cuffed the back of his head. "No. We went through them already. Here, have a drink and act like a man."

He tossed the scroll aside, poured out the amphora and they all chinked cups. Some dark wine spilled out of one of them and splashed the table, blotting some of the instructions on the parchment, which ended:

… burn this immediately after reading.

VIII

Ambrosius was grateful for the unexpected gift of a few hours of sleep. Though tired, he was at least able to function and he went to the Basilica direct from the public baths. And, when he saw Rufinus waiting for him, he was also grateful that Poppeia had insisted upon him wearing his best (and only) toga, which Anna had cleaned for him whilst he was in Ostia. He had experienced a pang of regret for her that Poppeia had not failed to notice when she mentioned her name.

The forum was already busy and, though the air was crisp, the clear skies suggested a warm day was in the offing.

"Good morning, sir. Not been waiting for me long I hope."

"Salve. No, don't worry," he said. "Ready?"

They strode across the shaded porticoes of the Basilica, skirting past an official lecturing a small group of traders – one of whom was asleep - about changes in weights and measures legislation, and headed towards a door with 'PRAEFECTVS VRBANVS' chiseled above the stone lintel.

An officious looking commentariensis was seated at a desk to the left of the door. He glanced up at them as he pared the nib of his quill pen with a knife.

"If you're here to see the City Prefect, you've no chance. He's busy."

"And his deputy?"

"In Portus."

"Then I'm afraid you're going to have to put down your quill and disturb him."

The secretary looked up at him. "And you are?"

"Junius Rufinus, Prefect of the Watch. This is Ambrosius Milo, tribune of the Fourth Cohort. It's urgent."

He put down the knife. "I'm sorry, Prefect. I'm under instructions that he should not be disturbed. By anyone."

"That's fine. I'll take my chances," said Rufinus, approaching the door.

"No! Just … for the sake of the gods!" he said, throwing his hands in the air and rising from his desk. Ambrosius looked at Rufinus and rolled his eyes. He was the sort of man they both despised.

After the knock on the door, there was a brief pause followed by an irritable 'yes?'

"Sir, I'm sorry, they insisted on seeing you. It's–"

"Yes, yes, I know who they are. Thank you."

The City Prefect's large office was a study in order and tidiness that bordered on the obsessive. Apart from a single piece of parchment and an inkpot, his desk was entirely free of clutter. The shelves running around the room were almost mirror images of each other, and each scroll holder was capped and labeled with the tag at the same height. It smelled of pine, wax and leather, with no scent quite dominating the room.

Fabius Clio eyed the Prefect and his tribune as they entered, his sharp gaze lingering on Ambrosius for a moment with the faintest of frowns. He nodded at his secretary who closed the door behind him.

"He's right you know," said Clio in his nasal voice, "I am extremely busy."

"I wouldn't have disturbed you if it wasn't important, you know that."

Clio leant back in his chair, pressing his fingertips together. "Go on."

"I'll get straight to the point. I need your authority to view a document in the Records Office."

"Which document and why?"

"An innocuous enough one – an architect's plan of a very old building. I need absolute discretion on it, that's why we've come to you."

Clio glanced across at Ambrosius and a thin smile straightened his lips.

"Oh come on, Junius! You'll have to do better than that! What's he doing here? What are you both up to, eh?"

"I know who murdered Terentia, senator Piso's daughter, and the final proof of it lies in that Records Office," said Ambrosius.

Clio leaned forwards and fixed Ambrosius with his shrewd blue eyes. "Oh does it now? Tell me, what have you had planted there?"

"And what's that supposed to mean?" he said, giving Rufinus a look of exasperation.

"It means I know about you and your outlandish methods. I've no idea why you have broken your exile – perhaps the less said about that the better – but your timing is uncanny. Are you quite sure you're not trying to deflect attention from your own misdemeanours?"

"I'm sorry? My outlandish methods?"

"Sir, you misunderstand both of us," interrupted Rufinus. "I myself recalled Ambrosius from Ostia, where there were credible threats his life was in danger. And as for his methods, it's fair to say we have not always been in agreement, he and I. However, though much of what I have heard is circumstantial, it is extremely compelling. I strongly recommend you hear it."

Clio looked from one to the other and sighed. "For what it's worth, I believe that you both think you are on to something. But the matter is already closed."

"Closed?"

"Yes, the Praetorians found the man responsible for the murder of young Terentia a number of days ago. He signed a confession but died following interrogation. I hope that puts your minds at rest. So, if there is nothing more …?"

Ambrosius and Rufinus shared incredulous looks. "With respect," said Rufinus, "that is bilge."

Clio looked up at Rufinus in surprise. "Excuse me? I perhaps ought to remind you who you are speaking to and about."

"And you talk of uncanny timing, sir! The murderer is caught, only to conveniently die during interrogation, having been beaten into signing a worthless confession, is that it? Were there any independent witnesses?"

"As a matter of fact there were, not that I have to divulge to you. The very insignificant trio of the Divine Emperor, his son and Terentia's own father, Senator Terentius Piso. None disputed the evidence: I suggest you follow their lead!"

"No," Ambrosius shook his head, "I just can't believe that. It's a set up! They saw a staged confession from someone beaten senseless, it must have been!" A look of enlightenment crossed the tribune's face and he shook his head. "How have I been so blind?"

"Look, I'm going to have to stop you there. I just don't have …"

Ambrosius turned to Rufinus. "I never even thought to ask where you got your information from, about what happened at the docks."

"What are you talking …?"

"I assumed all along that you were acting on instructions from the Praetorian Prefect, because you said your orders were from much higher than Fabius Clio here, so I didn't even consider the possibility of the City Prefect's involvement! Tell me, did you motivate Plautianus against me, because I snubbed your offer to join the Urban Cohorts? Was it you that sent informers sniffing about after me?"

Clio's face turned a shade of crimson and he stood behind his desk, his fists trembling. "How dare you slander my name in this way! I'll have you flogged for this, you damned villager!"

271

Junius Rufinus surprised them both by the anger in his voice. "Enough! You've gone way too far, tribune! Step outside; we'll do much better without your sharp tongue in this room!"

Ambrosius glared at both men before stalking out of the room and slamming the door shut. In the cool portico people stopped what they were doing and looked at him, but he ignored them and found a shaded step to sit on whilst the throbbing between his temples subsided. He became reflective and tried to remember if his temper had always been so volcanic. There were, as he saw it, two Ambrosius Milos: the first died years ago along with his wife. It was all he knew that the man he perceived himself to be today was different; and not in a good way.

Gradually, the ambient noises, sights and smells of the busy forum washed over him. He watched a fig seller with a wide-brimmed hat working his way through knots of people, boasting about the quality of his wares. He was doing a roaring trade today. Ambrosius envied his simple task in trying to shift as many baskets of fruit as he could before it grew dark.

It was nearly an hour later that he heard the footsteps approach him and felt the tap on his shoulder. Ambrosius braced himself for a haranguing but Junius Rufinus had the same distant look as he did the previous evening.

"You have a curious appetite for self-destruction for someone with a child, tribune," he said, sitting next to him on the step.

Ambrosius looked away.

"You were way off the mark in what you said in there. If I'd known you were going to launch into that little tirade I'd have stopped you from coming."

"I don't know what to think anymore."

Rufinus took a deep breath. "Let me help you then. The orders to have you sent to Ostia came in a letter to me written by Gaius Plautianus. Clio had nothing to do with it. He knew about it, he'd been told to take action against you but Plautianus pre-empted him."

"And the people sent to assassinate me in Ostia? The same people that informer told you had been given some contract? What about them? Who sent them?"

"I don't know. Nor does Clio."

"He says he doesn't know."

"No, Ambrosius, he doesn't know. It surprised him when I told him. You were barking up the wrong tree there and you saw yourself how angry you made him. You don't know Clio as I know him. He can be a difficult, obnoxious character at times but the man's as straight as a tent pole."

"I don't know … well, it doesn't matter anymore, does it? In a couple of days, this forum will be filled with people falling over themselves to vote for disbanding The Watch and giving the reins to Plautianus. Then he'll have them all in his pockets and Clio will probably benefit in some way, too."

"He's got his own private concerns about that, for what it's worth."

They were silent for a few moments and Ambrosius closed his eyes to enjoy the feeling of the breeze against his face. It came from the right direction, carrying the scent of pine from the lower slopes of the Palatine opposite rather than the prevalent whiff of dirt, dung and sweat from everywhere else.

"So, what about you, sir? What will you do with yourself?"

"That very much depends on what we find in the Records Office."

Ambrosius looked at him in confusion.

"When I say 'we', I mean to exclude you from that of course. There's no way Clio wants you along."

"You mean you've convinced him?" A grin crossed Ambrosius' face. "How in Hades did you manage that?"

"With a great deal of effort. I've offered to fall on my sword if you're wrong. I don't mean literally, tribune, you're not that important, but it was the only assurance of my conviction he'd accept. He's under the misguided impression that my career – whatever's left of it - means more to me than life itself, which was a convenient impression for him to have."

"And you'd do that … for me?"

"Don't get ideas above your station!" he said with a frown. "There's more at stake here than just you! And you'd better be right, or we've all had it."

"I think I am."

"Thinking isn't enough!" Rufinus got up and dusted off his toga. "I'm to come back this evening and meet Clio here. Do us all a favour. I don't care where you'll be, just promise it won't be here. Whatever happens, I'll have a message sent to you at your home or the Watch House, not that there seems to be any difference these days. Good day, Ambrosius."

The tribune watched him leave and tried to clear his thoughts, as the sun crept stealthily over his legs. He pondered the old saying that problems diminish in the daylight and found himself in agreement. For so long he had preoccupied himself with things that had spiraled out of his control: vengeance for Larissa, retribution for Terentia, the fate of his career … the nexus of these three things, and Fate itself, had achieved what? Nothing positive, that was for sure. And the one constant in his life, Poppeia, was at home and perfectly alone. He closed his eyes and shook his head as a ripple of shame passed through him. Throughout it all, his daughter was the only thing that mattered and he had neglected her too.

IX

Five more mercenaries arrived in Rome via the Porta Raudusculana as Ambrosius sprinted off to find Poppeia. They adjusted the position of the poles on their shoulders, carrying what was left of their provisions and a change of clothes, and wiped the sweat from their faces. Though they tried to feign indifference as they trudged under the stone arch, the glances they exchanged told of the same thoughts.

This city was vast.

X

Ambrosius had thought that bringing his daughter to Titus' cremation might spook her but her maturity and resilience again gave him cause for surprise and admiration. He gave her frequent glances as she walked alongside the bier, carried by him, Bulla, Ludo, Chest and two other close friends of Titus. Though the sorrowful atmosphere and the wail of the professional mourners must have made things difficult for her, she still managed a sad smile for him and gave him an encouraging nod. And that look gave him all the strength he needed.

The procession had been predictably sombre but what had impressed everyone was its length. People who didn't know Titus joined in as the bier was carried through the streets of the Aventine on its loop to the pyre set up inside the courtyard. His cortege had grown as rumour circulated that the huge man laid out on the bier was the same watchman who had led efforts to extinguish the recent inferno and who had been responsible for saving dozens of lives. Lucia followed the body with her head bowed and concealed beneath a black veil. Nobody had been able to get a word out of her throughout. She resembled a wraith trailing the man who had been her physical and spiritual soul-mate on his final journey to Elysium.

And now a hundred or more torches blazed inside the packed courtyard, as the pallbearers made their way through the narrow channel made by people stepping aside for them. With some difficulty, they managed to slide the bier atop the pyre, and then all save Ambrosius melted back into the crowd.

He had delivered funeral speeches before and it had never been easy for him. But this was something different altogether. Throughout, he had to keep his eyes averted from the shrouded body, and at times he even had to imagine that he was watching himself make the speech from a safe distance, for he knew that one tear would start a deluge.

He described Titus as a 'Colossus amongst men', 'the bravest, most honourable man he had ever seen, to whom saving rather than taking lives came most naturally' and he quoted a few fond anecdotes from men with whom he had fought in the legions. It was as he was delivering one of these that he noticed the face near the front of the crowds next to Poppeia. It made him falter mid-sentence and, though to everyone else it seemed like a catch in his throat, to him it felt like his heart leaping from his mouth. Anna was watching him intently as he spoke, her hand resting on Poppeia's shoulder. When he hesitated, she gave him a sad smile and he somehow managed to continue to the end. Bulla handed him a torch and he drew his cloak over his head, whispering a prayer of deliverance.

Then he lit the pyre.

It was perhaps the frightening speed of the flames that obscured Titus' body which stoked Lucia's anguish. Her lament was so heart-rendingly profound that she took other onlookers with her. She pushed past Bulla and Chest, and stalked over to Ambrosius, jabbing him in the chest.

"You took my man from me!"

He lowered the hood to his cloak.

"I'm so sorry, Lucia, he–"

She slapped him so hard that the blow resonated from the walls of the building and made him stagger backwards. "His blood is on your hands! You killed him! I hate you! I hate you for what you did! I curse you!"

Then she burst into tears and fell to her knees, tearing at her hair. Seeing it all, Anna hurried over to her but she brushed her off and stumbled towards the pyre.

"No!" shouted Ambrosius.

She took a step into the flames and tried to claw her husband back. Several watchmen dragged her back, screaming, and smothered the flames in their cloaks. Another doused her in water, and the clothes hissed and steamed as if the malign spirits of her possession were leaving her body.

From being subdued and reflective just moments before, the courtyard became a scene from the underworld filled with the keenest wailing and crying, the muted roar of the fire, faces illuminated in grief, tendrils of smoke and flames that danced like impish sprites.

XI

Junius Rufinus had seen the flickering torches of the procession as he and Fabius Clio made their way across the forum towards the Tabularium. The Records Office was tucked against the lower slopes of the Capitoline hill, behind the great Temples of Concord and Vespasian, but its austere face soared above them. The thought of entering the vaulted rooms that echoed like a mausoleum was never appealing at the best of times, but in the dark of night it made him shudder.

Clio, however, didn't seem to care. Rufinus could only guess that he had spent many hours inside to become so accustomed to the dry, dusty air that smelled of decaying leather, parchment, ancient stone and, if it was possible, age itself. They plunged into the twilight between the sacred buildings with their torches and felt the ground rise beneath them but, on rounding the Temple of Concord, they saw something that made them check their steps.

An armed Praetorian was guarding the entrance.

Before they had chance to retreat and form a plan, the Praetorian turned to look at them. He was a young officer with a wispy beard and clear blue eyes. He was also a little jumpy: Rufinus knew the look well, however much the Praetorian tried to dissemble it. Being on sentry duty alone in the dark was enough at times to make even the stoutest of hearts pound harder.

"I'm sorry, gentlemen; the Tabularium is closed for the night. To everyone."

Clio bristled as he approached. "Not for me it isn't! Do you know who I am?"

"No," the guard squirmed, "I don't, but it doesn't matter. I have my orders."

"And I have mine! And a key, given to me by a consul of Rome, no less. So please step aside," said Clio, fixing him with a haughty stare.

The guard looked to the floor. "I've been told to let nobody past."

"What have you done to upset your supervising officer, young man?" said Rufinus soothingly. "If the Tabularium is closed then why have you been posted here?"

"Break-ins, I suppose."

"I really don't think so," Rufinus looked over the guard's shoulder at the solid oak door and its studded iron ribs. "And this is the only entrance. Look, I think you may have had a practical joke played on you. You're not long in service are you?"

The guard shook his head.

"No, I didn't think so. It's a common prank played on new-comers – I've had it done to me – to see how willingly you obey orders. I remember many years ago I was posted outside the gladiator school and I wondered why they were all laughing at me when I returned to barracks, but I didn't think about it at the time. Sixty of the toughest, meanest, most battle-hardened fighters for miles around and me thinking they needed protecting from somebody!"

The Praetorian looked Rufinus up and down. "Were you in the Guard?"

"No, young man, I wasn't." He smiled at him. "I take it you don't recognize me, either. I'm the Prefect of the Watch and this gentleman is the City Prefect, the commander of the Urban Cohorts. We have worked here for many years and would like to finish up before we go home. It's getting late."

Clio and Rufinus waited while the Praetorian procrastinated for another few seconds before fumbling for his keys and muttering something under his breath.

"No need to bother. As I said, I have my own key."

"Sorry," he said, stepping aside. "And Prefect? Do you think I should return to camp and let them know I was set up?"

"No, no," said Rufinus quickly, "you should never desert your post, joke or no joke. But when you are relieved in the morning, let it be known that you had merely played along with it. Or even better," he said with a wink, "say that you actually caught a burglar and handed him over to The Watch. That'd surprise them alright! I'd be prepared to write you a good service report to return the joke."

The Praetorian's face brightened. "Thank you, Prefect! Do you need any help in there? I mean, it's a bit disordered."

Rufinus shook his head as he followed Clio inside. "You're right, it is. But we're used to it. Shouldn't be too long in here but we'll call if we need you. I'll shut the door behind us, keep it secure."

After the door was closed, they let out a ragged breath.

"What in Jupiter's name is he doing there?" asked Clio in a hoarse whisper as they stepped into a dark corridor.

"I'm only glad it was him and not someone with more about him."

Clio nodded. "You did well, Rufinus."

"Afraid that's where my contribution is likely to end. I've never been in here before: I have no idea where to start."

"Fortunately I do. There's an aediles' repository on the first floor. Should be where all the documents about buildings are stored."

They pressed on along a confusing warren of corridors. Even though Rufinus knew that the curved ceilings were high, he felt an instinctive need to stoop as he walked. The torches ripped the stagnant air, illuminating inscriptions carved into the travertine blocks in narrow, archaic letters. Occasionally Clio would stop and examine them and drum his fingers on his mouth, then set off again with purposeful strides. Rufinus had always know he was the sort of man who was naturally disposed to arguing against suggestions that were not his own but who, once he had come to a particular way of thinking, would pursue it relentlessly. It made him a doughty opponent but an equally effective ally.

Eventually they came to a stone staircase, at the bottom of which was a rack for holding oil lamps. They both took one and climbed the worn steps, the distorted echo of their sandals giving the unsettling impression that they were not alone. The acoustics in the building was just one of a number of aspects of it that made Rufinus shudder and he began to feel a vague sense of panic. Perhaps he was unwittingly being led into an ambush and would be made to disappear without a trace? He doubted there was any place more suitable in the entire city for such an end. Maybe Fabius Clio had been in on it all along, as Ambrosius had dared suggest? Is that why he had become so touchy when challenged?

"Right, I think this is it. Be careful with the torches in there. The vellum and parchment are as dry as kindling: the place would go up in no time."

Rufinus thrust his torch into the doorway and his heart sank. This place was even more of a jumble than he had imagined. "After you."

Clio shrugged. He set his torch into an iron bracket in the corridor and lit his oil lamp. Rufinus copied him and they plunged into the forest of crates and document holders.

"We could be here all night sorting though this lot. I hadn't reckoned on the size of it."

Clio gave him a look. "Are you being serious?"

"Of course," he said, frowning, "just look at it!"

"I don't know what you were planning to do, Rufinus, but I had absolutely no intention of wading into that morass!"

"I'm sorry? I thought you were willing to help."

Clio let out a bemused laugh. "This isn't a children's library, Rufinus. Finding some order in this little room – and it is a little room compared to some in this building, let me tell you – is a lifetime's work in itself. It's a fool's errand," he said, stepping between stacks of crates and disappearing from view. "And I'm no fool. Whenever I need access to some long forgotten law, I get someone else to find it for me. I'm hoping that the work has already been done for us by whichever unfortunate clerk gets to spend his life in here. The trick is to find his register. Should be easy enough, or it would be if you didn't just stand there like a statue."

Unaccustomed to being spoken down to, Rufinus rolled up the sleeves of his tunic and got to work. "So what's this register likely to be? A scroll? A wax tablet?"

"A scroll, or set of them. No permanence in a wax tablet of course."

"Of course," he muttered.

They scanned the tags on the various document containers in silence but the task was rendered impossible at times due to the faded inks and crumbling parchment. After an hour, Rufinus' back was sore and he began to feel a dull throb behind his eyes that developed into an enervating headache. To make matters worse, the tongue of flame from the spout of the lamp was shrinking as the font of oil was used up, and he regretted not bringing any replacements. He wasn't even sure he would be able to find his way back to the staircase.

"How are you getting on?" Clio's voice was distant. Rufinus wondered just how sprawling the room was.

"Not so well. And the oil's running low. How about you?"

"Same."

There was a brief silence. "I expect you'll be wanting me to go and get some more lamps, Rufinus?"

He chuckled. "Well, you'd never find me again if I was to …" His voice trailed away.

"What is it?"

"Hang on a minute."

"Come on, man, what have you found?" Clio's voice grew louder as he came to find him.

"Over here," said Rufinus, raising his lamp.

281

When Clio joined him, he pointed to a niche in the wall, inside which was an uncapped leather cylinder. Behind it were four glass paperweights.

Clio looked at Rufinus and nodded. "Certainly worth a look."

The Watch Prefect edged between piles of crates to retrieve the cylinder. It was heavier than it looked and contained numerous tightly rolled documents. They set their lamps aside and Rufinus extracted the parchments with trembling hands.

"Top one. Top one first. Most recent, I shouldn't wonder."

But the scrolls were so tightly bound that they curled up at the corners and he struggled to hold them open. "Here," said Clio impatiently, "give me the bottom."

They scanned the itemised lists of names and titles, annotated with extra letters and numbers.

"What do they denote do you think?" asked Rufinus. "Receipts?"

"Yes. They're initials but the rest of the handwriting is absolutely appalling. I can barely read it in this light."

"RES MANCIPI ... RES NEC MANCIPI ... what on earth is that?"

"Conveyancing," muttered Clio. "Irrelevant."

"Sale and transfer of domestic animals and sheds; sale and transfer of domestic animals; same; same; farming equipment and warehouses; same ..." Rufinus read the list aloud but Clio's eyes scanned the list like a hawk's, his forehead furrowed with creases.

"There," he declared, stabbing the parchment with his finger, "'AEDIFICIA PVBLICA: R iv: VIGILVM COHORTES ...' Public buildings: Watchmen's cohorts ..."

Rufinus followed his finger across the entry. Their eyes fell upon the endorsing initials scratched against it but, for an agonizing second, their brains failed to register their significance.

"No! Surely ... no!" Clio let the roll slip through his fingers and Rufinus dropped it altogether.

They exchanged looks of disbelief and Rufinus stooped to pick the scrolls back up to confirm what they had just seen. Just then, footsteps approached along the corridor. A silhouetted figure appeared in the doorway.

"So, did you both find what you were looking for?"

XII

The last of the foreigners arrived at their allocated safe-houses and retrieved the key from under a loose cobblestone by the doorstep.

Taking a final look round them, they entered and deposited their few possessions in the atrium. There were two pitchers waiting for them on a table, containing water and wine, a basket of fruit and a scroll parchment. They read the instructions and ignored the refreshments, only wanting to splash their faces and find their sleeping pallets. They had already settled this on the way in and discussed little else. Their task was a matter of mere hours away. At the same time the following evening, there would be cause enough to celebrate, for the old Emperor would be dead and they would be able to count themselves amongst the most powerful, richest men in the empire.

XIII

Rufinus and Clio filed out of the building into the cool night air and counted their lucky stars that the Praetorian guardsman really was one of the most gullible fools they had ever met.

"We need time to process this … to … make sure we've not simply made a hasty assumption."

Rufinus guided him into the inky darkness by the senate house steps. "I feel suddenly very trapped out here, don't you?"

Clio looked around him and he, too, felt the impossible weight of the buildings looming over him. "I see what you mean: like the darkness has eyes. What do you propose?"

"Those initials were signed the very day young Terentia's body was stolen, and that was some time ago now. Who knows what might be about to happen? I think we have to enlist some help, lots of it and very quickly."

"I think I'd like to sleep on it. We should reconvene first thing tomorrow morning and compare thoughts."

Rufinus mulled it over. He was shattered and the thought of getting some rest appealed strongly to him. It was also a sensible option. However, he could almost feel the significance of the document he had secreted inside his tunic burning his skin. The initials were two weeks old and such a lot had happened in that time … His senses screamed at him to press on, spurning sleep.

"No."

"What do you mean 'no'? It'll be midnight soon!"

"I think we have to do something now. Right now. For the first time since all these troubles started I actually think we've stolen a march. It'd be criminal to squander it now. You're not going to like this but I think we should make representations to the Emperor."

Clio snorted. "You're right, I don't like it! Not one bit!"

"Are you saying, Prefect, that you still don't believe me? Is that it?"

"No," he said after a time, "that's not it. I think this had something to do with an affair between Terentia and the Emperor's son, Caracalla. That's why she was killed. So you can see why just to go rattling Severus' door at this time might be a bit … risky. After all, the Emperor may have been the one who sanctioned it."

"That's a bit extreme!"

A chilly breeze picked up, carrying the distant clatter of cartwheels rattling over cobbles. Rufinus had not brought a cloak with him and he shivered.

"Well we can't very well stay out here arguing about it. I think we should make our way to our tribune's Watch House. There'll be plenty of support there, should we need it. And I think that Ambrosius deserves to know about what we've just found. It was his thinking that took us there after all."

Rufinus expected a vehement disagreement but, to his surprise, none came. Clio looked away.

"He still owes me an apology."

"And I'm sure he'll give one, in time. Go easy on him, Prefect. He's not had an easy time of it."

Clio sighed. "Lead the way then, Rufinus."

XIV

Prior to the funeral, Ambrosius had not supposed that he could feel any more wretched, but Lucia's feral despair knocked him into a dark abyss. He waved away anybody that tried to console him and wrapped his cloak tight about him, seeking the quiet solace of the courtyard's furthest corner. He dropped onto a bench and allowed the shadows to envelop him, brooding over the decisions he had made. In hindsight, every choice had been so patently wrong and he found he was now unable to rationalize any of them.

So distant was he that he failed to notice that he had been joined on the bench.

"That was a very touching speech," said Anna. Her quiet voice made Ambrosius start.

He shook his head and didn't reply.

"Ambrosius," she said, touching his cheek, "you look like you haven't slept properly in days."

He flinched, as if she had stung him with a nettle. "Most of us haven't", he said after a time.

"Lucia didn't mean those things she said. That wasn't her …"

"Please … just … don't."

The buzz of conversation, punctuated by the spit and hiss of the flames, drifted over to them. More people entered the courtyard. After a few minutes, Anna stood up.

"I'm sorry. I had to come, but I didn't mean to make it any harder for you. I'll just say goodbye to Poppeia."

She turned to leave.

"Don't go," he croaked. "Please. Not just yet. Sit down."

She wavered, as if uncertain what to do for the best and looked back towards Lucia, who was being tended by one of the cohort's medics. Ambrosius followed her gaze and noticed two men approaching them carrying shaded lanterns. There was no mistaking the worried looks on the faces of Fabius Clio and Junius Rufinus.

"I'm sorry Ambrosius, I know this must be a bad time for you," Rufinus, glanced over his shoulder at the smouldering funeral pyre and closed his eyes in sadness.

"Tribune," acknowledged Clio, with reluctance.

"Perhaps we might have a brief word?"

"I'll be with Poppeia if you need me."

"Thank you, madam."

When there was no one in earshot, Rufinus spoke again. "Ambrosius, we've just returned from the Tabularium."

Screened by the shadows, Ambrosius dried his eyes on his tunic and quickly composed himself.

Rufinus removed a document from his tunic. "You were right: somebody did make considerable efforts to locate the plans of your barracks. Look."

"What's this?"

"An index of documents signed out."

"Bring your lantern closer: I can hardly read it." Ambrosius scanned the entry by the Watch Prefect's fingernail. "The handwriting's bad. Is that … wait a second, is that …?"

"We think so."

Ambrosius felt nauseous. The script was spidery but the initials were clear enough.

LTP

LVCIVS TERENTIVS PISO

Ambrosius glanced over at Poppeia and then wheeled away to retch. How could Terentia's own father do such a hideous, unspeakable thing?

A few watchmen looked over at them and Rufinus slipped the document back inside his tunic. Ambrosius felt as though the blood had drained from his entire body.

"That bastard," he said in a hoarse whisper, "dared enter this building hours after he'd had her body stolen and accused me! I want him! I want him to beg me for his life as I choke it out of him!"

"Ambrosius, you have to control your emotions. This has to be done properly or we'll lose the slender advantage we have."

"Tribune, please. We've all been made fools of. You may get your chance or you may not. Either way, you were wrong to think I was complicit in some way. And, I suppose, I was wrong about your motives."

Ambrosius clenched his jaw. "So what do you want to do next?"

"Senator Piso needs to be arrested; and now, whilst we may still have an element of surprise."

"I'll do it."

"Just slow down. Piso needs to be arrested but we must assume he'll not be alone, so that means you'll have to take some people with you."

"What about Gaius Plautianus? He's obviously involved."

Rufinus looked to Clio. "It's a fairly safe assumption." said the City Prefect in his lawyerly manner, "Arresting a senator is one thing but it's another matter entirely trying to bring in the Praetorian Prefect. It's almost an act of sacrilege. That's why we'll be trying to get an audience with the Emperor Septimius Severus. If Plautianus is to be arrested, that's his decision to make, not ours."

"And what do you make of the chances?"

Clio pursed his thin lips. "Yours, slim, and you should expect vehement resistance. Ours … even less so."

Ambrosius rubbed the bridge of his nose, ransacking his memory for something he may have missed that would trap Plautianus conclusively. But it was no good: he was too exhausted.

"Fine, I'll get a small group together."

"Good," said Rufinus, as his eyes followed a watchman stumbling past. "And try to find some that aren't already drunk. When you have, we'll give you directions. Come and find us by the gate."

Ambrosius set about speaking to his men, trying to gauge those that were fit for the role. In the end, the team chose itself. Bulla and Ludo had been involved at the outset and wanted to bring it to its conclusion: Chest and Stilicho had proved their worth since, and both provided some muscle. Though all save Ambrosius had been drinking, news of the senator's involvement in his own daughter's disappearance had a sobering effect. Ambrosius told them to wait by the gate whilst he looked for Anna. She was stood with Poppeia next to Lucia, who was staring into the ashes of the pyre.

He touched her elbow and she stepped away.

"I'm sorry, Anna, but there's been some news and I need your help, though I know I don't deserve it."

"You want me to look after Poppeia?"

He looked at her in surprise. "Yes. Can you?"

"Are you going to tell me what this news is?"

"We're going after senator Piso."

"What, the girl's father?" Anna frowned. "Why?"

"We think he had something to do with her death. Or at least that he was involved in stealing her body, for some sick, twisted reason."

Anna put her hands to her cheeks in astonishment. Ambrosius put his on top. It was an instinctive gesture but she did not resist. "Can you do that for me?"

She nodded. "Thank you for telling me."

"And if I don't come back … please swear to me you would take good care of her."

"Ambrosius! You will …"

"Please, Anna; I mean it."

"Of course. Of course I would."

He looked at her for a moment more and then turned away.

"And Ambrosius?"

"Yes?"

"Poppeia wants to say something to you."

Poppeia stepped forwards, wringing her hands. "Please be careful, daddy." She glanced at Lucia. "And I'm very proud of you."

He stood, lost for words for a moment, before sweeping her up and kissing her forehead, breathing in the scent of rosemary in her hair. "And I love you so much." He put her down and she ran to Anna, watching him wide-eyed with concern as he jogged over to the group by the gate. Rufinus had been watching the scene and gave him a brief smile.

"Just the five of you then?"

"It's enough to be getting on with. Don't want to draw too much attention to us."

"Agreed. Does anyone know Piso's town house?" asked Clio.

The question was met with blank looks.

"I assume someone here knows where he lives? Are you not paid to patrol the streets all night?"

"He doesn't live on our patch," Ambrosius said, "I'd never seen him before he came knocking here."

There was more head-shaking.

"Not a great start is it, Junius?" Clio frowned at the Watch Prefect. "Hardly a ringing endorsement of watchmen's fabled local knowledge."

"What?" snorted Ambrosius. "There's over a million fucking people …"

"I know where his house is," Clio dismissed the tribune's indignation with a patronizing wave. "So tame yourself, please. It's off Via Latina, beyond the Capena Gate and the fork with Via Appia. I've dined there."

As Clio gave directions, Ambrosius' anger was only checked by a barely perceptible shake of the head from Rufinus.

After he had finished, Fabius Clio cleared his throat. "Whatever happens, one of you will have to get a message across to us on the Palatine. It's to be hoped that we will at least have made it as far as the reception chamber of the Imperial Palace."

"Then how are we supposed to reach you?"

"The chamber is near the entrance. Give two short whistles. If we don't respond immediately, two more. One of us will come outside to meet you. Failing that, ask the Praetorians at the gate nicely."

Ambrosius looked away. It was a rickety plan but it would have to do under the circumstances. "Fine."

Rufinus nodded. "Any more questions, gentlemen? Excellent. Not a word to anyone else for now. Good luck to you all."

The meeting broke up whilst the watchmen prepared themselves and fetched their kit. Inspired by a late moment of piety, Ambrosius approached the shrine to the guardian spirits of the cohorts. He pulled the hood of his cloak over his head and sprinkled some oatmeal onto the flames of one of the votive candles, watching them spit and hiss. He closed his eyes and whispered several fervent prayers and added some vows of deliverance to Mars the Avenger and to Mercury for good measure. He returned to the small group of watchmen and led them out of the gates.

There was a full moon and a bright canopy of stars so he branched off The Street of The Public Baths at the first opportunity, leading the group through the forbidding alleyways of the northern Aventine. The conversation petered out as they attuned themselves to the cloying darkness and the scurrying of unseen animals. A rising hum of raucous conversation and laughter ahead of them suggested an all-night drinking den tucked into one of the sidestreets. The din peaked and then faded occasionally as its doors admitted new customers or disgorged paralytic revelers into the night.

After a few minutes, they emerged onto the narrow street that skirted the tiered stands describing the northern end of the Circus Maximus. They had to step aside to allow a desultory stream of wagons and carts of produce to trundle past them. The sleepy muleteers that led them gave them only the most cursory looks. Further down the street, a trio of wretched looking women leaning against boarded-up shops stirred at their approach and then, seeing their watchmen's garb, sagged backwards in disappointment. As the pale light from Ambrosius' torch crept over the face of one of them, she turned aside self-consciously but failed to conceal the terrible sores on her cheeks. He glanced from her to her two friends, and the looks he received were not friendly. To their left, the hulking silhouette of the Imperial Palace blotted out the entire length of the southern Palatine. The Emperor Severus had a reputation for working throughout the night and surviving on a paltry amount of sleep. The rumour was it had aged him prematurely and that his health was in rapid decline: Ambrosius wondered if he was even remotely aware that there was a danger far more deadly than exhaustion waiting for the right time to strike him down.

Eventually they came to the Septizodium, a tall shrine to the seven planetary deities, which marked the eastern aspect of the Palatine. The street ahead widened and, as they emerged from the shadows of the shrine, they saw a group of men on the other side of the crossroads. They were wearing cheap-looking cloaks and had only one lantern between them. The men froze as they saw the watchmen then turned back, glancing over their shoulders before disappearing from view.

Ambrosius caught Chest's cloak as he was about to sprint off after them. He shook his head in response to Chest's look of surprise.

"Whoever they were, they're not part of the plan."

Ludo shifted on his feet. "I can't help thinking we're being led into a trap, tribune. That Clio ... he doesn't look like he should be trusted."

"Pompous bastard," offered Stilicho.

Ambrosius rasped his stubble with his nail and closed his eyes, trying to recall Clio's words just before they left the Watch House. What had he said?

Your chances are slim?

Was that some sort of reverse psychology, knowing that Ambrosius would do the opposite of what Clio himself suggested? He was so shattered that he could happily have kept his eyes shut and slept where he stood.

"We've got no choice. But we can take a different route. Chest, didn't you grow up somewhere near here?"

"I did."

"Get us to Piso's house via the back streets and you can have a night shift off."

"We will soon be having every night shift off!"

The group turned to Bulla, who had been virtually silent since Titus' death. Ambrosius slapped him on the shoulder. "Lead on, Chest."

Grateful for the opportunity to show his worth, Chest took the group off Via Appia into the malodorous labrynth of backstreets skirting the Caelian hill and the spur of high ground behind it. Forbidding tenement blocks now reared up on all sides of them, fronted by faceless shops that were boarded up for the night. The cut-throughs were so narrow here that there was barely room for them to walk in single file. Chest strode on, undeterred, until the group felt the ground begin to rise beneath their feet. After a few minutes, the buildings began to thin out and gave way altogether to a small copse. The ancient street steps faded into the hillside and they felt wild grasses snagging their sandals, slowing their progress. More than once there was a sharp curse followed by the muffled thump of one of them tripping over. Then Bulla stubbed his toes on a slab of rock hidden under the long grasses. He yelped in pain.

"For fuck's sake, Chest! Where do you taking us?"

"Sorry, should have warned you. Remains of some old temple strewn about: watch your feet."

Up the slope they scrambled and a break in the trees rewarded them with an elevated view of the silvery river as it caressed the banks of Tiber Island to the west. The air here smelled clean and crisp, with just the faintest hint of wild lavender. Chest called them to a halt.

"We've done a bit of a loop to avoid the main road. That house down there, with the old wall round it, is the one I think Clio was on about."

They all looked down. Even in the dark, the scale of the house certainly suggested it might belong to a senator. Ambrosius wondered if the single Poplar tree that soared into the night sky above the tips of the other trees around it appealed to Piso's sense of self-worth when he first acquired the property.

He shrugged. "We'll know, soon enough. Any questions?" The other four shook their heads. Ambrosius took a deep breath. "Extinguish two of the torches, then let's go."

As they descended in silence and approached the walls, Ambrosius scanned across the high windows. Nothing stirred. They skirted the perimeter walls and emerged onto a private track off Via Latina, and gravel crunched beneath their sandals making them slow to a creep. Once he was at the doorstep, Ambrosius slipped a thin metal wedge into one of the grille slats. Then he hammered on the door for a few frenzied seconds.

He stopped and waited and they all listened. After a few moments there came the sound of padded footsteps and dark mutterings. The grille slider rattled as whoever was behind the door tried to open it.

Then there was silence.

"Who is it?"

The tone was irritable but tinged with wariness.

"Pennus!" replied Ambrosius in his most gravelly voice.

Another uneasy silence, then a tut and the door was unbolted from within. They braced themselves and judged the moment to perfection. When the third and final bolt had been withdrawn, Stilicho and Chest dropped their shoulder into the door, and it crashed against the inner wall, making the frame shiver. There was a yelp of surprise.

"Watchmen, Fourth Cohort!"

"Piso? Where's Piso?"

But the old janitor who had been soundly asleep just seconds before could not speak. He backed against the wall with his eyes bulging and his mouth agape.

"Leave him," ordered Ambrosius, looking around. The layout of the house was similar to that of the Praetorian Captain, Pennus, though it was much larger, and lining the walls were sombre rows of wax death masks, impressions of Piso's illustrious ancestors stretching back into the hazy days of The Republic. The flickering light from their torches cast the faces in eerie, contorted expressions and animated the painted frescoes on the walls behind them. Ambrosius considered the options: five men was too few by half.

"Ludo, Chest, remain down here and watch our backs. Bulla, Stilicho, follow me."

But before he even reached the foot of the stairs, a small pool of light appeared at the top.

"What is the meaning of this outrage!" The flame exaggerated a severe face and vulture-like nose. He extended a trembling finger towards the tribune. "You again!"

For a fleeting moment, even though he was dressed in a nightgown, the magisterial tone of the man stopped Ambrosius in his tracks.

"Back from the dead to bind you over for conspiring to murder. Come down here please."

The senator's body convulsed with rage. "How dare you break in like this? Get out of my house!"

Ambrosius gave him a cold smile. He had been scrutinising his face and there was no mistaking the twitch as he uttered the word.

Murder.

It was like a small bird had pecked at his cheek, as sure a sign of guilt as he had hoped to see.

"No, senator. And when we leave, it will be with you."

Piso glared at him for a few long moments and swayed on the top step. It dawned on Ambrosius what was going to happen next, but he was too late in shouting a warning.

Ludo and Chest had beaten him to the same conclusion and had already bounded half way up the steps, three at a time. As Piso pitched forwards, Ludo dived at him. Instead of dashing his body against cold marble, Piso now fell onto the altogether softer back of the watch centurion, crushing his body against the cold stone. The senator slid down his back and would have clattered against the steps were it not for Chest. Using his bulk as a shield, he gathered him up before his head struck stone. Piso shrieked with pain and indignity as he was bundled down the stairs and deposited on the floor. Ambrosius produced a leather strap and bound his wrists in front of him. The senator's body was as thin and tough as a whip, and he struggled like a polecat, but the score was too great to settle and at that moment Ambrosius could have bound up an unbroken horse.

"Easy does it old man!" he said through gritted teeth. "We just saved your life!"

"You damned near killed me, breaking into my house, making me faint! I'll have you crucified for this, you peasants! All of you!"

Whilst Piso fulminated, Ambrosius glanced at the stairs.

"Ludo, stop slouching, I need you."

The centurion groaned and peeled himself away from the steps. "I think I've popped a rib."

"That's fine then, nothing you can do about a rib. Just be grateful it wasn't someone like Bulla that fell on you. Help him up Bulla," he said with a wink.

"And you," he jabbed his finger into Piso's chest, "will tell us where your personal correspondence is kept."

"I'll do no such thing! You're just petty thieves! You're a disgrace to your ranks! Well now you're in trouble!"

"Tribune," said Chest, reaching for his cudgel, "we have company."

Ambrosius looked around him. Slaves had appeared out of every doorway, surrounding the watchmen, perhaps fifteen of them, and at the head of the stairs now stood a woman.

Piso's wife.

Only a few of the slaves were armed but one brandished a meat cleaver.

"We are watchmen of the Fourth Cohort. Your master has been arrested and you should go back to your rooms, unless you want to come with us too. We have no argument with you but we will use force if we have to. So go!"

The slaves looked at each other, waiting to take their lead from someone else.

"Go!" bellowed Ambrosius, raising his baton.

They all flinched and took a backwards step.

"They take orders only from my husband and I."

Piso's wife was a mousy, unprepossessing woman in her night stole but, as she crept down the stairs, her beady eyes focused on the tribune, he realised that her appearance was deceptive. Her voice was cold and devoid of fear, and he noticed she was carrying something behind her back.

"That's far enough, madam," he said, raising his hand.

"And I certainly don't take orders from the likes of you!"

She was on the bottom step now. Ambrosius made eye contact with Ludo and the centurion frowned at her back as she passed him. He shook his head. She had no weapon.

"Why are you here?"

He looked at the slaves around him. "In front of these?"

"Yes."

That stunned him. A senator's reputation, and that of his forebears, was painstakingly established on the pillars of dignity, courage, authority, gravitas and piety. And those pillars were about to come crashing down in front of his slaves.

"Darling? Why?"

"Fine," Ambrosius cleared his throat, "we believe, with good reason, that he was involved in stealing your daughter's body from our crypt ..."

"Disgusting slander ...!"

"Silence!" her tone made all of them start. "Go on."

"... and that he therefore had a part in her death."

"How can you let this creature say these things?"

She stalked over to Piso and slapped him hard about the cheek. The resonance of the blow made the slaves draw breath.

"And what is your 'good reason'?"

Ambrosius had a vision of Terentia's bent fingernails, and the signs of her brave struggle. He could see now where she had inherited such spirit.

"We think your daughter was taken by means of the … by means of tunnels underneath our barracks that even I had no knowledge of …"

Her face hardened. "You are referring to the sewers."

"Yes, the Cloaca Maxima. The original plans for the building were held in the Tabularium, where access is tightly restricted. We recently gained entry and checked the records. The plans were signed out on the day Terentia's body was stolen," Ambrosius pointed to Piso, "by him."

She turned to him, and her breathing became laboured.

"Why?"

Piso looked at the floor.

"Why? Why? Why?"

She screamed and flew at him like a bird of prey, swiping his face with the document cylinder she held behind her back. The blow knocked him to one side and Chest and Bulla had to struggle to tear her away from him.

"What are you all looking at? Go away!" The slaves scurried away to their quarters. "Go!"

Then the anger drained from her and she went limp in the watchmen's hands. They let her sink to her knees and she broke down in tears, dropping the document holder. It rolled away from her and came to rest by Ambrosius' feet.

Piso's eyes darted to it but before he could reach it, Ambrosius snatched it up.

"What's this, eh?"

"Give me that back! That's private correspondence!"

Ambrosius tossed it to Stilicho, who removed several rolls of parchment. He read them and frowned.

"Well?"

"I think they're addresses, tribune. See what you think."

Bulla took Ambrosius' place guarding the senator and he looked for himself. "Seems you've not just been looking at plans for our barracks, eh senator? What are these, vacant houses for you to view today? Have a little side-line in property do you, or is that just a cover story in case you were asked why you were so interested in ours? Madam, how did you get hold of these?"

Ambrosius turned to Piso's wife but she was rocking on her haunches, sobbing quietly. "Just go, please. Take him and go."

Ambrosius considered her potential impact as a witness but did not want to push his luck. He dragged Piso up by his arm. "At least allow me to change."

"There'll be no banquets where you're going."

As they approached the door Ludo, who was wincing as he moved, turned back. She cut a pathetic, forlorn figure at the foot of the stairs, like an unloved child. "Tribune, shouldn't we take her with us or something? We can't leave her like that."

"Madam?"

She waved them away without looking up. Ambrosius shook his head. "Let's go."

They stepped out into the cool air. The commotion had not woken any of the neighbours. He had been worried that the sight of a fellow senator being dragged off into the night would have sparked a riot.

"Ludo?"

"Yes tribune?"

"Can you go and report to Clio and Rufinus? We need to regroup."

"I think I can manage that."

"Take Chest here as support and send him back when you get there. Come on, man. You've just picked up a few bruises. Suck it in!"

Ludo nodded and hobbled off down the private path with Chest, gripping his side and wheezing like an old man.

XV

After he had returned to barracks and handed over Piso to the quaestionarius Vitalis, Ambrosius closed the door to the study and poured himself and Bulla a cup of wine. They were both now reeling from exhaustion but they also knew they were in possession of items of great importance. Yet, as they looked at the documents set before them, they didn't know what to make of them.

Architects' original plans for three buildings.

Deeds for the three buildings, annotated in a fresher ink.

Ambrosius leaned back in his chair and rubbed his eyes. "I should've kept some of us behind to search the house. I can't believe I didn't search the house."

"No point worrying about it now. Always we can go back."

Ambrosius considered the possibility of Piso's wife systematically rummaging through his private correspondence and burning it. He didn't think it likely, given her attitude towards her husband.

"What did you make of her?"

"An old cuckold." Bulla made a face. "She wasn't very happy with him, no?"

"No, I mean the way she already seemed to know something. She was almost expecting us. Or if not us, someone else."

"Think we should also have brought her in?"

"I don't think that would've helped." He leaned forwards and stared at the documents again. "I just wonder why she had these in her hand."

"She wanted us to have them?"

"Or she'd been waiting for the opportunity to have a look herself. My mind is playing tricks on me," he said, pointing to a scribble in the margins of one of the pages. "That's definitely today's date, right?"

"Let me see. 'a.d. xviii Kal. Apr.': eighteenth day before Kalends of April, yes. Day before the end of our Sebaciaria."

"He'd have been busy today. These three are all in different regions."

"He's a senator," Bulla shrugged, "and rich. He himself doesn't have to visit them. He didn't view this place but he still took the plans."

Ambrosius got up and retrieved a vellum map of Rome's fourteen regions from a shelf beneath the water clock.

"That's because it's not vacant. We're here."

"Not for much longer. Day of the assembly vote today, no?"

Ambrosius scratched his forehead. He had forgotten about the vote on The Watch.

"Good point." He cleared his desk and held down the corners of the chart with paperweights. "Those three houses ... help me plot them on this map."

Bulla scratched his head. "I only recognize one of them ... this one here, south of the Aventine."

"I should hope you do," Ambrosius gave him a look. "It's on our patch, right on the border between Regio XII and Regio XIII."

"I knew that."

"And this one's here," he said, marking the street with an 'x' in charcoal, "on the lower slopes of the Viminal, just above the Subura."

"That place is shithole." Bulla looked closer at the map. "The street divides the second and third cohorts' boundaries, no?"

"Looks like it."

They struggled to place the third house and refilled their cups before having another go. The surge of being on the point of identifying something significant but elusive dimmed their fatigue.

"Shall I get Vitalis? He knows every streets," said Bulla.

"Just wait a minute. He's busy with Piso."

A minute passed in near silence. Water dripped from the clock's outlet into its bowl and Bulla began to count how many times he could repeat Get Vitalis to himself before each soft plop. Ten seemed to be the nearest answer.

"Got it!" Ambrosius stabbed the map with his finger. "Here, just off Via Tusculana."

"That's Scaurus' region."

"Not quite: it's the other side of the road."

Bulla tutted. "You're looking at Piso's sheet wrong way up." He turned it round to face Ambrosius.

"Well, whatever, but the point is it's on the border, yes?"

"Could just be a coincidence. They're not exactly the nice areas, are they? Probably cheaper to buy, no ?"

"This one wouldn't be, off Via Tusculana." Ambrosius took a deep breath and stretched his arms above his head. "So if he didn't want the buildings for himself, who or what did he want them for? To sell on at a profit? For other women?"

"That explains his missus' anger!"

"For status? To stop somebody else having them? To run a private cult?"

"For the storage?" offered Bulla.

"For … for what?"

"Storage. I dunno, for all his wine and stolen statues or something."

Bulla's remark triggered another question he had put to the back of his mind. He remembered the night he and Longinus had chanced upon the swarthy foreigners loading up the stolen merchant vessel. And there was a lot of cargo. Enough weaponry to equip a private army, they had remarked.

In the courtyard, the bugler sounded the next hour, Conticinium. Dawn was just three hours away.

"Oh shit!"Ambrosius jumped up from his chair and frantically gathered up the documents.

"What? What is it?"

"How could I be so fucking stupid?"

"What?"

"We need to get to those houses and take possession of them before other people do!"

*

All told there were twenty one vigiles stood to attention in the small courtyard. That was all Ambrosius had been able to muster from those not already out on patrol. They looked keen and ready, if a little anxious. He doubted they were even half as anxious as he was.

"Gentlemen. There are less than three hours before dawn. And when dawn breaks, our careers will be finished. It's the nature of time, day by day, hour by hour, to take more than it gives. That's just how it is. But today the Praetorians want to take our livelihoods away from us. It is in their nature to give nothing back: nothing, in return for more than two hundred years of duty and sacrifice and devotion. And sometimes death. And now, here am I, standing before you – with possibly just hours left as watchmen – asking you to give again. I wouldn't blame you if you told me to stick it and walked away. Right now, out of this courtyard." He walked down the ranks of watchmen, all listening intently, and felt a surge of pride tinged with sorrow.

"I … er …" he faltered and scratched his head, "My wife was taken from me, five years ago. I nearly gambled and fought and pissed away my life in the days and weeks that followed but two things saved me: my daughter … and the knowledge that the man who violated and murdered her, even after she'd given up all her money, may still be walking these streets."

The silence in the courtyard deepened as the watchmen looked on, agog, at these revelations. "And as long as those two things are so – along with my respect for you all – I will keep going until the the sun rises and the vote is taken and the Praetorians come knocking. And then they will have to enter this building, our Watch House, over my dead body! So … who is with me?"

The roar of support made Ambrosius reel backwards. He felt energy seep through his bones, dispelling his exhaustion. He waited for the shouting and stamping to fade before he continued.

"We have three addresses, gentlemen. They've been chosen to create confusion and cause delay because they're sat on cohort or region boundaries. We'll split into three sections led by me, Stilicho and Vitalis."

There were a few murmurs and exchanges of puzzled looks. The grizzled gaoler met them with a grin and Ambrosius slapped him on the shoulder. "Vitalis here assures me he still has one last patrol in him! Be sure of this; the man's knowledge of the city streets is second to none. And, yes, before you ask, Piso is still under guard and he remains silent. Vitalis will take his nine to the nearest house, south of the Aventine. Stilicho, yours will go to that on the Viminal hill and I'll lead the rest to the Caelian." They all murmured their understanding. "Unfortunately, time is very short. We don't have enough to waste negotiating back-up from the tribunes of the various cohorts. I will speak to tribune Scaurus of the Fifth myself en route to the Caelian, but that's the lot. Needless to say, your whistles are the only means of drawing help, should you need it."

He walked slowly along the lines and checked that they all had one secured by twine around their necks. "I have asked you all to arm yourselves, but do not be careless with your lives. I have seen the weaponry with my own eyes and I only hope we encounter nobody wielding any of it. The tactics are up to each section leader. Stilicho and Vitalis have both seen the plans of their buildings. Listen to them. They are experienced watchmen, with the grey hairs to prove it. We need the houses securing by dawn at the latest. After then, nobody will enter unless authorised by me." He stopped and looked at them. They were silent with concentration. "Any questions?"

There were none.

301

"Then Fortuna be with you."

XVI

After some fuss, and only after his kit belt was taken from him, Ludo was admitted to the reception chamber of the imperial palace by the Praetorian sentry. As the surly guard led him through, he surveyed its opulence with wide-eyed astonishment. The display of wealth and power was overwhelming, oppressive even. He had never seen anything like it and he could only imagine that in the daytime, when light was streaming through the soaring arches, the gold, silver and delicate, priceless tapestries would present an even more magnificent sight.

Junius Rufinus greeted him and led him into an ante-room whilst the guard turned back without a word.

"He's a charmer," said Ludo.

"Well he was no brighter for us, if that's any consolation." Rufinus frowned at him. "What's wrong with you? You're virtually bent double."

"Nothing serious, sir. Where's the City Prefect?"

"Through here, take a seat."

Fabius Clio looked him up and down, noting his awkward gait without comment.

"Well? What happened?"

Ludo leaned closer and described the encounter with the senator and his wife in hushed, conspiratorial tones. When he was finished, Clio arched his eyebrows and let out a soft whistle.

"Well now, there's an interesting development. And where is the honourable gentleman now?"

"Under the close watch of our gaoler Vitalis, I'd guess."

"What are your thoughts, Rufinus?"

But before he could reply, a tall, slim figure appeared at the door to the ante-room. The three rose instinctively.

"You are here to see my father?" He had an intense gaze and his voice a deep tone that belied his youthful appearance.

Clio cleared his throat. "Your Highness. We have met before but this is the Prefect of The Watch, Ju–"

"Yes, I know very well who Junius Rufinus is." His eyes turned to Ludo. "You are?"

Ludo extended his hand. "Ludo Postumus, Your Highness. Centurion of the Fourth Cohort."

Caracalla ignored it. "Come with me."

He led them across a marble hallway, past a gilt throne, flanked by giant candelabra, and into a richly painted study, decorated with tasteful antiques and scrolls. "Sit, please. My father has been working throughout the night, as he often does." There was the faintest trace of reproach in his voice. "But he will see you now. He will expect proskynesis, as would I."

As Caracalla took his seat by a long desk, Ludo looked to Clio and mouthed 'expect what?'

Clio made a surreptitious bowing gesture. Caracalla noticed it and his frown deepened. He looked to each of the men in turn without saying anything. He gave the disquieting impression that he was reading their thoughts and, given his expression, disapproved of them.

After several minutes of deepening silence, he tilted his chin and Clio looked behind him as the stooped figure of Septimius Severus entered the room. The Prefects got to their hands and knees and bowed, their foreheads briefly touching the floor, as he shuffled by: Ludo dived between them and remained face down even as the other two stood up.

"You fool, get up!" hissed Clio

The centurion rose sheepishly, clutching his bruised ribs. He couldn't take his eyes off the Emperor. He had only ever seen marble statues portraying him as a tall, broad-chested soldier, with powerful shoulders, thick hair and beard. These representations bore no likeness to the swarthy, wizened figure that eased himself down opposite him.

"Or perhaps this fool's reverence for his Emperor, Fabius, happens to be greater than your own." Severus permitted himself a brief smile. "So. What pressing matter brings together the three of you at this ungodly hour?"

"Your Highness," began Clio, "please accept that this is as … difficult for us to deliver as it will be to receive."

"I doubt it."

"Well … it concerns a sensitive matter – a series of them, actually – relating to the recent death of Terentia, the young daughter of senator Terentius Piso."

Severus frowned. "Surely you know that my Praetorian Prefect has already dealt with that?"

"Yes, I heard, Your Highness. But the individual he caught, whoever he was, had nothing to do with it."

"Nonsense! I saw the evidence with my own eyes. He confessed!"

Clio glanced at Rufinus: Severus' temper was already cracking.

"I suspect, Your Highness, that the confession was beaten out of him."

Severus rolled his eyes. "I don't recall seeing you there. And a confession, young man, is a confession whether voluntary or beaten out of someone."

"And is a shameful lie when the man doing the beating is in fact the guilty party."

Rufinus had not intended to use such a cutting tone and Severus stared at him for a few moments. "An especially distasteful comment in light of the fact that he appointed you to your current position," he said with quiet menace. "So you had better be prepared to qualify that spiteful slander, Junius Rufinus."

The Watch Prefect felt Caracalla's eyes boring into him. No point holding back now, Rufinus, he thought to himself, choosing his next words carefully. "Are you aware, Highness, that senator Marcus Maracanthus has gone missing?"

Rufinus was sure he saw a flicker of interest in Severus' eyes. "Go on."

"I received a coded message from him that he had overheard a plot against your life following a session of the senate. He sought my counsel; however when I went to see him I was told by his distraught wife that he had not been seen in several days. She, too, had become worried by his behaviour after he had told her much the same thing. None of my sources heard anything either."

"Then your sources must be deaf. Rumour had it he eloped. With a courtesan."

"Marcus' wife stated that he had overheard the Praetorian Prefect in a heated exchange with another man in an ante-room of the Senate House, and that he thought he was seen as he left. We believe we now know the identity of that man."

But there was no prompt from Severus. His inscrutable eyes were locked on Rufinus.

"Just continue!" said Caracalla irritably.

"Of course. Terentia's body was stolen from the crypt of one of our barracks within hours of it being embalmed there. One of my tribunes, Ambrosius by name, has since proved that it can only have been taken by someone entering the building by means of the sewer network. A level of knowledge that detailed can only have been attained by either those

305

involved in its construction, who are of course long since dead, or by someone looking at various architects' plans. Earlier this evening, the City Prefect and I gained access to the Tabularium and were able to establish that someone had indeed looked at those plans, on the very day her body went missing."

The light in the room seemed to fade with the dark look that now occupied the Emperor's face. He stroked his beard but said nothing.

"Damn you and your pauses, man! You seem to think of yourself as some sort of stage narrator!" snapped Caracalla, jumping to his feet. "Who was it? Who looked at it?"

"Your Highness, it was senator Piso himself."

Severus looked away in disgust and Caracalla, his legs shaking, sat back down. A thick silence settled upon the room. There was more, of course, but Rufinus held back, looking to Clio.

"I'm very sorry, Your Highness, but we saw no alternative than to come to you immediately."

"Piso!" whispered Caracalla. "My Terentia …"

Ludo looked at him in surprise. He had not been told of the affair with Terentia. "Begging your pardons, Your Highness … Highnesses, you may be relieved to know we have just arrested the senator at his home."

"What?" snapped the Emperor.

"And I think it was just as well, too. He tried to throw himself off his stairs when we entered."

Clio and Rufinus glared at Ludo. They had no intention of disclosing that yet.

"He did what?" Now it was the Emperor who rose. "Let me remind you that the man is a former consul of Rome and is only guilty when a jury of his peers or I damn well say he is guilty!"

"Ludo, just …" said Rufinus.

"Yes, Your Majesty, but he obviously knew the game was up and tried to prevent us taking him. But then his wife came downstairs and smacked him with a document cylinder, demanding to know how he could possibly have done such a thing. The point is, though, we think something important - involving him - was going to happen today."

"And how do you know this, boy?"

"Because the documents had three more building plans on them, and descriptions, and notes had been added which mentioned today's date. My colleagues are back at the Watch House now, trying to work out what that will be …"

"Ludo …"

"… and Vitalis the quaestionarius will probably be teasing that out of the senator as we speak." He gave a satisfied look to Rufinus and Clio, whose head was in his hands.

"A common gaoler interrogating my consul?" Severus' face had turned crimson. "Then I hope for your sake that your colleagues find something. Because be sure if they don't," he lowered his voice and it rumbled with menace, "this time tomorrow evening you will be nailed to a crucifix on the Appian Way."

XVII

"Scaurus?"

Ambrosius looked from the portly tribune of Cohort V to Red and the rest of the watchmen. They were all grinning.

"What are you doing?"

"I'm not missing this one. I had my regrets as soon as I saw my lot off the last time: I swore I'd have one more dash before I was put out to pasture. Here, help me with this kit belt would you, young man?"

Ambrosius tried to fasten it but such was the tribune's girth that the end wouldn't meet the buckle. Scaurus breathed in until he was red in the face but it was no use so he slung it over one shoulder instead.

"There," he said, wiping the sweat from his brow before replacing his helmet, "fits perfectly."

Red and Chest sniggered and it became infectious.

"I'll show you, you disrespectful girls! Watch and learn from the old master!"

The gates closed behind them, a low profile exit with no fanfare: Scaurus, Ambrosius, Chest, Bulla, Pollo, Red, Viator and Valens. Scaurus had offered more but Ambrosius had declined on the grounds that the group would draw enough attention to itself as it was.

As they descended into the quiet streets, the men talked in hushed tones like old acquaintances. Scaurus' men mentioned that they had all paid casual attention to the house of the Praetorian captain following their visit the night before but there had been no activity since. The house they were now making for was not far, at the bottom of the north slope of the Caelian hill, and was barely within their patch but Scaurus, whose knowledge of the streets of Rome was second only to Vitalis', said that he knew exactly where it was.

They soon reached the colonnades that ringed the Temple of Claudius. Scaurus took Ambrosius aside. Despite being overweight and sweating freely, he had not uttered a word of discomfort.

"What sort of entry were you planning, Ambrosius?"

"I've been thinking about that all the way here. We have to assume the place is locked up and, whether there's anyone inside or not, knocking on the door is a waste of time. So I think we force entry with mattocks."

Scaurus grinned. "Good lad."

"Worth posting anyone round the back?"

"No. If it's the street I'm thinking of, it doesn't have a garden. It's up a steep cobbled slope where the houses are back to back."

"Good, makes it easier." They rejoined the group and Ambrosius explained the approach: two watchmen to break the door's hinges and locks. They would step aside and the rest would file in, splitting to clear upstairs and downstairs at the same time.

There were no questions. They now reached the north east of the Caelian in silence, using the contours of the hill and the concealment of the crowded buildings to their advantage. As before every step into the unknown, the watchmen began to feel the fluttering conflict between danger and excitement, leaving a queasy feeling in their stomachs. They checked that everything was ready to hand on their belts and that nothing had worked loose. And, when they were called to a halt at the foot of the street, they checked each other's kit.

Satisfied, they gave the final thumbs up and approached the house. The street was quiet and the shutters all closed for the night. Only the hissing of their torches and their own laboured breathing broke the stillness. Ambrosius had studied the plans so intensely that it had morphed in his imagination into a fortress, and yet here it was in reality, a white-washed house with a faded green door and small windows, much like any private residence in the city. He looked up at it again and then put his ear against the door.

It was faint but he was sure he was not imagining it.

Scrape ... scrape

Like something was being dragged across floorboards.

He stepped back with his finger raised, the signal of at least one active occupant. Red and Valens removed their mattocks and hefted them onto their shoulders. They looked at each other, nodded and brought them both crashing down onto opposite sides of the door, shattering the tranquility of the night.

The door splintered but did not yield. They repeated the dose and then stamped it with the flat of their boots. It clattered to the floor, skidding into the darkened hallway. Red and Valens stepped aside and Scaurus was first across the threshold, his torch thrust in front of him and his baton at the ready. Chest was next into the hallway, followed by Ambrosius but that was as far as they got.

It was their eyes that Ambrosius saw first; wide, startled but fierce. There were at least four of them; bulky, swarthy figures materializing out of the gloom, howling like wolves. Something invisible hummed though the air and thumped into Scaurus, who grunted in surprise and pain.

It all happened so fast there was no time for thinking, only reacting. One of the figures, bristling with body hair, lunged forwards, a dull glint of metal in his hand. Scaurus' cudgel found its mark, thudding into his assailant's shoulder but it was a hopeless mismatch and the tribune stumbled backwards, taking Chest with him. The air hummed and reverberated as another object slammed into the doorframe behind the watchmen.

"Back! Back!" screamed Ambrosius, gripping Chest's belt and dragging him towards the street.

A shrill whistle, repeated three times from the street and the mercenaries hesitated, anticipating a flood of attackers.

Chest had gripped Scaurus by the cloak as he himself was tugged backwards and the three of them stumbled back through the doorway. Scaurus was clutching the shaft of an arrow embedded in his left arm. Dark blood dripped from the tips of his fingers.

"I dropped my cudgel," he wheezed.

Red gave three more whistles, deafening his colleagues as he supported Scaurus over the threshold and away from the house. The watchmen glanced fearfully at the doorway as they scrambled back, bracing themselves against a volley of arrows. Instead, there was a flurry of activity and the door was raised and banged shut against its frame. And then they began to tremble with delayed shock.

"Bastards got me!"

"Just a flesh wound old friend!"

Ambrosius legs screamed at him to stop backpedalling and, he sank to his knees and laid the old tribune against the cobblestones. The arrow wound was not the worst of it. He peeled aside his sodden cloak and grimaced at the blood seeping from another ragged slit in his tunic.

"Just a scratch is it?" Scaurus chuckled at the look on Ambrosius' face. "You'd better warn your friends before it's too late."

"I'm not going to leave you here! Just hold on and keep your hand against that nick! Chest, Bulla … you need to get a message to Vitalis and Stilicho to hold back. And we need the Urban Cohorts. And medics. Right now!"

"Tribune, only you and Bulla know those other two places and, no offence, but he's a bit slow. We can summon help from here though, no problem."

Ambrosius' fist was shaking as panic seized him; he clenched and unclenched it and tears stung his eyes. He froze, unable to make a decision.

"Do what you can, young man," whispered Scaurus, "and end it for me."

XVIII

Driven by a desperate urgency, Ambrosius hared through the dirty streets overlooked by the sprawling Baths of Trajan, haunted by the images that had just been seared onto his mind. He plunged into the slums of the Subura without a care for his own safety, his torch making shadows dance against the filthy walls as he sprinted on. And even when his legs began to feel leaden and his lungs burned, the sickly memory of that first arrow and the deadly hum of the second drove him onwards. He soon realised that, in his haste, he had paid no attention to where his legs carried him and he stopped, braying for air. He removed his helmet and squeezed the felt cap within it. Sweat drizzled from it. He ran his fingers through his damp hair in mounting panic.

Where in Hades am I?

Images of his unsuspecting colleagues, his friends, being picked off and butchered by more hulking mercenaries pricked him over and over.

Think, you fool!

He was in a small square of boarded up shops. Tenement blocks reared up on every side of him, obscuring his view. He darted into an alleyway straight ahead and his view narrowed further. It stank of putrefying food and he felt something greasy brush past his calves as he pressed on, committed to the haphazard twists and turns of the path that soon disorientated him.

Then the alleyway abruptly ended and he was disgorged onto a broad street that skirted sloping ground directly ahead.

The Viminal hill.

Encouraged by this lucky break, he set off around the spur of the hill and clattered into the backs of some patrolling watchmen.

"Watch it, you cocksucker!"

He was shoved to the floor by the furious vigil, who stood over him. Ambrosius scrambled to his feet, unable to speak.

"Shit, it's the tribune! Zeus' great hairy bollocks, I'm sorry! Here - get him his helmet – I didn't recognize you trib!"

"Demetri, you Greek arsehole!" said Stilicho, throwing back his head with laughter. "Cloakroom duties for you, I think!"

But their smiles faded when they saw the grim look on Ambrosius' face. "Is everyone in this section here?"

"Er, yes," said Stilicho, after a quick head count, "what's wrong?"

He propped himself on his knees. "Our house was occupied ... by some, I don't know who they were, soldiers, mercenaries, I think. I'd seen them in Ostia – they're well armed – they beat us back when we'd forced entry and we took a casualty, Scaurus, tribune of the Fifth. I don't think he's going to make it. We need help."

At that moment, from somewhere behind them, came the faintest peal of a whistle, followed moments later by another.

"Shit. It's all going off."

The watchmen looked at each other in consternation.

"Well you may just have saved our hides, tribune," said Stilicho, patting Ambrosius' shoulder. "Right, who fancies a jog to the Praetorian Camp?"

"I'll do it," said Demetri.

"Just hold on. Tribune, didn't you say earlier they might be involved in all this?"

Ambrosius straightened and pulled the damp tunic away from his skin. "Too late to guess, Paulus. Brutus may not be but it's they and the Urban Cohorts or nothing. Think you can swing it, Demetri?"

"Of course. I'm from Athens. We invented talking."

"Then I'll go with you," said Paulus, "You seem to have lost the art."

"Good. Don't take no for an answer. We'll wait for you here but you have to hurry."

*

Paulus and Demetri had never encountered the sentries of the Praetorian Camp before. They wasted precious minutes demanding that the gates be opened and were jumping up and down in frustration before they finally parted. They sidled through the gap as the doors creaked apart and came within a heartbeat of rushing onto the points of two spears.

"Just slow down, watchmen. You're not coming in armed."

"Malaka, we're not armed!" protested Demetri, throwing his arms into the air, "You call a pick axe and rope armed? What's wrong with you? We're on the same fucking side, remember?"

"Lose the belt kits."

"What?"

"Your friend here has a baton."

"An oak baton, right, so I'm hardly gonna take on a spear and long shield am I, my friend?"

The Urbanus had a flat, puggish face that was devoid of warmth. "You'll get 'em back on the way out, just take 'em off."

Demetri looked at Paulus in disbelief. He unbuckled it with fumbling hands and tossed it to the floor in disgust. Paulus followed suit.

"Happy now?"

"Enough. Come this way."

"Please, run!" said Demetri, already jogging.

The flat-faced sentry inclined his head to the gate and his colleague resumed his post. "Don't try anything, mind," he called after them, "I have this pointed between your shoulder blades!"

The sight of two watchmen being followed by the sentry as they jogged towards the Prefect's quarters caused some merriment amongst those on late night fatigues. They stopped and pointed at them, making lewd gestures as they passed, but Demetri and Paulus ignored them, thinking only of the time they had already wasted.

When they reached the camp's headquarters, another pair of sentries, Praetorians this time, barred their route. One of them was the tallest man either of them had ever seen. He looked at them in amusement.

"What's the rush ladies? Everyone's asleep."

"Then wake them," said Demetri, out of breath, "right now."

He raised an eyebrow and looked at the soldier who had escorted them. The Urbanus nodded gravely.

A few minutes later, the lofty Praetorian emerged looking less than happy. "The Prefect says if this is anything less than a dire emergency, he'll roast your kidneys over a camp fire. Come in."

He led them through a Spartan reception room to a chamber with a desk, chairs and an impressive suit of parade armour that glinted in the light cast by several oil lamps. They could hear someone muttering and moving about in the room beyond. The door opened and Paulus and Demetri stopped in their tracks. The Prefect was barefooted and wearing an under-tunic, but they were unable to take their eyes from the blood soaked lint square over his nose and the bandage around his head. He was also sporting two impressive black eyes.

"Well don't just stand there, damn you, what do you want at this hour?"

"I'm sorry … I didn't expect …"

314

"Gaius Plautianus is away. I'm in charge for now." He watched them falter and stare at his injuries.

"Which cohort are you from?"

"The Fourth, sir."

"Ah," Brutus' tone softened, "Titus' cohort. Why are you here? Why are you not mourning him?"

"The city's under attack from mercenaries. Men from our cohort have been wounded during raids, at least one is dead, possibly more. We have no weapons, we need your help." Paulus' words sprayed out like water from a burst pipe. "And we need it quickly."

"What? Is this some sort of joke, watchmen?"

"The gods! Please don't make me explain again, sir! We're losing time!"

Brutus glared at him.

"Where?"

"There are three places we know about: the Viminal, the Caelian and the Aventine. Only the tribune and two others have seen the plans. The tribune waits at the Viminal."

"Plans," asked Brutus, retrieving his under armour, "what plans?"

Paulus turned to Demetri with a look that said 'Should I tell him?' Demetri was beyond caring.

"Our tribune arrested Senator Piso a couple of hours ago. The plans were in his house."

Brutus spun on his heels. "Piso?" He winced in pain as the frown aggravated his shattered nose. "What business did he have there?"

"It's a long story, sir. Perhaps you'd better ask tribune Ambrosius yourself."

"Oh I will, watchman, don't you worry," he strode past them and gave orders to someone outside before returning. "Wait for me out there."

*

When he emerged a few minutes later, he was wearing full battle armour and had removed the bandage. Demetri and Paulus could not help but stare at the angry swelling around his nose and the scab that still wept droplets of blood. If ever there was the image of the scarred warrior, this was it. But he seemed oblivious to any pain as he barked orders at the officers dashing about the camp, relaying commands of their own to their subordinates.

The tall Praetorian sentry reappeared looking worried and whispered something to Brutus.

"What?" roared Brutus. "You can't find both my infantry and cavalry captains? Have you tried the cookhouse? Have you asked the gate sentries?"

"All the usual areas, sir. Pennus hasn't returned since yesterday. Alexander likewise."

"I only gave them a few fucking hours' leave!"

Whilst Brutus fulminated, the two watchmen fidgeted, counting the vital minutes ticking by. And still soldiers of the Urban and Praetorian cohorts assembled in columns with impressive efficiency. A handsome cavalry officer with a silk neckerchief hurried past them, still attaching his armour as he jogged to the huddle of other officers being briefed.

"This is taking too long," mumbled Demetri. He approached Brutus just as the meeting dissolved and the officers assumed positions.

"You're coming with me, watchmen," said Brutus, not looking at them as he strode past. A line of cavalry galloped past and, ahead, the gates of the camp creaked open in response. They noticed the young officer near the front and could only imagine aristocratic ladies swooning at the sight.

When the horses were clear, the three columns, headed by section leaders wearing distinctive cross-plumed helmets, broke into a jog. There were no commands and no signals, and yet within just a few paces the rattle of hob-nailed boots pounding the floor settled into a perfect rhythm, with only the sounds of the watchmen's own irregular strides and their panting to disrupt it. The lines swung south out of the camp and then west, compressing without fuss to pass underneath the ancient stones of the Viminal Gate. On they jogged, past rickety tenements and locked-up shops, the click of boots on cobblestones not missing a beat. Paulus and Demetri experienced a surge of power and exhilaration and they felt the hairs on the backs of their necks stand on end.

"Where now?" growled Brutus.

"To the right … first, no … second road to the right," said Demetri, out of breath, "doesn't pass the house. The tribune should be waiting there."

Brutus grunted and barked out the directions. After forty more paces, the columns reached a crossroads. They swung right, onto a curving, dirty street and, on the right, lights dotted here and there described the rise of houses up the Viminal hill. Somewhere in the distance they heard a shrill whistle.

Ambrosius and the men of Cohort IV heard it too, and their sense of desperation deepened. It was an agonizing choice: to await the arrival of help that might never come or to abandon their own raid to lend a hand to their colleagues. As they waited, the mood became tense and fractious, with some of the men threatening to disobey orders.

But then the click of boots approaching at the double silenced them and three columns of soldiers swung into view. The powerfully built man at the head of them raised a clenched fist and, in just three strides, the soldiers came to a smart halt. Brutus strode over to Ambrosius, removing his helmet. The tribune winced at the welt across Brutus' misshapen nose, and the purple rings around his eyes.

"Why am I not surprised to find you at the middle of all this, watchman?"

Ambrosius retrieved the property deeds from his tunic, where they had become damp with his sweat. Whilst the watchmen and the soldiers eyed each other, Ambrosius explained only what he had experienced at the Caelian and showed Brutus that and the Aventine address. The Praetorian listened without comment and, at the end of it, gave him a wry look.

"When this is over, watchman," he said quietly, "you and I need to talk."

Brutus issued clipped orders to his captains, who saluted him. And then their two columns set off again at a brisk jog.

"Praetoriani!" he walked along the line of soldiers, thirty strong, as he spoke. "Rapid entry, longshield wall. Unknown number occupants. Armed resistance probable. Questions?"

There were none. He turned back to Ambrosius. "Lead on, tribune."

XIX

"You sure that's the right street, Vitalis?"

"It's the one I was shown. I started walking these streets when you were still hanging off your mommie's teat, you little shit."

"Alright, point taken." The watchman shrugged. "Never had a problem here, that's all."

Vitalis frowned at him. The young vigil had a reputation for laziness. He doubted he'd ever been near it. "Quit grumbling. All you do is grumble, Antonius. Come on lads, let's just get this over with."

They were silent as they approached the door. A weak glow filtered through the shutters. Vitalis looked at the other houses in the dark street. They weren't the only early risers: one or two other lamps had already been lit. One of the watchmen produced his mattock and stepped forwards. Vitalis looked at it for a moment and shook his head.

Is this definitely the right door? Have I lost it after all? Why would mercenaries want to plot up here?

His leg throbbed from the pace he'd forced and his efforts to disguise his limp. Feeling the mounting impatience of the other men, he had another look round and noticed a man lurking in the gloom at the entrance to the street. Vitalis stared at him until the other watchmen turned round. The man sloped away.

"What was he up to?"

Vitalis shrugged but felt a flutter of unease. "Dunno. Beggar?" He turned back to the door. "Oh, fuck it," he muttered, and banged on it, cupping his ear to it. He thought he heard faint voices but then there was silence. Footsteps approached and the door opened a few inches. A swarthy young face appeared, and his blue eyes glanced at each of the men outside.

"Yes?"

"City watchmen. How many of you are in there?"

The youth looked at him and raised his eyebrows.

"Do – you – under - stand - Latin?"

Silence.

"Is there anyone inside who can?"

Now the youth was staring at him.

One of the watchmen behind him muttered. "Are – you – a – moron?"

"Do – you – blow – goats?" There were a few nervous sniggers.

"Alright, that's enough," said Vitalis, turning to the jokers. The youth frowned and then disappeared, letting the door swing shut.

Vitalis jammed his boot by the frame to prevent it locking and pushed it open. The watchmen followed him inside. A fire was burning in a small hearth to the left and there was a table in the middle of the room with wine cups on it. Otherwise the room was empty. Ahead was a flight of stairs and to the right an open door. As their eyes adjusted to the gloom, they realised that they were being watched from the stairs, though the man's torso was in shadow.

"Do you understand Latin?" repeated Vitalis.

"Yes," came the reply from the stairs.

"That's an unsupervised fire. It's an offence in Rome."

Silence.

"Apart from that kid, is anyone else staying here?"

A pause. "No."

The hissing of the torch flames filled the uncomfortable silence.

"Right, mind if we have a look around?"

"No."

"Are you going to come down then?"

A sigh. "Moment please."

Another watchman took a few steps towards the door but it burst open. A huge foreigner and the youth that opened the street door charged out of it, brandishing glinting blades. One of them skewered him through his heart before he could even yell in fear. An arrow from the shadowy figure on the stairs slammed into Antonius' throat, the force of it knocking him backwards, spattering Vitalis' cheek with blood.

"Out! Out! Out!"

The gaoler's screams spurred the watchmen at the back to empty their lungs in whistling for help. He bent down to drag Antonius over the threshold, but as the man writhed and groped at the arrow he caught the door with his shoulder and it closed, trapping his own arm. He let go of his cloak and glimpsed one of the men inside shouting at the youth. Then he turned and they all ran for their lives.

After a few lumbering strides, Vitalis risked glancing over his shoulder.

What he saw horrified him.

Three burly foreigners emerged from the house wearing the equipment and yellow cloaks of watchmen. They chased them for a few paces and then hesitated, as if they were unwilling to leave something behind.

"Drop torches! Drop torches!" yelled Vitalis.

His eyes searched the gloom for a place to hide. He could see a dark, cobbled alleyway across the street, still thirty paces ahead, but he couldn't remember if it was a dead end. He looked back at the house. To his astonishment, the foreigners had stopped and were shouting at each other. Then they stormed back into the house, their arms flailing.

"In here!"

He pointed to the alley and the seven men darted across the street towards it. They hunkered down in the shadows of some rotting crates, wide-eyed and struggling to control their ragged breathing and the pounding of their hearts.

Moments later, they heard gruff voices in the street and the approach of footsteps. The watchmen sunk lower into the darkness, gripping the pommels of their cudgels. Then they saw them, at the very entrance to the alley, where they stopped barely ten strides away. Vitalis was sure the noise of his thudding heart would give them away. All of the foreigners were now also wearing watchmen's helmets and were talking amongst themselves. One of them stopped and pointed into the alleyway. The others turned to look. The watchmen froze and held their breaths. All but one took a step towards the alley. He barked something at them, shaking his head and pointing down the street. The others stopped, threw their arms in the air and trudged after him, moving out of sight. The watchmen sagged and breathed a ragged sigh of relief.

XX

Ambrosius looked to Chest, counted to three and they smashed either side of the door with their mattocks. They stepped aside to let a bull-like Praetorian pass. There was no finesse in the way he dropped his shoulder into the bowl of his circular shield and charged the door. It gave way as if it was made of straw, and he burst through with a roar. An arrow slammed into his shield but the Praetorian did not check his advance into the atrium. Two longshields followed, flanking their comrade and then Brutus himself entered the fray, clearing space behind him.

The dimly lit atrium, stripped of furniture, was full of men dressed in watchmen's garb, but the weapons they carried were certainly not Italian. Two more Praetorian longshields crossed the threshold before the fight-back began. At the periphery of his vision, Brutus caught a glimpse of a familiar purple tunic before one of the mercenaries brought a scimitar crashing down upon his shield. The blade sang as it was turned aside by the boss of Brutus' shield but, despite the obvious weight of the weapon, his assailant somehow had it arcing down again towards his skull in the blink of an eye. This time he met it before it gathered momentum, driving up his shield with both of his powerful arms. The impact checked the path of the blade and momentarily exposed the mercenary's face. Brutus swept the edge of his shield downwards at his opponent's skull and it opened up his flesh like a gutted fish, sending him twitching to the floor. He brought up his shield instinctively, anticipating another attack, but none came because the four longshields had now linked to advance on the foreigners. One of them slipped away, darting towards the temporary safety of an inner door but a Praetorian spear thrown at point blank range skewered him to the lintel.

"The stairs!" shouted Ambrosius, pointing with his old spatha sword. Brutus saw a flash of purple tunic scampering up the wooden steps.

"Take them alive!" he roared. More Praetorians streamed inside, amongst them Paulus and Demetri, and the old steps clattered and groaned under the combined weight of the men swarming up them.

There were only four mercenaries now, cornered but unbowed. They threw themselves upon the advancing shield wall with unswerving bravery, hacking at the Praetorians until there was no space left to wield their blades. Then they leapt upon the shields, trying to rip them away and gouge the eyes of the men holding them. But the advance was inexorable. Short swords, hidden behind the frames of the shields, darted out and withdrew, as quick as lizards' tongues. The mercenaries slid down the faces of the shields, their lips frozen in agony and surprise, their fingers grasping at thin air.

Above them, the floorboards thudded in sudden commotion. The shouting intensified and more Praetorians now hurtled up the stairs to assist. Knuckle crunched on bone and screams of pain and surprise rent the air. Brutus hawked at the floor and his spittle was flecked with the blood trickling from his gashed nose. He kicked the mercenaries in turn to ensure they were dead: two of them groaned and he dispatched both with a sword thurst through their necks.

"Stop fucking about up there and bring them cowards down!" he yelled, wiping the blade on a tunic.

A few minutes later, one of the Praetorians came downstairs, a grim expression on his face. "You'd better see this for yourself, Prefect. You'll never guess who we've just found up here."

XXI

Gaius Plautianus breezed through the reception chambers of the imperial palace, giddy in anticipation of his historic moment. The tension of the past, secretive few weeks had stretched his nerves to the point of exhaustion but he was now on the threshold of grasping the sacred prize.

The palace was blanketed in silence but there was something subtly different about the feel of the place. He couldn't quite put a finger on it: perhaps it was a foretaste of revolution or the internal strains of the imperial family reaching breaking point. After all, it was common knowledge that relations had never been worse between Septimius Severus and his son Caracalla.

He passed by the vacant throne that would soon be his, flanked by the candelabra aflame with the eternal fire said to have been lit by a priestess of Vesta centuries before. He looked around him. All was still. Then he frowned as he noticed a weak stripe of light coming from underneath the door to an ante-room across the chamber. He listened intently but could hear nothing.

Strange, he thought. The Emperor was famous for his indefatigability and ability to survive on minimal sleep, but Plautianus was one of the intimate few who knew this to be an untruth or, at least, an outdated image. It had been some years since the vigorous new Emperor had been able to battle singlehanded through the daunting bureaucracy that went with running the empire. He relied upon help from several trusted clerks, scribes and advisors working in the imperial civil service, not to mention his own son.

Plautianus added the clearance of that room to his plans and made his way towards the gardens within the old stadium of Domitian. He passed by the flowerbeds and the topiary, enjoying the sweet smell of the night air. Neat rows of fragrant orange and plum trees materialised out of the darkness. Perhaps he would not dig them up, or the Emperor's herb garden, after all.

The light from the moon and the stars made him feel exposed as he moved into the open, away from the high colonnades ringing the stadium, and for a moment the hairs on his nape stood on end. He turned around to see if he was being watched but the palace was a dark mass, pricked here and there with the glow from oil lamps. Then something else caught his attention and he stopped in his tracks, his ears straining against the ambient noises of the night.

An owl?

The note had been distant but steady, though it was gone by the time he attuned himself to it.

And then he heard it again, faint but unquestionably not a bird or other creature.

A whistle.

He glanced at the high walls that marked the eastern edge of the palace complex. For the first time, he felt a pang of doubt and ran through the arrangements in his mind, checking them once again for weaknesses. Pennus himself had assured him that the final preparations were in hand and that the mercenaries would only have to turn up for things to go according to plan.

A twig snapped behind him and he span around.

"The night passes slowly, does it not Gaius?" The Emperor's face cracked into a crooked grin. He gave Plautianus his candle and pulled his cloak tighter around him. "I heard your distinctive footsteps as I was writing. Come, walk with me."

Brutus' heart thumped into his ribcage. He stuttered to speak as he tried to read Severus' expression for some trace of suspicion but the old man could be utterly inscrutable when he chose.

"Well?"

"I often take the night air. It clears my head, gives me space from a nagging wife."

The Emperor's smile didn't waver but his eyes glimmered. Plautianus wondered if he had read the fleeting question that had entered his mind: if he throttled him now, would anybody hear? He glanced over his shoulder: Severus appeared to have ventured out alone.

"I didn't question your habits but no matter." He led him by the elbow and his old fingers were as cold as Death's. "Come."

They strolled for a few moments in strained silence. "So how was your break from Rome, Gaius?"

"My estates thrive. I was able to leave sooner than expected."

"And yet you did not pay your respects here when you returned?"

"The hour was late, Your Highness. I didn't want to disturb you."

"Ah," he said distantly.

They were heading towards a familiar tree stump, shaped into a bench, and Plautianus felt a knot form in his stomach. The thought once again occurred to him, stronger this time, that he might need to bring forwards his plan to kill the Emperor by half an hour or so, and his hand twitched in response. He decided to bide his time: the old man might yet retire to bed.

Severus lowered himself gingerly onto the stump and bade the Prefect sit down next to him.

"We are yet to talk about your plans for The Watch. I expected to hear more of this. The assembly votes today?"

"It does," Plautianus relaxed a little. "Though you are right, of course. The issue became ... buried under more immediate concerns. Finding Piso's daughter and so on."

"Yes ... concerns. Always concerns in life." Severus gave him an enigmatic look. He patted the bench. "I made this myself, did you know?"

"You told me," said Plautianus, glancing towards a dark patch of woodchips between the columns.

The Emperor caught his look and chuckled. "I also told you about the hidden escape passage under that wall, did I not? Domitian must have been a very suspicious Emperor, back in the day."

Before the Prefect could answer, Severus slipped off the bench. He ambled over towards the patch, a forlorn looking figure.

"Perhaps I should just let them get on and finish it, should I?"

Plautianus stared at him in disbelief. Had he somehow missed the signal from his men? Had the old man finally taken leave of his senses? He stood up, caught in a moment of indecision, as a soft banging came from somewhere underneath the earth. Then a large hole yawned open and woodchips rained into it, causing somebody to yelp in surprise. The Prefect looked on in horror as first Junius Rufinus, then Fabius Clio, another man he didn't recognise and lastly, fixing him with a malevolent grin, Caracalla himself emerged from the trapdoor.

"I'm sorry, Prefect. Were you expecting other guests?"

Plautianus clenched his jaw.

"Answer me only this," said the Emperor, stepping forwards, "why?"

Plautianus raised his chin but could only glare back: words had deserted him. Severus shook his head and looked away.

"Bind him up."

Caracalla produced a blade from his sleeve and for a moment it appeared he would plunge it through the Prefect's heart. He pressed the flat of the blade against his ribs.

"Please. Try and escape!" he cackled.

XXII

Brutus prodded Pennus between the shoulder blades with the butt end of a spear, making the Praetorian stumble down the street. The disgust etched on Brutus' face did not even come close to reflecting the revulsion and shame he now felt as he watched two of his most respected officers, an infantry and a cavalry captain, their wrists bound in leather thongs behind their backs, walk ahead of him with their heads hanging low.

The mood should have been one of jubilation as the enemy mercenaries, only moments away from striking out on their treacherous mission, had been eliminated without the loss of a single Praetorian. But the presence of two traitors in their midst, two of their own mess-mates found trying to hide in an upstairs room like scared mice, had cast a sombre spell over the party as it now marched towards the imperial palace.

Brutus called a halt as Ambrosius approached him.

"I need to go and find the rest of my men."

Brutus regarded him for a few moments before nodding. "You're out on your feet. You'll have two of mine accompany you."

Before Ambrosius could refuse, two Praetorians bearing round shields were stood next to him. They all set off at a gentle jog towards the Caelian.

"Tribune!"

Ambrosius turned around.

"No more heroics," said Brutus, "I'll see you at the palace."

*

When they rounded the corner, Ambrosius and his Praetorian escort were greeted with the scene of a battle's aftermath. A score of the Urban Cohorts and at least twice as many vigiles were busying themselves with the dead and the wounded, and ushering away morbid onlookers. The screams of hysterical bystanders and those men gasping in pain as medics attended to them shattered the night.

Ambrosius knew where to start. He saw Bulla and Red stood beside a body with a dirty white sheet draped over it. Red's eyes matched the colour of his hair and brimmed with tears. There was no need to question whose body it was. The five men embraced in a huddle.

"He was a brave man, and he died how he lived, Red. He wouldn't have had it any other way."

327

Red nodded and looked away, fighting back his tears. Ambrosius turned to Bulla. His face, usually so expressive, was haunted and pale. The tribune supposed that the horrors of the last two days, not soothed by any sleep, had pushed him well beyond any reasonable limits. He would have to keep a careful eye on him.

"Tribune?" said one of the Praetorians. "There's someone wants to see you."

Ambrosius turned to see another watchman waving at him outside the house they had raided shortly before.

"What's with the big grin, Chest? Did you have your eyes shut throughout this?"

The smile only faded for a moment. "Tribune, you need to see some of the weapons these pigs had! Look at this one," he pointed to one of the bodies lying face down, with a spiked mace in its hand. He flipped it over with his foot. "Strange: he's not a foreigner."

Ambrosius glanced at it without enthusiasm. He saw that Chest was right, however. The face seemed familiar, though he couldn't say why. Ambrosius shrugged and turned away.

"Anyhow, there're more weapons like that in the crates inside. I'm going to have to take something."

"I've seen them. Is that all you wanted?"

"Well, no," he put his hands on his hips, "but ... we did all this, we stopped something big."

"We did. But remember the cost. Is that why you're not down there with the rest of them?"

Chest glanced down the street at the men next to Scaurus' body. "I know but ... I didn't want to become too depressed, I suppose."

Ambrosius frowned at him but didn't comment on the disrespectful gesture. Perhaps now wasn't the right time to curb his youthful enthusiasm: time and experience would do a good enough job of that.

"What do we do with the bodies and the building?"

Ambrosius looked at the dark interior of the house and shuddered at the memory of what had happened there. "Give it a final sweep and then just have it boarded up for now. I don't see what else we can do with it. What about these?" he said, thumbing towards the blood spattered corpses of the mercenaries. "Did you see what happened to them?"

"I did. Not long after you went for help watchmen from most of the southern regions started arriving and we made sure they couldn't escape, though we didn't get too close. Then the Cohorts arrived and sent them packing across the Styx, though they took some punishment themselves. The stiff with the mace there was a bit handy and did a bit of damage before he copped one in the belly. I've never seen the Urban Cohorts at work before but they were good. Damn good."

"Don't go getting any ideas, young man. You'll have to earn your probatio first. Have the bodies piled up on a cart: they can be burned with the others when we get round to it."

"I'll get it done."

"And Chest?"

"Tribune?"

"Good to have you with us. You did well."

Chest's face beamed with pride.

XXIII

The watchmen's game of cat and mouse, led by Vitalis, was about to come to a violent end. Any remaining doubt that the mercenaries were lost had disappeared when the vigiles watched them meander through the dark streets of the Aventine in an irregular circle, almost walking right into the watchmen as they spied on them from behind the low wall of a shrine. With every step the foreigners took, it become more evident they were beginning to panic. Voices were raised and there was even a brief scuffle. Wherever they were heading, Vitalis didn't envy their task: the streets here were a rabbit warren. Had luck been favouring them, they would eventually have encountered the Circus Maximus, one of the city's most conspicuous landmarks from which they would surely have been able to orientate themselves. But now they were heading out of the city towards the Emporium and the warehouses by the Tiber.

"What the fuck are they doing?" whispered one of the watchmen.

Vitalis looked on. The mercenaries hesitated in front of the ruins of the Lavernalis Gate. Inaudible words passed between them and then they straightened and their gait changed as they walked through the ruins and out of sight.

"They've seen something and I think I know what it is. Move forwards, either side of the gate posts."

The watchmen split into two groups and broke into a crouching run towards the stone blocks. As Vitalis stumbled past the opening, his guess was confirmed. Another patrol of vigiles was heading towards the mercenaries. It occurred to him that their colleagues might be fooled by the imposters' disguises and be attacked when their backs were turned.

"Shit."

"What do you reckon?"

Vitalis took a deep breath. "We have to warn them."

At that very moment, the watchmen heard something that changed the game completely.

Horses' hooves.

They swivelled on their haunches. "Don't tell me the treacherous bastards have cavalry too?"

"I doubt it." Vitalis narrowed his eyes. "Fuck it." He stood up and emptied his lungs into his whistle.

As the first of the Praetorians swung into the street behind them, there was a flurry of activity outside of the walls.

The captain led the charge, the cross-plumes on his helmet bending as he gathered pace.

"They're dressed as watchmen!" bellowed Vitalis. "They're armed – take them down!"

Though the captain didn't acknowledge, Vitalis knew he had heard him. In one fluid motion, he withdrew the sword from the scabbard around his mount's neck and the Praetorians behind followed suit. The line of horses swept past and then the watchmen dashed after them, fanning out.

The mercenaries were caught in an open stretch of ground. With the presence of mind, they might even now have turned the few moments of frenzied shouting to their advantage. The other party of watchmen, hurrying from the south in response to the whistles, had no idea what they were running to and had frozen in confusion. Before their eyes, a troop of Praetorians was about to massacre a group of fellow watchmen, urged on by another group of vigiles. Instead, the mercenaries reached inside their cloaks. One of them produced a small compound bow and had notched an arrow in the blink of an eye. As he raised his arm and took aim, the Praetorian captain scythed past him. With a flick of the blade, the bowman was left with a stump for a forearm, from which arterial blood spouted in a graceful arc. He dropped to his knees, looking at his severed limb with a look of mild surprise.

The Praetorians dispatched two more mercenaries with a similar economy of effort, leaving just two more. They closed back to back as the horses slowed and spread out into a circle and the riders smartly dismounted.

"Put down your weapons and you will be taken alive! Put them down now!"

The pair wavered, giving Vitalis a chance to see the strange quarry at close quarters. They were both dark skinned – darker than most native Italians – without having the colour of other men they had seen from the black continent of Africa. Their eyes were an icy shade of blue and they had smiliar pointed chins and bulbous noses. The elder of the pair had his cold eyes fixed on the captain and began chattering in a guttural tongue. He bent his knees and reached out his weapon. The younger mercenary dropped his scimitar to the floor.

"You, throw it in front of you and raise your arms! Watchmen," shouted the captain, turning his head, "give me a pair of leather binds, if you carry any."

The mercenary leapt up and charged the captain.

"Look out!"

The Praetorian saw the blade but even his keen reactions were not swift enough. His weak parry only deflected the scimitar away from his heart by a few inches, but it saved his life. The blade opened a deep cut across his bicep, making him stagger backwards.

Two Praetorians charged the younger mercenary before he had time to react and slammed him to the floor.

"Baba!" he shrieked.

Having broken through the inner ring, the mercenary now turned to Vitalis, who had read what was about to happen and whose mattock was already out of the loop of his belt. With a feral shriek, the mercenary raised his sword but the pointed end of the mattock was already swinging towards his stomach. It buried itself deep into his organs with a wet thump and held fast, stuck in his ribs. Vitalis let go of the handle and the foreigner crumpled over it, tugging weakly at it. He dropped his sword and slumped to the floor, still struggling to remove the mattock even as he breathed his last.

Unsighted by the mass of cavalry officers restraining him, the screaming young mercenary redoubled his efforts to break free. A powerful fist to his chin silenced him. The Praetorians bound his wrists behind his back whislt others hurried over to the captain, who was now clutching his wound. Dark blood dripped through his fingers.

"I'm fine! I'm fine! Just get it bound up would you!"

He wiggled the fingers of his right arm and they responded, suggesting no permanent damage to nerves or tendons. One of the officers retrieved some padding and bandages from a pouch on his horse and dressed the wound without fuss. Meanwhile the group of responding watchmen wandered over to Vitalis and his men.

"Here, let me help you take it out," said one of them, pressing his foot on the lifeless mercenary.

Vitalis and he worked the handle until the head of the mattock popped out of the corpse. He wiped it on the mercenary's clothing.

"So, mind telling us what the hell this was all about?"

Vitalis tossed the mattock aside and hobbled away to lean on a stone wall that circumscribed a sanctuary. The surge of adrenaline had dissipated and now his bad leg felt like it was on fire.

"Someone? Anyone?" The watchman turned and looked to Vitalis' men, who shook their heads gravely.

"No!"

The three Praetorians lifting up the unconscious mercenary turned to Vitalis.

"What?"

"You're not taking him anywhere like that?"

"Why not? What's the matter with you?"

"Look at him! He's wearing our damned equipment! There's no way we're being associated with that!"

The Praetorians looked at him as if he was deranged. "Well you better fucking well take it off then, hadn't you?"

XXIV

Dawn broke the colour of a livid bruise as the last of the plotters was dragged into the octagonal colonnade surrounding one of the courtyards of the imperial palace. Extra detachments of Praetorian guards, interspersed with soldiers of the Urban Cohorts to ensure their loyalty, had been posted at every door and archway of the entire complex.

It was a macabre line-up: a distinguished senator, the Praetorian Prefect, two bruised Praetorian captains, a petrified young Libyan mercenary. Unlike the others, whose heads were hung in shame, Publius Terentius Piso and Gaius Plautianus were staring defiantly into the distance, and would not meet the gaze of anybody in the courtyard.

Until Brutus entered.

"Gaius?"

Brutus checked his stride.

"Gaius?"

Only now did Plautianus twitch.

"Tell me this is a mistake? You're here just because of them, right?" he said, pointing to the two Praetorians.

The silence in the courtyard deepened.

"No, Brutus," said Caracalla as he emerged from the half-light of a portico. "He's here because he's a treacherous shit and he's going to be executed with the rest of them."

Brutus' mouth fell open. He tried to form words but none emerged.

Plautianus' lips curled into a sneer. "Go on, ask it! You want to know why I didn't consult you, my loyal deputy, don't you?"

Brutus froze.

"Well, don't you? Let me put you out of your misery then. It's because you have no vision, Vibius, that's why. You're a simple soldier, a good one, but just a soldier all the same."

Ambrosius almost felt sorry for the man. He watched him step back, registering the faces in the courtyard in bewilderment . The moment of triumph the man had expected was instead the moment that his entire career turned into a hill of sand. The ferocious back-hand swipe that snapped Plautianus' head to the side, lifting him clean off his feet and sending him spinning to the floor, surprised everyone. Brutus stood over him and spat into his face before striding out of the courtyard with his fists clenched. None of the sentries dared stop him.

The sound of a girl's sobbing broke the ensuing silence. "D'you see that, dear wife?" Caracalla spat out the words and pushed Fulvia Plautilla into the middle of the courtyard. "That's your beloved, treacherous father! Go on! Bid him farewell! This will be your only chance!"

Plautilla fell to her knees, shrieking hysterically by her father, who had begun to stir. It was a pathetic scene and Ambrosius could not bear to watch it. She was just a young girl, barely any older than Terentia had been and, by sheer accident of birth, was now destined to see out the rest of her years in misery.

"Enough!" The Emperor now stepped forwards. "Enough of this theatre. Guards! Take them all away and have them thrown into the Tullian. Their presence here sickens me. And Clio! Have some of your men follow them. Who knows what they might attempt otherwise?"

"Father, wait!" said Caracalla as soldiers moved in to round them up. "Not that one! I want that one kept behind."

All eyes turned to Pennus. For the first time, the Praetorian looked worried. Caracalla's sinister gaze now fell upon Ambrosius, and an icy rivulet trickled down his spine. The thought struck him that he might blame him for some of his anguish.

"Ask – watchmen," he said slowly, and his thin lips curled into a smile.

Ambrosius glanced at Ludo, Bulla, Clio and Rufinus, whose faces reflected his own concern.

"I'm sorry, Your Highness?"

"Ask – watchmen. Those were the last words of the prisoner that he," he said jabbing his finger towards Plautianus, "executed to cover up his own disgusting treason. Yes, that's what he said, I get it now! It's been bothering me ever since I heard it! Well? I'm asking you, watchman: what is it you have for me?"

What was he talking about?

Ambrosius' exhausted mind could entertain no more twists and turns. It went blank.

"Well, what's wrong with you? It seems you're the man that exposed all of this, and yet you have nothing to say? Or were you part of this treachery and are now turning on them to save yourself?"

Ambrosius could feel the combined stares of the prisoners boring into him. It was as if they were willing him into a state of numbness.

335

"Tribune."

He heard Rufinus' voice piercing his fuddled thoughts.

"Tribune!" said Rufinus, with an encouraging nod. "Now might be the time to show him what you found."

And then his mind lit up.

"I have this, Your Highness," he said, rerieving a rolled-up piece of sailcloth.

Caracalla snatched it from him. "What is it?"

"Please. Unroll it."

He did so and then grimaced at it. "Is that blood?"

"It is."

"Whose blood? Where did it come from?"

Ambrosius glanced at Pennus and Piso, and he felt his anger stir.

"From inside a disused building by the docks. It's Terentia's blood."

Caracalla gaped at it and spread it out in the middle of the courtyard with an awed reverence, his whole body shaking.

"Go on," he whispered.

Ambrosius stepped forwards. "That boot print, Your Highness, was lifted from the very spot where she was raped, beaten, slaughtered and tossed away, like a slab of unwanted meat."

The colour drained from senator Piso's face and he swayed where he stood.

Caracalla's body began to convulse with grief. "Whose print is it?"

"It's his."

Everyone turned to look at the bull-necked Pennus. He took a step backwards. "That's nonsense, I tell you! I wasn't there!"

"Take off your sandals."

"What?" he growled, screwing up his face, "I don't take orders from a watchman!"

"Do it! Do it now!" shrieked Caracalla, storming towards him.

At first, Pennus backed away but then, seeing that he faced the inevitable, he stood his ground, tensing his powerful shoulders.

"Guards!" ordered the Emperor, who had been watching, stony faced, from the colonnade, huddled inside his cloak.

The soldiers made short work of his resistance. One of them applied a choke hold and two others swept his legs away from him. After a brief struggle, he stopped thrashing about and the veins in his neck stood out proud as his chest heaved. Another soldier cut the straps of his sandals and tossed them towards the centre of the courtyard. Caracalla pounced on them and flipped them over, comparing them, side by side, with the bloody print.

"They match! What else, watchman? How can you prove this is her blood, and where it came from?"

"Your Highness? Please, don't torture yourself any more, this is …"

Caracalla leapt up, his eyes blazing.

"Lift up his sleeve?"

"What?"

"Guards, lift up his sleeve!"

Pennus tried to resist but, with his hands bound, it was futile. The guards rolled him to one side and pulled up the left sleeve but his thick forearm was unmarked. Ambrosius experienced the tiniest sliver of concern: would the deep scratch marks have faded in two weeks? One of them pulled up his right sleeve, tearing it in the process. Ambrosius saw the guard lean closer, peering at something.

Caracalla stalked over.

"Some of Terentia's fingernails were bent during her struggle, and there was skin under one of them. His skin."

"He bears the marks!" Caracalla's voice reached a frenzied pitch and his eyes flared wide. "More, watchman! I want to hear more! I want to hear all of it!"

There was one more thing. Ambrosius was glad he had remembered to go back for it before entering the palace. He reached into his pocket, his fingers brushing an unfamiliar oilskin bundle, and he flinched as if it had pricked him. He fumbled in his other pocket, retrieving a small leather pouch. He gave it to Caracalla, who frowned at it and tugged the drawstrings apart with trembling fingers. He gasped as the Sardonyx ear stud dropped into his palm

"Where did you find this?"

"In the same room, between the floorboards. We think it might have come off during the struggle."

Caracalla gave him a strange look. "You fool: it's not hers! It's mine!"

He spun on his heels and approached Pennus. "That's where we used to meet, she and I! That's where we would escape! Her from her wretched father, and me from here, from these … expectations, that cling to me like burrs to a dog! And you knew she'd be there because you'd been watching

337

us! You tricked her, didn't you? You lay in wait for her by the warehouses! Well, is that not so?"

Plautilla, who had been rocking on her haunches, let out a renewed howl. Caracalla wheeled on her.

"Stop your snivelling, daughter of a traitor!"

He produced a knife from within a fold in his robe and, for a horrifying moment, it looked like he would plunge it through her heart. Instead, he turned back to Pennus and rammed it, handle deep, into his throat. A fountain of blood sprayed onto the bare arms of the soldiers still restraining the Praetorian and they jumped back in revulsion.

Pennus' body went into a frenzied spasm and Caracalla let go of the knife, leaving Pennus trying to clutch at it with his bound hands until his efforts gradually subsided and he lay still.

That was enough for Ambrosius, who had shielded his eyes. He inclined his head towards a doorway. Clio, Rufinus and the other watchmen followed him in stunned silence. Ambrosius expected to be challenged and ordered to return but no such command came. And, even if it had, he would have carried on walking: his only thought was to escape from the madness of that courtyard and to be free once again.

XXV

At about the third hour of the day, a freedman of the imperial civil service threaded his way through the knots of chattering people in the forum. Nobody paid any attention to him, even when he made his way to the notice board by the steps of the speaker's rostrum. He tore down the note advertising that afternoon's vote upon the motion of one Rabirius Felix, that control of The Watch be transferred, with immediate effect, to the Praetorian Guard. Nobody even noticed how he tore it up into little pieces and tossed it into the air, and how the light breeze scattered it across the dirty paving stones.

Nobody noticed because they were too engrossed with the rumour that a prominent senator, the Praetorian Prefect, two of his captains and an unknown mercenary – little more than a boy, it was said - had just been executed inside the Tullian prison.

EPILOGUE

Day XXX of Sebaciaria

"Uff, you're far too heavy for this!"

"Daddy, you're just too old!"

"So are you: you're twelve! I've not lifted you up since you were little!"

"Yes but the poor thing's stuck. Come here pretty puss!"

The cat raised a lazy eyelid and looked away. "Poppeia, she's a cat. She's perfectly content up there. Or she was until we came along."

"Ps ps ps ps!"

The cat had had enough. She scurried along the branch of the pine tree and darted down the trunk and away into a flower bed. Anna clapped her hands and laughed out loud. "Your poor father! He's only had two hours sleep!"

"Just as well we're only clearing out the barracks tonight before the next lot starts Sebaciaria. A whole week off before day duties start." Ambrosius groaned and put down his daughter, "Which is just as well: I think I've put my back out!"

The three carried on walking up the path. The balmy afternoon had breathed life into the Hill of Gardens. Peals of contented birdsong and fragrant scents filled the air, and the first butterflies of the season flitted across their sight, free at last from their cocoons. Poppeia went on ahead, gathering wild flowers. Ambrosius watched her with pride.

"Very ladylike!" said Anna.

He smiled. They walked on in companionable silence for a few minutes. He was about to offer her his arm when his fingers encountered the oilskin in this pocket. He stopped in his tracks.

"Gods! I'd forgotten!"

"What is it?"

"Titus gave it to me before his fight," his hand trembled as he looked at it. "He wanted me to give it to Lucia in case anything happened to him."

"You should open it."

"No! He insisted she should have it."

"Come on, Ambrosius! He would have wanted you to know what was in it first."

Ambrosius nodded. "Knowing him, I suppose so."

340

He unfolded it. A simple but beautifully cut silver crucifix glinted in the sunlight. Anna put her hand over her mouth in complete surprise.

"Well, well, you secretive old dog," said Ambrosius, grinning. "I knew you were hiding something from me!"

"Something that could have had him killed! And landed the rest of you in serious trouble!"

He shook his head. "He would have given nothing away. Loyal to the end, that man."

"Will you give it to Lucia? I can, if you like."

"I will. It's something I need to do, but not yet. Not just yet."

They strolled on. "Listen, I appreciate you agreeing to come for a walk with us, especially here. I needed it after this morning."

Anna shuddered as she remembered what he had told her. "Out of all the horrible things that you've described, I still can't get over that one thing."

"Terentia?"

"Yes," her voice dropped to a whisper. "The gods know we're all familiar with greed and ambition and all those other stories we're told as children. But to allow your own daughter, your own flesh and blood, to be killed just because she's threatened your career … it's like a story from one of those horrid Greek legends."

"She threatened his name with her affair, and broke the weak marriage bonds between Plautianus and the Emperor. I can't imagine it either, but if you'd also been inside his house and seen those damned wax death masks watching your every move, you'd start to see the expectations those families drag about with them. And Plautianus' offer of him being made head of his new senate as a compromise, the second most powerful man in the empire, was just too tempting for him."

"Yes, they say power corrupts, don't they?"

Ambrosius and Anna flinched and turned in shock.

"Power," said the stranger, glancing at the bundle in Ambrosius' clenched fist, "and religion."

"Who are you and what do you want?"

"Forgive me! My name is Primus." The man held up his hands defensively. "And sometimes us messengers are just too light on our feet, like Mercury himself. I merely wanted to relay to you the heartfelt thanks of Their Imperial Majesties and, I might add, the Roman People."

Ambrosius weighed him up and tried to control his pounding heart. Had he seen him somewhere before? Regardless, he had encountered enough of this sort in recent days to know a little of what lay beneath the well-groomed appearance and the brittle smile.

"They would, of course, have preferred to thank you for your efforts in person but ..." he tilted his chin in Poppeia's direction, "I shall explain that you were anxious to spend time with your family. I'm sure they'll understand. And, who knows, perhaps one day they will deign to call upon you again."

The man's smile did not crack under Ambrosius' glare. He bowed courteously to Anna, glanced once again at the bundle before giving Ambrosius a knowing look and walked away. He did not turn back.

Ambrosius clenched his jaw and turned to face Anna. He saw the fear in her eyes and suddenly remembered how wretched he felt when she walked out on him. "I'm so sorry about those things I said to you. I'm sorry that I took your being around for granted. But it's not like that. You're a part of our lives, come what may, a big part. Please come back and stay with us?"

Anna looked into his eyes but she didn't have to search hard for signs of his sincerity: it shone from him. She put her arm around his waist and they carried on walking up the path.

*

Partially concealed from view, Poppeia had stopped what she was doing to turn and watch them. She smiled distantly and tucked her hair over her ears. Then she removed one of the flowers from her bundle – a sky blue Forget-Me-Not – and laid it against the base of a tree.

A butterfly with translucent scarlet wings fluttered onto her arm. It paused for a moment, twitched its wings and Poppeia watched it spiral away towards the treetops and out of sight.

If you enjoyed *The Consul's Daughter,* please share your thoughts on Amazon by leaving a review.

For more free and discounted eBooks every week, sign up to the Endeavour Press newsletter.